for Karen

RIDIN' AROUND

TAILLIGHTS IN CHROME, 8-TRACKS ON WHEELS...

ELAINE FIELDS SMITH

Elaine Smith

BLAZING
STAR BOOKS

Ridin' Around — Taillights in Chrome, 8-Tracks on Wheels
Copyright © 2010 by Elaine Fields Smith

For information about this title or to order other books and/or electronic media, contact the publisher:
Blazing Star Books
www.blazingstarbooks.com

Library of Congress Control Number: 2010908401

ISBN: 978-0-9827690-1-0

First Edition

Cover Design by Kelly Mason, Stephenville, Texas
Book Design by 1106 Design, Phoenix, Arizona
Sketch Art by Tarena Major, Granbury, Texas

Dedication

To my husband, Glenn — the love of my life.

To my deceased parents — Glenn and Betty Fields.

Dad taught me the wonder of words...Mom drilled
into my thick skull I could do ANYTHING, if I
put my mind to it. As usual, she was right.

Acknowledgments

A BIG THANK YOU goes to all the friends, family and acquaintances who contributed to this project.

Special thanks to Tarena Major, the artist whose sketches enhance the pages of this book. Also, credit goes to Kelly Mason for the cover design.

Ridin' Around would not have been possible without help from Arden and Sherry Knight. Further, editing services by Mr. Knight and Word Journeys, Inc. taught me the error of my grammatical ways. 1106 Design was instrumental in producing this book. Every contributor's work is greatly appreciated.

Preface

RIDIN' AROUND: *Taillights in Chrome, 8-Tracks on Wheels* was written to celebrate a wonderful time in life—young adulthood. It also offers the opportunity for the reader to spend a few hours feeling good. People need to laugh more. With so much negativity in the contemporary "entertainment" world, I felt compelled to create a book filled with fun and good-hearted spirit. *Ridin' Around* also emphasizes close relationships and the treasured support of close friends. Though coming of age can be confusing and sometimes tragic, kids should be able have lots of fun. My book showcases this concept with the goal of allowing readers to chuckle, smile, and possibly shed a few happy, and sad, tears.

When folks ask what triggered me to sit down to write this book at age fifty, I actually have a good answer. The mind-awakening breathing exercises learned in yoga and practicing some beginner meditation allowed my brain to perceive a wider spectrum of possibilities than ever before. Plus, an epiphany transpired when describing my enviable work situation, an insurance underwriter working from home, in an interview with a volunteer organization. Details such as having a thirty-hour work week with all benefits in place, the freedom to hop out of bed to go to work in my pajamas, and earning a higher than average salary made my employment atmosphere seem very favorable indeed. However, after admitting to this "bird nest on the ground," the statement that quickly followed, "but I hate my job," truly shook me to the core. Collectively, these realizations coalesced into the desire to pursue a dream—write a book. A few weeks later, a great idea sprouted in my head. What better topic to write about than the memories and experiences from our younger days? Thus, the inspiration took root and budded into a glorious blossom. Before long, an entire garden of memories and imagination filled a spiral notebook.

My husband and I met with friends, remembering "the good ol' days," gathering new adventures from just about any source. Every story and character is fact-based, though not necessarily historically accurate. One anecdote was obtained while I was at a convenience store in a small town with my motorcycle girlfriends. Six of us were resting and eating ice cream when a guy approached us. (Not an unusual situation with six to eight ladies riding motorcycles, I might add!) The story he told was so unique and fit in so well with one of my characters, I decided to use it. Though I do not know his name, this encounter serves as a good example of how additional events outside our own personal experience were gathered.

There were some major bumps along the *Ridin' Around* road. About two-thirds of the way through the writing project, volunteer work brought a fifteen-year-old foster child into my world. Virtually all of my energy and focus went into helping this teenager for almost a year. That in itself was a separate journey. Also, Glenn (my husband) and I opened a business. More time and brain power were placed into that—leaving the book on the proverbial back-burner. But then I met some local people with publishing experience who were willing to help me—a novice, but willing author—by revealing some of the secrets of the publishing world. The *Ridin'* road transitioned, becoming long and much smoother, and now stretches far into the distance with possibilities.

Ridin' Around: Taillights in Chrome, 8-Tracks on Wheels is set in a small, Texas college town during the fall of 1980. This setting is appropriate because that is where most of the happenings contained in the following pages actually occurred. The sketch art featured in each of the chapters was specifically created by a local artist for this book. Each illustration represents an actual location or feature mentioned within the story. Generally, dramatic license has been taken, since the attempt to be as authentic as possible in dialog and storyline posed the exhilarating, and impossible, challenge of having a memory with exact recall.

Nonetheless, my college friends and acquaintances did indeed have numerous unique "word play" expressions (which became part of our everyday vocabulary) that were preserved in this retelling. The actual events are compressed in time. Tender memories and anecdotes—both comical and adventurous—are blended into a representative trueness of the age, the cars, the music, and the attitudes of days gone by.

It was a time of trust. Rarely were doors locked. Neighbors didn't fear one another, and young people knew how to make their own fun. Long-standing friendships were strong, and new friends were easily won—all that was needed was to stop at a local "hang out" and "start talkin'."

Also, "wheels" were most helpful to have—along with the mobile music provided by the in-car 8-track cassette tapes. These players were infamous for the mechanical sound made when changing tracks on the tape. It occurred to me that a representation of this pause could be used to indicate transitions within a chapter. That idea's result was use of the following symbol:

So sit back—shift gears to a time when there were no cell phones, no Internet, no satellite radio, and young folks had to find their own way...by *Ridin' Around!*

— Elaine Fields Smith
July 2010

Chapter One

*T*HE GRAND OLD HOUSE TOWERED more than two stories above the carefully transplanted and tenderly maintained native shrubs and wildflowers growing at its foundation. Three stone chimneys emerged from the sharply pitched roof, stretching majestically into the cloudless sky. On the front porch, a man sat rocking in a squeaky metal glider, watching activity on Main Street. Close beside the glider was a small table which held an almost empty tea glass conspicuously in need of a refill.

He just rocked, glided actually, quite content to sit on his front porch. The somewhat heavy Sunday afternoon traffic was tapering off as local drivers and church-goers got off the streets, returning to their homes to prepare for the upcoming work week.

The man awaited the evening parade of vehicles filled with younger people. It was September, and the college kids were back in town. The locals kept riding around doing the drag all summer, but things really got hopping when college was back in session.

A solid black four-wheel drive pickup passed by, complete with a Blue Heeler dog riding along on the toolbox in the bed of the truck. The young man's window was down. While passing by the house, he stuck his arm out to wave casually at the man on the porch. The dog looked toward the house. His head seemed to nod in a friendly greeting. The older gentleman smiled, raised his hand, and waved back in a nonchalant manner. It's what they did every time the young man drove by. Somewhere along the line, the man had named the young fellow in the pickup Rowdy and the ever present four-legged passenger Rocky. He had no idea what the driver's real name was. To him it was just Rowdy waving, with Rocky riding along in the back. It was awfully nice of them to acknowledge his presence in the world.

Turning his attention to gliding, he leaned forward a bit, to gain some momentum on the forward stroke for the cautious rise to his feet. His mobility was hampered by an old knee injury he had sustained in World War II while climbing up a rope net on the side of a battleship. In the rush to get aboard he slipped, then hung upside down with his leg in an unnatural twist for quite some time. That knee was never the same.

The man picked up his empty glass, turned, and walked into the house to get a refill of sweetened iced tea. As he opened the screen door, he froze in place. A motorcycle was screaming in his direction. Close behind, a police siren shrieked. The clamor shattered the afternoon's serenity. The gentleman looked back toward the street with concern; a familiar figure zoomed past, with a police car not far behind. His eyes crinkled a bit with amusement, as he sent a silent wish of good luck to the motorcycle rider. It was no surprise the motorcyclist was in that particular circumstance.

As he again attempted to enter his home, another sound grabbed his attention—a horn—barely loud enough to be noticed. Turning toward the street again, he saw a couple of college girls in a little gray car. They waved enthusiastically at him. He waved back, recognizing the car and the girls from the previous school year. The man watched the taillights retreat, until the red glow could no longer be seen. A second later, he couldn't see the car at all through the smoke pouring out of the tailpipe. He shook his head.

"I'm glad to see Mr. Rocker outside. It looks like he's doin' all right," said Tanya, the driver of the gray car. She was beginning her sophomore year at the university and had come back to school with a new short and sassy haircut.

"Yeah, he's always rockin' just like us. Hey, Mr. Rocker!" the passenger, Janie, shouted out the car window with a big wave.

Mr. Rocker's face crinkled up even more when he smiled, especially around the eyes, as he walked into the house, the screen door slamming behind him. *Slam-slam.* If a screen door with a spring attaching it to the frame is left to close on its own, it invariably bounces when hitting the wooden framework and makes a double-slamming noise. Nobody seems to know why—it just does.

As the man disappeared, the girls continued happily "making a drag." They drove from one end of Main Street to the other (nobody knew exactly how far it was, and they certainly didn't care), turning around at each of the two Dairy Queens conveniently located at opposite ends of the "drag." A block or two past Mr. Rocker's beautiful home were several small, white frame houses which also faced Main Street, otherwise known as "the drag." Most were rental property. All were somewhat run down.

"Well, Glenda and Kevin are still there," said Tanya. She pointed to her right, almost clipping Janie's nose. An old, rusty AMC Matador sat in the driveway beside the house, a hideous hulk. A bright yellow Camaro was parked in front of it, almost out of sight. "I wonder how long he'll be in town. I'll be really mad if he doesn't come see me."

Janie glared at the two parked cars with a frown. "I was surprised when Kevin didn't come back to school this year. He was always so much fun to have around. I wonder why they're at that ratty old place. Glenda said on Friday she was goin' home for the weekend, but her car's been there since late Saturday mornin'."

"Ha! I suspect they've been pretty busy. Don't you remember she said she didn't hear from him just about all summer?" Tanya asked mischieviously. "We'll see her after while."

Janie shrugged and shook her negative thoughts away with a few tosses of her head, her full curly brown hair flying in the air. She turned her attention to the road ahead.

Tanya drove past Central Texas State University's seemingly ancient stone front entrance and around the corner, where the boys' dorm stood three stories high next to Main Street. It was a stately red brick building with casement windows cranked open in every room. Janie leaned out the car window; her curls blew wildly in the wind. "Flesh—we want FLESH!!!" she yelled in the general direction of the dorm.

Tanya quickly stepped on the gas. The car accelerated slightly but left a getaway smoke screen before any guy in the dorm could look out his window. The girls laughed, because they really didn't want to see any actual bare flesh. It was just great fun to drive by and yell at the guys. The girls noticed several people sitting on the low, rock wall bordering the sidewalk that seemed flabbergasted at Janie's antics. They simply stared. Janie again leaned out the window, waving her cupped hand slowly as if in a parade—the queen wave.

"Don't stare at me, or I'll wave at you!" Janie yelled. The people sitting on the wall laughed at her behavior. This type of antic was normal for Janie. She ducked her curls back into the car with a giggle.

Tanya drove up to the Dairy Queen and pulled in behind several other cars also making a drag. They steered their vehicles around the back of the building and up to the front of the parking lot next to Main Street. Like stock cars going around a race-track curve three wide, Tanya and two other drivers jockeyed for position. All darted onto the street. Within a block, they fell into single file before the first traffic light. The quicker car was first, but Tanya was next. The third car lagged behind—the latest victim of the little gray car's getaway smoke screen.

"Let's go back to the dorm and see if anybody else is around," Tanya said. "The getaway smokescreen strikes again!"

Janie was tickled. "Yep, we left 'em in a fog. Head out to Horne Hall, Tanya. I need a potty break anywho."

Tanya whipped her little car between the stone pillars that marked the front entrance to the college campus. The road was one way going in and one way back out again. It was divided throughout by a wide center median with grass on the inside and parking places all along the edges. The drive followed a horseshoe path to the left of the median just past the girls' dorm, Horne Hall. At the second bend of the U, the road split. To the left was the one-way lane out to Main Street. To the right was a two-way street which ended in a T intersection at a neighborhood, serving as the back entrance. The U loop through the middle of the campus was officially part of the drag. Anybody and anything could drive through—and just about everybody in all kinds of vehicles did.

Tanya noticed a pickup coming up slowly behind them, so she quickly parked her little car close to the front of their two-storied, elderly dorm building—right next to her friend Glenda's yellow Camaro.

"Hey, look-it! Glenda's here already. She must a' come in the back way!" Janie exclaimed, as she crawled out of the car and hurried toward the steps. "Hi, Glenda...hi, Candace. Hey there, Barb-oh...and hey, hey, Months of the Year! Be back in a minute," she called to the girls standing next to the yellow Camaro.

Janie ran at full speed up the stairs and into the building. The "Months of the Year" were coeds and very close cousins: April, May, and June. They also lived in Horne Hall.

Tanya walked up to Glenda slyly. "Ah ha! So, there you are...how was Kevin? Well...Glenda?"

Glenda made a show of looking confused—gradually altering that look to innocence. She glanced at Candace and Barb-oh mischievously, but still didn't answer the question.

"Oh, come on. Your car was parked in front of his rusty old wreck in the driveway of that little house on the drag since early yesterday. Don't play dumb with me," Tanya said accusingly.

"OK. KO. I confess." Glenda's face brightened. "He called me at Mom and Dad's just as I got home Friday night and asked me to come down and spend the weekend with him. I was so excited I could barely wait till Saturday mornin', and then I nearly got a speedin' ticket gettin' down here from Dallas. It was SO good to finally see him. I missed him so much this summer I almost couldn't stand it. He got use of that house from a guy he knows. Man, you can't get away with anything in this small town!"

Tanya tried to elbow Glenda in the ribs. "Not hardly. Not when you're parked right out on the drag! Is he comin' by here? I haven't seen him in a long time either."

Glenda dodged the jab and furrowed her brow. "I don't think so. He said he was goin' back to Stonehill to get ready for work tomorrow."

Her attention was drawn to the street by some loud music. She turned toward the noise, finding two jocks in the white pickup that had been behind Tanya. Kent and Matt were testing out Kent's new stereo and playing air guitar to the Dire Straits hit, "Sultans of Swing." The jocks saw the girls on the sidewalk in front of the old dorm. They stopped to turn up the music even louder, showing off the new stereo's sound.

Matt noticed the brunette standing among the girls on the sidewalk. "Hey, isn't that Kevin's old girlfriend?"

"Yeah, it sure is," Kent said, turning down the music and slowing to a stop in front of the girls. "You know, when he didn't show up for football camp this summer, I knew somethin' was up. I guess now we know why."

"Hey!" Matt didn't know the name of the girl with thick, shoulder-length brown hair, but he knew she was Kevin's girlfriend. "Hey, I heard back in Stonehill that Kevin's gettin' married."

Glenda stepped up to the door of the pickup, soft blue eyes shining happily. "Yeah, that's right. We're gettin' married right after I graduate next year."

Matt suddenly slumped back into the seat, glancing over at Kent with a strange look on his face. He slowly looked back at Glenda. "Uhh, yeah. Well...we gotta go." Matt avoided eye contact with the girl who looked so happy. He motioned to Kent to get moving, reached over, and turned the volume back up, to cover the uncomfortable silence.

The pickup pulled away slowly, driving around the U, sharing the Dire Straits music with the entire area. The jocks drummed on the dash as they graced the campus with their presence and made their way back out to Main Street.

"Hmm. I wonder what that was all about?" asked Tanya. She frowned and walked over to stand beside Glenda.

"I don't know." Glenda's brow also creased with sudden apprehension. "It's weird he should say somethin' like that. Kevin practically begged me to run off with him to San Antonio and get married this weekend. I told him I only had one more year of school—that we could wait that long." Glenda shook off the frown and smiled. "It was such a relief to see him. You know, I didn't hear from him all summer and had no idea where he was!"

Candace gazed at Glenda, surprised. She quickly took her car keys out of her pocket and jingled them. "I've gotta go. I've gotta go get somethin' from home. Come on, Barb-oh—ride with me. We'll be back after while."

Candace turned away so fast her long strawberry blonde curls swirled around her head. She took off running toward her truck with Barb-oh trailing.

The girls on the sidewalk watched their friend's pickup truck drive very quickly around the U and speed off toward Main Street.

Tanya turned to Glenda. "Hmmph. What's up with her?"

"No tellin'." A strange sensation came over Glenda and caused a shiver.

"We're outta here. See y'all later," April said. The three cousins disappeared around the corner of the building.

"Hmm, she must a' parked up front today," Glenda mused.

Janie appeared in the upstairs window and looked down at her friends. "Hey, what's goin' on?" she yelled through the screen.

Tanya tilted her head toward the window. "I don't know. But I'm hungry. Grab Queen *Jazz* and come on down!" She turned to Glenda. "Let's go in your car, OK? Mine probably needs a quart of oil by now. Mmmm, I feel like a corny dog."

"Sure." Glenda smacked her lips together several times. "Yepper, I believe I feel like a corny dog and a cherry limeade, too. Let's go!" She pressed her hand on her chest and took a deep breath to shake off the uncomfortable sensation. "But we gotta make a drag first. You know it's a rule."

"Of course!" Janie voiced her approval. She bounced down the concrete steps of the dorm and joined the others.

The three friends loaded up in the yellow 1975 Camaro. The car had no air conditioning, but that was all right. Since the windows stayed down, they could see and hear everything that was going on. The car did have an under-dash 8-track tape player with great speakers installed in the back deck, so the girls could play their very own choices of music very loudly. It was wonderful to have mobile music at your fingertips. It was practically impossible to pick up rock and roll radio stations from the big cities in a small town out in the boonies like Dairyville. The only station that would tune in clearly was local and played twangy old timey country music. That kind of sound was all right to dance to, but for ridin' around, these girls wanted rock and roll.

Tanya plugged in the Queen tape, as Glenda backed out of the Amen Corner parking place she had claimed earlier in front of the dorm steps. "Fat Bottom Girls" kicked off right in the middle of a word. That's the way 8-track tapes worked—the tape would start off where it had previously stopped. Sometimes a song paused and then continued, as the tape changed from one track to the next. But it was certainly better than the girls singing on their own. Besides, it helped a whole lot having Freddie Mercury sing lead.

As she left the campus, Glenda gazed at the house where she and Kevin had been together for the past twenty-four hours. She sighed, happily joining in the singing with her friends, as they made their way down the drag. They passed through downtown with the old stone courthouse positioned right in the middle of the square. There was a great dime store and a really old hardware store, but mostly the courthouse was surrounded by lawyer offices. All the stores and offices were closed up tight, as it was late Sunday afternoon.

They made the turnaround at the old Dairy Queen and noticed a guy in a faded brown Malibu parked over to the side—under the DQ sign. "Hey, that's Charles," said Tanya, offering up a "queen wave" out the passenger side window. Charles nodded in greeting but stayed in his car.

"He must not be feelin' good, or maybe he's just about outta gas," Glenda said. She was very glad her daddy had provided her a gasoline card and didn't fuss about the bills.

As the Camaro rumbled back up the drag toward Mr. Rocker's house, Glenda looked thoughtful. She stretched her left hand out the window and relished the feeling of the warm air rushing around her fingers. She wiggled them, letting the wind massage her hand, then quickly grabbed the steering wheel and pointed to the large Victorian house with her right index finger. "I love that old house. It's so grand," she said dreamily. "Oh look—they got a historical marker!"

"Hey, yeah. I didn't notice that earlier. Good for them! Now it should stay just like it is forever," Janie said.

"I'd love to see the inside sometime. I hear it has three fire-places with fancy tile and twelve foot ceilings. And I bet the stained-glass windows are even more beautiful from the inside lookin' out!"

"Yepper. I noticed earlier they put in a circle drive this summer—at least I don't remember 'em havin' one before. You know, I bet it *is* a royal pain in the butt to hafta back out of your driveway straight onto the drag!" Tanya noted. The other two girls nodded in silent agreement.

They rode back up Main Street to the Astro Drive-In—the local hangout strategically positioned in the middle of the drag. Glenda whipped the car through a gap in the traffic, and then made a fast left turn into the entrance.

"Way to shoot the gap! Hey, there's a spot on the *un-nerd* side," Tanya said, making exaggerated quotation mark signs with her fingers.

"Good deal." Glenda drove slowly around the back side of the little white brick building positioned between the rows of ordering stations. "Do you see her?"

Tanya peered around the area. "Her car isn't here. It should be all right." Their archenemy worked as a car hop at the Astro; they avoided any contact with her when possible.

Glenda pulled up to the ordering board on the "un-nerd" side. It was extremely uncool to park on the nerd side. Common knowledge. That's why spots on the un-nerd side were sometimes hard to grab. Even if the only place to park was on the nerd side, one would keep going. It was best to make another drag and swing through the Astro on the next pass-by to try again. It was a rule—never, ever park on the nerd side.

"The usual?" Glenda asked of the other girls. "Let's get it to go, OK?"

"KO. Hit the button," Janie said brightly.

The voice in the box answered Glenda's call. Glenda spoke loudly to the speaker. "This is three separate orders. We need one with a corny dog, tater tots, and a cherry limeade—one with a corny dog, cheese tater tots and a cherry vanilla lime Sprite—and the third order is a just a corny dog and a Dr Pepper. To go please—and thank you!"

"OK. We'll have that right out," squeaked the tinny voice.

"Get your checks ready," Glenda instructed. They'd ordered like this enough times that they knew exactly how much each total would be, and they always wrote checks. They had to save their meager cash stash for places that wouldn't take personal checks.

After the food arrived in three separate sacks, Glenda gave up the coveted un-nerd spot and headed back to the dorm. "I'm sure my Amen Corner parkin' place will be gone," she said between sips of cherry limeade with the straw still in her mouth.

Sure enough, as Glenda drove in the college entrance, past the Student Center, the "quack shack," and the dorm—there were no available parking places in front of the building. As Glenda made the U turn, the girls looked toward the old World War I cannon on the lawn of the Administration Building and saw some friends sitting there. Glenda honked twice. The girls all waved at the two guys, Boots and Gene. Boots, whose name was actually Jim, was a real cowboy and the best country dancer around—thus the nickname. Gene was an all-around nice guy. The girls didn't really consider either of them boyfriend material, but they were great guys to have as friends.

Glenda parked her car on the opposite side of the median from the dorm. The girls piled out with a clamor. They continued singing the song that had been playing on the stereo even after the music stopped. The car windows were left down, the doors unlocked. Dairyville was that kind of town—nobody would mess with your stuff. They spotted another friend and walked toward an old bench anchored to the center of the island. CTSU tradition buffs called this structure the Shoe Bench. Perhaps this name was given because the backs of the benches were quite high—perfect for leaning back. Plus, there was a concrete and pipe centerpiece just right for propping up shoes.

"Hey, Brent. What's happenin'?" asked Tanya.

Brent didn't answer. He just sat very still.

Janie plopped down beside him, putting her food sack in her lap. "What's up with you? You think you're a bunny, and if you sit very, very still we won't see you? How about an explanation—and hurry up about it. I'm hungry, and my cheese tater tots are gettin' cold!"

Brent turned in an excruciatingly slow manner toward Janie, his face devoid of expression. It was almost a surprise to hear him actually speak out loud. "How do you know it is me? Or even who 'me' is? Or that anybody is actually sittin' here? I may or may not be real, and this place may or may not exist. I might be a figment of your imagination."

"HA!" cried Janie. "Let's see!" She reached over and pinched the inside of his knee with vigor. Brent offered no reaction. His sometimes odd behavior was well-known around campus. "Ah yes, KO—I see. You *are* a figment of my imagination." Janie rose to her feet from the bench. "I'm goin' upstairs to eat my cheese tater tots, and you can sit here and act like you're not here if that's what makes ya happy. See ya, Figment!"

With eyes rolling and giggles galore, the girls walked to their dorm. As they hopped up on the sidewalk, each paused in mid-step in a personal imitation of an Egyptian pose. The funny maneuver always caused them to laugh out loud.

After the interlude, they noticed Candace and Barb-oh were back from their errand. The two girls were walking toward the dorm steps with purpose.

"Hey, did ya get whatcha went after?" Tanya asked.

"Yep," Candace said. Barb-oh stood by in silence. "Glenda, I hate to do this, but I thought you should see it."

She nervously handed a folded newspaper to Glenda. A confused Glenda put her bag of food and her drink down on the top step. She took the paper from Candace's shaking hand. Then she looked down at the *Stonehill Gazette:*

A picture of Kevin. *Her* Kevin, looking back at her with his bedroom eyes and crooked nose, wearing the shirt she had given him for Christmas. Her Kevin and a blonde girl sat side-by-side, shoulders touching, smiling happily.

The caption below the photograph provided more information:

Mr. and Mrs. Weldon Waring proudly announce the engagement of their oldest daughter, Kelly Ruth, to Kevin Ray Curtis. The casual double ring wedding ceremony will be held in the Waring home in Stonehill, Texas, at 3:00 p.m. on the fifteenth of September. Friends and family are invited to attend. Reception will follow.

Glenda stared at the picture for a few seconds, and then slowly sank down as her knees gave way, wilting onto the bottom step. Tanya caught the paper as it slid from Glenda's limp fingers and looked at the page. "That butt-face!" She glanced at Glenda and whispered, "Oh, Glenda. Oh, my God."

"I'm *so* sorry," Candace said. "Folks in Stonehill say she's pregnant." Barb-oh looked on with concern.

Slowly raising her face toward her friends with a look of shock and disbelief, Glenda closed her eyes. A cry of grief, loss and pain rose from deep within her heart. The sound was like that of an injured animal. It was a moan, a muted scream that rose above the group of girls and out into the darkening sky. It was the kind of sound that could raise the hair on the backs of necks. And it did.

"What in the world was that?" asked Boots. Gene jumped down from where he had been sitting on the cannon. Boots didn't expect an answer. He hurriedly joined Gene, who was already running toward the disturbing sound.

The Figment also heard the disconcerting cry. He dropped his figment façade, hurrying across the parking lot toward the dorm. The three guys arrived on the sidewalk where the girls were gathered but stopped short. Their eyes met with the common masculine purpose to protect, then moved ahead as one toward the group of girls. But as they reviewed the situation, each observed no one was bleeding or otherwise in mortal danger. Wary eyes relaxed and gave way to willing ears as the guys stayed in the background and listened.

"I don't believe it," said Glenda. "Just this mornin' he wanted me to go with him to San Antonio and get married tomorrow. He begged me!" She looked up at her friends with pain and tears in her blue eyes.

"Yeah. Oh, Glenda, he wanted to marry you so he wouldn't hafta marry HER!" Tanya said bitterly, pointing at the picture in the paper.

The guys looked at each other quizzically. They moved in closer to stand among the group of girls huddled around Glenda, who was trembling on the bottom step. "What's going on?" asked Gene.

Janie took the newspaper from Tanya and thrust it at him. "Take a look at that." She moved past him to sit beside her shocked friend on the step. Glenda had begun to sob. Janie put her arm around her.

"Glenda...I'm sorry, but I have to say I'm not surprised," Gene said quietly, handing the paper to Boots. Janie looked sharply up at him, but he was looking at Glenda compassionately.

"Oh, man," the Figment spoke after he took the paper from Boots. "Damn him. I always thought he was a son of a bitch." Boots remained silent but looked off into the distance.

"You're not helpin'," Tanya said with a slap to the Figment's arm.

Glenda was quiet, but they all could see she was about to completely fall apart. She seemed to be on the edge of hysteria.

"Come on. Let's go upstairs," Janie said gently. She motioned to the others to pick up the food and drinks and follow. Barb-oh grabbed the paper from the Figment before the girls disappeared into the dark hallway of the dorm. The guys stood abandoned on the sidewalk in the fading sunlight.

"Hmm," grunted Gene. "Back to the cannon and do some thinking, Boots."

"Right." Boots looked at the Figment. "Comin'?"

"Yeah, sure—might as well watch the cars go by." Brent was such a notorious loner, Boots and Gene were suprised he agreed to join them. But they shrugged and started walking.

The three guys moved slowly back across the parking lot, noticing the sunset through the trees over the dining hall. Avoiding the concrete steps that led to the Administration Building, each took the shortcut by hopping up onto the stone retaining wall in front of the cannon, and walking across the freshly mowed grass. While Boots and Gene regained their perches on either side of the barrel, the Figment leaned casually on one of the cannon's wheels.

"Hey, there's that crazy guy in the big Thunderbird," said Boots.

Gene nodded. "Yeah, that guy can really drive. I've seen him turn that land yacht around on a dime. I wish I had a car like that. It looks new—must be a '78 or '79 model."

"Sorry about that," the Figment said. "Your role is the starvin' college student, and for wheels like that you gotta have a real job."

Gene considered the remark. "True. You speak the truth, oh wise one."

The silver Thunderbird made the U turn in front of the cannon to head back out of the college drive. The driver, with his right hand resting lightly on top of the steering wheel, casually lifted his index finger in greeting to the shadowy figures on the cannon. The three guys returned the acknowledgment with almost imperceptible nods in unison—the most noticeable being when Boots' beige felt cowboy hat turned slightly orange with reflected light from the flaming sunset.

"He's by himself. Seems like that's kind of unusual," Gene said.

"The night is young," said the Figment.

"Again, my unusual friend, you speak the truth. You know, there's really no telling what goes on in that car."

Boots tipped his hat in agreement.

Directly behind the Thunderbird, the four-wheel drive pickup rolled up with the dog in back. They, too, were about to make the U turn in front of the cannon and its attendants.

"GRRRRR!" The Figment growled loudly, quickly gaining the dog's attention. The large Blue Heeler moved menacingly over to the right side of the pickup toolbox and stared straight at the source of the noise.

"GRRRRR!"

The dog stood tall and alert, ears up, locking his eyes on the Figment. As the truck made the turn to move away from the object of his attention, the dog moved his legs to keep his balance on top of the toolbox. He moved back-and-forth as needed to keep his sharp eyes focused on the irritating human. The pickup moved further away—completely out of sight in the relative darkness that took place between dusk and the delayed activation of the streetlights on campus.

The Figment let out a yell. "HA! I WIN!"

"Win what?" Boots asked impatiently.

"The starin' contest—I win."

"Just because he couldn't see you anymore. That's the only reason, Brent. He'd still be here staring at you if the pickup under him hadn't driven away." Gene laughed at his own words.

"I still win," the Figment said indignantly. "Tell me again where you're from. One of those 'I' states?"

"Indiana, Brent. I was born in Houston, but my folks moved to Indiana when I was little." They'd been over this before.

"Right. Illinois—Indiana—one of those 'I' states." The Figment's drawl was a bit snide. "I wondered why yew tawk funny."

Gene ignored the comment, though it was true. He tended to put the "g" on the ends of words, whereas his friends usually dropped it. He couldn't help the way he talked, and neither could they.

A few other cars drove by, but the people in them didn't pay any attention to the guys at the cannon. Next a big white station wagon with three girls in the front seat rounded the first turn of the U. The passenger waved enthusiastically from the open window.

"Hey, there! How's about takin' us for a drag?" yelled Boots.

"In your dreams, cowboy!" Laughter erupted from the car. The large vehicle that was obviously somebody's mama's car pulled away.

"Good grief, man. They're in high school!" cried Gene.

"Jail Bait," the Figment stated with a snort.

"I can dream, can't I?" asked Boots.

"Just make sure there's no cop in that dream, buddy, or you'll be lookin' at a statutory rape charge!" the Figment said.

Gene nodded. "Yeah, Boots. You know, he's right. You'd best stick with consenting adults—real women."

"Now if you could just get one to notice you, Boots, you'd be in business!" The Figment's voice carried its usual sarcasm.

"Shut up, Brent!" Boots said with equal venom. "I don't see you hangin' out with any real women, bubba."

"Now Boots. Don't get your panties in a wad. I believe it's time for this smart young man to go find a beer or somethin'. See y'all later."

With that, the Figment made his exit into the darkness.

Gene and Boots settled back to silently watch the world go by. The guys made no noise, but the campus wasn't at all quiet. They heard country music coming from pickup trucks, ZZ Top from a Roadrunner, loud exhaust pipes, and a lot of noise caused by a pair of motorcycles that seemed to be chasing each other around the island. Finally, they rocketed out of sight. The parade of passing vehicles seemed continuous.

"You know, there's really a lot of cool cars in this town," Gene said.

"Yepper. Here comes that Thunderbird again. Ah ha, the driver is no longer alone. Surprise, surprise, surprise. He has picked up a friend."

The silver Thunderbird rounded the start of the U, with the driver saluting in the same manner as before. A young man with a slightly fuzzy blonde afro coolly flashed the two-fingered peace sign at the guys from the passenger seat. He also tipped his chin upward in acknowledgment and then dropped his hand, drumming his fingers on the outside of the door to a Ted Nugent tune. Suddenly, the driver goosed the car around the other corner of the U. The exhaust pipes rumbled, and the car fishtailed slightly before it straightened, proceeding calmly down the road on the way out of the campus.

"Not impressed!" shouted Janie as she returned from Glenda's car. She'd been sent to retrieve the Queen tape for Tanya.

The driver revved the engine again, and the tires chirped briefly. Giggling, Janie heard the occupants of the car laughing over the sound of the tailpipes. After she ran past the Shoe Bench, the Thunderbird came to a slow stop behind a parked car.

"Hey, Fuz. There's the yellow Camaro. Seems like that girl back there rides in it, and I think she lives up there in that end room with the bright light," the driver commented coolly.

"Yeah," agreed the passenger, the guy called Fuzzy. "I've seen her ridin' around before, and that car is always parked around here if it's not out on the drag." He looked over toward the girls' dorm and nodded.

The driver, nicknamed "Evel Knievel" by those who knew him best, looked intently at one of the end rooms on the second floor of the dorm. He saw figures moving around behind filmy curtains but couldn't really see much from that far away. The room on the other side had some kind of poster hanging on the back wall. He'd have to look closer next time around. Evel wondered if the girl was up there, the one who drove the yellow Camaro. Shaking the thoughts away so hard that his longish hair stood out a little on either side wildly above his ears, he stepped on the gas, rapidly exiting the college.

The Thunderbird motored on past the boys' dorm and up to the north end of the drag at the new Dairy Queen. "There's some girls pullin' out, Evel," said Fuzzy. "Do the Dairy Queen Turnaround in front of 'em."

A roguish expression crossed Evel's face. He grabbed the emergency brake and turned the steering wheel in an expert move that flipped the big car around "one-eighty," the perfect spin ending when the car headed calmly back the way it had just come.

"Perfect! Maybe they'll chase us," Fuzzy said hopefully.

"Question is—do you really wanna get caught?"

Fuzzy leaned out the window to eye the carload of girls. His frizzy hair blew into his face, as he noticed the car make a quick right turn off Main Street. He ducked back inside. "Hell, they turned off," he said dejectedly. He made a partially successful attempt to put his hair back in the right places.

"That's your luck, Fuz—always bad," Evel said with a snicker.

Fuzzy gave his friend a brief dirty look, but then relaxed to enjoy the ride. "Hmm, that's weird—it's kinda quiet through here."

"It's fixin' to not be quiet. Look up ahead. It's Ben in the Trans Am, and he's flashin' his headlights."

"Oh, no. Not that." Fuzzy gripped the armrest firmly with his right hand while bracing against the dash with his left. Casting an uneasy glance at Evel, Fuzzy read the expression: something exciting was about to happen. He ducked his head and focused his eyes on the floorboard.

Evel flashed his headlights back at the approaching car and sat up straighter in the seat, squinting his eyes into slits. His lips opened a bit, and he pressed his tongue against the right corner of his mouth. The cars approached each other at equal speeds. At what seemed to be a predetermined cue, each driver switched lanes across the yellow line onto the wrong sides of the road.

Fuzzy closed his eyes and held on even more tightly.

As the two vehicles passed, each driver could hear the other yelling with excitement. As soon as they were clear, the cars steered back onto their proper sides of the road.

Evel threw his head back and shouted with joy. Fuzzy released his death grip on the armrest. Consequently, he waved his arms excitedly back-and-forth above and beside his head inside the Thunderbird. "I HATE it when y'all do that!"

Evel quieted his laughter to a chuckle. "Would you rather me stay on the right side of the road when Ben's on the wrong side?"

"No! I guess not, but it's still crazy."

"Yep. It is. Oh, it's not so bad here in town, but it really gets interestin' when he wants to swap lanes out on the highway goin' eighty or ninety miles an hour."

As the car bounced over the railroad tracks, Fuzzy did a double take out the passenger window.

"What is it?" asked Evel.

Fuzzy frowned. "I don't know—somethin' with the Marlboro Man. Let's take a closer look when we come back by."

"No problem. He's been there for years, and I bet he'll still be there when we roll past here again."

"Yeah, it's not like he's gonna walk down to the Quick Stop!"

"Nope. He's pretty well stuck right there. In concrete."

Evel continued driving down the drag. Fuzzy looked out the window. "Hey, Moo Lah," he called to the fiberglass Holstein cow that stood on a platform in all her black and white spotted glory, some fifteen feet above ground. The platform was planted atop a pedestal on the corner of the courthouse square, bearing a sign that proclaimed the total gallons of milk produced yearly from the local dairies rounded up to the nearest 10,000th. "Someday, Moo Lah," Fuzzy called out the window to the cow. He turned to Evel with a meaningful look.

Evel ignored his passenger and drove past the businesses in the downtown area. One had a reflective coating on the glass facing Main Street, which served as kind of a sun shield for the interior of the building and created a mirror for those on the outside. If the traffic light at that intersection caught him, Evel always took the opportunity—day or night—to look in the mirror to check out how the car looked—and was never disappointed.

He drove to the old Dairy Queen and noticed Charles' Chevy Malibu backed in under the DQ sign. Evel nosed in the Thunderbird beside the faded brown car so the drivers' windows would be facing each other, then shut off the engine.

"Hi there," said Charles brightly.

"Outta gas again, buddy?" Evel asked. Fuzzy made a funny face at Charles.

"Yeah, almost. Stop lookin' at me like that, Fuz. Well, I got just enough to get to and from work till payday Friday." Charles was most times broke and had terrible luck in general. But he was a good friend—good for a lot of fun.

"You wanna ride around with us?" *Why ask?* Evel already knew the answer.

"You bet, thanks!" Charles climbed out of the Malibu.

Fuzzy and Evel had also exited the Thunderbird and were leaning on the trunk. "First—let's git a Dipped Cone," Fuzzy suggested. "I'm buyin'."

"You're on," agreed Charles.

The three crossed the pothole-filled parking lot and entered the building through the glass door. A short time later, they walked out carrying flat-bottomed cones with soft-serve vanilla ice cream coated with a hard shell of chocolate. The workers at the Dairy Queen hand-dipped the ice cream in melted chocolate. It was almost magical to watch the way the chocolate hardened as the cone was handed to the patron wrapped inside a white piece of tissue paper.

The guys returned to their cars, nibbling and slurping on the ice cream cones, as they relaxed in the dim yellow glow of the streetlight. They watched the parade of cars, their silence interrupted only by slurping noises.

"Hey, Evel. There's your little brother," said Fuzzy. Evel caught part of his dipped cone's chocolate shell with his teeth before it slipped off the ice cream and plunged to the ground. Ice cream melts fast in September in Texas. "Don't that Nova run purdy good?"

"Yep. Watch this." Evel balanced the flat cone on the trunk of his car and raised his hand in greeting. Larry's face took on an impish expression, as Evel pointed at him—twirling his finger in circles. Larry's grin grew to a wicked smile. He pulled out of the parking lot and came to a stop on Main Street. After a moment, the engine roared, and the back wheels started spinning. Smoke rolled out from under the Nova in clouds that drifted over the Dairy Queen parking lot. Larry let off the brake, allowing the car to move forward out of the tire smoke.

"Weee Haw!" called Charles, as Evel and Fuzzy cheered.

"Not a bad smoky burnout for a kid!" Fuzzy said.

"Yeah, I helped him rebuild the engine, and it's pretty stout. You know, I love the smell of tire smoke in the evenin'." Evel retrieved his ice cream cone before it melted into a puddle of sticky goo on his freshly polished trunk lid.

Nervous, Charles asked, "What if the cops hear?"

"Or smell," Fuzzy added.

"He knows what to do. He *is* my little brother," Evel calmly replied.

Larry screamed the Nova up the drag for a bit—and then quickly turned off on a side street to disappear into a residential neighborhood. The locals knew their way around town much better than the college kids, who rarely veered from the drag or the main roads. Occasionally, they would venture off into the neighborhoods if there was a party somewhere. But afterward, they likely couldn't remember how they got there or how to get back again.

"See what I mean?" Evel asked proudly.

They heard a noise from the museum grounds next to the old Dairy Queen. Sometimes a cop sat back in the darkness by the little historical chapel to sleep or try to catch people pulling in to park. Sure enough, a police car appeared. It seemed to be in a big hurry, but with no lights or sirens. The car had begun to gain speed but abruptly slowed in front of the Dairy Queen. The officer noticed the fresh black tire marks on the road. He looked over at the guys leaning on the Thunderbird. All three had innocent, though somewhat amused, looks on their faces. Each gave the officer a friendly salute with what was left of their ice cream cones, as if they were saying, *hey, we didn't do it. We're sittin' here eatin' Dipped Cones.*

The cop glared at them and took off toward town. "I guess Larry better stay off the drag tonight," said Charles.

"Yeah, he's gotta get up and go to school tomorrow anyway," Evel said. "He'll take the back-roads home. Let's make a couple a' drags to see what's happenin'. There's somethin' I wanna look at."

"Yeah, the Marlboro Man," said Fuzzy.

"And somethin' else," Evel added.

Charles cast a questioning look at Fuzzy and received a shrug in response. The Thunderbird pulled out onto the drag behind a few cars that were completing their turnarounds in the parking lot. After passing Moo Lah and the courthouse, the car travelled toward the railroad tracks.

"Can we stop here? Let's take a look," Fuzzy asked of Evel.

Evel checked the rearview mirror and confirmed no headlights were approaching. He brought the big car to a stop in the road where they could get a good look at the Marlboro Man. This icon was a billboard unlike any other around—a thirty-foot cutout of a rugged cowboy smoking a cigarette. He was very big and very cool—a unique landmark on the drag. Or, for that matter, a unique icon on the national landscape.

Fuzzy noticed something wrong. "Somebody shot him! There's an arrow in his...pants!"

The three were outraged that someone would shoot arrows into the Marlboro Man. But it was doubly shocking for him to be skewered in that tender area. "Ouch," said Charles with a cringe. "They got him right in the...zipper."

"Good shot," noted Evel, "or maybe just lucky. Oh, great—now everybody will be shootin' arrows at him. I sure hope they don't miss and hit somebody over at the Rastro."

The guys had nicknamed the Astro Drive-In after George Jetson's dog. Evel often lapsed into Astro talk. Sometimes other guys mimicked the old space cartoon, too.

"Rat's ror sure, Ralph!" Fuzzy added.

They nodded their heads—first in agreement—then slowly side-to-side in sympathy. Evel bounced the big car over the railroad tracks. At the college entrance he turned right, slowly cruising up to the girls' dorm. He stopped to point up at a well-lighted room on the second floor. The back of the wall could be seen perfectly through the open window. "See that poster up there in that end room with the light? What is it?"

Fuzzy squinted and peered into the room. He let out a hoot. "Wow, it's a picture of a bunch of naked girls on bicycles!"

"Queen *Jazz*," said Charles knowingly from the back seat.

Fuzzy turned around to look at his buddy. "Huh?"

"You know the song 'Fat Bottomed Girls'? The poster was in the Queen album with that song on it. *Jazz*. Tanya, the girl that lives up there, listened to it all the time on 8-track last year. I know her."

Evel turned sharply around. "You know the girl up there—the one with the yellow Camaro?"

"No. Well, yeah sorta'. Tanya drives a gray Vega that smokes." Fuzzy and Evel both looked at Charles like he was nuts. "I mean exhaust smoke. You know—it burns oil—I mean *really* bad. But she rides around a lot with the girl who has that Camaro. I think she lives in the other end room. It's dark over there right now. Her name's Glenda."

Charles pointed across the median to where the yellow car was parked, then back up to the darkened room.

"Hmm, OK," Evel said coolly. The dark stillness gave him a strange feeling. He shook his head to banish the odd sensation, and his hair again stood out a bit. "Let's go."

Fuzzy leaned forward to turn the volume knob to max. "Queen's OK, but let's crank up Ted."

Within moments, all three were drumming to the screaming sounds of Ted Nugent's guitar—Evel on the steering wheel, Fuzzy on the dash and Charles on the back of the seat. They loved ridin' around. There was no better way to spend a Sunday evening.

Chapter Two

GLENDA SAT ON THE WOODEN LEDGE of the large open window at the end of the second floor hall. The window was right next to her room—she'd sat there many times before watching the cars go by—waiting for Kevin. All the girls on the second floor of Horne Hall liked to sit there when they could; almost all had gotten into trouble at one time or another for doing so. The Dean came up with all sorts of lame reasons why they should stay away from the window. Like they were destroying the screens—university property. Or it was dangerous—they might fall out. Or it wasn't ladylike—as if any of the Horne Hall girls cared about that. It was a major rule infraction to sit there, but Glenda just didn't care.

In fact, she didn't care about much of anything anymore. The previous two weeks were a complete blur in her mind. Her friends had made sure she got up in the morning, went to class and even practically carried her to the dining hall for lunch and supper. But she couldn't bring herself to eat and could just barely keep a Dr Pepper down. She considered that it was a good thing she didn't care for alcohol; otherwise, crawling permanently into a bottle of spirits may have been a real possibility. She shivered at the image of what happens to the brain—the risk of addiction. Besides, the taste of alcoholic beverages always gave her chill bumps and shudders. She didn't need that sort of thing. Normally, she was silly enough without chemical assistance. But not lately.

Glenda stretched her legs out on the wide sill. Crossing her ankles, she leaned her head back on the frame. The windows in the old building were huge, designed to let in as much air as possible since the dorm was built long before some really smart man somewhere invented air conditioning. While leaning against one side of the window, stretching her legs, her tennis shoe clad feet didn't come close to touching the other side. Her head fit comfortably under the raised sash. She was average in height, weight, in shoe size. Glenda believed herself to be very average all around. On the other hand, Candace, being a much bigger person, had to slump over when she sat in that same place, her chin almost resting on her ample chest, as she wedged herself in the window. That image caused Glenda to feel almost sociable. It was Sunday afternoon and all right with her that things were quiet. She'd come back to school early after leaving home while her folks were still at church. All day Saturday her mom kept throwing clichés around, saying "shake it off" and "stop mopin' around about Kevin." "Good riddance to bad rubbish, I say." Glenda heard that one at least five times that day.

It hurt. It hurt badly. There was nothing left to do but go through the motions.

Glenda sighed, closed her eyes and let her mind wander. She examined the past two years, how she'd fallen into—and seemed trapped inside—such a miserable mental state. Memories of past incidents ran through her mind like a movie: hickeys on his neck, girls claiming to be his dancing partners, his asking for money to be dropped out of her window so he could treat his friends to a midnight hamburger. It was really amazing—there were so many things he did that should have opened her eyes long before. Glenda finally realized Kevin's explanations for such actions, explanations that seemed so logical and acceptable at the time, were really just downright deceptive. Time-after-time, she accepted his lies as gospel truth. Totally oblivious to his duplicity, over-and-over she forgave, forgot or simply ignored his behavior—each time taking him back into her arms.

Blind love. That's what it was. Stupid, blind love. He did so much that caused her pain. Yet, it took the ultimate betrayal to prove that her love was misplaced. He used and hurt her deeply. Glenda decided at that moment no one would ever treat her like that again. Never.

Her quiet emotional analysis was disturbed by the sound of a car rumbling slowly up the lane. It was a baby blue two-door Buick or Oldsmobile. Sometimes she thought of those cars as Oldsmobuicks. But she'd never seen this car before. The guy in the passenger seat looked up at the window and seemed surprised to see someone, or maybe he was surprised to see her specifically, sitting there. He smiled ever so slightly, raising his right hand in a hesitant greeting. Glenda cocked her head to the side a bit and froze for a moment. She lifted her eyebrows in surprise, then felt her face relax pleasantly. She was also astonished to find her hand rising to wave back at the guy—a numbed instinct seemed to almost awaken.

Tanya came out of her room and was surprised to see her friend showing more life than she had in over two weeks. "Who is it?"

"Oh, I don't know. Just some guys in an Oldsmobuick." Glenda lowered her hand but kept her gaze focused out the window.

"Hey, that's the guy that drives the silver Thunderbird!" Tanya exclaimed.

Recognition sparked for Glenda. "Yeah, you're right. I think it is. That's strange. He usually drives his own car."

"I've never seen that car before. Maybe a friend of his got some new wheels."

The blue vehicle pulled away, slowly making its way around the U. It continued on the one-way down the other side of the median, and then slowed even more while rolling past her Camaro. She'd parked on the far side of the island, since she didn't plan on going out anytime soon. She reasoned there was no need in hogging the Amen Corner parking place.

"Glendee-girl. You haven't done anything lately, and you're not eatin' even when we make you go to the dinin' hall." Tanya leaned on Glenda's shins to look out the window. "You're losin' weight and if you don't look out, you're gonna get sick."

The two girls watched the blue car drive away. Glenda sighed. "So what? I *feel* sick...sick all the way down to my bones." She resumed her gloomy look.

"We need to get you out, Glendee-girl. When everybody gets here, let's do somethin'," said Tanya firmly. The pet name, Glendee, had come from a combination of Glenda's name and her middle initial: "E." Glendee.

"I really doubt I'll feel like it. I've gotta study for a chemistry quiz tomorrow, anyways."

"Quiz? That shouldn't take much studyin'. So, go on and study now. At least we could go out and sit on the cannon later, KO?"

"I guess so. Maybe." Glenda unfolded herself from the window sill and heard Tanya groan. A horn honked, as Glenda looked through the screen. "Oh, great," she whispered disgustedly.

An old Dodge station wagon had stopped in front of Horne Hall. After honking and looking to be sure she was seen, the person inside moved over and stuck her hand out the passenger side window flashing an obscene gesture known as "shooting the finger." The car moved away.

The gesture irked Tanya. "Gee-eez, Lou-eeze. What a low-life. We make a point to avoid her in town, and then she comes in here and does that. Why does she keep botherin' us?"

"It's an old feud, meaningless now. Except even as bad as I feel, I still cannot stand her guts," said Glenda with little emotion. She slowly shuffled into her room.

Tanya nodded and listened to Glenda plopping down on her bed with a squeak. She sat in the window in the same position that Glenda had just left, daring anyone to say anything about it. She grabbed that spot every chance she got. It was the best vantage point on the whole campus. From there you could see everyone driving in and out—not to mention anyone who was walking toward the dorm, sitting on the cannon or hanging out at the Shoe Bench. The powers that be had tried to stop them from sitting in the window, but they all had failed. Rarely was the window sill unoccupied, except in the middle of the night—sometimes insomniacs used it even then. All the girls avoided touching the screen in any way, but in her opinion Dean Stickler could go suck an egg.

Tanya had heard the dean's husband was the Principal of the local high school. She silently sent condolences to the teenagers of Dairyville. She chuckled disdainfully to herself. If Dean Stickler was bad, she could only imagine how grumpy Principal Stickler must be.

But the girls of Horne Hall had persevered together. It was part of the reason this dorm was special. That, and rarely did they lock or even shut their doors. The girls answered each other's phones, borrowed each other's records and tapes and sometimes clothes. At night, the building sounded like an airplane about to take off. With at least two box fans in each room plus all doors open for the greatest air flow, the collective hum resembled the howling of a jet engine. At that time of night, when the only sound was the roar of the fans, the building seemed almost alive. Another form of life appeared in the winter when the boilers kicked in, filling the radiators with warm water to heat the cold rooms. The pipes banged and popped and cracked until you'd swear it was the building's bones creaking in the cold morning air. Everyone suspected it was actually somebody down in the basement banging on the pipes with a wrench to coax the system to pump some heat into the ancient radiators.

Tanya felt a genuine affection for this dorm. It was the best home she'd ever had. She sat in the window in blue jeans and her Superman T-shirt, which she'd had since high school. Her name was on the back in black heat transfer letters. She reclined, daydreaming, purposely avoiding her biology book and the upcoming test. It just didn't seem all that important. The sun shone brightly. Traffic was picking up. More people moved around the campus than earlier. Tanya heard Boz Scaggs singing his heart out—"What Do You Want the Girl to Do"—the usual Sunday afternoon serenade from downstairs. The upstairs and downstairs residents engaged in stereo wars every now-and-then. Too much dancing and playing music loudly upstairs caused those below to pound a broom handle on the ceiling, communicating the displeasure of the occupants. Likewise, too much Boz Scaggs was liable to cause a bunch of jumping up-and-down and banging around from the upstairs to send the same signal from above. But it was OK right now—it fit the time. Her mood.

Tanya noticed a figure walking down the hall toward the end window. "Hall-oh!" Linda called in her very own version of "hello."

"Hey. Did you just get off work?"

"Yeah, and am I glad. What's goin' on? Is she in there?" Linda bobbed her head toward Glenda's room.

Tanya nodded her head. Linda nodded once, turning silently to go in. It was her room, too.

"Hall-oh, Glendee. How are you doin'?"

"Hi there, Linda Lou. OK, I guess. I'm just tryin' to study this organic chemistry and havin' a hard time keepin' my mind on it," replied Glenda with her head bowed. Her eyes were closed. It looked like she was praying; the pained look on her face spoiled that image.

"Well, try to keep at it for a while. I've gotta go run some errands. When I get back we'll do somethin'—KO?"

Linda was truly worried about her friend.

"OK. I guess so. Tanya wants me to go sit out on the cannon later. I'll try to go," said Glenda glumly. "I've gotta finish readin' this chapter, but then I can go. You know, I think I need to."

"That's for sure! I'll be back in a little while. Do you need anything from the store?"

"Naa. Mom fixed me up yesterday—I'm restocked, thanks." Glenda looked at Linda with gratitude. It was sure nice to have people who cared about you.

Now, if she could just care about herself again.

Linda grabbed her purse and walked out of the room, her key ring jingling. She stopped the racket for a moment to move silently over to Tanya at the window. "Let's definitely get her out this evenin'. She's wastin' away, and we've gotta do somethin' about it."

"Definitely," Tanya whispered back. Then, in a more normal tone of voice, "No thanks—I don't need anything. See ya when you get back."

"KO," Linda replied aloud. The two girls flashed conspiratorial expressions.

On her way out, Linda called a "Hall-oh" to Janie, who was be-bopping down the hall on her way to the room she shared with Tanya. She tossed her laundry bag through the doorway, slid up to the window and tapped Tanya's shoe with her finger.

Tanya got the message, and bent her knees to pull her feet up close to her butt. That made room for Janie on the window sill. Neither girl was considered tall, so they both fit nicely into the window even with outstretched legs. They looked something like bookends facing the wrong way, backs to either side of the vertical frame with knees slightly bent and sneaker soles touching in the middle.

"We're gonna get Glenda out and go sit on the cannon after while," said Tanya softly, holding a finger up to her pursed lips to keep her usually boisterous roommate quiet.

"Does she know? Why are we whisperin'?"

"Yepper. She agreed to go a little while ago. I don't want to disturb her studyin', so she can come out with us later, silly."

"Oh," Janie whispered back. She covered her mouth to stifle the laughter. Tanya quickly caught her friend's case of the giggles. Sometimes they did that—just cracked up.

"Hey, what's so funny?" a voice called from below.

They looked down to see Gene peering at them from the sidewalk. They immediately stopped laughing, glanced at each other, then returned their eyes to him. "Stay right there!" Tanya yelled.

The girls ran down the hall, hit the stairs at full speed, sprinted past the blaring Boz Scaggs and rushed through the open double doors. They flew down the steps to land beside Gene on the sidewalk.

"Where's Boots?" Janie asked.

"Over at the Shoe Bench," Gene replied.

Each girl grabbed Gene by an arm. They headed to the Shoe Bench.

"Why, there are two of my favorite ladies!" called Boots to the approaching trio.

Janie ran over to join him. They sat side-by-side on one bench while Gene and Tanya took the other side. All eight feet—four small and two large sneakers, and two cowboy boots—were soon propped up on the pipe footrests.

"We're gonna make Glenda come out tonight, and we're gonna start by sittin' on the cannon. So, you guys gotta stay off it," Janie said.

"Sure thing, your highness," Gene replied sarcastically. "Gosh, can we at least sit here?"

"Yepper. That'll be just fine. I don't know what'll happen, but I hope lots of people drive through so there'll be somethin' to look at," said Tanya.

Hopefulness filled Janie. "Maybe The Guy With The Hair'll come by."

"The Guy With The Hair?" asked Gene. "Don't most guys have hair?"

"Not like this guy," Tanya said. "His is always perfect. Plus, he's blonde, cute and he's a football player. And he has a really nice car."

"Oh, just my type," stated Boots, rolling his eyes.

Tanya stomped her feet on the ground. "Shut up and teach me to waltz, Boots." She had tried several times to talk him into teaching her to waltz—country style.

The cowboy stood up. Being a gentleman, he gallantly reached his hand across the footrest toward Tanya. She, in turn, elaborately placed her hand in his. He led her over to the open area on the concrete pad, where they assumed the standard dancing position.

"Just put your right hand in mine up here," Boots held his hand out in the air at shoulder height. "And hang on to my back belt loop with the other. I'll put my arm around you...here." He gently placed his right arm around her waist.

"Hey, watch it, buddy!" cried Tanya jokingly. Everyone knew Boots wouldn't take advantage of any girl, especially Tanya.

"Hush," Boots chided. "Now just think big step, then two little steps. Step—two—three, step—two—three. Right, like that. Hey, Gene, hum us a waltz."

"Yeah, right. Hum it yourself," Gene replied acidly. Everyone knew he couldn't carry a tune in a bucket. They wouldn't even let him sing along with a tape in the car. Back home, the church music director always said they had a full choir: Soprano, Alto, Tenor, Bass—and Gene.

Boots smiled mischievously. He did the humming, directing Tanya in their waltz around the Shoe Bench. His movements were so smooth and confident. It was truly a beautiful thing to dance with him. They kept waltzing as cars passed by the Shoe Bench. Some honked in approval.

"There, you got it! See, it ain't so hard," he commented happily.

"For you...maybe," said Janie. She seemed ready to pout.

"OK. You next, little miss," Boots said. After this comment, he gracefully turned Tanya around, right in step, back to the bench. He released her. She floated down to sit by Gene. Boots put his hand out to Janie. In no time he had her waltzing, turning circles and laughing in the grass. The concrete pad wasn't big enough for this lesson.

"Step—two—three, step—two—three," Janie chanted. "Hey, this is easy!"

"And so graceful," Gene said with a sigh. He couldn't dance either. No rhythm. Tanya gently patted his knee in support. They all loved Gene—even if he couldn't sing or dance.

"Hall-oh!" a voice called from behind Janie and Boots. "Turning circles? I want to!" Linda put her grocery bag and purse on the bench beside the sulking Gene. She jumped up-and-down a few times. Skipping over to the dancing couple, she tapped Janie on the shoulder. "May I cut in?"

Boots looked down at Janie with amusement. He twirled her around quickly, holding her hand above her head. Janie fell giggling and a bit dizzy down to the bench.

Linda was an excellent dancer, and she loved to dance with Boots. He could turn her in circles like no one else. He started humming while waltzing with her out to the asphalt drive. They proceeded to dance their way up the street and toward the U.

"Hall-oh, Glendee!" Linda called up to the room, as they passed by the dorm.

Glenda leaned over to look out the window at the sound of Linda's voice. Linda waved at her roommate—then she and Boots danced their way through the first turn of the U with several tight circles. Glenda continued to watch them with wonder and amusement. She shook her head side-to-side good-naturedly. One never knew what one might see out that window.

Several sorority sisters sat on the cannon. They whooped and applauded as Boots and Linda danced by. A car drove past playing a Lynyrd Skynyrd song, prompting Boots to change dance styles as he sang "Gimme Three Steps" to Linda Lou. They jitterbugged around the rest of the U, moving in circles this way and that. They performed the special move where she turned, grabbed his hand—he turned, grabbed hers—then they pirouetted each other around in a circle. When they finally ended up at the Shoe Bench, both dancers were out of breath.

"Thanks Boots. That was great fun!"

"Any time, Linda Lou. Always a pleasure." He bowed, ever the gentleman.

Linda began gathering her things. "Whew! I'm goin' on up to the room. Hey, I got Glenda somethin' special. Y'all come up in a little while, but don't wait too long, OK?"

Tanya popped up to her feet. "I peeked, Linda. You got ice cream!"

"Hey, Tanya. You lost your Y!" Gene exclaimed. Tanya turned around with a confused look.

"Lookee. Here it is!" Janie reacted. She quickly retrieved the letter from the concrete, slapping it onto Tanya's back. She stood back to review her work. "Ha, now you're Tan-ay. The 'Y' is at the end! You know, like Sund-ay—only you're Tan-ay!"

"Yep," continued Linda, apparently ignoring the conversational drift. "Strawberry, Glenda's favorite, I thought it might help. I have some spoons in the room. Janie, you and *Tan-ay* come on up in a few minutes," she said with a giggle. She had noticed the rearranging of Tanya's name after all.

"KO. We scream for ice cream!" exclaimed Janie.

Linda walked toward the dorm awash in good feelings. She hoped Glenda would respond to the strawberry ice cream. Still exhilarated from the dance around the U, she was about to walk out from between two parked cars when she noticed a vehicle moving slowly in her direction. It was the silver Thunderbird with the guy she'd heard was considered to be the King of the Drag behind the wheel. He was looking over toward the dorm. But he must have noticed her out of the corner of his eye. The driver turned his gaze to her pleasant and somewhat astonished face. As he passed by, Linda nodded slightly and adjusted her bag of cold tubs of ice cream. She noticed the guy had nice eyes with a hint of wildness in his good-humored expression. She'd never seen him up close like this—only occasionally out on the drag.

The car cruised smoothly away. She ran across the road to make her way up to the room.

Glenda saw Linda pause beside the slow moving silver Thunderbird. She watched the car closely. Charles was looking upward in her direction. She told herself, *what the heck—make an effort.* She waved at him with a shake of her hand. He waved back as the car went on around the U.

"She waved at me," Charles said.

"Who?" asked Evel.

"Glenda. The girl in the room up there. You know, the one with the yellow Camaro. She's Tanya's friend. She waved at me. Come to think of it, I haven't seen her car out for a few weeks."

"Me neither." Fuzzy popped up from the back seat. Charles had called "shotgun" at their last stop, so Fuzzy lost his usual front seat position. "You're right. Her car is always parked—I never see it out anymore."

Evel let the conversation sink in, as he made the rest of the U. He glanced back up at the second floor end room but was too far away and the light was wrong to see much of anything.

"There's Tanya!" Charles pointed toward the island, then raised himself out of the car window to sit on the door frame. "Hey, Tanya!" he called across the red vinyl roof.

At the sound of her name, Tanya popped up from the Shoe Bench. Seeing Charles' head bobbing above the Thunderbird, she ran across the grass, and between two parked cars. Evel pulled Charles back inside by his shirttail, just as she shuffled over to the passenger side.

"Hi Charles, what's goin' on?" she asked, leaning her forearms on the car door. "Hi, I'm Tanya. You're Evel Knievel, right?"

"Hey there," Evel said playfully. She knew he was a bit crazy but could see his smile expand into his very blue eyes.

Charles felt hopeful. "Wanna go ridin' around?"

"Sorry, but no. I can't right now. We're gonna eat some ice cream and then get Glenda to come out to the cannon. She's been feelin' pretty down lately."

"What happened?"

"Long story—maybe later. We're tryin' to help her feel better and get her over a complete butt-face."

"Oh," Charles said, disappointment and confusion mixing in his voice.

"Maybe we'll see y'all later," said Evel. "We'll be out ridin' around."

"KO! Stare at me, and I'll wave at you!" Tanya ran around the front of the car on the way back to the Shoe Bench.

"Man oh, man. Is she cute!"

"Sure is. A Supergirl named Tan-ay," Evel remarked.

"Huh?" Charles asked with crossed brows.

"Her shirt. Didn't you see the name on the back? It said Tan-ay." He pronounced the new nickname just like Janie and Linda had, and stepped on the gas a little harder than necessary.

"Oh, I didn't see that. I was lookin' at the front!"

"It's not a bad view from the backside either, buddy," remarked Fuzzy, as the Thunderbird took off. The motion of the car set him involuntarily back in the seat.

Back at the Shoe Bench, Gene was asking Tanya a question. "You know that guy—the driver? He's the King of the Drag!"

"Not really. But I do know his friend, Charles. We rode around a little with him last year," Tanya explained.

"Let's go eat the ice cream before it melts," said Janie. She stood up to stretch her arms above her head.

"Righto—let's go," replied Tanya, as she popped up onto her feet. "See you guys later. Remember—DO NOT sit on the cannon tonight, OK?"

"Gotcha. Can we at least visit?" asked Boots.

"Sure. Anything to cheer Glenda up. Hey, on second thought, when those girls over there leave, y'all could go claim it for us and save our places!"

"There's a good idea, Tanya," said Gene. "We'll grab it as soon as it's vacant. When you gals show up we'll move out, so your butts can sit on warm seats."

"That'll work," said Janie. She stood on her tiptoes to give Gene a hug, pleasantly surprising him.

"See ya'!" Boots called to the twosome hurrying to the dorm.

The girls raced down the hall, roaring into Linda and Glenda's room. They plopped down on either side of their depressed friend with a mighty squeak of the bedsprings.

"OK. Glendee, I got you a little somethin', and we're all gonna share," said Linda, pulling the two small tubs of ice cream from the paper sack. "Strawberry, of course."

She handed Glenda an open tub and a plastic spoon with a flourish. Glenda looked back-and-forth at the two girls at her sides expectantly.

"Hurry. It's gettin' soft after Linda's soirée around the island!" Janie said anxiously. Linda pulled out the other tub and three more spoons.

The girls huddled together in the room. Linda sat barefoot on the floor; the other three stayed on Glenda's bed. Each girl dipped out a big spoonful of the luscious strawberry ice cream, then rotated the cartons among them. "I remembered how you loved to go to the Udder Delight to get a strawberry ice cream cone last year. I thought it sounded good on a hot day like this," Linda said.

"Dee-lish!" exclaimed Glenda. "You know, my junior year in high school the school sponsored the foreign language classes on trips to Europe. Somehow my folks managed to come up with the money, and I went to Spain with that group. I was so shy." She saw the puzzled looks shot her way. "Yes, really—a terribly shy child. Anyway, between my bad Spanish and their bad English, I couldn't order off the menus, so it seemed I got the same fish and rice dish just about the whole week. When I got back to Texas, man, was I glad to see real food again. I ate a whole half gallon of strawberry ice cream plus seven ham and cheese sandwiches the first few days after I got home. You know, I think I could do that now, too." She looked fondly at her friends.

Linda, Janie, and Tanya glanced at each other with satisfied looks. It was working. The real Glenda was coming back!

After polishing off the ice cream, each girl got a coke from the little fridge in the corner of the room by the sink. It might have been a grape or orange soda, or a Dr Pepper, but it was still a "coke" to them.

"Let's do our studyin' now. Then we can go out to the cannon, KO?"

Glenda looked at Tanya. "Don't you have a biology test tomorrow? You shouldn't stay up all night studyin'. Go do some now. We'll go out about dark-thirty."

"OTay! Sounds good to me. Come on Janie," said Tanya. The girls carried their drinks across the hall to their room.

"Thanks, Linda," Glenda stated meaningfully. "I really needed that!"

"No prob. No prob at all. Now, where the heck are my shoes?"

The roommates snickered at each other, as Linda was notorious for losing her shoes. Both realized it was the first time Glenda had smiled or laughed in days. Linda hugged her. They were interrupted by the stereo across the hall playing the Earth, Wind and Fire song, "September." Glenda let her head fall back to gaze at the ceiling. Linda closed her eyes in a cringe.

Janie stuck her head in the room. "Go on and study. I've gotta work on my modern dance project."

Oblivious to her friends' reactions, she bounced happily into the hall. The unwilling audience could hear steps and jumps and occasionally an "ouch." She'd been practicing the self-choreographed dance routine for a week. "You know, I'll be glad when this is over. I mean this dance project to 'September' and the whole dang month. Mom would say 'don't wish your life away', but I'm sick to death of both," Glenda said.

"I know whatcha mean," replied Linda. "I'm glad you're feelin' better, but I'm certain Janie is in for a big headache if Tanya breaks that record over her curly head."

"If she doesn't do it, I will!" exclaimed Glenda. She lay down on the bed to finish an organic chemistry chapter. Linda opened a book she was reading for a literature class.

Outside the dorm, the parade of noisy vehicles continued— a distant din the girls had learned to ignore when necessary. They shut out Earth, Wind and Fire, the traffic outside and the worries of the day to concentrate. They didn't see the ratty old Matador stop below their window, or hear the honk. That sound blended in with everything else. The car moved away around the U.

Boots and Gene had claimed the cannon as soon as the sorority girls vacated the area and were comfortably saving Glenda's and Tanya's seats. They saw the Matador stop briefly in front of the girls' dorm. They recognized the car. Then the driver pulled around toward them.

"Oh my God—it's Kevin!" exclaimed Gene.

"So it is. Look over here at me, Gene. Don't let him think we saw him or even care to see him," Boots said coldly.

Gene physically turned his body away from the street to look straight at Boots, listening for any sign of the car stopping. They both breathed a sigh of relief as they heard the rattling vehicle fade away.

Boots was concerned. "OK. He's goin' out. Oh, boy—this is gonna be interestin'. Who knows what'll happen if Glenda sees him. You'd better go tell Tanya or Janie first."

"I'll go over and yell at them," Gene said. "One of them will come down."

"Just don't get Glenda lookin' out the window, bubba."

"Right. Thanks for the warning. I'll throw a rock or something."

Gene hopped down from the cannon seat. He walked across the grass looking for something to throw at Janie and Tanya's window. As he jumped off the retaining wall, he noticed some dirt clods that had apparently fallen off of a four-wheel drive truck or some such vehicle. Picking up a few dried mud balls, he headed over to the dorm to take aim at the room. He reared back and chunked one dirt clod at the open window. It hit the screen, exploding into a puff of dust and dirt that rained down on his head.

It worked though. Tanya's head appeared. "Hey! What's the big idea, throwin' dirt up here? It landed on my sheets!"

Tanya saw Gene motioning for her to come down. She jumped at the chance to leave the room but ran into Janie's path. They sidestepped each other, barely avoiding a collision. Tanya moved quickly to get away from Janie's fussing.

"You ruined it. Now I hafta to start all over again!" She stomped into the room to reposition the arm of the record player at the beginning of "September." As it began, she heard a bang— Glenda's door had been slammed shut. Cringing at the sound, Janie persevered by striding into the hall to do the routine again.

Tanya arrived at Gene's side, breathless from running down the stairs. "What is it?" she huffed.

"Come over here, away from the windows." He grabbed her arm.

They walked over toward the Shoe Bench. It was unoccupied, so they sat down.

"We just saw Kevin," he said to her gravely.

"Oh, no! He's in town? He should be married by now!"

"It was him all right. He stopped right in front of Glenda's room and honked. I guess she didn't notice. I hope she didn't see him and freak out."

"I don't think so. They were concentratin'. When they concentrate, they shut everything out—even Janie's modern dance homework," Tanya said with a sarcastic shake of her head. Her manner turned more serious. "Whatever could he want?"

"I'm not sure—but you're about to find out. There he is again." Gene's eyes widened. He tilted his head toward the street.

Tanya turned her body slowly in that direction. Kevin was peering directly at her. She felt like running as fast as she could in the opposite direction. Kevin motioned for her to come over to the car. Tanya glanced at Gene with dread. "Come with me," she whispered.

Gene took her arm. They walked slowly together toward the rusty old car. He released her, so they could squeeze between two closely parked cars to get to the stopped vehicle. They stood side-by-side to look at the person who had turned out to be the ultimate betrayer. This guy broke their good friend's heart—they didn't like it one bit. Dread and disgust showed in their faces as he got out of his car.

"Hi. Where's Glenda?" Kevin acted as if nothing had happened—like it was any other Sunday afternoon.

"What's it to ya?" asked Tanya coldly. "What 're you doin' here?"

He dropped the happy go lucky act. "I want to talk to Glenda. Tanya. Go get her for me—OK?"

"Humph. Fat chance. Go away, Kevin. Go back to your *wife*." Tanya's voice burned like acid. "Come on, Gene." She grabbed Gene's hand firmly, and they turned their backs. Kevin pointed toward the dorm room. "I'll find her. Even if I hafta go up there! I know the way, ya know."

Tanya ignored him, but noticed she was shaking. "God, please make him go away," she whispered. She needed to talk to Janie and Linda.

The car behind them started up with a dreadful noise. They heard it drive away, as they walked toward the Shoe Bench. They looked around to watch it making the U. Tanya took that opportunity to break away. "Go back to the cannon. I'll see you after while," she said, turning away. "Thanks, Gene. You're a good guy."

He playfully wiggled his fingers at her. "Go. Handle it gently."

When Tanya got back to the second floor, she looked in her room. Thankfully, Janie had finished with her rehearsal and was turning off the record player. She went over to Glenda's door, opened it a bit, and stuck her head in. It was weird to find the door closed.

"Hall-oh! Is the music over? Open the door, Tan-ay," Linda called from her desk.

"Linda. Uhh...could you come over here for a sec?" Tanya asked in a forced even tone.

Glenda looked up and shrugged. "Two more pages, and I'm done."

"Be right back." Linda walked in her bare feet across the room. She left the door open as she walked across the hall to Tanya and Janie's room.

"What's up?" she asked a bit too loudly.

"Shhh. I just saw Kevin. He's in town and wants to talk to Glenda."

"That butt-face! He should stay in Stonehill!" Anger peppered Janie's voice.

Linda stood still for a moment, her brow furrowed in thought. She took a deep breath and looked at the girls. "Five minutes. Then we go out to the cannon. Be ready—it might be rough. But we've gotta face it. Just act casual, OK?"

"KO," the two smaller, younger girls said in unison. They looked at each other in silent agreement to stand together with Glenda through whatever would happen. Linda exited the room, shaking her head side-to-side.

"It'll take five minutes for me to find my shoes!"

Tanya and Janie glanced at each other with amusement. Janie went into her closet to change. She had been wearing a dance leotard—not exactly "go hang out at the cannon" attire. Living in the end dorm room with no curtains had taught the girls to use the large closets on either side of the door as a dressing room, phone booth, or anything that required privacy. Either that or get dressed lying down on the bed—which was sometimes necessary to zip up the tight jeans they often wore.

"I hate all my clothes!" Janie's voice was muffled by the closet door.

Tanya dropped onto her bed and landed in the dirt Gene had thrown through the screen. She scooped it up as best she could, placing it pinch-by-pinch in the windowsill—flapping the sheet to shake off the rest onto the floor. She'd sweep someday. Tanya turned back to the window. There were little holes in the bottom of the screen—from the installation or something. They were handy to stick small items through, if you wanted to send something below. Like a message. Glenda used to roll up dollar bills tightly to push through the opening at Kevin's request. Tanya poked the dirt clods through the holes and dusted off her hands.

Janie exited the closet in fresh jeans and T-shirt, suddenly exuberant. She went to the mirror to arrange her curls, or, at the very least, to put them into some sort of order. Tanya joined her and brushed her own short hair. "Easy to manage," the beautician had said—"Short and sassy," her mother observed.

Tanya agreed with her mother's side on this point—she was short and sassy but certainly not easy to manage!

The girls walked over to Linda and Glenda's room to see if they were ready. Surprisingly, they were. Linda had found her shoes, plus Glenda looked lighthearted—two rather rare happenstances. Tanya and Janie's eyes met in a moment of dread, as they headed down the hall to face whatever might happen.

Candace came out of the community bathroom with dripping wet hair and a towel wrapped around her body. "Where are y'all goin'?"

All four girls stopped at the top of the stairs, turning their heads in unison to look at the source of the voice. "Y'all go on. I'll catch up with ya," Janie said. The other girls continued their way down the stairs.

Janie turned to Candace. "We're all goin' out to sit on the cannon and try to cheer Glenda up. I think she's feelin' better, but that might not last long."

"Good. Wait a sec...Huh?"

"We just heard that Kevin's in town lookin' for her."

"Oh, no. That low-life. He got married last week. My mom's neighbor was there!"

"Yeah, well—he's here now. I have no idea what's gonna happen. I'd better go catch up with 'em. You comin' out later?"

"Sure. I'll be there in a little while. I gotta dry my hair and stuff," replied Candace.

"KO. See ya in a bit." Janie turned to race down the stairs. Candace stood there for a moment, feeling the dread that Janie had shared. She shook her head slightly. Drops of water released from her curls dripped a trail on the linoleum all the way to her room.

Chapter Three

*T*HE GIRLS MANEUVERED THROUGH the parked and moving vehicles, then on to the cannon area. Glenda slowly walked up the steps in front of the flagpole. But the other girls took the shortcut, agilely hopping up onto the stone retaining wall. They met up on the walkway and converged on the cannon. The sun was sinking behind the buildings, but there was still enough light to see Boots and Gene saving their places.

"Hey, girls! Gosh, Glendee, it's good to see you somewhere besides the dining hall!" Gene said. "I'm glad you're feeling better."

"Come over here on this side, Glenda. You can have this seat," Boots suggested. He knew an outer limb of the 100-year-old live oak tree that stood nearby would shade that side of the cannon from the streetlight. He and Gene had a discussion while waiting on the girls. They decided it was best to not have a spotlight on Glenda. He hopped down from his cannon seat—his boot heels making a loud thud on the concrete foundation. He gallantly gave Glenda his hand to help her climb up, assuring she was safely seated on the perch between the wheel and the barrel of the cannon.

"Thanks, Boots. Hey, the seat's still warm!" Glenda jovially commented—making an effort to put on a happy face.

"Here, Tanya. You take this one," said Gene, as he, too, hopped down to the ground. Tanya climbed up to the seat on the other side of the barrel from Glenda before Gene could lend his hand. He leaned forward. "Did you tell her yet?" he whispered. Tanya widened her eyes with alarm and quickly shook her head side-to-side. "You'd better," he stated flatly. "And soon." They turned their attention to the street.

"Lookee *there*! It's The Guy With The *Hair*. Oooh baby!" yelled Janie, as a red Firebird drove past. The driver gave the standard one finger salute and a friendly nod at the party at the cannon.

"Good one, Janie. You made a *rhyme*...every *time*," Tanya said in fun.

"Yepper. You was a *poet* and didn't even *know it*!" Glenda added. "But don't y'all get started about *Longfellow*, please!"

Traffic was pretty steady. Lots of high-schoolers drove by in their mamas' cars with music blaring. There was a van with a rather shady looking character, quite a few hot rodders, and the jocks in the white pickup went by, too. Dire Straits music was playing loudly from the cab.

"Is that the only tape they have?" Janie joked. Tanya and Glenda snickered.

A motorcycle approached from around the first curve. There were two people on it, but something didn't look right.

"Hey, that's Evel Knievel, but who's on the back?" asked Tanya.

All they could see behind the driver of the motorcycle was a puffball of hair and a couple of elbows. As the motorcycle passed by the cannon, the situation became clear.

"It's Fuzzy. He's ridin' backwards!" Janie exclaimed.

As the motorcycle passed by the cannon, Fuzzy noticed the girls waving at him. He raised one hand in greeting. He held on very tightly to the back of the bike with the other and was apparently enjoying seeing people's reactions. He'd been watching a car load of local girls with amusement who were following the motorcycle. They were yelling out their windows at him.

"Man. Those guys *are* crazy. I bet they'll do just about anything," said Gene. He leaned against the barrel of the cannon.

The girls all laughed at Fuzzy's antics and watched the motorcycle make the turn and head on out of the college. They turned their heads in unison, looking back to the left to see what was next.

"It's the girl in the VW bug," Glenda said quietly. "We'd always honk until we couldn't hear each other anymore. You know, I still don't have a clue who she is."

"Me neither. But it's a really cool car," replied Janie. She sat down cross-legged on the concrete pad.

The Volkswagen was black with large polka dots—red, blue, yellow and green. We're talking big dots—ten inches in diameter—all over the car. The girl beep-beeped her horn, as she passed by. Everyone waved at her and wondered who the heck she was. They never saw the car anywhere but on the drag. It was a mystery.

Tanya cleared her throat. When Janie heard the signal, she stood up beside Linda. Both looked back at Tanya, who nodded once. They had to tell Glenda now before it was too late.

"Uhh, Glendee. I need to tell you somethin'," Tanya began hesitantly.

"KO. What is it?" Glenda asked curiously. She leaned over the barrel of the cannon toward her friend. Tanya could see the outline of Glenda's head in the glow of the streetlight and could feel her good-natured presence. She gulped and took a deep breath.

"I saw Kevin a while ago. He was lookin' for you," Tanya said, closing her eyes in a grimace.

"Where?" Glenda asked flatly. The good humor faded, and she slowly sank back into the shadow of the tree limb.

"He drove through when you were upstairs. He wanted Tanya to go get you, but she told him to go back to Stonehill," Gene said, continuing the breaking of the bad news.

"Really. Well, hopefully he did," said Glenda coldly. She fell silent, but her breathing had quickened.

Candace walked up and joined the group. As she approached, Glenda prepared to get down from her place on the cannon.

"Oooh baby. Here comes The Guy With The Hair again!" Janie exclaimed in an attempt to change the subject.

"Here, Candace. Keep my spot warm." Glenda jumped off the cannon.

"Where you goin'?" asked Tanya with concern.

"You'll see," Glenda said. She walked quickly to the edge of the retaining wall, and hopped to the pavement below. Simultaneously, the red Firebird came around the first part of the U. Glenda boldly walked up to the car. It stopped, and she placed her arms on the roof above the open passenger window to look in. Her friends stared at her with their mouths hanging open.

"Hi. If it's not too much trouble, would you take me for a drag?" Glenda asked of The Guy With The Hair.

"No problem. Hop in," he said casually, like it happened all the time. Maybe it did for all Glenda knew.

"Aren't you Kevin Curtis' old girlfriend," the handsome jock asked. He unsnapped the cuffs of his plaid western shirt and rolled them up. The car was now in motion.

"Old? I take offense to that. However, it is a true statement. Well, it is since he went off and got married without tellin' me," she said sarcastically but with a forced grin. She wondered if it came out more of a grimace.

"Really? I heard he got married over in Stonehill and wondered what happened. Shotgun weddin'?" he asked. He adjusted his shirt collar, but the wind blew it right back where it had been.

"Yeah. That's the story. And this is the second girl I know of he's gotten pregnant while goin' with me. I've been such a fool," Glenda told him quietly. She was struck with the oddity that it was easier to say these things to a stranger than it was to say them to her own best friends.

"That's rough," the driver said compassionately. "But if you don't mind me sayin' so, you're much better off." Glenda realized this was a nice guy. And he really did have very nice blonde hair—maybe a little too much hairspray, but nice. She sighed.

"Thanks. I just heard he's in town lookin' for me. I thought makin' a drag incognito might keep him from seein' me first," she explained.

The Guy With The Hair looked over at his passenger to assess the odd situation. She was pretty cute, but he had a girl back home. The story sounded logical—he shrugged. "You like AC/DC?"

"You betcha. Plug it in and crank it up," Glenda felt more comfortable. She settled in and placed her elbow on the open window frame. This was fun—weird—but fun.

They exited the campus, turned right past the stone columns, then continued up the drag past the boys' dorm. Glenda saw people sitting on the wall and casually waved at them. They made the turn around at the new Dairy Queen, making their way back toward downtown. She continued looking around, watching for Kevin's rusty Matador. Or maybe he was driving his wife's car. A grimace crossed her face, as the thought crossed her mind. *Dirty Deeds Done Dirt Cheap* was the tape in the 8-track player. She nodded as if agreeing this, too, was dirty business.

They went past Moo Lah and on down the drag to the old Dairy Queen. As they turned around there, she saw the silver Thunderbird parked between two other cars, but nobody was around. Glenda released a sigh of relief—realizing with surprise she didn't want the Thunderbird driver to see her ridin' around in this red Firebird. She looked around the area again.

The song "Ride On" came through the speakers, catching her conscious attention. It was a slow, haunting blues tune that made her relax and lay her head back against the headrest. Her dark brown hair was a stark contrast against the white bucket seat. The Guy With The Hair glanced at her, as he turned into the college.

"Wanna go 'round again?" he asked pleasantly.

"No, thanks. This was a big help. I'll just hang around a while and see if he shows up. Then I gotta go study for a test tomorrow," she answered. The car came to a stop in front of the cannon.

"Well, it was nice. Glad I could help. Good luck," he said genially.

Glenda got out of the low-slung car. "Thanks a lot. See ya!" She tried to sound friendly. It occurred to her that he didn't tell her his real name, nor did she ask.

"No problem," he answered, moving the gear shift into Drive. "See ya 'round."

Glenda stepped back from the car. As it began to move, she made her way back to her friends at the cannon. She was very surprised to see them all staring at her with shocked faces. Candace got down from the seat without a word. Glenda hopped back up. She patted her tall friend's shoulder in casual thanks.

"What the heck was that all about?" Tanya asked, leaning over the barrel of the cannon.

"Glendee! That was The Guy With The Hair! What was he like?" asked Janie excitedly.

"Nice. I simply asked him to take me for a drag, and he did. No big deal."

"Come on. Details, give us details!" Janie couldn't believe her friend just politely hopped in the Firebird with The Guy With The Hair.

"He was nice. He had an AC/DC tape. It's a nice car, and we made a drag. It was nice. That's it." Glenda shrugged casually.

Gene had moved over to lean on the wheel beside Glenda. "Did you see him?" he asked quietly.

Glenda sighed sadly and simply shook her head side-to-side. She realized he knew why she had ridden off in that red Firebird. Gene nodded and moved around the cannon to stand next to Tanya.

Evel and Fuzzy rode by again on the motorcycle, except now the passenger was facing forward. For some unknown reason Fuzzy removed his T-shirt and held it up above his head like a flag. However, it became more like a sail, because as Evel cracked open the throttle, the bike surged forward. Fuzzy's feet flew up, as the wind-filled T-shirt pivoted his upper body backward. The group at the cannon drew a collective gasp. They saw tennis shoes—and Fuzzy falling backward. But his feet somehow caught on Evel's elbows. This kept the rest of Fuzzy from tumbling off the back of the bike. He let go of the shirt with one hand. It deflated, and he grabbed at Evel's shirt to pull himself upright. He rested his forehead on his friend's back. His sigh of relief was visible. Janie and Tanya also sighed. Everyone at the cannon cheered.

"Whew! That was close. Don't fall off, Fuzzy!" Janie called.

A friendly hand lifted in recognition to cover a sheepish look before the bike disappeared around the corner.

"What's happenin'?" asked the Figment. He snorted with amusement, as Janie practically jumped out of her skin. He had walked out of the shadows toward the cheering, sitting unceremoniously down on the concrete beside her. Janie glared at him. Her visage altered and she calmly looked away. After all, he claimed to be a figment of their imagination, so she could ignore him. But her expression changed sharply upon seeing what was out on the road.

"Oh boy. Here we go," said Gene softly so that only Tanya heard him.

"Glendee…" Tanya stopped short.

"I see him. Hang on—let's see what he does," said Glenda coldly. Tanya looked at her friend to see if she was crumbling. What she saw instead was a young woman with steel in her blue eyes. Tanya sat back in the seat to wait for whatever might happen. She watched the rusty car pull over close to the retaining wall.

"Glenda! Glenda! Come here," Kevin yelled. It seemed he didn't dare or bother to get out of the car.

"Janie. Would you do me a favor and go ask what he wants?" Glenda made the request slowly and softly. Janie popped up on her feet.

"You bet." Janie walked painfully slowly across the grass toward the rusty car. When she got to the edge of the wall, she squatted down like the catcher in softball that she was. She said nothing and waited with a slightly hostile look on her face.

"Janie. Please get Glenda for me. Please," Kevin pleaded.

"Why?" Janie asked coldly.

"Come on, Janie. I just want to talk to her. Please, I need to see her." Janie noticed he was turning on his old charm. It didn't work.

She said nothing in return, rose from the squatting position, and walked slowly back toward the cannon. A few cars drove by. Some honked for fun, but others honked because the Matador was in their way.

"He said he just wants to talk to you, Glenda. I'd tell him to go jump in the lake if I were you," Janie said with anger. She turned on her heel and plopped down to sit by the Figment. "He thinks he is so suave. He had us all fooled."

"Yepper. That he did," Glenda commented evenly. She hopped down to the ground from the cannon seat.

"You're goin'?" Tanya asked with shock.

"Might as well get this over with and see what he has to say," said Glenda with a shrug. She turned toward her friends. "I gave my heart and two years of my life to him—I'd kinda like an explanation as to why he threw it all away."

Her friends were silent. Janie got back up on her feet to walk over to Glenda. She stood on her tiptoes, hugging her friend firmly. "Good luck. Please come back," she whispered softly to the older girl.

"Thanks. I'll see y'all in a few," Glenda said evenly. She walked casually toward the old Matador. Her mind was struck with a flashing thought of chrome and silver—she'd never really thought about what an ugly rattle trap Kevin's car was before.

"Glenda. Sweetheart. Come here. I've gotta see you," Kevin called, leaning across the bench seat.

"Well, here I am in all my glory," Glenda answered blandly. She stopped on top of the wall, calmly looked around the area, then jumped down onto the pavement. She leaned on the car door to speak through the open window. "Why are you here and what the heck do you want? Why aren't you at home with your wife?" she asked with cold anger in her voice.

"Come on, baby—get in. I need to talk to ya. Just get in. Let's go somewhere and talk." Kevin was practically begging. He leaned over and opened the door. "Please."

Glenda closed her eyes, steeling herself to what she had to face. She drew a deep breath and looked back at her friends at the cannon for a brief moment. After another breath, she got in the car, and they drove away.

"Baby. It's so good to see ya. I've missed you so much," Kevin stretched his hand toward her shoulder.

"Do not touch me."

He pulled his hand back quickly—a sign that perhaps he realized getting to her wasn't going to be so easy this time. "You wanna make a drag?" he asked.

"No. Go to the park. We can talk there," Glenda told him. "I don't really want to be seen ridin' around town with a married man."

"I'm not married."

Glenda remained silent. She didn't want to have a big scene in the car out on the drag. Kevin turned off Main Street and drove into the city park. He pulled over at a picnic table at the far end of the park. It was out in the open—not a tree around. He turned toward Glenda, holding out his hands in entreaty. "Oh, baby, I *really* need you," he said softly.

Glenda again said nothing. Instead, she got out of the vehicle and sat on the picnic table top with her feet on the bench. He climbed up beside her and moved in close. Too close. She pulled away. "Please don't touch me."

"OK. OK. Glenda, I'm not married," Kevin said again.

"Oh, Kevin. It was in the Stonehill paper. I saw it. Candace brought the engagement announcement, and she knows people who were actually at the wedding. She even heard you were workin' for your father-in-law. You are married," Glenda said with her eyes closed.

"I know. It kinda…well…it did happen. But it was annulled. You gotta believe me. It was annulled." He seemed quite upset.

"What about the baby?" Glenda asked patiently. She ignored the act. It had worked before—but not this time.

"Baby?"

"Oh, come on. Yes, baby. The unborn child. Your fiancé—excuse me—that was me. Your bride was pregnant. Everyone up there in Stonehill knew that. The engagement announcement and the actual wedding were only two weeks apart. You married her. There's no doubt she's pregnant," Glenda said with growing impatience.

"OK. Well, yeah. But...but she lost the baby. She had a miscarriage, so we got the marriage annulled," he said firmly. "I love you, Glenda. You're my baby, my only baby."

Glenda nodded slowly and breathed deeply. "Annulled. So you can move back here, and we can see each other every day," she said with a quiver in her voice.

"Well, no. I mean, I have my job in Stonehill, and I need to stay there. I could get away every now and then and come see you."

"Ah. Perhaps I could drive up there to see you?"

"No. No. That wouldn't work. I live in my boss' garage apartment, and I'm sure he wouldn't like it," Kevin answered nervously.

Glenda again nodded her head and sighed. She could finally see through his lies. "Well, this is a lot of stuff to take in. I need time to think. Please take me back to the college," she said, hopping lightly down from the table. She slowly turned around to face him. "I loved you, Kevin. I need time to see if I can trust you again," she said, falsely giving him a little hope. He didn't seem to notice the expression of love was in the past tense.

"OK, baby. OK. Hey, I'll give you a phone number, and you can call me after six o'clock when I get home from work. That way we can talk every day," Kevin said. He attempted to embrace her but she pulled away. She almost cried—but held the tears inside with a great effort. He tried to kiss her—but she ducked, and he kissed the top of her head instead. "I love you," he whispered. "Let's go back to the house. That guy left it unlocked for me." Glenda gasped and pulled away without looking at him. That's where they had been when he had tried to convince her to run away with him to get married. She shivered, as she realized what he was saying, shaking her head in a silent but definite "no." He sighed in defeat. They walked back to the car.

"Please do write down the phone number for me, Kevin," Glenda said. She pulled on the car door with more force than was necessary in an effort to release some tension. Plus, the effort wasn't wasted—the door had to be completely shut, as there was a real danger one could fall out of the old Matador.

Kevin found a carpenter's pencil in the back floorboard and wrote the phone number on a scrap of paper. He started the car and drove out of the park. They remained in silence, though he tried several times to reach for her hand or to touch her leg. But Glenda withdrew as far away from him as she could—right up against the nasty door panel. She wanted to fly out of the window and escape, and seriously considered getting out of the car at the earliest opportunity.

As they pulled up to the stop sign at Main Street, Glenda looked around for a means of escape and saw the silver Thunderbird drive by. Instead of getting out of the Matador, however, she dropped her head, so that her long brown hair covered her face. For some reason she didn't want anybody in that car to see her anywhere near this car. She peeked out to see if the Thunderbird was gone and watched several other vehicles pass by before Kevin was able to turn left onto the drag.

They drove in silence onto the campus. "Do you want off at the dorm?" he asked in a low voice.

"No. Go on up to the cannon—everybody should still be there."

"Waitin' for you," he said, looking at her.

"They are my friends. They were your friends, too. They've taken care of me while you were off doin' whatever it was you were doin'," Glenda remarked coldly.

"I know—I know. Please forgive me. I love you—I need you. Baby, please call me." Kevin pressed hard on the brake pedal. The car squealed to a stop. Glenda struggled with the door handle. Finally, the latch creaked open. She got out, but leaned down to look at the liar who had so earnestly proclaimed his love for her.

"By the way, isn't this boss you mentioned earlier your supposedly former father-in-law?" she asked slowly through the open window.

"Uhh...well...yeah," Kevin answered hesitantly.

Glenda nodded and slammed the door shut. She stood still for a moment to fight off the nervous shaking. She slipped the note with the phone number into her back pocket, hopped up on the wall and walked quickly over to her friends. Everyone was standing or sitting on the edge of their seats.

"What happened?" asked Janie. "What did he say?"

"I've...gotta go...get a...drink" said Glenda, avoiding the question. "I think I'll go up to the room." She looked around nervously. "Linda, you wanna come with me?" she asked of her roommate with a bit of a plea in her voice.

"Sure thing. Let's go," Linda answered, gripping her friend's arm gently and leading her away. The group at the cannon watched them walk past the flagpole and down the steps to the street.

"That sorry son of a bitch. I'd like to kick his skinny little ass," said the Figment. Gene nodded his agreement.

"So would I," said Candace with malice.

"I would, too. But I'm sure a *healthy* gal like you could do a much better job of it, Candace," said Gene impishly. He teased her a bit to lighten the mood and assumed a fighter's stance. Candace turned and took a swing at him, but he ducked, running into the shadows.

"I'll healthy you, you turd!" she called to his retreating figure.

Tanya hopped down from her cannon seat, and Candace stepped over beside Janie. They all felt the night was ruined.

Candace turned to the guys still visible. "See ya later, Boots, Figment," and turning to the shadows, "and you, too, Gene wherever you are—you chicken butt. We gotta go be with Glenda."

The guys remained silent. Gene walked back into the light and stood beside Boots, but there was nothing to do or say except watch the three girls walk away.

Up in the end dorm room, Glenda opened a Dr Pepper and sat down slowly on her squeaky bed. Linda placed a record on the player. The Little River Band song "Cool Change" filled the entire room with sound. The strong piano and clear vocals always touched both of the girls deeply. Glenda placed the canned drink on her desk so she could lie down on her bed. Linda turned off the overhead light, but Glenda covered her eyes with her left forearm anyway. She let the musical sounds and positive vibrations wash over her, trying desperately to calm her fast-beating heart. Janie heard the music from across the hall. She wandered into the room to sit beside the prostrate Glenda. She gently touched the heartbroken girl's right hand. Glenda knew right away that Janie was beside her and took comfort in that simple gesture. The song ended—in the silence each girl could hear the other's breathing. Linda Lou took off that album and was searching for another.

Glenda uncovered her eyes to look at her little friend with the big heart and golden brown curls. "Janie. Would you go get Candace for me, please?" Janie nodded—she accepted the mission. Candace and Barb-oh's room was just two doors down—so very quickly the three girls entered the end room. "Candace. Would you please go call your mom and ask her to look up the County Clerk's phone number in Stonehill?" Glenda asked, after sitting up on the edge of the bed. She took a sip of her Dr Pepper.

"Comin' up." Candace turned to leave the room and winked at a confused Janie. Barb-oh joined her little friend on the bed with the now upright Glenda.

Linda Lou had listened carefully to the conversation and looked thoughtful. She turned to put on the record she had picked out. The Eagles song "Already Gone" started playing and got the atmosphere in the room jumping after the calming effect of "Cool Change." Barb-oh and Janie sat tapping their toes to the beat. Linda Lou looked hopeful, as she slid down into her desk chair. The song brought the girls' spirits up a bit—Glenda took strength from the defiant lyrics and strong harmonies.

Candace joined singing the last lines of the song, while walking back into the room with a piece of notebook paper. She handed it to Glenda without a word but with a slight smile. Glenda reached up slowly and took hold of the piece of paper. She glanced at the writing on it briefly before placing it on her desk under the lamp, to keep it from blowing away. "Thanks much. Everybody at home OK?" Glenda sounded like she was feeling better.

"Oh, yeah—crazy as ever. Mom just looked the number right up and gave it to me. She didn't even ask why," Candace replied. She at first gazed very seriously at Glenda, but her expression quickly softened. "Hey, y'all. I've got some readin' to do. Nighty-night everybody." She waggled her fingers at the girls and left the room.

"Me too," said Linda Lou. "I hate to—but I have to."

"I could work on my 'September' dance," Janie reflected. Suddenly, pillows, pencils, and whatever else was handy were hurled in her direction. "It's due Tuesday. Then it'll be over! Well, until the big recital."

"Thank goodness," said Linda. "I used to like that song."

"Y'all go on. I'll be OK. I need to reread a chapter, too," said Glenda. "If I can keep my mind on it, that is," she added softly.

Janie had run out of the room, dodging projectiles with Barb-oh in hot pursuit. But Tanya stayed behind and eased down on the bed beside Glenda. "You OK?" she asked with concern.

"Yeah, I guess," Glenda answered.

"What did he say?" Tanya had known Kevin as long as Glenda had. She had dated Kevin's best friend for a while before he left the area. She knew the history between them better than anyone else.

"He said the marriage was annulled—said he wasn't married." Glenda replied weakly. "He claimed she had a miscarriage."

"That sorry s-o-b. He's tryin' to win you back?" asked Linda with anger.

"Apparently," said Tanya. "Glendee, what 're you gonna do?"

Glenda sighed and replied, "I don't know, Tan-ay. I just really—don't—know."

Tanya sighed, too, and said, "Good night." She walked across the hall to find Janie putting on the dreaded record.

"Ear plugs! Anybody got ear plugs?" Tanya called out into the empty hall.

Linda Lou got up and quietly shut the door. The only light in the room was from the two small desk lamps. The girls settled down to their studies.

Outside, the silver Thunderbird slowly drove by. The driver was alone, as his comrades had turned in for the night. He peered up at the second floor dorm rooms. His brow furrowed at the contrast of the brightly lit room next to the darkened room on the other side. The picture reminded him of another night. Foreigner's album *Head Games* was playing in his 8-track player. His favorite song, "Rev on the Redline," had just finished, and there were a few seconds of quiet, as the tape deck changed tracks. He heard "September" playing from the brightly lit room on the upper right. A glance down at his open tape box confirmed his Earth, Wind and Fire 8-track was in its place. Surprisingly pleased, he began to drive around the U, but not before sending a silent "hello" up to the darker room.

Janie finally stopped the record player after rehearsing the dance routine three more times. The dorm settled down for the night. Linda reopened the door to allow air to move through the room. It was late September and still quite warm. She looked down the hall, listening to the combined sounds of the thirty or so fans for a moment. She knew everyone in this hall and knew they wouldn't live in the air-conditioned dorm even if they could. This place was special—with friends that were like family. Sighing, she retreated into her closet to get ready for bed.

After her last class Monday afternoon, Glenda was back in her room, alone with two notes with two similar, but different, telephone numbers. She picked up the larger piece of paper and took a deep breath. She walked over to the black wall phone beside her closet, picked up the receiver to hesitantly dial zero. The operator came on allowing Glenda to request to charge a third billing call to her folks' telephone bill. She called out the phone number for the Stonehill County Clerk to the operator. Even though no one else was around, she stepped into her closet for privacy.

"Hello? Yes—I'd like to find out if there is an active, legal marriage license for a certain person. Can I do that? Thanks. That would be a big help. The name is Kevin Curtis." Her hands shook, as she waited for the answer.

"Yes. That's his birth date. It is active? No annulment? I see—well, thank you very much." She came out into the room and hung the phone on its cradle on the wall. Leaning on the closet door, it closed with a loud click. She slid down the smooth wood surface to the floor, hung her head on her knees and cried silently. She had been in that position for quite some time when Tanya found her.

"What happened? Are you OK?" Tanya asked with concern. She sank quickly down on her knees beside her friend.

Glenda took a deep breath. "He's married. I called the County Clerk. The marriage license is active—there's no annulment. There's no doubt, Tanya. He's married."

Tanya slid down onto the floor beside her friend. Her head fell back with a thud against the door. "Oh, Glendee," she said softly. "He's a low-life—a sorry, no good lyin' son of a bitch."

With eyes brimming with tears, Glenda looked at her close friend.

"I loved him, Tanya. Blindly. Foolishly. I loved him with everything I had, and he threw it all away."

"Shows what he knows. I hope he realizes what he's lost," Tanya said firmly. She sighed. "But you deserve better anywho. Well, what now?"

"I don't know. I have his number, and may call it. But first, we should make a run to Riverview."

Tanya looked at her friend with surprise. "Really? Well, whatever you wanna do, I'm in. Let's go," she said, pulling Glenda to her feet.

Janie danced up to the pair. "What's up?" she asked.

"We're gonna make a run, wanna go?" Tanya asked, as she went to her room for her wallet.

"Certainly!" exclaimed Janie with delight before noticing Glenda's reddened eyes. Tanya put her index finger on her lips to halt any conversation. Janie nodded understanding.

The girls got their money and IDs, and the three were heading down the hall when Candace came up the stairs.

"Need anything from the beer store, Candace? We're makin' a run," Tanya informed.

"You betcha. Let me get some money—you can get me a cherry sloe gin." Candace hurried to her room.

Armed with money and a full tank of gas, the girls pulled out of Dairyville to drive the twenty-five miles to the nearest liquor store. The legal drinking age was eighteen which allowed almost any college student to buy alcohol. Glenda, at age twenty-two, still got carded. They entered through the glass door and stopped in their tracks. Somewhere from the back of the room Ted Nugent's "Wango Tango" was playing loudly. After a moment the volume was decreased, but not before the three had each taken up positions in the three aisles. They were dancing with arms up high and a jumping action that was quite frenzied. The store clerk stared in amazement. The song ended—the record player apparently cut off, as no more music was playing. The girls made their way to the back of the store. They placed their choices on the counter with stone serious faces.

College girls were a common sight for the store clerks in Riverview, but these three were uncommon. The zany dancing—followed by the abruptly straight faces—confused the young man behind the counter. Janie leaned over to whisper to the other two girls. "We gotta get outta here. I hear this guy has a Licker License!" The trio dropped the serious act and laughed out loud. They made their purchases, including a large bag of tortilla chips, and piled back into the Camaro.

Tanya plugged in Glenda's Steve Miller Band tape and "Jungle Love" screamed from the speakers. Each girl had popped the top of her favorite beverage. Glenda had no favorite, but she tried to drink it anyway. Tanya and Janie liked to drink beer. Glenda had purchased a small bottle of cheap wine and stifled a shiver after each sip. She ate the chips to be able to drink her beverage. She drove back to Dairyville carefully, joined the daytime traffic on Main Street and drove the half mile or so to the Astro Drive-In. The dreaded Dodge station wagon was in the employee parking area. The driver, who made a habit of flipping people off, was definitely on duty. Glenda saw Jacqueline Ann carrying a tray to a car. She liked to be called Jan, but Glenda and the girls called her Jackal Ann. She had a fling with Kevin a year before that had allegedly resulted in an abortion. Jacqueline Ann and Glenda had been flipping each other off ever since.

Glenda exited the Astro without stopping and drove on. The girls made a complete drag—but not much was happening. After all, it was the middle of the day. They got burgers at the new

Dairy Queen, then drove out the back way. Glenda steered her car into the exit lane of the Taco Hut drive-thru just for fun, but mainly to wave at their friend Justin going the wrong way. The maneuver was successful—she headed back to the dorm.

"Let's get this stuff in the fridge and deliver Candace's goods," said Glenda after they had toted their various bags of burgers and beer to the second floor of Horne Hall. She was drinking slowly, since she wasn't very good at it. "I'm hungry."

Back at the room they ate their burgers and chips and partied the afternoon away by playing records, dancing and drinking. Linda Lou came in around 5:30 p.m. She found three giggling females lying in her floor. "Hall-oh! What in the world's goin' on here?" She laughed at the sight.

"We made a run!" exclaimed Janie.

"Ah ha! And what did you bring back for little ol' me?" Linda stood with her hands on her hips.

"In the fridge, Linda. For later," replied Glenda from the floor.

"OK. OK. I know. Dang it, I've gotta go to work. I'll be back after nine. Don't drink too much and throw up or anything," Linda advised.

"Righto. We'll be good. We promise!" Tanya called happily. Linda left the room.

"Oh, crap. We'd better go to dinner before they close the dining hall. Come on, y'all," said Janie, rising unsteadily to her feet. Apparently, the burgers and chips had worn off.

"You two go ahead and get me somethin' to go. I'm stayin' right here," Glenda said in a forced cheerful tone.

"KO. We're gone," called Tanya. They hurried out of the room.

Glenda rose up to a sitting position with a clear head. She had actually not consumed all that much alcohol and had eaten almost the whole bag of chips. But what little that was coursing through her veins raised her courage level enough to pick up the smaller scrap of paper from her desk. Sitting cross-legged on the bed, her shaking hand held the note for several minutes. At 6:02 p.m., she went to the phone and dialed zero again. "Yes, operator, I'd like to make a third billing call, please." Glenda read the number aloud that was scribbled on the paper. She wished the call didn't have to be made—but it had to be done. The receiver almost dropped from her hand when she heard his voice on the other end of the line. "Hi, it's me." Glenda barely managed to get her voice working.

"Hi," Kevin said quietly.

"Hi. How are you?"

"Fine." He obviously couldn't or wouldn't talk openly.

"Kevin...you are married," she said shakily.

"I am?"

"Yes, you are. I called the County Clerk's office, and they said the marriage license is not annulled. You're married," Glenda stated firmly but sadly.

There was a long silence on the other end of the line. "Don't call here again." The phone line went dead.

Glenda stood there holding the black handle of the receiver tightly for a moment—eventually releasing her grip and placing it quietly on the hook. A shuddering breath escaped from her chest. "Well, that's that." She walked over to her desk, eased down into the chair and put her head down on her crossed arms. The tears had been flowing for some time when she heard Tanya and Janie coming down the hall with their usual clamor. As they turned into Glenda's room, she looked up at them. Coming to a standstill upon seeing their friend had been crying again—they backed quietly out of the room. Glenda put her head back down.

"She must a' called him while we were gone," said Tanya to Janie, as they walked quietly into their room.

"Apparently. And it didn't go well. Damn him straight to hell. We knew this would happen," answered Janie. Tanya nodded sadly.

They left Glenda alone for a while. But half an hour later they convinced her to go with them to sit on the wall that faced the drag. Glenda had washed her face, and Janie insisted she change into her favorite top—a white T-shirt with purple baseball sleeves with the CTSU logo on the front. Despite all this preparation, Glenda walked almost aimlessly. The little bit of alcohol and a lot of shock and pain had completely numbed her senses. Tanya and Janie steered Glenda toward Boots and Gene. They all sat on the wall facing the street. Cars were passing by within six feet of where four of the five sets of feet were swinging. One set was just hanging there.

Daylight was fading as dusk fell. Traffic was getting heavy. Sometimes a line of vehicles backed up in front of the people hanging around at the wall. The favored place to sit was within 100 feet of a traffic light. Thus the sitters could get a good look at whoever was stopped in front of them. They, in turn, got looked at quite often.

"Don't stare at me, or I'll wave at you!" Janie's favorite saying rang out. The cars moved away and became more spread out. There were honks and waves, but Glenda seemed oblivious. Suddenly, she stood up and walked out onto Main Street.

Gene was looking at Janie and shading his eyes from the glare of the streetlight above them. Janie's face abruptly changed from a pleasant expression to one of alarm. She saw the back of Glenda's white T-shirt between the headlights of an oncoming vehicle.

Janie screamed. The tires of the fast approaching car screeched, as the driver slammed on the brakes. Gene had looked toward the street at the first hint of panic in Janie's eyes and moved very quickly. He ran to Glenda, grabbed her arm, and pulled her out of the path of the white station wagon just before the vehicle slid by. The high school girls in the big car were shrieking. But when the driver realized she hadn't hit anything or anybody, she took off with another screech of the tires. Gene and Glenda collapsed almost breathless in the grass in front of the wall.

"What did you do that for?" Gene asked with great concern.

"I don't know. I don't think I care," Glenda said numbly.

Gene raised the miserable girl to her feet and set her down on the wall. "Listen to me, Glenda Meadows. He isn't worth all this. You are a beautiful, wonderful woman who deserves a whole lot better than you've been getting for the last year. Look at me. Look at all of us here. We love you—we need you—and we want you back to being yourself!" he said with deep feeling.

Glenda looked up at him with tears in her eyes. "What—what did I do?" she asked with confusion.

"You walked out in front of a car! That's what!" cried Janie. She grabbed her friend's hand and held on tightly.

Glenda looked at Janie in confusion. Gradually, a look of anxiety came over her, realizing what had just happened. She gazed with alarm at Tanya, Gene and Boots, and gripped Janie's hand tightly. "Oh, my God," she said shakily.

"Let's go back to the dorm," said Tanya. She rose to her feet.

"No. No. Sit back down. I wanna stay here for a little while. And think," Glenda said softly. "Go ahead and do what we always do. Do it for me."

So, the little group stayed quite somber for a time. Slowly, as more cars drove by and honked and people waved and yelled, Tanya and Janie began reacting by yelling back and waving when appropriate. Glenda was clear-eyed and eventually her dimple appeared, as she gazed fondly at her friends. At one point she looked up, noticing the silver Thunderbird coming toward them from the direction of the traffic light. She was watching when the driver looked her way. Her lips widened into a smile—her hand rose slightly to wave at him. She saw his amicable reaction—the slight nod of acknowledgment just before he disappeared around the corner. The friends sitting on the wall did not notice the exchange. They kept up their antics until it was nearly midnight.

"You feel all right, Glendee?" asked Boots with his hand on her shoulder.

"Yepper Boots, ol' buddy. I think I'll be OK. Thanks," she answered. "And thank you, Gene. I don't know what else to say. Girls, let's go." She climbed up on the wall and balanced on one foot, held the other out in front—with arms making a "Z", like a figure in an Egyptian hieroglyph. Janie and Tanya did the same in turn. They jumped off the wall, and the girls laughed together all the way back to the dorm.

Chapter Four

SATURDAY AFTERNOON WAS PERFECT: sunny, not too hot, not too cool, not too windy, not too anything. Evel, Charles and Fuzzy had made their usual beer run to Riverview. On the way back to Dairyville, they stopped at a convenience store for ice and snacks, backing the Thunderbird into a parking spot close to the front door and next to a sports car. While Evel made the necessary purchases for a successful Saturday night, Fuzzy and Charles were at the pumps, flirting with a girl named Janet who was pumping gas into her Plymouth Volare.

"Hey, Janet, do you have a Bandaid? I just scraped my knees fallin' for you!" Janet giggled at Fuzzy's joke and her attention was drawn from the gas pump.

"Forget him, stick with me and we'll go places together!" Charles added. Janet responded with a short laugh before she squealed and jumped back from her car—the gas tank had overflowed. Gasoline pooled on the pavement at Janet's feet. Fuzzy calmly reached over, flipping the lever on the gas pump upward to stop the flow of fuel and gently took the handle from Janet's shaking hand. He quickly hooked the nozzle on the pump.

Janet tried to calm herself. She attempted to ignore the incident as she walked into the store to pay for the fuel in her tank—plus the half-gallon or so that spilled onto the ground. Charles and Fuzzy stayed by the Volare, waiting for the chance to compete for her attention again. After returning, Janet hurried into her car and told them she'd see them later, leaving the two guys standing next to a puddle of gasoline.

Evel came out of the store with his purchases and paused to stare at the roadster parked next to his vehicle. The size difference was substantial. The object of his attention was a two-seater with no roof, whereas the Thunderbird was practically a land yacht. The sports car was painted British Racing Green with pearl white racing stripes over the hood and trunk area. The owner of the roadster exited the store. He halted to stand quietly beside Evel. Both gazed at the beautiful car with admiration.

Evel turned his eyes to the proud owner. "Man. That's quite a vehicle. You know, it's not a car you could have sex in, but it sure is a sexy car. I hope someday I can own a Cobra."

"That there's an AC Cobra. You will, my friend, if you really want it." The owner, who appeared to be in his fifties, had an air of roguishness. "Plus, you will if you're lucky enough. See ya 'round!"

Evel watched the man fold himself into the roadster and felt his heart pound when the engine roared to life. He very nearly fell to his knees in awe as the Cobra pulled away. He sighed while opening his trunk. After dropping in the sacks of supplies, he poured ice into the cooler over the cans of beer. With that task done, he closed the trunk lid. Evel looked toward his friends, hearing their voices near the gas pumps. Each was tossing a cigarette lighter into the air with his hand, catching it again in the same hand. They were looking intently at each other.

"If you don't light it, I will," Fuzzy said, challenging Charles. "I'll do it!"

Evel had begun to walk toward the gas pumps to join the guys, but upon hearing those words he ran while yelling, "NOOO!" The warning was cut short. He came to an abrupt stop when a huge ball of flame appeared between him and his friends. Another vehicle quickly pulled away from the pumps, narrowly escaping the explosion. Evel stood on the verge of panic when the smoke cleared. Fuzzy and Charles were still near the gas pump. They weren't blown to pieces or on fire. They seemed stunned, but all right.

He looked quickly around the area for trouble—then back at his buddies. "Run! Damn it, RUN! Get in the car!"

Evel hurriedly ran back to his car and dove in. The Thunderbird started with a roar.

After hesitating, Fuzzy quickly decided it was indeed a very good idea to run. Off he sprinted, circumventing the still burning puddle of fuel with an awkward shuffle. He glanced at Charles, who was jumping around in a vain effort to stomp on the flames. All Charles actually managed to do was catch the bottoms of his boots on fire—so instead of jumping, he did a strange version of a goose step, trying to kick the flames off his boots. He yelled something, but the words made no sense.

"Charles! Stop speakin' in tongues and come on! But put your feet out before you get in the Thunderchicken." Fuzzy had regained his sense of humor once he knew they were safe from the fire.

But it was time to make tracks. Through the glass they could see the clerk was on the phone. No doubt the police and fire trucks would soon be on the way.

Charles scuffled and skidded his feet on the concrete enough to douse the flames from the soles of his boots. He hastily jumped in the front seat beside Fuzzy. Evel slammed the Thunderbird into Drive and stomped his size twelve foot on the gas pedal.

"GO!!!!" both of the other guys yelled in unison.

With a screech of tires and rumble of mufflers the car flew out of the store parking lot, its occupants breathing sighs of relief.

"What in the holy hell did you do that for?" Evel exclaimed. He glanced in the rearview mirror to check for flashing lights. "It was—oh, man—it was right by the gas pumps. You nearly blew yourselves up!" He was still very agitated and nervous. "Not to mention the entire gas station!"

"But we didn't, did we?" Fuzzy's voice was so calm it was casual. "Where's the cooler?"

"In the trunk." Evel's eyes squinted in concentration. "Let's go out on the highway and let me clear my head."

His lips opened just a slit, as he pressed his tongue against the right corner of his mouth in the familiar sign that something exciting was about to happen. Charles and Fuzzy looked at each other in anticipation.

Just outside the city limits, Evel put the pedal to the metal. The speedometer needle registered 70, then edged up to 80, 90, and ultimately to over 100 miles per hour. Fuzzy let out a whoop. Charles held tightly to the passenger door armrest. Evel had a rather wicked look on his face as the car continued to accelerate. As he approached 110, he took a deep breath and let off the gas. The car slowed—if one can call 90 slow—until it was finally cruising at a much more legal 55 miles per hour. He kept the big car at the speed limit for a while, then slowed even more and safely made a U turn at a wide spot in the road. By the time Evel drove back into town, he was much calmer and a lot happier.

"You know, my car is down at the old Dairy Queen. If y'all wanna go get it, we could sneak back by that store and see what's happenin'," Charles said.

Fuzzy turned to Evel. "Good idea. Let's go."

Evel nodded and made a quick left turn to traverse the outskirts of town. He stepped a little harder on the gas pedal when he heard sirens in the distance. But just as quickly, he slowed back down. It was probably best not to get caught speeding after almost setting fire to a gas station. The Thunderbird took its good, sweet time.

They made it to the far end of the drag without incident. The Thunderbird was parked securely out of sight behind the old Dairy Queen. Everyone quickly piled into the brown Malibu. Charles started the motor, calmly pulled out onto Main Street and drove nonchalantly up the drag. Evel hung his elbow casually out the passenger side window, coolly flashing the index finger salute when appropriate. Fuzzy leaned up between his friends to peer out the windshield. The Malibu went past the college and through the traffic light, but instead of turning around at the new Dairy Queen like he normally would, Charles went straight. This unexpected action caused a few cars trying to pull out onto Main Street in the normal stock car fashion to dodge this way and that. Several horns honked. Charles steered the car into the left-hand lane, ignoring the irritated motorists. That's when they saw the emergency lights up ahead.

Charles grew flustered. He looked around nervously. "We're cool. They won't recognize this car—just drive by slow," Fuzzy hoarsely whispered from just behind Charles' shoulder.

"Then why are you whisperin'?" Evel whispered back to his friend in fun. Fuzzy squinted his eyes, glaring briefly at Evel.

Charles tried to ignore both of them, slowing the car a bit as he approached the flashing lights. The guys casually looked over at the store. Two cop cars, one fire truck, and plenty of men in uniform were milling around an area that had obviously been sprayed with foam.

"Wow. This is great!" Charles exclaimed, obviously somewhat relieved.

"Speak for yourself," Evel said sharply. "You could a' blown up this whole side of town!"

He nodded his head and waved ever so slightly to the cops and firemen at the store. Evel worked for the City of Dairyville—he was well-known. The emergency personnel waved back at their fellow city employee, not knowing that his accomplices were the actual perpetrators of this particular fire.

"Whew. I guess that *was* pretty stupid. Charles, you'd do *anything* if we dared ya to, wouldn't ya?" Fuzzy asked.

"Just about, I guess. I didn't notice we was that close to the gas pumps—I was thinkin' about Janet."

Evel rolled his eyes and shook his head slowly side-to-side. "Sometimes I wonder...oh, forget it. Just get me to the beer."

Charles turned around and drove back toward town. Traffic was fairly light. After an otherwise uneventful drag, he parked his car in its usual space under the old Dairy Queen sign. The three guys piled back into the Thunderbird.

Evel took off for the West Side Park, a quiet, secluded, yet conveniently located little park on the opposite edge of town. It had decent restrooms, trash cans, and was a very good place to lay low. "We'll drink a few here—then make plans for tonight," he said, backing up to a picnic table.

He unfolded his large frame from the driver seat, walked back to open the trunk and in less than two seconds had an open beer can raised to his lips. The others quickly followed his example. Fuzzy and Charles sat on the bench, facing Evel, who was sitting half in the trunk and half on the very wide back bumper of his very large car.

Evel closed his eyes and took a deep breath. "Man. I thought your little cotton swab head was on fire, Fuz."

"Hey, look. It is singed a little bit!" exclaimed Charles, pointing at Fuzzy's head.

"What?" Fuzzy thrust his hand into his blondish afro. "Where?"

"Just kiddin', Fuz." Charles and Evel laughed. It didn't take Fuzzy long to join in. They were laughing so hard they almost didn't hear a car pull up next to them. Fuzzy poked his head around the edge of the Thunderbird to see who it was. The baby blue Oldsmobile GS slid to a stop in the gravel.

"Hey, Daniel. Come have a beer," Fuzzy said to the tall, young man getting out of his very low car.

"Talked me into it. What've y'all been up to?"

He was taken aback at the reaction to that casual question. All three of his friends were practically hysterical—Fuzzy even fell flat to the ground and bounced up-and-down in an odd display of mirth. Charles doubled over with laughter. However, Daniel seemed unmoved. "Well, it must a' been really somethin'," he said evenly, reaching into the cooler. "Tell me."

They told the story of the fire in great detail, which led to other stories and jokes. Even though most had been previously related on other occasions, the guys didn't really care. They still loved the telling and the hearing, as the stories and jokes were all very funny. The group stayed in the park for over an hour trading comical tales; each guy reached into the cooler regularly. Evel was an experienced drinker and almost never drank enough to impair his driving. He only overdid the drinking when there was someone around he trusted to drive. And that list was very, very short.

The sun was going down, but the guys' courage was rising. They figured the excitement at the convenience store had probably died down, so they broke camp—they were ready to hit the town.

"Wanna ride with us, Dan?" asked Evel.

"Naa. I'm packin' it in early tonight. I gotta get up and go to work at the grocery store at five in the mornin'." Daniel got in his car and started the motor.

"Too bad for you!" exclaimed Fuzzy. "More beer for us!"

Daniel and his blue car pulled away. Fuzzy was already feeling pretty good. He and the others piled into the Thunderbird.

"Hey, Evel. Let's drive by Trish's house. I wanna see if she'll go ridin' around with us."

Evel looked over, good-natured concern flashing in his intense blue eyes. After a moment of thought, he shrugged and nodded in agreement. Ten minutes later, Fuzzy and Trish sat in the back seat with the cooler. Charles rode shotgun. The Thunderbird was on the drag on Saturday night. Everyone was ready to party.

They drove through the college, which was fairly deserted since most people went home for the weekend. But the coeds in the second-floor end rooms had apparently stayed around, as both windows were lit up like beacons in a lighthouse. Charles peered at Tanya's room to catch a glimpse—but didn't see anything except the poster with the naked bicyclists. He sighed and turned his attention to the cannon, thinking maybe she was there. But no girls were in sight. "Where are all the girls?"

A male voice from that general area answered. "That's what we'd like to know!"

Charles glanced to his right and saw two guys step out into the glow of the streetlight. He lifted his hand in greeting. They did the same. Sighing, he took a little comfort in the fact that he wasn't the only one without a date on Saturday night.

"There they go—party in progress," said Gene jealously, as he resumed his perch on the cannon seat.

"Now, Gene. Note—three guys and one girl isn't a real party. Except they probably have a lot of beer which, in some cases, makes up for the lack of female companionship, come to think of it," Boots said.

"Let's go out and sit on the wall. There's *bound* to be more going on out there than there is here." Gene hopped down and started walking.

"Whatever your highness desires," Boots bowed and removed his cowboy hat with a flourish as the exasperated Gene passed by.

"Oh, come on." They walked side-by-side.

"There goes Boots and Gene," Janie stated to Tanya with a sigh. They were sitting toe-to-toe in the window. The girls had watched the Thunderbird pass slowly by. They'd seen Charles—but he didn't see them. He wasn't looking in the right window.

"Dang. It's boring tonight. Let's go catch up with 'em." Tanya swung around, her mood brightened. Her feet hit the floor.

Janie also jumped down from the window sill, and they walked into their room to freshen up. The girls didn't like to go out on the drag without looking halfway decent—might as well make an effort and wear mascara. You never knew when Mr. Right might come along. Turning to check each other's appearances, each nodded approval of the other.

They walked across the hall to Glenda's room. "We're goin' out to the wall, Glendee. Wanna come along?" asked Janie hesitantly. Since the frightening incident the previous week with the car on Main Street, Glenda had avoided the wall on the drag. "Boots and Gene just walked out that way."

"Oh, yeah? Well, maybe I'll come out there in a few. Right now, I've got laundry downstairs. Go on—have fun." Glenda waggled her fingers at her friends.

"KO. We sure will." Janie shook her finger at Glenda. "And you be sure to come out!" The two girls walked calmly down the hall for a change.

Glenda crinkled her nose in amusement and got her laundry basket ready. "I might just do that," she said aloud, glancing at the clock. "Linda should be off work, and she'll be here directly." She lifted the laundry basket off the floor. "Besides, there's gotta be some rule against talkin' to yourself and doin' laundry alone on Saturday night!" She snickered at her own joke, shuffling off to retrieve her last load of clothes from the dryer.

Janie and Tanya approached the stone wall in front of the boys' dorm on Main Street, hoping to sneak up on the guys. Each girl picked out her target. Janie took Gene, and Tanya took Boots. They jumped on their victims' backs. Gene grabbed at

Janie and bodily pulled her up onto the wall, plopping her down beside him. Boots offered no such reaction, so Tanya beat on his back. He still didn't move. "You're no fun," she said acidly.

"Is somebody back there?" Boots asked with a glance over his shoulder. Tanya chose that moment to climb up on the wall to strike the Egyptian pose. Several cars honked at the comical sight. She hopped down and sat between Gene and Boots. "What's happenin'?"

"Same o' same o'," answered Gene. "People driving by, mooning us, throwing beer cans at us—some even throwing kisses!"

"Hopefully just the girls!" exclaimed Janie. Unexpectedly, she leaned over and kissed him sweetly on the cheek. A wolf-whistle came from a dark blue pickup driving past. Janie waved grandly and settled in to watch the cars go by. They heard a loud rumble approaching. A souped-up Nova sped by with a "pickle-green" Roadrunner chasing it closely.

"Go...Go...GO!" Tanya yelled at the passing cars. "Now this is much more interestin'. Look! There's Evel Knievel. Hey, what the heck is that?"

The Thunderbird was indeed approaching—and something was flapping out the passenger side window. "What the...?" a perplexed Gene asked.

What they had seen flapping had suddenly taken flight. A red T-shirt and lacy white bra floated eerily through the air, landing softly in the grass at Boot's boot tips. The four shocked friends sitting on the wall looked in unison down at the clothing lying in the grass—then back up at the retreating taillights of the Thunderbird.

"Oh, my gosh!" cried Janie. She leaned down to pick up the items.

"No. No. Don't touch anything," said Gene. "We'll leave 'em right there. I bet they'll be back. I think those things should stay right where they are. Man, I told you those guys know how to party!"

The others burst out in laughter.

Meanwhile, Fuzzy leaned over the giggling Trish and tapped Evel on the shoulder. "Uhh...buddy...please go back. We gotta go back there," he said with dread.

"Oh, no. Not again?" Evel groaned. He made a quick right turn and diverted the rearview mirror up to where all he could see was a reflection of the red headliner. It was one thing to have a girl take off her clothes for you, but quite another when the girl is with your best friend.

"Yeah. Back there at the wall, where those people are," Fuzzy said. He hurriedly took off his own shirt to cover Trish's bare breasts. This girl had a very bad habit: after about three beers, she tended to take off her top. Sometimes, she took off the bra, too. And sometimes—everything went out the window. "I just hope they didn't run off with her shirt."

"And bra!" laughed Trish. She was wiggling around and making it difficult for Fuzzy to pull the T-shirt over her head. He finally succeeded and firmly instructed her to leave it on—he didn't want them both to be topless.

Back at the wall, Tanya watched the traffic carefully. No passersby seemed to notice the clothes lying on the side of the road. As the minutes passed, the wall-sitters grew more and more concerned. Everyone jumped when Tanya squealed and pointed at the incoming traffic. The Thunderbird had apparently sped around the block, as it suddenly was stopped on Main Street—right in front of the friends sitting on the wall. Cars approached from behind, but there would be a few seconds before they, too, would have to stop.

A shirtless Fuzzy jumped out of the Thunderbird, left the door open and ran to the wall. He looked at the people sitting there, then down at the clothing in the grass.

"We left them there for you. We figured you'd be back," said Gene.

"Thanks, man—I don't know why she always does that!" Fuzzy said with exasperation. "It's pretty damned embarrassin'!" He scooped up the clothes and ran back to the car to slide behind Charles into the rear seat with the giggling Trish.

"Hey, Tanya!" called Charles, but he had to shut the door, and the Thunderbird lurched forward.

"Charles! Hey!"

Charles craned his neck to see Tanya. "You wanna go ridin' around?" he yelled out the window.

She waved frantically. "YES! Come back!" She turned to Janie. "What the heck? It'll be fun. Besides, they may or may not come back by."

Wide-eyed, Janie said, "Yeah, right. Of course they will. I couldn't go. I don't have the guts!"

Gene looked over at her with surprise. "What, this from the girl that hangs out of car windows yelling at guys? The girl who usually demands to be the center of attention? Janie Gentry doesn't have the guts? Pal-leeze..."

Janie squinted at Gene. She reached out, politely pushing him backward. He fell off the wall and into the grass on the other side. Janie, who stood just over five feet tall, agilely hopped over the wall and squatted down on his belly.

Tanya and Boots got on their feet to see what was going on behind them. Tanya bowed her head, covering her eyes in mock exasperation at the sight of the two tickling each other on the ground behind the stone wall. They turned back toward Main Street and sat down on the wall. Tanya shook her head and looked toward the sky.

"You two quit that," called Boots over his shoulder at Janie and Gene. "You're embarrassin' me."

"Go for it!" Voices came from the upper floor of the boys' dorm.

Janie suddenly realized what it looked like they were doing. She quickly scrambled to sit beside Tanya on the wall facing the street—away from the guys in the windows. Gene stayed down on the ground, enjoying the moment. "You know, you can really see quite a few stars from this angle, even right here in the middle of town," he said dreamily.

Tanya and Janie looked at each other with raised eyebrows—then nodded in silent agreement. Each hopped up and over the wall and lay down on her back on either side of Gene. Boots was now all alone on the wall.

The landscaping crew had mowed earlier in the week, and dried grass was all around. Tanya grabbed up a handful and started turning her body from side-to-side. "Hey, is this what they call rollin' in the hay?"

Janie and Gene both rolled with her—laughing—and throwing the dried grass at each other.

"I don't think so. But, Gene, that's probably as close as you'll get to rollin' in the hay with two pretty girls your whole life!" Boots said in fun. He turned his attention to the oncoming traffic. "Hey, Tan-ay—here come your friends."

"Which ones?" Tanya was disinterested. She was still happily rolling in the hay.

"The guys in the Thunderbird. I think they're slowin' down again."

Tanya hopped quickly up, dusting the dried grass off her jeans and T-shirt. She jumped over the wall and leaned toward the street in an "on your mark" stance—just as the silver Thunderbird slowed almost to a stop in front of her.

"Come on—hop in!" called Charles, opening the car door. The vehicle was still slightly moving. "Come on—hurry!"

Tanya ran the few feet across the grass and took one jumping giant step to launch herself into the car. She pulled her feet in just as the door shut. The Thunderbird hastily disappeared around the corner.

"Well. How do ya like that?" complained Janie. She and Gene had resumed their positions on the wall with Boots. Her hair was a mess. Gene reached over to pick a leaf off the top of her head. She slapped his hand away with her own. He looked slightly tickled.

"It'll be fine. Don't worry. She won't be gone long." He pulled on one of the grass clippings stuck in her unruly curls.

Janie sighed impatiently, shaking her head with great purpose. She yelled into the air, "QUIT IT!"

Brusquely shaking off Gene's attentions, she noticed something approaching from her left. "Lookee there! It's Glenda!" Janie jumped to her feet and was hopping up-and-down.

"Hall-oh!" Linda Lou shouted. Her head was thrust out the open window, as they slowly passed by. "Stay there. We'll pick you up the next time around!"

"KO!"

Janie was truly excited to see her friend finally out in her car. "Hoorah, Glenda's on the drag! The Camaro's on the drag and it's Saturday night!"

Gene and Boots nodded at each other knowingly. This was the way it was supposed to be, seeing these girls happy—without a care or fear.

The parade of vehicles continued, some familiar, some not, some friendly, some too friendly. Eventually, the silver Thunderbird came back by with Tanya waving from her place in the middle of the front seat.

"Hey, Tan-ay! Glenda's out on the drag!" Janie hollered as they passed by. She thought she saw Tanya look back and hoped she heard. All of a sudden, a familiar sounding honk got her attention. It was the yellow Camaro. She got ready.

"Hall-oh! Hop in back!" Linda Lou called to Janie. The car slowed to a stop, "Hurry!"

Janie slipped into the back seat of the Camaro, quick as a flash. Linda Lou made a funny face at Boots and Gene, slammed the door, and they took off. She ran her fingers over her forehead, and flicked her hand out the window, as though wiping sweat off her brow.

"That was excellent, Janie. You are a 'Speedy Gonzales'—Ándale! Ándale!" exclaimed Glenda. She watched the rearview mirror to see if anyone behind was unhappy about the unscheduled stop in the middle of Main Street, but everything looked all right. "Where's Tan-ay?" She shifted to peer at Janie in the rearview mirror.

"Arriba! Arriba! Ándale! Would you believe the guys in the Thunderbird picked her up a little while ago? Just like you did me?"

"Are you cereal? Corn Flakes or Froot Loops?"

"Corn Flakes. I mean really—they did!"

"Who was in there—I mean besides the driver?" Glenda was really curious now.

"Let's see...there was Charles and Evel Knievel, of course. Oh, and Fuzzy was in the back seat with a girl. She took her shirt and bra off and threw it at us."

Linda Lou looked quizzically over her shoulder at the lively girl in the back seat. Janie nodded her head so hard her curls bobbed up-and-down. She leaned up between the bucket seats.

"Don't look at me in that tone of voice. It was so weird. We were just sittin' there, and this shirt and bra came flyin' outta the Thunderbird and landed in the grass right at our feet. Gene didn't let us touch anything and sure enough—directly here came the Thunderbird. Fuzzy got out and picked the clothes up." Janie giggled. "Oh, and he didn't have a shirt on either."

"A topless twosome?" asked Linda Lou.

"Yeah! And I think she did it on purpose. We all could hear her laughin', but we couldn't really see her. But we sure could hear her. It was strange. I mean—don't ever let me get that drunk. OK?"

"Like we could stop you!" replied Glenda with a backwards snort.

She turned up the volume on "Jungle Love." The girls loved that song. They were in traffic at the new Dairy Queen. Glenda studied the arrangement of the vehicles to determine what the best position would be. She picked her spot, maneuvered into it and shot out in front of everyone else with a triumphant whoop.

Tanya watched the Camaro zoom away from traffic. She bounced on the seat. "Hey, there's Glenda! Oh, my gosh. Glenda's out on the drag!"

"What's so strange about that?" asked Charles. He tried to put his arm around the bouncing girl.

"Oh, man. You wouldn't believe it. She's been so depressed. It was really bad. I mean she actually walked out in front of a car last week, like she was tryin' to commit suicide or somthin'." Tanya craned her neck back-and-forth to look up ahead for her friend. When Tanya leaned up, Charles took the opportunity to drape his arm over the back of the seat behind her. He also bent over a bit.

"You know, we noticed her car hasn't been out lately," he said with interest. All at once, Tanya's words sunk in. "Wait a second. That was *Glenda* that almost got hit by a car? I heard about that!" Charles pulled his arm back. He sensed it wasn't the time to make a move. "That was her? I don't believe it!"

"Hmm. My brother was a few car lengths behind a station wagon that nearly hit somebody the other night. That must a' been it," Evel said thoughtfully. "Did it happen right back there—where you and your friends were sittin' on the wall?"

Tanya turned to face Evel, who was a mystery to her. "Yes. Janie and I were so scared. If it hadn't been for Gene, Glenda mighta' got run over." She saw an expression of concern cloud what appeared to be a usually happy face.

Evel glanced at her with a flash of his very blue eyes before turning them back to the road. "Why'd she do that?"

"Well, she found out her fiancé had gotten another girl pregnant and was married. Actually, first he tried to talk Glenda into runnin' off to get married, but she didn't. Thank goodness." Tanya sighed. "Last week he even tried to convince her he wasn't married—when everyone knew he was. It was terrible."

Evel and Charles remained in shocked silence for a second or two. "That's rough," Charles finally said.

"Man. That *is* awful," Fuzzy said from the back seat.

"Is she OK now?" asked Evel evenly. "I mean—that's why you're glad she's out tonight?" He peered intently at the traffic in front of them.

"Yeah. She's gettin' better little by little. This is the first time she's been out in her car in weeks," Tanya explained. She leaned toward Evel to look up ahead for her friend. He glanced down at the side of her face—then focused on the traffic ahead.

"It looks like she's turnin' into the college. You wanna catch up with her?" Evel asked.

Tanya quickly leaned back with surprise. "Could we?"

"You bet," he said in an affable tone. "Hang on."

Suddenly, the big car pulled onto the wrong side of the road and passed several vehicles. The T-bird cut back into traffic one car length before the left blinker coolly announced the intended turn into the main entrance. The Camaro was already moving up the drive toward the Student Center, but the Thunderbird had to wait for some traffic to clear. Evel floored the accelerator as soon as an opening appeared and slid the car across the pavement into the entrance. He stayed on the gas, quickly catching up with the Camaro.

"Hey, lookee back there. There's Tan-ay in the Thunderbird!" Janie proclaimed, after she'd heard the Thunderbird approach from behind.

"Where?" Linda Lou asked.

"Back there! Glenda—STOP!"

Glenda slammed on the brakes and the car slid to a short-lived stationary position. But she heard a screech of tires from behind. With a quick decision, she stepped on the gas pedal so hard that her back tires squealed before the Camaro surged ahead. Linda and Janie were tossed frontward with the abrupt stop, then backward with the sudden movement forward. Glenda watched in the rearview mirror. When she saw the Thunderbird had come to a halt, she stopped too—more mindfully this time.

The big car's passenger door opened. "Thanks for the ride. See y'all later!" Tanya told Evel and Charles, as she quickly exited the car. She ran around the front of the Thunderbird, waved at Evel, and shuffled up to the driver side of the Camaro.

"Hi, Glendee. Can I go with y'all?" Tanya was hopping up-and-down.

"Don't be a goober, Tan-ay. Get in!" Glenda opened the car door and stood up.

Tanya reached in—tilted up the seat—and slid into the back with Janie. Glenda eyed the big car behind her. She couldn't really see much beyond the glare of the headlights, but she smiled and raised a hand in greeting before sliding back into the driver seat.

"So...that's Glenda," Evel said.

Charles looked over at him. "Yeah. She used to be a lot of fun. Well, maybe she will be again now that that dick-brained son of a bitch is outta her life." Evel looked over, wondering about the venom in Charles' voice as he kept talking. "Well, I mean, he must have dick for brains if he messed around on that girl. Tanya thinks Glenda's real special."

Evel took that in silently, nodding slowly. He drove on around the U and followed the Camaro out of the college. He watched the car load of girls and seemed slightly amused, until he suddenly remembered there was still a girl in his car.

Evel cleared his throat while readjusting the rearview mirror to its correct position. He hesitantly looked into the back seat. Charles turned around to look for himself.

"They're asleep," said Charles. "Can you believe it? All this goin' on, and they're both asleep!"

"Wake him up."

"FUZ!!" yelled Charles. He reached back and slapped Fuzzy's knee...hard.

"Wha—what?"

"Fuz. What time does Trish hafta be home?" Evel asked. "It's ten till eleven, and we're ten minutes from her house."

"GO!!" Fuzzy said urgently—now fully awake. Evel made for the back streets, which he knew well as a city employee.

"Trish—Trish! Wake up! Where's your shirt? It's almost eleven o'clock!" Fuzzy felt panicked.

Charles and Evel heard a commotion coming from the back seat and decided it was better not to look. Trish was a senior in high school; she still had a curfew. Evel felt a responsibility to deliver her home on time and in one piece.

At 10:59 p.m. on the Thunderbird's digital clock, Trish leaned up between the seats to give Evel and Charles each a kiss on the cheek. The couple exited the car, and Trish kissed Fuzzy goodnight on the lips. She ran up to the door, opened it and stepped in at the click of eleven.

Evel felt a measure of satisfaction, looking first at the dash clock, and then at Fuzzy, as he slid back into the Thunderbird's rear seat. He backed out of the driveway as quietly as possible.

The Thunderbird moved much more slowly through the neighborhoods on the way to Main Street than it had on the frenzied drive to Trish's house. Soon, Evel saw his brother's Nova in the new Dairy Queen parking lot. Larry waved urgently out the driver's window to catch Evel's attention. Evel quickly dodged a few cars and pulled into the parking lot against the oncoming traffic. He stopped next to Larry's car, so he could see his brother up close and turn his full attention to him.

"Hey, Brother Glenn. Roger's car is stuck in some trees on the drag down past town. He needs help, but I gotta git Chip home," Larry called to his brother from the Nova. "He's had a little too much, if ya know what I mean."

"Right—go on. I'll go check it out. See ya later!" Evel yelled back at his younger brother.

"Hurry! Before the cops git there!" Larry put his car in gear and took off.

"Let's go!" called Fuzzy from the back seat. Charles nodded his agreement.

Evel turned the T-bird around and hurried down the drag. He drove through downtown, steadily slowing down to locate the problem. "He said the car was stuck. That doesn't make sense. It hasn't rained lately. I wonder how he got stuck?" asked Charles.

Evel pointed to the left. "That's how. Larry said somethin' about trees. Well, I'll be damned."

He cut off the lights and turned into a driveway. The three jumped out of the car and hurried over to a vehicle that was in big trouble. "How in the world did that...?" Fuzzy stopped when Evel motioned for quiet.

They carefully walked closer and found the problem was obvious. Roger wasn't stuck in the mud. He had run his Pontiac into somebody's yard, and the front fenders were wedged between two trees. The back tires had scooped out little trenches in the topsoil where the driver tried unsuccessfully to back the car out of its predicament. Roger sat in the driver's seat, his forehead resting on the steering wheel in despair.

Evel took command; he had a knack for knowing what to do when there was trouble. "Fuz. Watch for Jackson. I think he was up ahead of us. Run out to the street and pull him over when he comes back by."

Roger's passenger, Thomas, was standing over in the shadows. "What can I do, Evel?"

"Pray, Thomas. Pray." Evel suppressed a chuckle.

"There he is!" Fuzzy ran onto Main Street to get Jackson's attention. The pickup pulled into the driveway behind the Thunderbird. The driver killed the lights and engine.

"I'm glad nobody's home here. Maybe we can get outta this OK," Thomas said to Evel. He looked around nervously.

"That's good news." Evel rolled his eyes before turning to the newcomer on the scene. "OK, Jackson. You got a chain?"

"Sure. In the toolbox. What the hell—the car is stuck? Between the trees?"

"Yeah—and stuck but good. Roger can't back it out, so we gotta pull it out. You hook up your chain and feed it back here to his car, OK?"

"You got it." Jackson jogged to the bed of his pickup. "Hop down, Rocky—outta the way," he called to the dog that always rode on the toolbox.

Rocky obeyed and jumped down into the bed of the pickup, but no farther, as Jackson pulled the chain from the toolbox. Rocky reclaimed his position as soon as the metal lid was closed. Jackson quickly hooked the chain to his trailer hitch, throwing the excess into the bed of his pickup. He backed slowly onto the lawn to within six feet of Roger's vehicle. Fuzzy secured the other end of the chain to the Pontiac's bumper. Jackson hopped in his four-wheel-drive truck and peered in the side mirror. "Say when!"

He didn't notice a car was approaching on Main Street.

"What the heck is goin' on up there?" Linda Lou asked, as the yellow Camaro rolled up to the commotion in the yard.

Glenda slammed on the brakes. "Hey, can we do anything?"

Evel looked up sharply at the unexpected interruption, but brightened when he saw the Camaro. "Run—run for your lives!" He waved his arm to indicate they should leave the area.

The girls in the car laughed at his actions. Glenda punched the gas pedal to move away from the scene.

Evel turned his attention back to the wedged Pontiac. "OK, Roger. Start the car and put it in Neutral. Make sure the emergency brake's off and hover your foot over the brake pedal. When you feel the car come loose, and I give the signal—step on the brake. Got it?"

"Yeah, OK." Clearly distressed, Roger sighed loudly, then turned the key and started the engine. "OK. In Neutral—brake off."

"Fuz. Charles. Y'all watch each side and holler when it's loose!" Evel yelled. He ran up to the cab of the truck and told Jackson to begin slowly pulling. The engine of the pickup truck started with a roar.

With Charles watching on one side and Fuzzy on the other, the chain drew tight as Jackson pulled forward. Unexpectedly, the back bumper broke loose from the car and flew toward the pickup. The abrupt release of pressure caused the truck to surge forward. This action luckily kept the bumper from joining Rocky in the bed of the pickup. It clattered and scraped to a stop on the driveway.

"Dammit, Fuz—hook to the frame. Man, I thought you knew better than that!" Evel said impatiently.

The guys pulled the bumper over to the side, and Jackson backed up again. Fuzzy took the chain, easily hooking it to the frame of the vehicle—now that the bumper was out of the way. Again they manned their stations. Jackson put his truck in gear. It surged forward a bit, but unexpectedly paused.

A terrible screeching sound began low—then louder—then even louder. Ever so slowly, the car began to move backward as the chain was pulled. Suddenly, with more metallic screeches, the sound of wood splintering and a loud CRACK, the car leapt from the trees.

Fuzzy gave the signal, "Clear!"

"Whoa!" Evel yelled.

Jackson stopped immediately, but Roger didn't. "WHOA!" Evel screamed. He ran toward the still moving car.

Roger's foot slammed down on the brake pedal, stopping the car about two feet from Jackson's back bumper. Fuzzy quickly moved in to unhook the chain from both vehicles. Jackson got out of his truck. Evel slapped him on the shoulder. "Thanks, man, way to go. Now get the hell outta here!"

"Right. Let's go Rocky!" The dog barked happily. He was always ready to go. Fuzzy threw the chain in the bed of the pickup. Jackson spun his wheels in the yard during his hurry to leave. Dirt flew all over Roger's car.

"Now you, Roger—back on outta here and go home," Evel said.

"It's wrecked. Oh, man, my dad's gonna kill me." Roger cringed, then he and Thomas got in the car.

"Here—you might need this," said Charles. He tossed a piece of chrome molding through the passenger side window into Thomas' lap.

"And don't forget this," Evel called. He opened the back door and—with Fuzzy's help—shoved the damaged chrome rear bumper into the back seat. Roger moaned when he heard the back door creak loudly, as it was closed. The end of the bumper stuck out the open window. He backed out onto Main Street.

Roger looked at the trio in the yard. "Thanks, guys. I owe ya one."

"Go!" said Evel. "And we better get outta here, too."

"Yeah, before somebody calls the cops," said Charles.

"That won't happen. Your uncle lives next door, don't he, Evel?" asked Fuzzy.

"Yeah. Uncle Dub lives there. It's a good thing this didn't happen in his yard, or we'd have never gotten away with it," Evel chuckled. He liked and respected his uncle and his house.

"We still won't if we don't go," Charles insisted.

"Right. Pile in, and we'll head outta town on this end for a change."

Evel backed out of the driveway, spinning the tires in an effort to quickly escape the scene. As the speedometer reached 35, he let off the throttle and held that speed. The yellow Camaro appeared, heading back up the drag. It honked, so he honked back. After the two cars passed each other, he pressed the accelerator pedal down to the floor to leave the area and swiftly disappeared into the darkness.

Chapter Five

REO Speedwagon's *You Can Tune a Piano, But You Can't Tuna Fish* played loudly from the 8-track player in Glenda's room. Tanya and Janie were lounging on Linda Lou's bed. Glenda was slouching comfortably in her desk chair, waiting for Linda to come back from gymnastics. At lunch, Linda told the group she wanted to go ridin' around that night. Since she usually worked on weekday evenings, it was a rare opportunity for her to go out with the girls.

"I'm sure glad Linda wants to get out tonight," Tanya said. "I think I'll die of boredom if we don't do somethin'."

Glenda smiled. "And it's only Tuesday."

She looked at a greeting card the girls had sneaked onto her desk. After gazing fondly at the girls, who were looking at her with anticipation, she reached over to the stereo and lowered the volume significantly. Glenda read the card aloud. "'To find your handsome prince, you have to kiss a lot of toads.' Ladies, that's a good one. In fact, I'm very lucky to not have warts of any kind, considering the toad I've been with for the last two years!" Her ensuing laugh was cynical, but pleasant.

"That's for sure. Talk about a guy that couldn't keep his pants on!" Janie pretended to fasten her jeans in jest.

"Yepper. I hope he has to change dirty diapers *and* pay child support for the rest of his life," said Tanya vehemently.

The girls nodded, looking straight-faced at each other. It was all true, sadly true. But unexpectedly Glenda began to laugh quietly. The other girls quickly caught the feeling and joined in. Before long, their giddy hilarity allowed a tumult of troubled emotions to release. Happy tears ran down quivering cheeks. An intangible page seemed to turn with a fresh, new chapter opening.

Quickly, their attention shifted to the sound of unfamiliar footsteps in the hallway. During the quiet pause and ꧁꧂꧁꧂꧁꧂ sound while the tape changed tracks, Glenda leaned sideways to peer out the open door. A girl peered into Tanya and Janie's room, but upon finding no one there, she walked across the hall through Glenda's doorway.

"Hey, everybody. Tanya, you know that guy Fuzzy, right?"

The girl, Melinda, was a fairly striking blonde who lived downstairs next to the end room that played too much Boz Skaggs. She was a freshman. The second-floor girls didn't know her all that well.

"Yeah, sure...well...kinda," stammered Tanya. "Why?"

Melinda sauntered into the room and sat in Linda's desk chair. She glanced around at her audience. "He asked me for a date. He's gonna pick me up, and we're goin' to the movies tonight. Where's the theater? Is it nice?"

"Ah, yes. Dollar night at the Monarch!" Glenda cast a meaningful glance toward Tanya and Janie.

Tanya understood Glenda's silent message and covered a comical reaction. "Right. Well, the theater is old but still pretty nice. It's just a couple a' blocks off the square in downtown. I think it was built sometime right after World War II, since it has that forties grand style and such a majestic name. But the crown jewel of the place is the huge stained-glass window up front. *It* is the Monarch."

"Monarch? You mean like the butterfly or like the king?" asked Melinda.

"Both!" Janie answered. "The window has a great big beautiful monarch butterfly, and he has a cute little golden crown on top of his head between his antennae."

"And the first time a person goes to the movies at the Monarch, they have to pat the butterfly on his crown," Tanya continued. "It's a rule. Hey, wait a second. Fuzzy's gonna' pick you up? I'm pretty sure I haven't seen him drivin' a car—ever. He always rides with somebody else."

Melinda frowned slightly. "Pat the butterfly's head?" She hastily smoothed her brow. "Yeah. Well, anyway. Yep, that's what he said. That he'd pick me up in a 'Vette. I'm pretty excited to get to ride in a Corvette." She grew more and more enthusiastic as she continued. "Is he nice? I mean…he seems nice enough to go to the movies with, especially in a 'Vette."

"Sure…well…I don't know him all that well, but he's probably OK." Tanya threw an expressive look at Janie who nodded imperceptibly.

"But…Melinda…you might need to watch yourself," Janie said, thinking mischievous thoughts. "We saw a girl's shirt come flyin' out of a car he was ridin' around in last Saturday night. It was pretty strange."

Tanya turned her attention to the wide-eyed Melinda. "Oh, peshaw! That was the girl's fault. He told me she threw it out after she'd had too much to drink. The real question is…" She paused and flashed the number one sign, shaking her index finger slightly. "Who took it off? Besides, if he's drivin' a 'Vette he'll be way too busy with the car to try to undress you, too!"

Melinda closed her mouth, looked at Tanya's smirk, frowned and rose to her feet. "Humph. Well, he's comin' by to take me the seven o'clock show. Y'all just watch out the window, and you'll see."

Melinda tossed her hair and exited the room in a huff. She turned so sharply out the door that her long blonde hair swung out, making a "swishing" noise as it brushed against the wooden door jamb.

"Don't forget to pat the butterfly's head!" Janie called out to the fast retreating Melinda.

The girls looked knowingly at each other and snickered. They silently agreed they would watch out the window for Fuzzy's Corvette. There were very few Corvettes in town. They knew one of the guys who owned one, and he wasn't Fuzzy. Glenda shook her head side-to-side and cranked up the music to kill some time.

"Roll With the Changes" was playing for the third time when Linda's digital clock showed 6:55 p.m. Close enough—Glenda switched off the stereo. The girls rose to their feet simultaneously. They tumbled cheerfully into the hall, where Tanya and Janie took up their toe-to-toe position in the window. Glenda stood between them, slumping over a bit to peer down to the sidewalk and street below. She saw their friends walking. "Looks like Boots and Gene are headed to the Student Center. Maybe they'll be out at the cannon later," Glenda said, bending down a bit farther to look out below the open sash.

"Yeah. We'll drive by after while and honk at 'em," Janie said.

"Or better yet, ignore 'em," said Tanya playfully.

"Oh, come on you two—quit it. Hey, hey, there's Fuzzy—right on time—but lookee—he's on foot." Glenda gently pushed the four tennis shoes out of the way, so she could lean directly on the window sill. Fuzzy must have felt their eyes on him; he looked up.

"Hey, Fuzzy! How's it goin'?" called Tanya.

"Hey, there. Just fine. Say, how do I pick up a date here? I mean...I can't just go in there—can I?" Fuzzy pointed at the door below the window.

Tanya snorted in sardonic amusement. "Ha. Not hardly! Normally, you hafta go up front to the lobby and leave a blood sample. But, hang on, I'll run down and tell Melinda you're here." Tanya hopped down before seeing Fuzzy's odd expression—he seemed surprised they knew why he was there.

But Glenda noticed. She continued with Tanya's joke. "Hey, Fuzzy. Don't worry. They don't take blood from a non-student. What's the dollar movie this week?" She seemed amused when he shrugged, as though accepting their knowledge of everything.

"They're showin' *The Jerk* with Steve Martin. It's supposed to be a riot," he said. "Who is that talkin'?"

"That was Glenda, and I'm Janie."

They saw his blondish afro nod, then watched his eyes divert to the door below them. Melinda ran down the steps to stand in front of him. "Hi! I'm all ready to ride in the 'Vette!" She hopped up-and-down a few times.

Fuzzy grimaced as pleasantly as possible and said, "OK, let's go." He led her to a little orange car in a parking space next to a green pickup. He opened the door for her to get in. Tanya had arrived back at the window, but the girls couldn't see what was happening on the far side of the green pickup. They all ran into the dorm room to look out the side window.

"That's not a Corvette!" Melinda shouted, a little too loudly. She looked around nervously.

"Hey, now. I didn't say it was. I said it was a 'Vette. It's a *Chevette*—my sister's car," he said with apprehension. He waited patiently with an anxious look on his face.

"Oh, well. It doesn't matter. Let's go."

Melinda seated herself as ladylike as possible in the tiny vehicle. She glanced up to see if anyone was looking out the window.

"That's even smaller than your car, Tan-ay!" said Janie with a slap on her roommate's shoulder.

Glenda rose to her feet. "I knew it wouldn't be a Corvette. But it was a pretty good joke!"

"Yepper. It worked, too. There they go—off to the Monarch!" exclaimed Janie.

The three laughed so hard they didn't notice the new arrival behind them in the hall. "Hall-oh! What's so funny?" asked Linda, her keys rattling. She kept her keys on a large metal hoop that resembled an old timey jailer's key ring. She often wore it as a bracelet in an effort not to lose her keys. It worked pretty well most of the time—unless the key ring was with her shoes.

"Fuzzy's 'Vette!" Glenda replied. Linda looked perplexed. "Oh, never mind. You had to be there. We've been waitin' impatiently for you, Linda Lou. When do you want to go ridin' around?"

"Hmm…in just a little while. I really need a shower after gymnastics. Oh boy, am I glad I don't have to work tonight! I'll take a quickie—I won't wash my hair."

"Good. 'Cause, you know, we really don't have that kind of time," said Tanya semi-seriously. Glenda and Linda's thick long hair was notoriously slow to dry. It seemed to Tanya like she always had to wait around for them. She silently thanked her mother for talking her into the short haircut.

Linda jingled her massive key ring in defiance. "OK. OK. I'll hurry!"

"Are they gone yet?" Glenda moved back into the hall to peer out the window again. "Look. There they go. You know… it is a really cute car."

Glenda waved at Melinda, who was looking up to see if anyone was watching. Melinda turned her head quickly and ignored the wave. The little orange car drove away.

Glenda turned to the other girls. "Y'all get ready. We'll go fuel up while Linda gets her shower."

She darted into her room to grab her keys and checkbook. She hated purses, and the checkbook case carried everything she needed: driver's license, college ID, cash, and checks. "Linda Lou, try to be ready in fifteen minutes. We'll gas up, make a drag, then come back and honk for ya, KO?"

"That'll work." Linda gathered her towel and shower supplies for the trek down the hall.

"All right. Let's go!" Janie exclaimed. The three headed down the hall ahead of Linda.

They stopped when the door on the opposite end opened. "Man in the hall!" a figure called.

"Where?" cried the three in unison. Two other coeds came out of their rooms, and everyone pointed toward the two people who had entered the hall from the lobby.

"There!!" Tanya pointed dramatically at the couple walking down the hall. "How much blood did they take this time, Alex?" she asked with a giggle.

"Y'all stop it," said Hope, the girl responsible for the man in the hall.

The girls chuckled as they moved down the stairs. It was a ritual to make a big deal of a male visitor to the dorm. Nobody could sneak a guy to their room, and it was actually a rule to yell "man in the hall", since there might be females in various stages of undress coming and going from the community bathroom. The guy had to hand over his driver's license and college ID to a watchful dorm monitor on duty in the lobby. At straight up ten o'clock, all the licenses and IDs had better be re-distributed back to their owners, or she phoned the room to which the boys were assigned. Or worse: she went to the room and banged on the door. It was unheard of to have a guy stay overnight in the girls' dorm; it just didn't happen.

The yellow Camaro drank the five dollars worth of gas that would last through the evening. After that, the girls made the obligatory drag. As they passed by the stone entrance... *KABOOM!* The explosion echoed off the buildings across from the college. "Wow. That was a big one," Glenda said. "I hope they didn't break the windows this time."

For several years, someone had been sneaking up to the old World War I cannon, loading it with a gunpowder charge and setting it off. It usually rattled the windows of the girls' dorm but never seemed to damage the old cannon. "Yepper. They're at it again, whoever they are," Janie said with a giggle. It was an ongoing discussion every time the cannon was fired. Theories of the parties responsible flew around for days. But still, no one knew for sure who fired the cannon.

Farther down the drag, Glenda noticed a blue pickup behind her car. As she pulled out of the new Dairy Queen, it stayed right on her bumper. She drove calmly down Main Street, fully aware of the vehicle in the rearview mirror. Glenda quickly pulled into the left turn lane at the college entrance with the pickup trailing. But when she shot through a small gap in the traffic, the pickup swerved out of the turn lane and continued heading straight.

Janie craned her neck around. "Who the heck was that?"

"No idea—never seen 'em before." Though Glenda's voice was calm, she cast an intense look down the street at the pickup's taillights. "Let's get Linda Lou." She stopped the Camaro behind some parked cars right outside the dorm and honked the horn.

"Hall-oh—be right down!" Linda called from above. Tanya popped out of the car and slid into the back seat. It was understood Linda rode shotgun—she rarely joined them, so she always got the best seat. Linda glided gracefully down the steps and hopped into the car through the still open door. "Let's go. What's playin'?" She pointed at the 8-track player.

"KC and the Sunshine Band." Glenda plugged in the tape.

The girls pulled out on the drag, waving and honking their way to the new Dairy Queen. If it were possible to dance while riding in a car, that's what they did. With each thumping disco beat, a hand would emerge with fingers wide spread out one window. On the next beat another hand would appear out the other window—and this carried on around the back side of the Dairy Queen and out to the front. Several people in the parking lot yelled approval at the antics.

The dance ended suddenly. The blue pickup reappeared, edging right up on the Camaro's back bumper. The driver began alternately gunning the motor and stepping on the brakes, making the pickup raise and lower ominously on the front suspension. Traffic crept toward Main Street little by little. The pickup was obviously targeting Glenda's car, as its bumper nearly grazed hers with the wild gyrations. The driver and passenger seemed to be yelling, but the occupants of the Camaro couldn't hear the words.

"Oh, great," said Glenda, as she glanced with irritation at the rearview mirror. Working her way to the front of the pack, she looked intently at the traffic on either side and out on Main Street. She picked a spot just large enough for her car, waited until the last second—then shot out onto Main Street, leaving the blue pickup mired in traffic in the Dairy Queen parking lot.

Larry watched the action from the passenger's seat of Evel's Thunderbird. "Wow, that was a good move." The big car was backed into a parking spot along the side of the restaurant.

"Yeah. I wonder what those guys are up to. Do you know 'em?"

"Nope. But I bet they're up to no good. Do you know those girls in the Camaro?"

Evel frowned. "Kind of...I'm pretty sure she...I mean...they can take care of themselves. But it might be a good idea for us to keep an eye out."

The two brothers had been sitting in the Thunderbird—just watching the cars go by. Sometimes that was entertaining enough; it also saved gas. "I've got a funny feelin'. Let's make a move and go down to Tim's Donut Shop and be in the middle of things—that is if anything interestin' happens."

Evel started the car.

"Way to go, Glenda!" cried Janie. "You left 'em in the dust. OK, well, in the Dairy Queen parkin' lot!"

"Yeah, for now. Hey, there's the VW." Glenda honked her horn in response to the honk she had heard.

BEEP-BEEP. The VW horn sounded like the Roadrunner cartoon. Glenda honked twice. Then they heard three beeps, and Glenda responded with an equal number of honks.

"Who was that?" asked Linda Lou. "I kind of remember the car."

"I have no earthly idea. I don't even know what she looks like. We just honk at each other like that until we can't hear each other anymore. She drives through the college sometimes, but I don't think she's a student. It doesn't really matter. We just honk our horns at each other."

Linda planted her elbow on the open window frame. This was much better than answering the phone at the hospital.

Glenda made several drags, but nothing unusual was happening. They did notice kids gathering in the open lot across from the Astro Drive-In. "A new hang out for the high-schoolers, I reckon," said Glenda. "I hope the cops don't chase 'em off." She stuck her arm out the window and drew waves back from most of the people there.

"Isn't this a lot of people out for a Tuesday?" Linda asked.

"Yeah. Ain't it great?" Tanya declared happily from the back seat.

They stopped in at the Astro Drive-In for some drinks and parked on the un-nerd side for a while. After she returned to the drag, Glenda moaned. "Hang on to your cups, ladies. It's gonna to be a bumpy ride."

"OK—C-cups under control." Linda jauntily supported her breasts with both hands.

"Me too!" Janie leaned forward to thrust her chest out.

"Y'all quit braggin," Tanya said flatly.

"Thanks Tan-ay. We B-cups gotta stick together!" Glenda replied over her shoulder, holding up her Astro cup. Tanya mirrored the action, and the Styrofoam cups touched in a toast.

Glenda turned her attention to the rearview mirror. The blue pickup was back. In the glare of the streetlight, the girls could see two guys in the cab peering through the pickup's windshield. The driver pulled up to Glenda's back bumper. She punched the gas pedal, and the Camaro took off. The car flew over the railroad tracks—passed by the donut shop in a flash—and sped down the drag with the pickup in hot pursuit.

"Look out—the chase is on," said Larry. He slid off the hood of his brother's car to stand on his feet and watch the two vehicles pass quickly by.

"Right. Keep a watch out for trouble," said Evel. He was casually leaning on the hood of the Thunderbird, but concern covered his face.

The girls were getting tossed about but cheered their driver on. "Let's try to lose 'em!" exclaimed Janie. "Glendee-girl. Go through the park!"

Glenda abruptly turned right, roaring down a side street. She only paused at a stop sign before the car accelerated into the grounds of the city park.

Tanya turned to peer out the back window. "Here they come."

"OK. And here we go. Hang on!"

Glenda slammed on the brake and spun the steering wheel—then got back on the gas. The half-a-donut in the large open area near the old stone recreation hall allowed the car to head back the way it had just come. They passed the blue pickup as it pulled into the park area. The pickup screeched to a stop. The girls laughed when Glenda tapped the horn twice to send a "bye-bye" signal to the stopped vehicle.

Glenda hastily looked around, resolutely steering the car into another sharp turn. "We'll go this way—then come out on the drag on the other side of the courthouse. Let's just see if they can catch up."

"Oh, my!" Linda held firmly onto the door panel armrest.

"Don't worry, Linda Lou. Glenda always gets away," said Tanya, as she patted her friend's shoulder from the back seat.

Glenda quickly made a block to get in the right position to drive casually back up Main Street. The blue pickup idled at the stop sign on the road leading in and out of the park when the Camaro passed. The driver glared at Glenda when she boldly waved her arm out the car window. He hesitated only a moment before pulling out onto the drag behind her. But Glenda was ready. She raced up the drag past the donut shop, flying back over the railroad tracks and barely noticing people on the vacant lot shouting encouragement. Driving as hard and fast as traffic would allow, she quickly turned onto a side street at the edge of the university property. She ducked into a back parking lot to disappear into the campus.

The pickup driver stayed right with her. He wasn't going to be that easy to shake.

Glenda spun her back tires up the lanes. The Camaro slid around the ends of five separate rows of parked cars with the pickup following very closely. Both vehicles weaved and turned, nearly out of control—but stayed right together up-and-down every lane in the parking lot. Glenda shot her car back out onto the side street and into the neighborhood that flanked the college. The driver of the pickup misjudged the turn—bounced over a curb onto the street—but regained control. The chase was on again.

The Camaro zigzagged through the streets of the neighborhood. Suddenly, Glenda was looking at the back entrance to the college. Making a quick decision, she abruptly turned the car to the left, speeding through the poorly lit entrance, past the quiet red brick buildings toward the U driveway and S curve in the center of the campus.

"What the heck?" Gene asked with alarm. He heard a car approaching rapidly from behind with screeching tires and a roaring engine. He craned his neck, looking back as far as he could from his seat on the cannon. "Oh, my gosh. It's Glenda. Hey!" He waved and called as they rumbled past. He thought he saw a hand wave from the back seat out the driver's window, but the car went by so fast he wasn't sure.

The blue pickup quickly caught up with the Camaro, as Glenda weaved through the S curve and onto the outbound driveway.

"Ah ha. Boys chase girls," commented Boots jovially.

"My money's on the girls." Gene settled back into his seat on the cannon.

"Mine too. Matter-of-fact, let's go down to the Shoe Bench. Maybe we can hear the story when they get back, unless somethin' else happens between now and then," Boots suggested. He slid down to the concrete.

"Well, they aren't stopping this time around. That's for sure. There they go—at a high rate of speed, I might add," Gene said. He pointed toward the retreating vehicles. "OK. Let's make a move. Knowing Glenda, it won't take long for her to shake off those low-lifes!" Gene also jumped off the cannon.

Glenda jammed the accelerator to the floor, praying silently that no one would back out of a parking space. The girls looked at each other to make sure each was all right. Linda very nearly lost her composure as they passed by the safety of their dorm building—but she looked at Glenda and saw a determined face. Linda nodded, looking through the windshield with renewed confidence. The girls in the back seat, however, had been severely tossed about.

"They're still behind us, Glendee," said Janie with a tinge of worry. "Maybe we should a' stopped at the dorm." She leaned up between the seats and placed a gentle hand on Glenda's right shoulder.

"No way!" exclaimed Tanya. "It ain't over till it's over. But I *am* glad we got lids for our drink cups!"

"Correct," Glenda said calmly, after she sipped from the straw in her cup, which had miraculously remained intact between her thighs. She patted Janie's hand with her own and turned left onto the drag, but not before silently thanking the traffic gods for the green light.

"We'll go back downtown. If they keep this up, I'll just go park in front of the police station."

Linda Lou nodded in agreement. "Good plan, but first let's try to lose 'em for good!"

Tanya slapped Linda on the shoulder with approval. Janie nodded eagerly.

"OK ladies—away we go!"

Glenda punched the throttle to easily pass a car on Main Street. As she sped past the high-schoolers, they yelled support to her. She stuck her arm out the window, making a fist to show she was in control. The blue pickup was stuck behind a few other cars, so she slowed down to cool it for a bit.

"Oh, crap," said Janie, looking out the back glass.

The two cars had turned into the Astro, clearing the way for the pickup to regain its position directly behind the Camaro. Glenda slammed her foot on the accelerator pedal and again flew over the railroad tracks.

"OK, everybody. Really hang on!" Glenda yelled over the roar of the air coming in the open windows of the car.

Linda noticed the silver Thunderbird with some people standing about at Tim's Donut Shop. In an effort to be cool, she casually waved at them. Glenda motored toward downtown. She was going pretty fast when she made a quick decision to turn left and head to the police station.

The Camaro fishtailed a bit, but Glenda regained control. She noticed some people walking across the street up ahead. She also saw in the rearview mirror that the pickup was sliding around the corner behind them.

"Oh, no. The movie's let out!" cried Linda Lou with alarm. "Glenda! People are in the road!"

"They'll hafta move! Here we go!"

Glenda punched the throttle. The people scattered quickly. She turned the steering wheel to maneuver the Camaro onto the intersecting street with a barely controlled slide. She regained full control and completed the turn. Her plan was to drive to the police station two blocks away. But a tremendous screeching noise on the street in front of the theater caused her to slam on the brakes, bringing the car to an abrupt stop.

The driver of the pickup completely lost control. Glenda and her friends looked back, watching in horror. The large vehicle slid in the roadway and crashed into a light yellow car which was parallel parked in front of the theater.

"Git back!" yelled Fuzzy, as he saw the pickup sliding toward the theater. He and Melinda had just left the picture show with big smiles—it was a very funny movie. His expression changed when the bright yellow Camaro sped by with the blue pickup gaining fast. Losing sight of the Camaro, his attention was focused on the pickup sliding out of control toward the sidewalk.

"OH, NO!" He jumped back from the sound of the crash, pulling Melinda with him. She buried her face in his shoulder. He fought his way through her blonde hair to risk a look toward the street. His sister's Chevette was all right. Fuzzy breathed a sigh of relief. The guys in the pickup were looking around frantically. By all appearances, they were about to bail out and run away from the scene of the accident. Fuzzy did not notice the Camaro slowly pulling away.

"Oh, my God!" cried Linda as Glenda drove away from the scene.

"That was great!" cried Tanya. "Way to go Glenda!" She banged her fists on the back of Linda Lou's seat with excitement.

"Yeah, well, maybe—even if those nimrods aren't hurt, they definitely made a *mess* outta somebody's *baby mess yellow* car!" Glenda sighed with relief and drove slowly down the street, as the girls laughed at her joke.

The last time the Camaro sped by the donut shop with the pickup in hot pursuit, Evel and Larry couldn't stay on the sidelines for another minute. The Thunderbird jumped out onto the drag to follow the vehicles. After the pickup disappeared around the corner on Monarch Street, Evel punched the throttle and was turning left onto the same street when he heard the crash.

"They wrecked!" cried Larry.

"Where's the Camaro?" Evel looked quickly around the area.

"I think I saw it go around the corner that way." Larry pointed to his right. He immediately pointed at the blue pickup. "Come on! Let's go see what happened!"

Evel nodded and parked the Thunderbird behind Fuzzy's borrowed 'Vette. He saw Fuzzy and his date on the sidewalk. They appeared to be OK, but the distressed girl was hiding her face in her hands. He looked back at the pickup. It had sideswiped a Plymouth Duster innocently parked in front of the theater. The passenger of the pickup had already bailed. The driver was crawling out behind him.

Evel and Larry walked toward them.

"Those bitches!" the driver yelled loudly. He looked around crazily. "Where are they?"

"Who?" Evel asked suspiciously. He noticed the fellow was unsteady on his feet—probably very drunk.

"Those bitches in that yellow Camaro. That's who. They made me wreck my truck!"

"No, friend. It looks to me like *you* wrecked your truck, *and* somebody else's Duster. There's not a Camaro in sight that I can see," Evel said firmly.

"If I ever see them again, I'll..."

Evel squinted his eyes, expanding his chest a bit. Larry raised both hands with palms out and stepped back. He knew that look.

"Where're you from, Jack?" Evel asked with a tone of voice which left no doubt he was dead serious.

"Schmittville." The driver spat and turned sharply toward Evel and Larry. "What's it to ya?"

Evel pulled himself up to his full six feet and made his two hundred pound presence known. "Jack Off, you'd best get in your wrecked truck and go back to Shitville. And stay there."

"Oh, yeah?" the driver was bowing up now. "And just who you callin' Jack Off?"

"Hey, look. There's the yellow Camaro!" Evel pointed to his right.

"Where? Where?" The driver turned slightly in that direction.

"Right here." Evel threw a hard right jab into the guy's face. The driver twirled around and landed in his buddy's arms.

"Awright! Way to go, Brother Glenn!" exclaimed Larry. Shortly thereafter, he cocked his head to one side. His expertly trained ears heard the distant siren. "Cops."

Evel nodded—but took a second to look up to the figures on the sidewalk. "Fuz. Y'all OK?"

"Yeah, we're all right. But you'd better git the hell outta here!" Fuzzy curled his arm around Melinda. They all turned their attention to the ever louder siren.

"RUN!" Evel delivered his usual "panic" command. "Larry—in the car—Fuz you go a different direction than we do. *Go!*"

The two brothers hurried into the Thunderbird. Evel threw the car into Reverse and squealed the tires, fleeing the scene. Fuzzy and Melinda left more calmly in the opposite direction.

Glenda stopped her car in the First Baptist Church parking lot a few blocks away from the theater and turned off the engine and lights. The girls sat in silence for several minutes, waiting for their hearts to stop racing and nerves to settle.

"Let's go back to the dorm." Glenda spoke breathlessly, still a bit shaky. "I need a coke." She held up her empty cup. "I'm out of cherry limeade, dang it."

"Me too, Glendee. I lost mine out the window somewhere along the way!" said Linda Lou. "Girl, I didn't know you could drive like that!"

"You need to get out with us more, Linda. It's like this all the time," said Tanya with a giggle.

"Really?" Linda turned to look incredulously at the girls in the back seat.

Tanya and Janie rolled their eyes dramatically. Linda reached back and whacked the knees she could reach with her hand. Glenda breathed deeply a few times and started the engine.

"Oh, come on. It's not always like this—sometimes it's even worse!" Glenda said. They all giggled, releasing tension.

"Lookee. There goes the silver Thunderbird. I wonder what they're up to. It sure looks like they're in a hurry," said Tanya, leaning up between the seats of the Camaro. The Thunderbird was on another street about a block away.

"Oh, *paleeze*. That car is always in a hurry," Janie said. "You think it's safe to go now, Glenda? I want..."

She stopped talking. They listened to the approaching sirens...cops.

"Hmmph. Sounds like the cops were across town at Mac's Burger or somewheres. Figures. We need 'em at the police station, and they ain't there!" Tanya said dryly.

"Yepper. Ain't that the truth? Time to go, girls. But—easy-like. We don't wanna to call attention to ourselves. So, I'll head right back down the drag like nothin' ever happened," said Glenda confidently. But her hands were still shaking a little.

When they passed Tim's, the parking lot was deserted. Up the drag, the kids across from the Astro Drive-In were still out. One pointed at them. "Everybody wave," Glenda said. "Be cool—act natural."

The kids cheered with a bit more enthusiasm than she would have expected. Finally, the girls got to the college campus and eased into a parking place near the Shoe Bench.

Gene and Boots popped up from where they had been waiting. They ran over to the car. "What happened? Are y'all all right?" asked Gene, clearly concerned.

"No dents, scrapes, or blood, so I guess you got out of that one pretty neatly," said Boots with approval.

Glenda hugged him vigorously, her adrenaline still pumping. Tanya and Janie grabbed Gene and began spilling out the story, as they all walked over to the Shoe Bench.

Glenda plopped down and heaved a great sigh. Everyone fell silent. "Crashed. I can't believe they crashed right in front of the picture show," she said, laughing quietly.

Linda collapsed beside her friend and slapped her on the thigh. All four girls started cracking up, releasing the emotion of the last hour of nervousness. Boots and Gene stood back, watching with amusement as the girls' hysteria peaked.

"It was wild!" cried Janie. "You should a' seen it. That pickup was chasin' and chasin' us, but it crashed! It was crazy, but we made it back OK. Thanks to Glenda!"

"As usual!" Tanya added cheerfully.

Everyone settled in their places on the Shoe Bench. Their story had wound down to only a few excited remarks when they heard a car stop. Most vehicles that cruised through the college did just that—cruised through. If a car actually halted, even briefly, it was worth a look. All four girls jumped to their feet to peer around to see who had stopped. They looked beyond the parked cars. A familiar blue sports car had pulled over. It was the only blue Corvette in town.

The driver got out. "Linda! Glenda! Hey, Janie. Hey, Tanya!"

"Jimmie Mac!" cried Janie. She and Tanya ran toward the Corvette to give him a hug.

"Hey, Jimmie Mac. We never see you anymore since you moved into that apartment!" exclaimed Tanya.

Everybody agreed Jimmie Mac was one of the good guys at college, but they hadn't seen him in several weeks. Each girl grabbed an arm and walked him to the Shoe Bench. When they arrived, Glenda and Linda Lou took the young man from their friends and also greeted him with hugs.

"Glenda. Are you OK? I mean, I heard about the trouble with Kevin, and some pickup was chasin' you a while ago on the drag. What the heck's goin' on?" They sat back down on the benches.

The girls relayed the story of the chase in four different versions from four different perspectives but with the same outcome—they were home safely. However, Jimmie Mac had to ask a few questions to get the story straight. Tanya and Janie dominated the storytelling while Linda and Glenda relaxed. Nobody noticed the silver Thunderbird drive quietly by.

Evel saw the Camaro was parked, appearing unscratched. The girls also seemed all right and were talking excitedly with their friends. He nodded with satisfaction. Maneuvering past the blue Corvette, he drove into the U but turned right to go out the back way—as if he didn't wish to be seen.

"Wow! What a night. I came by to see if y'all would want to come to a party Friday night at my place," Jimmie Mac stated to the group. "But it probably won't be half as thrillin' as tonight's escapade."

"All the better," Glenda readily agreed. "This adventure was plenty enough excitin' for one week! What's the occasion?"

"Star Channel is playin' *Animal House* at nine o'clock, so we thought we'd have a toga party. Snacks, dancin', trash can punch and all. Can y'all come?"

The girls eyed each other. Tanya and Janie stayed in the dorm every weekend, and Glenda didn't have to go home. The three shrugged and nodded. Linda looked thoughtful for a second, but nodded her head, too. "I can. I scheduled the night off work for a gymnastics meet, but it was cancelled, so I'm FREE!"

Jimmie Mac rose to his feet. "All right. Boots and Gene, y'all are welcome, too. You know where I live." Gene nodded agreement.

"Yep. Looks like we can all be there. Uhm umm, a toga party ya say?" asked Boots hesitantly.

"You bet. You gotta be in a toga to get in. Come on, Boots. You can show off those purdy legs! See y'all then. Somewhere around nine—or whenever. OK?"

"YES!" the four girls said in unison.

Jimmie Mac jauntily saluted before strolling back to his illegally parked Corvette.

"Toga? We hafta wear a sheet?" asked Boots, disturbed at the idea.

"Yeah—it'll look great with your *purdy legs* and cowboy boots!" Gene said sarcastically.

"The only sheet I have is blue, red and green striped. That's not very Roman. Oh my. Whatever do ya wear under it?" Janie asked.

Glenda and Tanya looked at each other and back at Janie, nodding agreement. "Tube top!" they answered in unison.

Boots held up his hands. "Toga fashion is not my department. Come on, Gene. Let's go in. I'm glad you gals are OK. You scared us pretty good drivin' through here like that." The guys accepted good night hugs before walking off into the night.

"Well, we know what to wear, but how?" asked Tanya.

"Safety pins, my friends—lots of safety pins!" said Glenda.

"I know," said Linda. "Let's go downtown to the dime store tomorrow afternoon. We'll see what cheap sheets and olive branches and stuff we can find."

"Outstanding idea, Linda Lou. Right after lunch, we'll do just that," said Glenda. "But I'm ready to go in. It's gotta be after ten o'clock. Might as well go around to the front."

The girls pulled open the glass doors and entered the big lobby with a big "Tah Dah" to announce their presence. Janie noticed the dorm monitor was dialing the phone, impatiently tapping an ID on the tabletop.

"Uh oh. Somebody's in trouble," said Janie softly.

"Yep," Tanya whispered. "I hope it's not Hope."

They walked toward the stairs but were stopped by an excited Melinda. She sprang to her feet from her perch on the bottom step. "Glenda! My God, are y'all all right? I was standin' right there!"

"Right *where?*" Tanya asked suspiciously.

"At the Monarch. When that truck that was behind you crashed, it was right in front of us!" she exclaimed a bit too loudly.

Glenda grasped her arm, pulling her toward some seats near the stairs. "Shhhh. What happened then?"

"Well, Fuzzy and I were standin' there talkin' about the movie. It was really funny, by the way. Anyway, that truck slid into the car parked *right* in front of the 'Vette," she said, looking around. "Then a couple a' guys in a big silver car pulled up and one of 'em socked the driver of the truck right in the mouth! Fuzzy knew the guy. They talked for a minute. Then we all ran to our cars and got outta there. It was really excitin'!" Her eyes glittered.

"Yeah, well. You should've been where we were. It was dad-gum scary."

"But Glenda had it under control, and we won the chase," Tanya said, brushing off Janie's sarcasm. "We made it, and they didn't—and that's what matters. Hey, what guy hit what guy? What did they say?"

"The guys that got out of the pickup looked drunk, and the guy from the silver car went over to one of 'em. I heard somebody say somethin' about *bitches*." Being the center of attention was new to Melinda—a freshman—and she was making the most of it.

"Who said we were bitches?" asked Linda, steel in her voice. "The guy in the silver car?"

"No. No. The guy in the pickup said it. Then the guy in the silver car socked him."

Glenda and Linda looked at each other with raised eyebrows, as did Tanya and Janie.

"Hmm. Perhaps this guy's not a toad!" Tanya remarked thoughtfully. Melinda looked confused, but the other girls shared the delicious inside joke.

"Well, I'm glad there's some knight in a shining silver car out there defendin' my honor," remarked Glenda grandly. She rose to her feet. "Bartender, I need a drink."

She headed to the stairs and went up the first few steps. "Thanks for the info, Melinda. I'm glad you had a good time on your date." She leaned over the railing to speak to the still-seated Melinda. "Did you like the Monarch?"

"Yeah. It was really neat," Melinda gasped. "Wait a second. Oh, no! I forgot to pat the butterfly!"

Janie and Tanya exchanged amused glances. "That's OK, Melinda," Tanya said. "Under the circumstances, I'm sure you'll be granted a second chance before anything bad happens to ya. Was Fuzzy nice?"

Glenda turned away, starting up the stairs to stifle a laugh.

"Yeah. But he didn't ask me out again—well, not yet," Melinda sounded disappointed.

Tanya leaned over to Janie and whispered, "That's because he probably doesn't know when he can get the 'Vette again!" She called aloud, "Wait up, Glenda!"

They left Melinda behind and stormed up the stairs.

Chapter Six

"HOLY MOLY. Look at that!"

Daniel and Evel were cruising through the college in the Thunderbird. His finger pointed past Evel's nose, toward the Shoe Bench and parked vehicles on the other side of the median. The yellow Camaro's passenger side door was open; music blared. But the sight to behold was four figures, dressed in what appeared to be sheets and tennis shoes with leaves in their hair, standing in a row doing some kind of weird dance. Evel heard the music and checked the rearview mirror. He saw nothing coming up from behind, so decided it was a show worth stopping for.

"What're they doin'?" Evel asked. "Mind ya—I like it—but it's kinda strange!"

"Looks like the 'Time Warp' dance." Upon seeing Evel's look of confusion, Daniel continued. "From *The Rocky Horror Picture Show*. You know—the midnight movie up in the city. See how they're jumpin' to the left—and steppin' to the right—and bringin' their knees in tight. That's what they sing and do in the movie." Evel still looked confused. "I guess you wouldn't have seen it. Not your style. Hey look—they're at the end." Daniel pointed again.

The music wound down, and the dancers all sunk to the ground, resembling a pile of leafy laundry. Except Janie. "If you don't mind, I refuse to ruin my carefully safety pinned toga!" she said with a laugh. "Let's go! It's almost nine o'clock."

The other three popped up and straightened out their togas. Each checked the fasteners holding the corners of the sheet on her shoulder. The costumes were in order, including confirmation that all tube tops were properly in place and out of sight.

Glenda's attention was caught by a slow moving mass of silver. She raised a hand to acknowledge the Thunderbird. Her dimple appeared, as she cocked her head slightly to the left, seeing a hand appear briefly from the big car's driver-side window.

She turned to lead her friends to the Camaro. Time to go to Jimmie Mac's toga party. Glenda popped *The Rocky Horror Picture Show* soundtrack out of the tape player. She watched for the Thunderbird, but it had disappeared. She shrugged and backed out of the parking space.

"How do ya like that?" Evel asked Daniel, his tone buoyant. "Ya never know what you're gonna see around here."

"Why you goin' out the back?" Daniel asked, surprised. "Runnin' from somethin'?"

Evel glowered. He drove down the back streets in silence, emerging near the railroad tracks and Tim's Donut Shop. He parked in his favorite manner—backed in. Daniel reached into the rear seat, returning with a couple of cold beers. Evel relaxed.

The two settled in for a time of drinking and watching the traffic go by. It was Friday night.

The girls walked around the pool toward Jimmie Mac's apartment and ran into Candace, Boots and Gene.

"Hi! Like my toga? I got it at Omar's Tent and Awning!" Candace exclaimed. She leaned on Glenda's bare shoulder. "I went shoppin' with Boots, see?"

Boots, dressed in a blue and white striped sheet draped across his left shoulder, bowed and removed his cowboy hat in musketeer fashion for the giggling girls. His toga must have originated as a very large sheet, as it billowed around the tops of his boots. Gene also bowed. His toga was light blue. He had his tennies on but no socks.

"Ooh baby—let's see those legs!" Janie tried to lift Boots' skirt.

He pulled away from her indignantly. "Oh, no you don't, young lady. Not on the first date!"

Janie laughed and brought herself up to her full, but not very tall, height to give him a big hug. Boots failed to notice Gene's frown.

"How's the punch, Candace?" Tanya asked.

"Outstanding. Come on in!" Candace took Glenda by the arm. She led the newcomers past the swimming pool in the courtyard and through an open sliding glass door into the apartment.

"Look everybody—it's the WWAB's!" Someone from the crowd in the apartment made this announcement.

"Who?" a guy in a polka-dotted toga asked.

"The Who's Who in American Bitches. That's who!" Candace exclaimed with a sweep of her arm toward the girls who had just entered the apartment. The WWAB's took a collective and flamboyant bow.

"Where's the punch? Come on, Janie," said Tanya, grabbing her roommate and heading for the kitchen.

"Wait up," called Linda. "How 'bout you, Glenda? Want some?"

"Maybe in a minute. Y'all go ahead."

Glenda felt somewhat subdued. This was the first time she'd been to a party without a date in over two years. One date in particular. She sat down on the couch; the movie was starting on TV.

Jimmie Mac appeared. "Hey, Glenda. You got the front row seat, I see. May I join you?" He plopped down, shifted a cushion and handed her a can of Dr Pepper.

"Hi, Jimmie Mac. Thanks."

Neither of them was much good at drinking alcohol, and they knew it. They raised their Dr Peppers in a toast, clinking cans. Some folks piled up on the floor to watch the movie, but most soon lost interest in favor of more live entertainment.

Glenda and Jimmie Mac spoke quietly together for several minutes. She told him about what she had been going through over the past few weeks, and he listened closely, much like a counselor. He didn't share anything about himself; he was always something of a mystery. Really nice, but really private. But he was a very good listener.

"Man. That son of a bitch. He didn't know what he was throwin' away. Or maybe he finally did figure it out, but it was too late." Jimmie Mac seemed angry, now very un-counselor like. He shook his head slowly side-to-side.

Glenda sighed. "Too late is right. Way too late."

Jimmie Mac saw her pain through the expression on her face. She remained still, staring at the TV screen. He waited a bit before he spoke again. "So, what's all this about WWAB?"

Glenda looked at him as if she'd been awakened from a dream. She took a sip of her Dr Pepper. "Oh—that. Last year we got so sick of all the pledging and hazing and butt-kissin' goin' on to get into sororities, and after the trouble we had with the Dean, we made up our own sorority. Secret—no one but us could be in it or even know what it was. Well, until Candace let the cat out of the bag a while ago. Our colors are black and red. The colors of rebellion."

"You—trouble with the Dean? I don't believe it! Are you serious?"

"Yepper. As cereal as Corn Flakes, my man. It's the honest to gosh truth. She even told me I shouldn't be so ugly and sour and have a chip on my shoulder!"

"Unbelievable," he said sympathetically. "Corn Flakes?"

Glenda laughed. "Never mind. You had to be there. Anywho, the trouble was all over the screen in the hall window in the dorm. It was a really big deal. They almost suspended us for sittin' in the window. It was really ridiculous, so we became the Who's Who in American Bitches." Glenda shrugged her shoulders.

Jimmie Mac nodded in understanding. "Cockroach!" someone yelled. Five or six guys fell on the floor on their backs. The group wiggled their legs and arms like upside-down insects.

Glenda handed her Dr Pepper to Jimmie Mac. "Not yet, you goofballs!" Glenda yelled through cupped hands to amplify her voice above the general din. "The movie's not at that part yet!"

But the guys paid no attention. They kept wiggling, so she relaxed on the cushions. Linda and Gene had taken up the rest of the couch on the other side of Jimmie Mac and were chatting. They were distracted by a familiar voice calling from outside the open sliding glass door. "Super—Man!!!"

The four people on the couch looked in unison to their left, shocked to see a toga clad figure flying through the doorway.

They leaned back as quickly and as far as possible into the cushions to brace for the landing.

"Super—Man!!!" Janie flew through the air some five feet and belly-flopped into the laps on the couch. She looked up at Glenda with wide eyes. "Hi!"

"Hi, there. Janie, are you OK?" She'd obviously been partaking of a good many cups of trash can punch. Glenda gently touched the golden brown curls in her lap.

"Sure. I'm fine, man!" Janie held up two fingers in a limp peace sign. "Thanks for catchin' me!"

Janie giggled loudly—then rolled off the laps and onto the carpeted floor. Those who remained on the couch chuckled at the sight.

"Looks like Janie's not too worried about losin' those safety pins now!" Linda leaned forward to peer across Jimmie Mac at her roommate.

Glenda laughed anew, and Linda also cracked-up. Janie was wiggling and giggling on the floor, so Jimmie Mac and Gene couldn't help but join in. Before long, they all were wiping tears from their eyes—they'd laughed so hard. Jimmie Mac looked up at the TV screen and abruptly stood up. He jumped over Janie into the middle of the floor.

"Hey, it's Otis!" Jimmie Mac leaned back, reaching across Janie to give Glenda and Linda each a hand up and over their little drunk friend. Janie struggled to her feet, and Jimmie Mac turned up the volume. He had the TV wired to his stereo. The Otis Day and the Knights song, "Shout," filled the room, spilling onto the patio. The music could be heard at the swimming pool.

More people poured into the apartment. Soon everyone was dancing in whatever space he or she could find.

The uninvited neighbors on the second floor must have been torn between envy and irritation. Or perhaps the view was just plain entertaining, as they looked down at the rocking apartment from their vantage point. Twenty or so people, dressed in sheets, were dancing, raising their arms in the air and flicking their fingers open like a magician's abracadabra gesture. The pace was frantic—then slowed—then picked up again toward the big finish.

The girls occupied the outer edge of the gyrating mass of bodies, jumping and dancing their way to the sliding door. They knew what was about to happen—it was best to move out of the way of the action.

The time had come—the signal was given: "COCKROACH!!"

Several guys and gals fell to the floor and wriggled their legs and bodies like bugs on their backs. Glenda and Linda stood in the doorway, noticing Candace standing on the other side of the room. She was smiling strangely, as she peered intently at the bodies moving about on the floor.

"What's she lookin' at? Oh, my! Lookee!" Linda said, pointing toward a guy wriggling nearby. "Fruit of the Looms, I do believe." She giggled and elbowed Glenda.

"Oh, ho. I reckon so. Lookee over there. Those gotta be Hanes," said Glenda, pointing to another guy who had also turned where they could see what was under his toga.

Tanya joined the fun. "Hey, this is pretty funny—funny ha ha, I mean—to look up guys' skirts!"

All three caught their breath at the sight of one thrashing fellow who twirled on the floor near their feet. "Whoa! And then there's Mr. Commando!" Tanya exclaimed.

This fellow wore no underwear at all. The surprised girls glanced at each other as his lower body rotated away. They saw his face and stiffly sprayed blonde hair. Linda caught Candace's attention, pointing to the guy going *au natural.* Candace nodded her head eagerly.

"Oh, my gosh! It's The Guy With The Hair!" cried Tanya. She jumped backward and out the door. Glenda very nearly fell over Linda to get out of sight. But The Guy With The Hair didn't notice the gawkers. Candace, on the other hand, remained where she could see up that particular skirt, until she found herself in the kitchen with the punch. She shrugged and dipped another cupful.

Some of the party moved into the kitchen with Candace and the punch. As more and more punch was dipped from the trash can, people grew wilder and wilder. After the cockroaches cleared the floor, the TV was switched off, and the stereo poured out disco music. Most everyone danced—either inside or outside the apartment.

Except Gene. He had seen all the crazy dancing bodies he cared to view. The thought crossed his mind the only person he wanted to see belonged to...Janie. She wasn't among the revelers. He rose from the couch, dodged the dancers, and moved into the kitchen unnoticed. Except by Janie, that is. She sat at the kitchen table looking at him with a silly grin on her face. Gene smiled back and joined her.

A good-sized crowd gathered at the donut shop. Larry's buddy, Chip, had dropped him off. Charles had arrived as well. Most of the guys regularly visited the cooler, except Larry. Only sixteen, he always tried to stay away from alcohol, especially out on the drag. The beer cooler sat on the asphalt behind the Thunderbird, with the guys gathered around it as though it were a campfire. Instead of warming their hands near a fire, they leaned down to withdraw cold beers. It could be argued, however, that though the beverage was cold, it warmed their insides. They told stories and jokes, laughing a great deal.

Suddenly, a siren was coming their way.

Larry looked sharply at his brother. "Run! Get outta here!" Evel ordered.

He pushed his brother and scrambled to put the cooler in the trunk. The other guys scattered about, hiding whatever needed to be hidden. It was serious trouble to have alcohol in public, and even worse trouble to have it in the presence of a minor.

Larry looked around wildly. He spied a car he recognized stopped at the traffic light just west of the donut shop parking lot. "Killer!" The guy in the four-door Pinto station-wagon looked over to see who was yelling. Larry again felt his brother push him from behind. He ran at full speed toward the car at the light. He jumped, diving head first through the open back door window into the back seat. His feet were still hanging out of the car when the traffic light changed to green.

"GO!!" Larry's muffled yell could be heard from the back seat of the slowly moving vehicle. His feet disappeared into the car.

Killer complied and stomped on the gas. The car quickly fled over the railroad tracks.

As feared, shortly thereafter a police car passed by. The officer turned off the siren, and all was quiet when he looked over at Tim's Donut Shop. He saw Evel, Daniel and Charles leaning on the front of the Thunderbird, innocent as could be. The cop grimaced sarcastically, shaking his head side-to-side. The guys waved congenially at him; he waved back, as he drove on by. They were up to something—of that he had no doubt. But he also knew they never hurt anybody or anything—it was usually all right to leave them be.

"Whew! Man, I'm glad Larry saw somebody he knows!" exclaimed Charles.

"Yeah, but who is Killer?" Fuzzy asked.

"I think he's a guy in Larry's class. He's a little...well...a lot nerdy—and supposedly really smart. Larry says he's all right. Killer always parks on the nerd side at the Rastro and doesn't seem to care what anybody thinks," Evel explained.

"OK, but why's such a nerdy, smart guy like that called 'Killer'?"

"I never really thought about it. But it's a good thing he was here, so Larry could get away." Evel calmly reopened the trunk. "They'll show back up later."

After an hour or so, Killer drove his Pinto wagon into the parking lot. Larry got out but left the car door open. "Is it safe, Brother Glenn?"

"Yep. No more booze. It's all in here." Evel rubbed his belly.

"And over there," Daniel slurred. He was pointing to the dark side of the building behind the drive-thru...the urinal area.

Larry bade farewell to Killer with thanks for the rescue and joined the other guys leaning on the Thunderbird.

"Hey Larry. Why's that guy called Killer?" Fuzzy seemed bothered by the subject of Pinto driver's name.

"Huh? Oh, his name's Calvin Killingsworth. He's the complete opposite of a Killer, so we call him Killer."

Evel chuckled. Soon everyone was joking around. More people and cars had pulled into the donut shop, joining in the fun.

One particular new arrival caused a sensation among the group. He was well-liked and always welcome. But he was just a bit different. Legend had it that his mama had a premonition when she named him.

Samson was a good-hearted, slightly shell-shocked Viet Nam vet—he was very strong and liked to pick people up. Not as in taking a person out on a date. He would literally put his arms around a person and lift him off the ground. After the struggle subsided, he'd walk around with his prize. Sometimes, he even held the person up over his head like a wrestler about to body slam an opponent. But Samson would never do that. Though he seemed like a rough character, he was actually as gentle as a lamb. When Samson was finished with his show, he always carefully placed the person back on his feet. He had quite a fan club, commonly known as the Samsonites, consisting of mainly high school kids who liked to dress in camo fatigues and listen to his stories. A few of them snickered as they watched him in action.

Quietly approaching from behind, Samson abruptly lifted Charles off the ground. "Hey! Put me down!" Samson whooped happily, tossed Charles in the air once—and caught him—then put him back on the pavement. The strong man pounded his victim on the back good-naturedly and bowed to the cheering Samsonites.

He turned toward Evel and Larry. "Larry boy. I thought you'd be ridin' your bike on a nice night like this. I started to ride mine, but they came by and picked me up." Samson gestured toward his fans. "Hey, how's that new paint job?"

Larry closed his eyes. A pained expression crossed his face. Evel chuckled softly. "Go on and tell 'em, Larry. Tell 'em about your little adventure the other night."

Larry turned to see quite a few faces, including the Samsonites, waiting to hear the story. He took a deep breath. "Well, in all honesty, believe it or not, last weekend me and Jason was racin' our bikes around town a bit and good ol' Sgt. Pettijohn witnessed hisself a wheelie or two. He took off after us with lights and sirens, but before long he was just chasin' me. Somehow Jason got away clean. So, I grabbed a couple a' gears and clicked the Kawasaki up to about a hunnerd and headed out on the Stonehill Highway. Shaun saw me when I passed by Action Automotive—you know, his dad's shop. Anyways, Shaun said I had to have been goin' 120. I just knew Pettijohn was back there, or he'd radio for the Highway Patrol or somethin', so I dove off onto Black Creek Road. You know it's paved for a while—then it veers left and turns to dirt. Well, I was still goin' about 90 when I realized I wasn't gonna make that curve. The Kawasaki launched across the bar ditch, took out the top two strands of barbed-wire fence near the road—but landed on two wheels. I kept on truckin', bouncin' over about a football field worth of tall rows of dirt—I guess that field had just been plowed. Anyways, when I finally did stop, it was by hittin' a huge wooden fence post—dead on. I stayed in the seat the whole time, until then, that is.

"And if that wasn't bad enough, I fell off the bike and landed butt first on a prickly pear cactus."

"Youch. But you weren't hurt—well, other than the cactus?" asked Daniel.

"Surprisin'ly, no. But the bike was bent up pretty bad, so I had to walk outta there. There I was, walkin' along and when I was almost up to the highway, I heard a car comin' up 'round the bend. I panicked and jumped over a fence and ran into an overgrown pasture to hide. Sure 'nough, it was a sheriff's deputy, drivin' real slow and shinin' his spotlight all around. I ducked down as far as I could and waited him out. It was then I felt stings. Ants, stingin' ants. I stayed as still as I could till he went away. As soon as he was gone, I slapped myself silly to git rid of 'em. I got outta there and ran as fast as my little legs would carry me—all the way to Action Auto. Shaun said I looked like hell. I told him that was awright—I felt like hell.

"So, to make a long story even longer, Shaun's pickup was broken down, so we rode into town in his mom's car and found Mike Campbell and got him to come out and help git the bike out of the field. It was a huge ordeal, but we finally got it outta there and into his truck and back to the garage. Mike has a police scanner, and he'd heard the cops were lookin' for a blue motorcycle. So, we put the bike, bent handlebars, flat tire and all, in the back room of the garage and covered it up with a tarp. Mike left, and then I realized my ass was hurtin'."

"Yeah, I bet. You was sittin' on cactus needles the whole time?" asked Charles.

"No, not exactly. I was sittin' kinda sideways." Larry's facial expression told everyone he remembered the pain. "Anyway,

Shaun said to drop my drawers, so he could see what was wrong. Then he saw the thorns and all. So, he went in the house and came back with some tweezers."

The flow of words suddenly stopped.

"Go on...keep goin'. This is the good part," said Evel mischievously.

Larry sighed. "Well, there I was—bent over the desk—Shaun was behind me with a magnifyin' glass and tweezers, and he was pullin' out the cactus spines. And who walks in? Killer."

"Oh, no," Charles snorted. The listeners stifled their laughs.

"Yeah, yeah. Anyway, he'd apparently been drinkin' a little, and he said, 'Whoa, boys...well...don't let me interrupt you. Uhh...well...I was just leavin',' and he backed out the door before we could explain. Man, it was embarrassin' as hell." Larry was shaking his head in disgust.

"Killer? You mean the guy...you jumped in with...a little while ago?" Charles asked between gasps. He wiped tears from his eyes with the back of his hand.

"Yeah, that's right. Thankfully, he came back to the garage a little later, because he couldn't believe he actually saw what he thought he saw. When he figured out what was goin' on, he ended up helpin' Shaun pick the thorns out of my ass." Larry paused before adding, "end of story."

The guys cracked up while Larry stood unmoving, a grimace on his face.

As they calmed back down, a rattling car pulled into the parking lot behind them. "Oh, hell," said Evel.

Silence descended over the group. Evel looked over at Daniel and Larry. "Jackal Ann," he said with dread.

Another sound grabbed his attention. "Hall-oh!" the passenger in the yellow Camaro yelled.

The car was approaching over the railroad tracks. The girl appeared to be waving and greeting the Marlboro Man billboard. Peering out the window, she noticed the group of people at Tim's

Donut Shop and waved her arm and hand in their direction. "Well, the toga party must a' been a roarin' success," Daniel said. The other guys looked confused.

Daniel glanced with amusement at Evel, who was about to respond when he noticed Jacqueline Ann standing out at the curb, shooting the finger with a flourish at the yellow car. Two more arms appeared out the open window, returning the obscene gesture. The driver of the Camaro gunned the motor. The back tires screeched. The car surged ahead and out of sight. Jacqueline Ann had an unpleasantly smug look on her face as she turned back toward the donut shop to join the group.

Larry let out a groan. He quickly walked around the Thunderbird to sink out of sight in the back seat. The girl walked up to Charles and locked her arm through his.

"Hi, guys. What's goin' on?" she asked sweetly. Too sweetly, considering the hateful expression that had been on her face only moments before.

"Just shootin' the bull—nothin' excitin' goin' on here," said one of the other guys.

She turned away from Charles—taking the speaker's arm instead. Charles glanced at Evel and shuddered—as if to shake off her touch. Evel cringed. He glanced urgently at Daniel.

"Let's get outta here and make a drag," he whispered. Without even a nod of acknowledgment, Daniel and Evel opened the car doors, quickly got in and closed them.

Larry sat up from where he'd been hiding. He couldn't stand Jacqueline Ann either. He saw enough of her at school—too much. Daniel locked the door. Evel had started the car by the time Jacqueline Ann realized they were leaving. She ran over to the Thunderbird and leaned on the open window frame. Daniel recoiled from her, mentally kicking himself for not rolling up the window.

"Where y'all goin'? Can I go?" she asked in that same sickening way—a pitiful attempt at a sweet voice.

Daniel turned toward her reluctantly. "We gotta go see a man about a car for Larry—a real good deal. Bye."

He signaled to Evel with a tap on the seat. The car pulled away, knocking Jacqueline Ann off balance. Just as Evel was about to exit the parking lot, the yellow Camaro again passed Tim's Donut Shop. The driver slowed the car. She looked intently at the scene—then a playful look could be seen on her face in the light from the Marlboro Man. She removed the silk ivy circlet she'd been wearing in her hair all evening, aimed and flung it toward the Thunderbird like a Frisbee. Not waiting to see where it landed, she looked ahead, sped up, and bounced over the railroad tracks.

Daniel and Evel were startled by the action, paralyzed for a moment, their mouths hanging open. The ivy circlet had made a perfect ringer on the Thunderbird hood ornament. It twirled around a time or two and stopped. The guys looked at each other in confusion. "You want me to get it?" Daniel asked.

"No time. Leave it there. Let's go." Evel turned right onto Main Street.

Jacqueline Ann was left standing in the parking lot with her hands on her hips. As she watched the Thunderbird move quickly away, the other vehicles in the parking lot began leaving. Before long, only two cars remained; one was the Dodge wagon. The Thunderbird passed by the donut shop on the way back up the drag.

Larry peered out the small oval opera window. "Boy. She can sure clear a parkin' lot in a hurry. Everybody's gone!" He exclaimed with a sarcastic laugh. "Even the Samsonites!"

"Standin' on the drag and flippin' people off wouldn't necessarily make her all that popular in my humble opinion," Daniel said with a snort.

"I do not care to be anywhere near that girl. That's just how I feel about it," stated Evel. The high school girl had propositioned him for sex once, and he cringed to think of her crudeness. "Remember, Larry," he said, looking in the rearview mirror at his brother. "Be selective in your choice of females. Very selective."

"Yeah, but it don't pay to be too picky—if'n you ever wanna get lucky, that is," said Daniel wisely. "Cruise through the Astro, Evel. Maybe somebody needs a ride home...with me!"

"R'all Right. Rang on!" Evel said in Astro talk. The brothers snickered as the car rumbled through the Astro Drive-In.

Suddenly, an urgent horn honking caught Larry's attention. He tapped on his brother's shoulder. "Hey, Brother Glenn, hold up for a minute. That's Killer again."

The Thunderbird stopped, with Killer close behind. The young man jumped out of his car, ran up to the Thunderbird, and pounded on the top of the car. "Larry! Evel! Chip's stuck in the drive-thru at Mac's Burger!" Killer was yelling like it was an emergency.

"Stuck? Oh, no. Here we go again. Man, don't hit the car. How's Chip stuck in the drive-thru?" Evel asked with surprising patience.

"Sorry 'bout that. Damn, I knew I'd leave somethin' out. He sent me to come find y'all. His car hung up on the speed bump, and it won't move. Com'on—let's go!" He saw Evel's nod and ran back to his car.

Daniel chuckled. "This I gotta see."

Larry was perplexed. "I heard they put in a new speed bump—but one big enough to high center on?"

They motored as quickly as possible to Mac's and saw the late model Camaro Chip had recently purchased. Evel parked in the diagonal space nearest Chip's car. Killer parked next to him.

Larry walked over to his friend. "Well...well...buddy boy. What's all this?"

Chip looked up from the driver's seat with a forlorn look on his face. "It's stuck. Like it's high-centered. It won't go in gear at all. Oh, man. What am I gonna do?" The car wasn't actually teeter-tottering, but it looked like it could.

"First, we get you out of the middle of the drive-thru. Please tell me the gear shift is in Neutral and not in Park..." Seeing Chip's nod, Evel took full control of the scene. "Good. And make sure the emergency brake isn't set. OK, everybody to the back of the car. We're gonna lift up and push—on three."

Five guys each grabbed two handholds on the Camaro's back end. On the count of three, they lifted. The rear tires came off the pavement, and the car surged forward. But it stopped when the back tires hit the bump. With another big push, the car hopped over the speed bump.

Larry stood on the offending hump of asphalt and jumped off. "That's way too high, man. Really overkill."

Mac's Burger had been in that location for years, but the management didn't want the kids driving around their place like they did the Dairy Queens or the Astro, so they put in a few mega speed bumps. People with low-riding cars who really wanted a Mac's Burger parked in the front, avoiding those speed bumps.

"Will it go in gear now, Chip?" Evel asked. "Try it." He watched the young man plop down in the driver's seat and turn the key.

"Nope. It's jammed. The gear shift won't move out of Neutral." Dejected, Chip got back out of the car. "What do we do now?"

"Make sure the key is off. Oh, hell, this was a clean T-shirt. I oughta know better than to wear white."

Evel opened the Thunderbird's trunk, retrieving a large flat-blade screwdriver, a hammer and a flashlight. He walked over to the white Camaro and lay down on his back to squirm underneath. "Man. This car is lower than a snake's belly in a wagon rut!" Evel grumbled as he wormed his way under the middle of the chassis. After various bangs and expletives, he wriggled back out in the open and shined the flashlight on Chip. He reclined on one elbow on the pavement, plopping one booted ankle over the other. "Try it now."

Chip fell into his car seat and turned the key. The engine came alive with a gentle roar. He pulled on the gear handle expectantly. It moved perfectly; the transmission slid into gear. He stepped quickly on the brake. "It works! What did ya do, Evel?"

"If I told you I'd hafta kill ya, or if I let ya live—ya wouldn't need me anymore. You knocked the linkage outta whack, and I put it back in place. But my advice is to not to come through here anymore!"

Pleased with himself, Evel rose to his feet, walked back to the Thunderbird and threw his tools into the trunk. Casually sauntering up to the front of the car, he removed the ivy circlet that had somehow kept its position around the hood ornament. Looking at his friends, he twirled it on his finger.

"Thanks, man. Only now I'm gonna hafta to find a way outta here that don't have a speed bump!" Chip said with a laugh. "Larry, you wanna come ride with me?"

"Sure. Hey, there's a back way out of everywhere. Brother Glenn, where can I catch up with ya later?" Larry asked.

"Probably down at the old Dairy Queen. We'll make a few drags then stop for a while there. Go on. I'll see ya later."

After getting in the car, Evel hung the ivy circlet on his rearview mirror. Daniel noticed it as he got in, glanced at his friend with a question—but shrugged when he saw no reaction.

All three cars found the back way out of Mac's Burger, encountered no more speed bumps and made their separate ways to the drag to ride around for a while. As predicted, Evel and Daniel parked at the old Dairy Queen. Things were pretty quiet; it was nearly midnight.

Eventually, Chip and Larry backed in beside the Thunderbird, and the guys got out and leaned on their cars. "Yeah." Larry was wound up about a subject. "With Jeremy's ticket last night, that's three guys caught this last week comin' out of the new Dairy Queen for exhibition of acceleration. That Sgt. Pettijohn backs up and hides in the cemetery and waits for somebody to spin out. Then...whooo ooo. He blows out from between those two stone columns with lights and sirens and gets hisself another ticket written. We just gotta do somethin' about that."

"Yeah, but what can ya do to the cops and not get in even more trouble?" asked Chip.

"I have an idea, but I need some help," said Larry slyly.

Chip perked up. "You know I'm in!" Evel and Daniel smirked at each other. They were liable to do just about anything.

"Here's the plan..." began Larry.

"Stop!" exclaimed Evel firmly. "I don't wanna to hear it. I don't wanna know nothin'."

At that moment, the group noticed a car driving into the parking lot from the convenience store that was on the opposite side of Main Street. The yellow Camaro entered through the opening in the curb the way cars usually pulled out. The car stopped right in front of the parked vehicles, and the doors opened. Toga-clad figures emerged.

"Janie. Linda. Change places, hurry!" cried Glenda, as she noticed the audience. She stepped in front of Evel. "Hi." She looked around him at the hood of his car—then back to him.

"Hi there," said Evel with a grin. "You want your ivy head-dress back?" He decided she looked pretty good in a sheet. The one bare shoulder caught his attention. He pulled his eyes back to her face.

"You have it?"

"Sure. You made a perfect ringer on the hood ornament. Now it's on my rearview mirror. I can get it if ya want it." She looked uneasy, but he flashed a winning smile.

Glenda looked up at him and saw the lines crinkle around his sparkling blue eyes. She liked what she saw, realizing this guy smiled a lot. "No need. You can keep it—if ya want to," she said with a twinkle in her own eyes.

"GLENDA!!" The cry for help came from the Camaro.

"Oh! Sorry, gotta go. Janie's about to throw up. We got her a 7 Up, but it's too late—she drank too much trash can punch at a party. We decided to put her in the front, so she could hang her head out the window if she needs to."

"GLENDA! HURRY!"

Glenda looked back at her car—then at Evel. She gave a little wave, about-faced and hopped into the Camaro. She quickly turned the car around, taking off toward the college.

"Hmm. I hope she makes it," Daniel said. He and Evel watched the taillights of the Camaro disappear into the distance.

"What the hell?" Larry was pointing urgently toward the street.

"Oh, shit!" exclaimed Evel loudly.

A full size pickup rolled across Main Street from the convenience store parking lot. The vehicle picked up speed on the downhill grade, headed for the old Dairy Queen building. Larry grabbed the front bumper and dug in his heels, as Chip gripped a door handle and did the same. Evel and Daniel raced behind the pickup to block its progress. They barely managed to stop the vehicle before it hit the second of four red painted metal poles which supported the restaurant's awning. Larry quickly found a loose red brick by the building. Placing it behind the driver side back tire kept the truck from rolling any farther.

"Oh, crap. That was close. Where'd this come from?" asked Chip.

"I 'magine from across the street at the little store." Evel tried the door handle. "Locked. It must a' slipped out of gear, or the brake didn't hold. Somebody'll come lookin' for it. Let's just sit back and see what happens."

They walked to their cars and waited. A police car stopped at the convenience store. Another pulled into the old Dairy

Queen and parked by the pickup. Chip and Larry took off running, escaping around the back of the building. Evel walked over toward the cop.

The officer shined his flashlight on the figure in front of him. "Hold it right there. Just what 're you doin' with this here pickup truck? It's been reported stolen!"

"Stolen? Hey, I'm not doin' anything with it—it just rolled in," Evel said cautiously. He stopped short—he didn't know this cop—must be a new recruit. The King of the Drag could sense trouble.

"Come over here. Lean on the truck and spread 'em."

Evel walked over to the pickup and did as he was told. The cop was getting his handcuffs ready.

"Man. I'm tellin' ya—this pickup just rolled over here from that store. Check the doors—they're locked. And look at the tracks in the gravel. You can see where it came from and that we barely got it stopped before it hit the buildin'," he said urgently to the policeman.

The cop looked across the street, noticing his cohort talking to an older man near the front door of the store. "Stay right there," he said roughly. Evel stayed but glanced over at Daniel, whose eyes were wide open with panic.

The policeman tried the doors, finding them to be soundly locked. He shined his flashlight at the tracks on the ground—then over at the store and back to the pickup. He saw the brick used as a chock for the tire, nodding his head. "Relax," the cop said to Evel. "Sorry about that."

"No problem." Evel heaved a sigh of relief and turned around to lean casually on the wayward pickup's fender. The policeman went to his car radio to call his buddy across the street. Evel could hear him talking.

"Yeah. Say, I found that stolen pickup. Well, if you'll look across the street, you'll find it, too," he said with a chuckle.

Evel looked over at the store. Several people were moving out toward the street. The other cop and the older man walked across Main Street to the Dairy Queen parking lot.

"I set the brake. I know I did!" the man was saying to the cop. He waved his arms in the air comically. Evel walked over to his car and finally relaxed. Daniel started to laugh quietly.

"Man. I thought they were gonna drag your ass off! You know that guy was lookin' at those girls in the togas when he forgot to set the brake!" Daniel said.

Evel nodded agreement—then looked around. He frowned. "Where's Larry and Chip?"

"They took off. Figures—first sign of trouble—they disappear."

The owner of the pickup unlocked it and drove off without a word. The cops stayed in the parking lot for a short while talking—then waved at the guys and left. Sometime later, Larry and Chip walked back to the cars.

"Where the hell were you?" Evel was irritated. "I need backup, and you haul ass!"

"Sorry, Brother Glenn. I wanna stay as far from cops as I can. We hid behind that historical church next door. Ya know, that's a pretty neat place—really old."

"Yeah, yeah—save the tour guide stuff. Let's go home. That's about all the excitement I need for one day. Besides, I gotta go help Uncle Dub tomorrow with some yard work."

"Drop me off at my car at the other Dairy Queen, will ya Chip?" Daniel asked. "I need a ride in that new car anyway."

"Sure," answered Chip good-naturedly. "I'll see ya tomorrow, Larry. About seven, right?" He and Larry had talked at length while hiding behind the old church.

"Right. Meet me at the Chicken House," Larry said.

Evel shook his head. He didn't want to know.

As the Thunderbird passed by the courthouse and Moo Lah, the clock at the top of the tower struck midnight. Bob Seger's

"Main Street" resounded from the in-dash player through the six by nine speakers in the back deck. A few cars were still out, but Evel and Larry headed to their folks' place outside Dairyville. Larry looked intently at the cemetery as they passed by. He and Chip had indeed come up with a plan while hiding behind the historical chapel. Evel's smile lines remained intact all the way home. Every time he checked the rearview mirror—which was often—his eyes rested for a moment on the ivy circlet swaying gently in the wind.

Chapter Seven

*L*INDA HAD PRETTY WELL RECOVERED from the toga party punch and was ready to clear her head. She and Glenda made a couple of drags—then Linda asked to escape town. Glenda picked a two-lane country road she knew wasn't well travelled and where it was safe to "air out" the Camaro.

Linda loved to ride fast. She would stick her head out the open window and let her long brown hair fly in the wind. Glenda was a hot-rodder from her high school days, so going fast was a natural thing. Both harbored a need for speed. "I love lettin' the wind blow through my mind!" called Linda into the wind.

Glenda cast an amused glance and commenced to drive the car like it should be driven—firm and fast. She took corners at twenty miles per hour over the posted, suggested speed. She and Linda almost experienced zero gravity going over some of the hills. Glenda loved roller coasters. The ride was pretty close to that thrilling sensation, except she was in control.

After zipping around the countryside for a while, they headed back to town at a more reasonable speed, mainly to avoid a ticket, and so they could hear each other talk. Linda had a new guy. She had kept pretty quiet about him, because he was younger than she had originally thought. She was more than a little nervous about the situation.

"But I'm in my last semester of college, and he has a year and a half to go," Linda was saying.

"So what? You can work or teach or somethin' while he's finishin', can't ya? Is that so long to wait? If I was you, I believe I'd go for a younger man. In fact, the three boyfriends I've had in my life were all younger than me."

"Yeah...but—well...I just don't know. I'm not sure." Linda stuck her head out the window, so Glenda punched the throttle again briefly.

"Yeaaaaaah!" Linda rejoiced in the freedom of the wind, trying to escape the conversation. It looked more and more to Glenda like Linda Lou was in love—she just wouldn't admit it to herself.

Glenda slowed the car as they rolled back into the city limits. "See that historical church? I'd like to go in there sometime. It looks...well...so quaint." They passed by the museum site by the old Dairy Queen.

"I've been to a few events there. They've got a nice little museum," Linda said, thankful for the change of subject. "The church is from the 1870s, and it's really well preserved."

"Sure looks like it. Doesn't look a day over seventy-five to me!" They laughed as they drove past the old Dairy Queen and on up the drag.

All of a sudden, Glenda caught her breath. A man was lying in the grass in front of the big Victorian house she had admired for so long. "Oh, my gosh! Mr. Rocker!"

She whipped the Camaro into the circle drive and slammed the car into Park, not taking the time to turn off the engine. She urgently jumped out of the car to hurry to the man. Linda was right behind her.

"Sir! Sir, are you OK? Do you need help?"

Glenda knelt down beside him. A pleasant face appeared. The man looked up with a crinkly smile.

"Well, hello! Help? Well, not really. But since you're here, y'all can help me up, slow-like," the man said, rising to a sitting position. He reached out with his hands.

Linda readily took the man's outstretched hand. Glenda gripped the other, and the girls gently helped him to his feet. They held on for a second or two to make sure he had his balance.

"Why, thank you, ladies. This is an unexpected pleasure." He seemed truly delighted.

Glenda noticed happiness shined from the man's face. She looked at him warm-heartedly. "We thought you'd passed out or somethin'. Gosh, I'm glad you're OK. Oh, I'm Glenda Meadows, and this is Linda Lou Garrett."

"I'm very pleased to meet you both. My name is Winston Walker Allen, but everybody just calls me Dub for havin' a couple a' double U's in my name, I reckon." He continued looking at the girls with his sparkling blue eyes. The smile lines deepened as he chuckled at his own joke.

The moment was interrupted when a passing car honked its horn loudly. Linda jumped a little, and Glenda turned to Mr. Allen. "Somebody's honkin' at you, sir," she said.

"More likely, they're honkin' at these two beautiful ladies in my driveway. Hey, my wife Bettie's inside makin' cookies. Do you girls wanna turn that hot rod off and come in for a minute? I need some iced tea myself." He turned to go up the steps, assuming they'd follow.

Linda and Glenda looked at each other with widened eyes. "Sure! I've always admired your house. I'd love to see the inside!" Glenda said excitedly. She ran over, clicked the car off and left the keys in the ignition.

He proudly pointed at the new bronze plaque. "Well, ladies. Follow me for the grand tour. I guess you've noticed the marker."

"Yes, that's great. This house deserves it," said Linda. She paused to read the inscription.

Glenda also stopped on the front porch, turned and looked out toward Main Street. She felt a bit strange, reminded of a character in *To Kill a Mockingbird*. Scout, the little girl, had expressed a unique perspective of observing the world from the Radley's front porch. Glenda had never seen the drag like this. A car drove by, and she noted how long she could watch and hear it. Almost in a trance, her mind's eye perceived vehicles from years gone by, driving past in various stages of glory.

Suddenly the scene went dark, with only the distant glow of a streetlight. One set of large red taillights cut a stark contrast in the virtual darkness. Glenda recognized those taillights—late model Thunderbird. The squeaking of the screen door brought her out of the reverie. The brown-haired girl nodded slightly and absorbed the odd, but good, feeling before follwing the others into the house. The old screen door shut behind the three with the tell-tale *slam-slam*.

"Bettie," Dub called. "Company! These damsels came to my rescue, though I wasn't necessarily in distress," he said with a chuckle.

"Mr. Allen. What *were* you doin'?" asked Glenda. "You must admit we were justified in being concerned. It was a bit startling to see an older man lyin' down in the grass like that."

"Ouch, that hurt. Though I will admit to bein' older than you, my dear. The logical explanation for my behavior is this:

We've got a water leak somewhere, and I can't find it. I thought maybe by gettin' down and listenin' to the earth I might hear water runnin'—or gurglin'—or somethin'—and narrow down where the pipe might be leakin'."

Bettie Allen walked into the living room, drying her hands thoroughly on a dish towel. "Sometimes I wonder about him..." she said with a mischievous glance and a wink toward the girls. "Imagine—listenin' to dirt!"

"Now, now. Be nice!" Dub exclaimed. "This here is Glenda," he said, pointing. He then thrust his thumb in the opposite direction at Linda. "And, Bettie Sue, this gal over here is Linda Lou!"

Bettie took her husband's arm in hers. She vigorously tickled him. "It's very nice to meet y'all. I declare. After thirty-five years of marriage, he still can't tell when I'm kiddin'. You girls come on in the kitchen and have some cookies—oatmeal raisin—and fresh out of the oven."

Glenda and Linda gladly nodded in agreement and followed the woman into the kitchen. "Ooh, it smells so good in here!" Linda Lou said softly.

"Oh, my, this is fantastic!" cried Glenda. "The ceiling must be twelve feet high and look at all the cabinets. I bet y'all have a whole lifetime of stuff on those shelves."

"You'd win that bet," said Dub with a chuckle. "My Bettie is an A Number One Pack Rat. She never throws anything away."

"One never knows when one might need somethin', and if you've got a place to keep it—well, why not?"

"I completely agree, Mrs. Allen," Glenda said. "My folks grew up during The Depression, and my mom's the same way. She says there'll be a use for everything she saves...sometime."

"I believe I'd like your parents, Glenda," said Bettie Sue. "It appears they raised a very nice daughter."

"Oh, I don't know about that. I could be a problem child, and you'd never know it," Glenda said playfully.

"Malarky! Bettie Sue, let's have some of those cookies and iced tea. Then I'll show these gals around," Dub said to the giggling group.

After sampling the cookies, the girls carefully carried their glasses of iced tea, following Mr. Allen around his big, rambling house. The three fireplaces looked resplendent in their Italian tile. There was also a music room and an intricately carved staircase to a mysterious second floor. "We don't use the upstairs much anymore. It's too much trouble runnin' up-and-down those steep steps. There are several rooms up there—but nothin' very special," Dub said.

"If it's in this house, it's bound to be special," said Glenda.

She couldn't look around enough—there was so much to see. The stained-glass windows she'd noticed from the street were stunning from the inside, with sunlight streaming in. Mr. Allen noticed her expression, how she took everything in; he saw something special in her, a love of beauty and passion, this one, and goodness, too. He was very glad they had stopped by.

"Everything is really beautiful, Mr. Allen. The house looks just like it should," Linda said approvingly. "And we're very glad you aren't hurt!"

"Ha! If I'd 'a known I could have had fine company like this, I'd a' laid down and played dead in the yard a long time ago!" Dub said happily.

The girls laughed. What a funny man.

"This has been a nice surprise for us, also, but we'd better get outta your way. Unfortunately, we have laundry to do," Linda said. "Mr. Allen, my parents have a similar place back home. I really feel it was a privilege to live in a home with such character. This house has character—even soul—doesn't it Glenda?"

Glenda readily nodded her agreement.

Bettie Sue appeared with a large plastic bag full of cookies. "Here, take these with you, and I'll take those glasses."

"Thanks, Mrs. Allen—that's very sweet of you. We'll have these later this afternoon while waitin' for our laundry to dry!" Glenda traded the iced tea glass for the bag of cookies. They all exited through the screen door and walked out onto the porch.

"That's your car, Glenda?" Bettie asked.

"Yepper. That's mine. I love it."

"Good for you, my dear. You know, I've been known to spin a tire or two in my time."

Glenda looked at her with surprise.

"I can vouch for that," said Mr. Allen. He held his hand up, as though he was swearing an oath in court. "That's how we met. She beat me."

Linda's eyebrows rose high on her forehead. "What? She beat you?"

"Not with a stick, silly girl. She beat me in a race. A car race. I was out at college in Lubbock, and I had the hottest '37 Ford around. She had a pretty nifty '32, and nobody thought she could drive it. But she challenged me, and we raced. She won." He shrugged. "That was back when ladies didn't drive much, and they certainly didn't race." Dub looked at his wife with pride. "But boy, I tell ya—this gal could!"

"Humph. And I still can! Plus, I never claimed to be a lady, I'll have ya know," Bettie Sue said with comic dignity.

Glenda moved closer to the older woman. "Me neither, Mrs. Allen. Sometimes I don't even much like bein' a girl."

"Oh, it has its advantages, my dear." She looked over at her husband. Glenda saw the love in their eyes as they gazed at each other. True love really *could* happen. It was a very pleasant sight.

"Thanks so much. We'll see you Rockers later," Glenda said, not remembering to use their real name.

"Excuse me?" Bettie was perplexed.

"Oh, geez, sorry. Well, before today we didn't know your names, and you were always rockin' on the porch, so we just called you Mr. and Mrs. Rocker."

"Oh, that's not so bad." Bettie sounded amused. "In fact, I kinda like the sound of that...The Rockers."

Dub laughed and patted Glenda on the shoulder. "You gals stop by anytime, ya hear? And when you're just passin' by, and I imagine you do that a lot, you'd better wave if you see us out!"

"That's for sure." Glenda said happily. "Thanks so much for the cookies and the tour. We'll see y'all later!"

Glenda and Linda waved and got in the Camaro. They looked back toward the house. The likable couple stood side-by-side on the porch, waving energetically. The scene was something like the *Beverly Hillbillies* in front of their mansion. Glenda and Linda looked at each other with raised eyebrows, realizing they had the same thought. They cracked up on the way back to campus.

About thirty minutes later, Evel parked his big car in the circle drive in front of the old Victorian house. A second passed before he realized his uncle was lying on the ground. Panicked, he jumped out of the Thunderbird.

"Uncle Dub! What's wrong? Do ya need help?"

Evel ran to his uncle's side. The old man looked up at him fondly. "Nothin's wrong, my boy. But since you're here..." Dub rose up a bit and held out his hand. Evel pulled his uncle slowly to his feet, and the two embraced briefly.

"Second time today I've been pulled to my feet. Good to see you Glenn—my favorite nephew." He always said that to both his nephews.

"Glad to see you, too—my favorite uncle," Evel said with his own crinkly smile. This was his only uncle, and he was a good one. He put his arm around the older man. "So, what's on the honey-do list today? Wait a minute. Second time? Hey, why were you lyin' in the grass? Gettin' a snake's view of things?"

"No. Though it is different lookin' up at EVERYTHING. Sometimes we feel small lookin' at the stars and such. Just imagine how the lowly spider or ant feels," Dub said dreamily. He noticed his nephew's long-suffering expression and shook his head. "Oh, never mind! I'm sure there's a water leak, and I was listenin' for it. Man, I'm tired of explainin'."

Dub frowned and shook his head again. "I know it's over here somewhere," he said, walking back to the area where he'd been lying in the grass. A honking horn interrupted them, and each automatically raised a hand to wave.

"Uh oh, Uncle Dub. Looks like you've got some admirin' fans there," Evel said mischievously. He watched the polka dotted VW motor out of sight.

"No. No. Not me, son. This is sort of a déjà vu, ya know. No. I guess you don't. OK, I'll play along. Oh, no, nephew. They must be honkin' at the fine, handsome young man standin' right there!"

He pointed at Evel good-naturedly. Evel laughed.

"I don't think so, Uncle. Now I know I really do love ya— but you *definitely* need glasses!" Evel clapped his uncle on the shoulder with affection. "Let's go find that leak."

The two went about their work with a surprisingly few number of trips to the garage refrigerator for refreshments. Evel found the water leak, and Dub fixed it. They each got a cold beer before relaxing in the glider on the porch.

"You know, rockin' and takin' it easy on this shady porch is one of my favorite things to do, Uncle Dub," Evel said with a sigh. He rested his head on the back of the glider. "I'll bet when it's dark, nobody can see you up here."

"Yep. Very possibly. For instance, when a certain car was in a certain predicament next door recently?" Dub threw an elbow into his nephew's side.

Evel turned to him with raised eyebrows and a shocked look. He tried an innocent approach. "You saw?"

"Yep. We sure did. You fellers made enough racket to wake the dead. Say, I don't know how I knew it, but I *knew* that dog's name was Rocky. Anyways, Bettie and me almost couldn't keep from laughin' when we realized you thought nobody knew you was over there. When the truth was, you didn't know we was over here!"

Evel shook his head in mock disgust. "Man. Ya can't get away with anything these days. Well, if ya don't need me anymore, I'll go on home and get cleaned up for tonight."

"Got a date?"

Evel let out a snort as he got to his feet. "Yeah, with a blonde!"

Dub's eyebrows rose with interest, but Evel held up his hands to halt that line of thought. "Not really. I'm pickin' Fuzzy up. It's Saturday night, so who knows? Need anything from Riverview? We're gonna make a run."

"Naa. I stocked up knowin' you'd be comin' over. Ya know—you can drink a man outta house and home!" Dub said good-humoredly. He didn't bother to rise to his feet; his knee ached a bit from all the getting up-and-down.

"So, you finally figured *that* out, did ya? See ya later, Uncle Dub!"

Evel gave the older man a salute before jumping in his car and pulling out of the driveway. The man waved his arm happily at the back of the Thunderbird. That was a good boy there, he thought. No, he's a man now—all grown up. He shook his head. *Well almost grown up—some of us never do.*

He felt better and whistled a tune while walking in the house to find his wife.

As Evel made his way through town, he made a razoo through the college. Looking up at the dorm, he noticed an illegible red sign hung somewhat crookedly over the building's nameplate.

He'd get Fuz to look at it later. After negotiating through the U, he saw the yellow Camaro was parked, apparently all right. Nodding his head, he decided the girls had made it home safely the night before—and hoped the one with the bellyache hadn't thrown up in the car.

His mind turned to preparations for the evening's activities. He frowned. Larry was up to something—that was for sure. Evel decided he'd keep a close eye on his brother. He was pulling out of the college as Tanya's gray Vega was turning in. The little car left its trademark getaway smokescreen, fogging the campus on the way toward the dorm.

"Look Janie. Look at the sign!" exclaimed Tanya, aiming for the open Amen Corner parking place.

"WWAB. I wonder who..." Janie looked at Tanya with widened eyes.

"Candace!" they said in unison. Tanya parked, and they hurried up to the second floor.

"Here they come," said Glenda, cocking her head to the side as if to listen. Candace and Linda Lou were each standing in the room eating Bettie Sue's cookies. Barb-oh was reclining on Glenda's bed—April and June were on Linda's.

Janie slid into the room. "That's great, Candace. How'd you do it?"

"Do what?" Glenda and the others struggled to keep straight faces.

"Oh, paleeze. The sign. The WWAB sign over the Horne Hall nameplate! Don't tell me you don't know about it," Tanya said with irritation.

"Yes, I know. We all know it's there. We don't know who did it, and it will stay that way," Candace said firmly.

Glenda tried to look innocent and munched on another cookie. She handed the bag to Barb-oh. "Right. Just like the WWAB and our initials in the new concrete over at the gym last year. That also never happened—right? We got away with that one, and we'll stick together and get away with this one, too," said Glenda. As she reached for her Dr Pepper, she shot a mischievous smile at Tanya and Janie. All the other girls except Linda laughed their way into the hall.

Tanya and Janie considered the situation for a moment. There was no doubt there would be trouble. Each nodded amiably. Glenda was pleased to see that they understood. They silently returned to their room to kill some time—then clean up for later. For what, they didn't know, but they'd get ready for whatever would come.

Glenda looked out toward the cannon. Someone was on the sidewalk below her window.

"Linda! Linda Lou—where are you?" a voice called.

Glenda moved closer to the window and looked down. An unfamiliar young man with curly brown hair was looking up at her.

"Hi! Hey, you're not Linda!"

"Correct. I am not Linda."

"Hi, whoever you are. Is Linda there?" he asked loudly but congenially.

"Perhaps...whom may I say is yelling?"

"Lee. I'm Lee! I drove up from A&M to see her. Wait a second. Are you Glenda?" he asked, a big smile on his face.

Glenda couldn't help but respond. "In the flesh. Linda was here a minute ago. Hold please, I'll try to find her."

Glenda turned around and collided with Linda Lou. She pointed at the window and got out of the way. Linda hurried over and looked down. "Lee! Hall-oh!" she called to the smiling young man.

"Linda! Come on down. Let's go ridin' around!"

Linda checked her watch and nodded. "OK. I've gotta go to work in a couple of hours...but...sure, I'll be down in a minute."

His face beamed when he heard her acceptance of his offer.

"So...that's him—the younger man?" Glenda asked with raised brows.

"Yep. We met last summer at a dinner thing his mom had. She was one of my professors last year. He's pretty nice and kinda cute. He goes to Texas A&M." Linda was almost whispering.

"He seems pretty darn nice to me, even if he is an Aggie. Get goin'!" Glenda encouraged her friend.

"Aggie yes, but he prides himself in bein' among the seven percent of the student body that does *not* attend football games!" Linda said proudly. She checked her reflection in the mirror, grabbed her purse and hurried out the door.

Glenda was overjoyed—she had never seen Linda so excited to see a guy. Good for her, she thought—outstanding in fact. She sighed and settled down to fold her laundry, as the late afternoon sun streamed in the window.

Over at the Chicken Hut, Larry's Nova was parked behind the building between Chip's white Camaro and a jet black Chevelle. A guy came out of the back door with two cardboard chicken buckets. He placed them carefully on the sidewalk. Larry walked up to him.

"Here you go—some fat and honey and grease. I left room for some other stuff." He snickered while handing two cardboard lids to Larry.

"Right. I'll let ya know how it works. Hopefully, you'll be long gone and in the clear by then," Larry said quietly. He picked up one of the buckets. Chip grabbed the other one a little too roughly. It sloshed a bit.

"Be careful! Jonathan, come up to the new Dairy Queen at nine-thirty sharp. Everything should be ready. I'll give you the signal if it's a go," said Larry. He was still speaking quietly.

Jonathan smirked, patted the hood of the black car and walked silently back into the building.

Larry smelled the contents of the bucket and made a face. "Let's go in mine. We don't want this stuff spillin' in your new car."

"OK. And if I was you I wouldn't stick my nose in there again!" said Chip. "Man, why didn't he put the lids on these things?"

"It's obvious, Chip—so we can add some of our own ingredients!" Larry said slyly.

Chip narrowed his eyes and nodded his head in understanding. They placed the buckets carefully in the trunk. Larry covered them loosely with the lids Jonathan had provided and drove the Nova out of town. They'd be back later—after dark.

Evel and Fuzzy were making the obligatory drag after the run to Riverview for beer. Evel sighed heavily as he noticed something. "Look Fuz—there goes that Cobra. Man, is that a magnificent automobile...or what?" He honked and heard a return honk from the driver of the green Cobra.

"Yeah. That's a nice car. But we'd better look out—there's Shakey's old Chevy," Fuzzy said nervously. He pointed at the car at the stoplight up ahead. They were looking into the setting sun. Evel strained to see through the windshield.

"Come on light—change," he said through gritted teeth. Evel was squinting at the red traffic light. It didn't obey his command, so he halted the Thunderbird behind the old Chevy to which Fuzzy had alluded.

Evel could see the outline of the figure up ahead. Shakey was a nice guy, but he had a palsy or some type of condition that made him shake, sometimes radically. It was a well-known fact that Shakey's car had a standard transmission—three on the tree. Evel checked the rearview mirror out of habit. He was distracted briefly by the ivy circlet that still hung there.

"I don't know how that poor guy keeps a driver's license... Oh, OH NO! Back—*back*—BACK!" cried Fuzzy. He saw what was happening just before Evel reacted.

"Huh? OH, SHIT!" exclaimed Evel. He saw the bumper of the old Chevy move toward the front of the Thunderbird. "Shakey's shaken the car into Reverse!" Evel threw the Thunderbird also into Reverse, but another check of the rearview mirror revealed a car had come up from behind. He had nowhere to go. "SHIT! SHAKEY!"

It seemed the shout from the Thunderbird was heard in the old Chevy, because Shakey apparently realized what had happened, slammed on his brakes and shifted his car back into a forward gear. He waved a sheepish, shaky hand at the car behind him. The light turned green, and he went on his way.

"Man-oh-man, let's not git behind him again!" cried Fuzzy with a sigh of relief.

"Ten-four. Damn, that was close. Let's cruise through the college. I want you to look at somethin'," Evel said, exhaling noisily through pursed lips.

They motored into the college. The Thunderbird slowed almost to a stop as it passed the girls' dorm. "See that sign, Fuz? What does it say?"

"Looks like black letters on red poster board. Yep, it's letters, all right. But it doesn't look like an actual word. It says W...W...A...B. These girls—they have a code, I guess?"

"Who knows—maybe we'll see 'em out later and ask. It's gettin' dark, and I'm positive Larry is up to somethin'. He told me to stay away from the new Dairy Queen, so I guess that means I'd better get over there and keep watch."

"What's goin' on?"

"I didn't want him to tell me, and I still don't. But I also don't wanna miss it. So, we'll hang out for a while in the Dairy

Queen parking lot. Keep your eyes peeled. Maybe we'll see somethin'," Evel drove past the wall in front of the boys' dorm and through the intersection. They started looking around.

Fuzzy was puzzled. "I don't see anything. Except there's a cop way up there. He's goin' kinda slow, ain't he? Hey, don't he park back behind those stone pillars sometimes? Wait, I think I see somebody walkin' over there in the cemetery, maybe. That's weird—they disappeared."

"Ummhmm," Evel mumbled suspiciously, driving around the back of the restaurant. He whipped the wheel and backed into a parking space that afforded him a good view of the entire area. They each grabbed a beer from the cooler in the back seat, settling in to wait. It wasn't long before they watched the police car stop near the stone columns, subsequently backing quickly between them. The vehicle retreated deep into the cemetery, fading into the darkness. Fuzzy peered across the street.

"Look over there. Is that Chip by that column?" Fuzzy was pointing but kept his hand below the open window, so no one but Evel could see what he was doing. "I knew I saw somebody!"

Evel shook his head. "Yep. And there's Larry by the other one. Man, that's purdy damn risky. The cop is right there!"

The two figures moved about—then disappeared. About five minutes later, they walked up to the back of the Thunderbird. Evel saw the younger guys approach in the mirrors and opened the door. Fuzzy also noticed and did the same. The two conspirators slid silently into the back seat of the big car.

"OK. It's all set. Now we sit back and wait for nine-thirty," said Larry. "Brother Glenn, what time is it?"

"Twenty after nine. Should we get ready to make a fast getaway?"

Larry and Chip chuckled. "Oh, I don't think so. We'll be OK right here. But, I'll need to git outta the car at nine-thirty," Larry said brashly.

The occupants of the Thunderbird waited in silence, watching the cars go by, acknowledging the people who noticed them sitting on the sidelines.

"There's that T-Top Monte Carlo. Man, that's a sharp car!" said Chip.

"Yep. College girls, my friend," said Fuzzy. "Outta your league!"

"I was talkin' about the car, not the girls."

"They are college girls and a lot of fun…matter-of-fact," said Evel.

Fuzzy turned to him with surprise. "You know 'em?"

"Sure. They rode around with me a little a few weeks ago. No big deal. They had funny names, like months of the year—May and June or April—somethin' like that," Evel replied casually.

As if to prove the point, the passenger in the Monte Carlo waved enthusiastically at the Thunderbird. Evel smiled and gave the standard response—the index finger raised casually off the steering wheel.

"Where was I?" Fuzzy asked, shaking his head. "Oh, never mind. I've got my college girl. Hey, Larry—it's nine-thirty on the dot."

"Lemme out, Brother Glenn." Larry patted his hand on the back of the driver seat.

All four guys got out of the car, converging at the front to lean on the hood. Larry intently watched the traffic coming out from behind the new Dairy Queen. Fuzzy edged closer to Evel. "Say, I can understand the Evel Knievel nickname, but why does Larry call you 'Brother Glenn'?"

"I don't know. It goes way back to when we were little kids, I guess. You know, Mom probably said somethin' like, 'Look Larry, there's your brother, Glenn', and he said 'Goo goo ga ga, Brother Glenn'—and it kinda stuck," Evel said. Fuzzy just nodded—the explanation made perfect sense.

"There's Jonathan!" Chip exclaimed.

A jet black Chevelle swung wide through the parking lot traffic trying to exit onto Main Street. It drifted toward the guys standing in front of the Thunderbird. The driver looked over expectantly. Larry gave him the thumbs up sign, and the twirling of the finger—the signal for "get on it." The driver gave the thumb and forefinger OK sign. He slowly pulled away.

"Watch this," Larry said to his companions with a smirk.

The Chevelle made its way to the front of the pack near Main Street. The driver floored the accelerator and the car's back tires began spinning. Smoke poured out from under the fenders—the engine roared, making the car fishtail radically. The driver allowed the car to move forward while still spinning the tires. In a matter of seconds, a police car came to life with lights and sirens. It raced out of the cemetery.

"Here we go," said Chip nervously. "Oh, man...I hope it works!"

"Wha—?" Fuzzy stopped talking when he saw something all over the police car. It screeched to a halt. Larry and Chip let out whoops of joy, falling into hysterical laughter.

"What is it?" asked Evel with growing enjoyment.

"We got buckets of grease—and stuff from the Chicken Hut—and mixed in some fresh cow shit from the dairy—where I work on weekends," Chip explained between gasps for air.

Larry also paused his laughter to provide more details. "We put the buckets of shit and stuff on top of the stone pillars at the entrance to the cemetery. After he backed in, we tied strings across the entry. So, when he came out, he hit the strings and pulled the buckets right down on the car. Look, he's runnin' his windshield wipers!"

Evel patted Larry firmly on the back. "It's everywhere! Oh, my, what a mess. Great trick little brother!"

Officer Pettijohn got out of his car, which was a mistake, because he hadn't turned the wipers off. The horrible looking sludge splattered all over his uniform. He glared at the Dairy Queen parking lot, but only saw a mass of headlights.

"Can he see us?" Chip asked, still wiping his eyes.

"Naa. I bet all he sees is red!" exclaimed Fuzzy. "And brown!" They were all laughing uncontrollably.

"Hey, what's so funny?" a voice called from a car nearby. The guys hadn't noticed the yellow Camaro approach for watching the spectacle across the street. Fuzzy pointed at the cop car—but then remembered something. He shuffled over to the Camaro.

"Hey, there. What's with the new sign on your dorm?" Fuzzy asked, choosing to ignore the near pandemonium around them.

Tanya was in the passenger seat.

"What sign?"

"The red sign—and don't tell me ya don't know what I'm talkin' about. It looks like somethin' you girls would do!"

Strange sounds came from the Camaro as the girls attempted to stifle their chuckling. Tanya looked over at Glenda for an OK and got a nod.

"It's our secret sorority," Tanya explained. "We don't tell just anybody what it means." She beamed pleasantly at Fuzzy.

"I'm somebody. Tell me!"

"OK. OK," Glenda said, looking around Tanya. "It's Who's Who in American Bitches, WWAB." She smiled at him. "Oh, and by-the-by, it's only OK for *us* to call ourselves bitches. So, now will you tell us what's goin' on here? There's a cop car comin' this way, and I've got a feelin' y'all better make tracks."

Fuzzy peered into the car at the driver seeing a very pleasant look, bright blue eyes—a mischievous air about her. He considered she might be right and looked over at the cop crossing the street toward the Dairy Queen. He focused back at the girls in the car.

"Right. Hey, we didn't do it this time. But it was a neat little trick with some buckets of shit landing on Officer Pettijohn!" Fuzzy patted the roof of the Camaro and backed away.

The police car worked its way against the flow of traffic in the parking lot. Glenda drove her Camaro expertly through the traffic and directly toward the oncoming police car. Fuzzy pointed to show the guys what was happening and ran to the Thunderbird.

"Let's git outta here! The cop's on the way, but those girls are runnin' interference for us—so, come on!" he exclaimed, practically jumping up-and-down.

Evel looked the scene over and gave his usual command: "Run!"

Larry and Chip scrambled into the back seat. Evel had the car started before Fuzzy had closed the passenger door. He spun the tires to leave the parking place and turned on his bright lights to show everyone he was moving against the regular flow of traffic behind the building. The cars parted like the Red Sea for Moses, as the Thunderbird slid through the mass of vehicles behind the Dairy Queen. Evel killed the lights as they went out the back way. The car disappeared.

Meanwhile, in the Dairy Queen parking lot, cars jockeyed for position. Glenda was stopped right in front of the police car. "Ha! That cop Pettijohn gave me the only ticket I've ever gotten. Everybody duck down!"

She was making a big effort to appear to be looking for something in the floor of her car. This delay tactic allowed her to block the only path through the traffic the police car could have taken. The other two girls slumped down in their seats, and struggled to keep quiet. The cop honked his horn, and Glenda looked up with an innocent, astonished face. After checking the rearview mirror to be sure the Thunderbird was gone, she held up an 8-track tape. She merged left into the traffic, waving the tape at the police car as she passed by. "Sorry about that, Officer Pettijohn!" Glenda called to the infamous policeman.

He glared at her for a moment—then turned his attention to his car. Spraying some washer fluid, he tried the windshield wipers again. But this only rehydrated the somewhat dried cow manure into a renewed sludge, as well as further smearing the chicken grease.

Glenda jumped out into traffic on Main Street, shouting with glee. "Ooooh Weee. That was great! Did you see that? Now that was a Crappy Copper!"

"Yeah! Pettijohn, the Poopie Policeman!" offered Tanya, after she popped up from her hiding place.

"On the Bull Shit Beat!" Janie gladly added.

As they drove past the boys' dorm, Glenda called out the window, "FLESH, we want FLESH!!"

"Screw you!" someone yelled from the third floor.

In unison, Glenda and Tanya yelled back, "Five dollars and a note from your mama!"

"And a *health* card to boot!" Janie added loudly. Boots and Gene were sitting on the wall, and the girls saw them laughing. It was a favorite joke.

They laughed and laughed. Glenda was back—all the way. It had been a great Saturday night—and part of Sunday morning, too.

Chapter Eight

GLENDA WOKE TO THE slapping sounds of bare feet and the ringing of a distant phone. The flap—flap—flap of feet hitting the linoleum-tiled concrete floor stopped about the same time as the ringing. *Yikes! Who's makin' all that racket so early on a Sunday mornin'?* Linda was on the early shift at the hospital and had left much earlier. The morning sun glared through the windows. Glenda covered her head with the sheet.

Janie entered the room. "Glendee-girl! Are you awake?" she whispered loudly.

Glenda pulled down the sheet to cast a rather grumpy look. "What?" she groaned. It had been a late night—fun—but late.

"Candace hasn't come in yet, and Barb-oh's worried about her. We're pretty sure she went to a party last night, but her truck is here. I mean, we all know she parties hardy, but she never stays out *all* night." Janie plopped onto Glenda's bed and held on to her aching head, wondering why she had a humdinger of a hangover.

Glenda rose to one elbow. A bare-footed Barb-oh entered and leaned on the closet door by the phone. "I missed it. The phone call, I mean. I know they say 'if it is important, they will call again,' but I bet it was her," Barb-oh sighed. "Janie said we could get you—get you to help look for her. Would you please? I have a feelin' somethin' is wrong and that was my phone and..."

Glenda's phone erupted into sound, interrupting her. Barb-oh picked up the receiver, as it was understood the person with the closest proximity to the phone was obligated to answer and stop the obnoxious ringing.

"Candace! Where are you? Are you OK? Thank goodness. What? Sure—yeah. I can do that. Here, Glendee—she wants to talk to you. I'm gonna go get her stuff ready. Holler when you are."

She flipped the receiver in a circle to untangle and get some slack in the extra long cord before handing it to the confused Glenda. Janie also cast a puzzled look at her long-time friend. Barb-oh just winked at her, quickly exiting the room.

"Candace? What's wrong?" Glenda was fully awake now.

"I need you to come get me, please. I'm at the old Dairy Queen. They're lettin' me use the phone—but only through the drive-thru window. Barb-oh's gonna get me some clothes together. I need you to bring her and them and please get here fast!"

Glenda flung back the sheet. "OK. OK—gimme a few minutes. I'm not even outta bed yet. Hold tight. We'll be there ASAP—Janie's motionin' she'll come, too."

"Sure. Whatever. Just get here with some clean clothes. And I mean everything: underwear, shoes, shirt, everything. And bring my hairbrush. Oh, and a sheet," Candace said impatiently.

"A sheet? OK. We'll hurry—but are you all right?"

"Yeah, yeah. No injuries—except to my pride. Just get here. I gotta go. They want the phone back and me far away."

The line went dead. Glenda handed the receiver to Janie to return to the wall cradle. "I've gotta put in my contacts. You make sure Barb-oh's gettin' a complete change of clothes, shoes, and a sheet—anything Candace might need. Oh, boy, I think this is bad. I sure hope she's not standin' stark-naked in the Dairy Queen parking lot."

Janie stared blankly for a second before shaking her curls wildly. She ran out of the room to help Barb-oh. Glenda hurriedly got ready; within a few minutes, the three were running down the stairs with a bed sheet bundled around the items Candace had requested.

Glenda drove the Camaro as fast as she could through the early morning church traffic on Main Street. When they finally got to the old Dairy Queen, they saw someone behind the building waving his or her arms. Glenda pulled slowly past the drive-thru but stopped suddenly. The three girls gasped at the sight before them. Each scrambled out of the car as soon as Glenda clicked off the ignition.

"My God. What happened to you?" asked Barb-oh, as she slowly approached her roommate.

"Oooowee, Candace! What's *that smell*?" Janie asked, making a big show of holding her nose with her thumb and forefinger.

"Lynyrd Skynyrd!" Glenda joked.

"No! It's Candace!" Barb-oh exclaimed.

"Y'all shut up and hand me the stuff. I found a water hose back here. Come on—help me guys, please," Candace pleaded.

"It's OK, Candace—it's all in the sheet. What on earth is all over you? Tell us what happened!" exclaimed Glenda.

"OK. Listen fast. Here's the short version. Y'all know I was at a party out in the country, right? And like a dumb-head I rode with some people out there and didn't take my truck. They...

well...we all got pretty well drunk, and the driver passed out. I had no way home. They didn't have a phone at the house, so somehow my extremely inebriated mind decided I should walk back to town. Somehow I ended up in a dairy lot, and I tripped and fell into the...oh, I don't know what it's really called, but it was a mucky bunch of manure."

"Manure?" Barb-oh asked. "You mean where they wash all the cow crap from the dairy buildings? The liquid shit they fertilize with?"

"Yep. That's right," Candace began stripping off the ruined clothing and kicking it away with her bare foot.

"You're gonna change right out here in the open?" Janie asked.

"Why not? They won't let me inside like this, and who's out this early on Sunday? Hand me that water hose, please, Janie. Barb-oh, turn it on full-blast!"

Candace turned the end of the water hose toward herself, clad now only in her underwear. After enduring the initial shock of the cold water, she rinsed her arms and legs off and finally her face and hair. As she dragged the brush through her hair, brown water splashed toward the other girls. Glenda jumped back. "You better get that crap off before you ride in my car, girl. Literally!"

"That's what the sheet is for, my friend. To catch the dripping bacteria," Candace said smugly. "Well, and for this!"

She threw the sheet over her head. The body under the sheet moved around a bit, and the girls heard two splats. "Hand me the unders, please," the muffled voice called from under the sheet. A hand emerged and Barb-oh put the underwear in it. A foot kicked the soggy garments toward the other pile of clothing. Directly, the hand came out again, and the rest of the clothing disappeared piece-by-piece under the sheet.

"Hee—hee. All that practice gettin' dressed in bed and in the closet comes in handy, doesn't it?" Janie giggled. Candace and Barb-oh's room overlooked the front lawn of the dorm, where a lot of people normally milled around. Like the girls in the end rooms, they had learned to get dressed in odd places.

"Apparently!" Candace came out from under the sheet—not exactly clean, but cleaner. "I forgot to ask you to bring a towel." She started to shake her head like a wet dog.

"Stop. Don't you dare. I've got one in the trunk. It's not all that clean, but I reckon that don't matter much!"

Glenda retrieved the towel and gave it to the dripping girl.

"Thanks, I think. I'll throw all this stuff in the dumpster, and we can get outta here."

"You're throwin' away your clothes—and shoes?" Janie asked with surprise.

"Yep. Trust me. It's all trash." Candace used just the tips of her fingers to pick up the ruined clothing. She carefully dropped each piece into the trash bin where it landed with a splat. She wrapped the towel around her head and sheet around her body, then tossed the hairbrush in the dumpster. Candace slipped into the flip-flops Barb-oh had thrown at her feet. "OK. I'm ready. Let's get outta here. But keep the windows down!" she said, giggling.

As they walked to the car, the girls released the laughter they'd been holding. Candace went up to the drive-thru window, knocked and waved at the people inside. The girls loaded up. Glenda sped away.

Janie laughed. "Oh my goodness. *Peeeeuuuu*, Candace. You still stink!" She moved as far from the offending smell as possible, cramming herself into the corner of the backseat.

Candace was still not in a very good mood.

"Hush—or I'll shake my hair on you, Janie!"

"Leave it to you to really end up shit-faced, Candace!" said a chuckling Barb-oh.

"Yeah, I'd say you got yourself in deep doo doo," Glenda exclaimed.

"Moo Lah, Poop Lah!" Janie called out the window, as they drove past the fiberglass icon of Dairyville.

Candace groaned. "Oh crap," she said disgustedly, letting out a backward snort as she realized what she had said.

The laughter didn't subside until the girls were back at the dorm.

Later in the morning, Candace smelled much better. She was passed out in her bed. Glenda and Tanya were getting bored. Janie and Barb-oh had gone with Janie's parents for lunch. Linda was at work. It was a beautiful, warm day, so the girls changed into their swimsuits to sunbathe in the courtyard. With towels spread out in a row with other sun-worshipers, they settled down to bake in the early afternoon rays.

"Can you believe the crazy things people use for suntan oil?" Tanya asked with a slow shake of her head.

"Amazin', isn't it? Baby oil and iodine—all kinds of exotic lotions. Lookee—that girl's usin' Crisco cookin' oil!" Glenda surreptitiously pointed at a coed slathering herself with vegetable oil.

"Oh, darn. I forgot my bacon fat," Tanya offered jokingly.

"And I failed to bring the margarine. No...no...it should be real creamery butter!" Glenda said. She had to be careful in the sun, as she was very fair-skinned. She lay back on her towel with a sigh.

Tanya relaxed in the sun and wondered if Janie was back. She also sighed and closed her eyes.

Janie had arrived at the dorm. Running excitedly to her room, she was quite disappointed to find no one there. A dry erase board hanging on the door usually held notes with pertinent information as to the girls' whereabouts. But this time there were no words—only a clue—a hastily sketched drawing of a sun above two prone stick figures. Frowning a bit while studying the rough sketch, her eyebrows rose with understanding. She scurried to the side window above her bed to look out. Below, in the courtyard between the two older dorm buildings, was a large grassy area, protected from the outside world by buildings on three sides and a wall toward the sidewalk. Janie saw a line of female bodies lying on towels in the grass. She peered at the bodies for a moment—then spotted Tanya and Glenda.

"Hey, Tan-ay! Glendee! What 're y'all doin'?" Janie called through the open window.

Glenda looked at Tanya mischievously. She rose up on her elbow and directed her gaze toward the originating point of the stupid question. "Silly gull! We're 'avin' a cuppa tea with the Queen of England!" Glenda said in her attempt at an English accent.

"And crumpets, too!" Tanya added. "Whatcha think we're doin'?"

"If y'all wanna get some sun, why don't we go to the lake? Mom and Dad are spendin' the afternoon with Barb-oh's sister here in town. They said we could use the Winnebago. I parked it on the street out back. And...it's stocked!"

Glenda and Tanya sat upright, looked at each other with surprise, nodding agreement. This was an offer they couldn't refuse. "Be right up!"

The girls quickly gathered their towels and lotions, slipped into flip-flops and cover-ups and started toward the courtyard door. "Hey. Take us with ya!" called one of the other sun worshippers.

Tanya flapped her hand in silent refusal and kept walking. "Remember when we first saw that motor home? We wondered who in the world would come to college in a Winnebago. I always heard 'the sun has riz, the sun has set, and here we iz in Texas yet.' But I never thought you'd hafta take your house with you to drive across it!"

"Yeah. Then when we got to know Janie and found out she was from El Paso, and Midland/Odessa was only half-way between home and here, and *that* was seven hours away—it made sense to make the trip in an RV. I guess her folks are on their way back to El Paso now?" Glenda asked.

"I think so. Janie said they went over to Louisiana for a while. And now they're workin' their way back to El Paso. This'll be neat. I've never been in a motor home."

"Me neither. Ooh, I hope Janie can drive it. Surely her parents wouldn't let her take it if she couldn't."

"Of course not—and stop callin' me Shirley," Tanya said, recalling a quote from the movie *Airplane*.

Glenda slapped at Tanya's arm with her towel, and they raced to their rooms. Janie and Barb-oh were ready and waiting. A few minutes later, they loaded up in the Winnebago.

"Hey ho—let's go. Go to the lake in the Winnebago!" Tanya sang. Barb-oh sampled the fridge contents, while Glenda relaxed on the bed in the back of the RV. Janie started the engine and began slowly driving down the side street. She turned onto Main Street, continuing carefully out of town toward the lake.

"Plenty of beer in here—no need to stop at the beer store, Janie," Barb-oh called from the easy chair behind the driver's captain's chair.

Tanya turned in her captain's chair to face Barb-oh. "Get me one, will ya? Boy. Candace will really be mad we left her sleepin' back at the dorm!"

"She sure will, but that's just *too* bad." Barb-oh rose and weaved her way to the fridge. "This must be what it feels like to ride on a train. Keep it between the ditches, Janie!"

Janie was happy. She felt this was a great opportunity. Not usually getting the chance to do much for her friends, she was going to make the most of this. They just had to be back before 7:00 p.m. Her folks said so. The dash clock read 2:30 p.m. so it wouldn't be a problem to be back on time. She sat up a little taller in the seat, trying to look like she knew what she was doing, as she herded the Winnebago toward an afternoon of fun.

"Whatcha wanna do?" Fuzzy asked.

"I don't know. What do *you* wanna do?" Charles responded lazily.

"Will you two stop it? Y'all do this every Sunday. I say let's make a run. I'm outta beer," Evel said grumpily.

"OK. I got a little money left, and we could ride around the lake, too," Fuzzy said, drawing an eager nod from Charles.

The guys piled into the Thunderbird. They had been sitting at Tim's, but nothing much was going on. Nothing except a new arrow protruding from the Marlboro Man. "Poor guy. He's shot full of holes." Fuzzy saluted the large billboard bristling with multi-colored arrows.

They pulled out onto the drag. It didn't take long for the speeding Thunderbird to catch up to the carefully driven Winnebago. Evel tried to pass, but there was oncoming traffic. "Damn RV. Grandpa, get outta the way!" he growled.

Suddenly, an opening appeared. He passed the motor home in a streak of silver. Fuzzy looked up as they passed and saw a young woman at the wheel. But that's all he could make out in the half-second it took to pass the large vehicle's small driver's window. "Uhh, that's no Grandpa. It's a..."

"Hang on. Ben's ahead. He's flashin' his lights," Evel said with growing anticipation.

"Oh, no! Oh, man, I'm closin' my eyes!" cried Fuzzy.

Charles leaned up from the back seat to look out the front window anxiously. He punched Fuzzy in the shoulder. "Don't be a wimp!" Charles trusted Evel's driving without reservation. He knew they'd be all right.

"Here we go," said Evel quietly.

Concentration creased his face, as his blue eyes almost disappeared beneath narrowed lids. He had slowed down after passing the motor home but was still doing 65. After a check of the rearview mirror, he returned the signal of flashing lights. Up ahead, the white Trans Am started across the center line. Evel eased the Thunderbird onto the wrong side of the road, but he peered ahead to make sure the way was clear. He knew the motor home was far enough behind to not be affected.

At 65 mph, it only took two seconds for the two cars to pass by each other on the wrong sides of the highway and safely return to their own lanes. Evel lifted his foot off the accelerator. He released the tension with a war whoop of excitement and triumph.

Tanya saw the two cars swap lanes. "JAAAAANIE! Look out!"

Janie caught her breath. Her eyes opened wide with panic. She lifted her foot off the gas and prepared to slam on the brakes. She didn't know how quickly the motor home could stop—and hoped it wouldn't spin out of control and kill everyone. Almost immediately, the car coming toward her changed to its own lane. Janie released the breath she had been holding, gently stepping on the accelerator pedal again.

"He's back over there. It's OK. Crap, that was scary—what in the world were they doin'?" Janie asked.

Glenda had grabbed a Coca Cola from the fridge after enduring the swaying of the Winnebago on her way to the front. "What happened?" She leaned on Tanya's seat.

"That Thunderbird...those guys...they passed us—then got on the wrong side of the road. That crazy guy in the Trans Am—he was comin' right at us!" Tanya exclaimed.

Glenda looked calmly out the front windshield. "Really? Well, everything looks OK, now."

Janie glanced at Tanya; both shook their heads with mock impatience. Glenda ignored them and asked a question. "Hey, Janie. Do you know where you're gonna park this big ol' thing?"

"Yeah, I've got an idea I think'll work. Trust me! Whew, I'm glad we didn't wreck! My dad would kill me…if I wasn't already dead, that is."

She lifted her hand from the steering wheel; it still shook. She flexed her fingers and wiggled them for a second before regaining a firm grip on the wheel.

Glenda slid down onto the little couch under the overhead cabinets. Noticing the retreating silhouette of the Thunderbird, she considered the possibility the driver really was a bit crazy. "I wonder what he's like, really?"

"What?" Barb-oh asked. "What did you say? I couldn't hear for the wind blowin' in my ears!" Janie had rolled the window down to let in some air.

Glenda shook her head slightly side-to-side. "Oh, nothin'—nothin' at all."

"Figures—they pulled into the beer store," said Tanya, almost to herself, but mainly to Glenda.

"Who?"

"The Thunderbird. You know, Evel Knievel in the silver Thunderbird that just scared the bejesus out of us. I wonder if they'll ride around the lake." Tanya turned to her roommate. "Hey, Janie, we will be where people can see us, right?"

"Oh, yeah. Don't worry about that. They couldn't miss this monstrosity. Hang on everybody. Here's the turn!"

Janie allowed the Winnebago to take its half out of the middle of the road, so she could make the right turn and keep the large vehicle on the asphalt. She drove into one of the many parks surrounding the lake, taking her time maneuvering into a large picnic area known for considerable parking space. She brought the big vehicle to a smooth stop next to a covered picnic table that overlooked the lake.

"Wow. Great spot, Janie. Way to go!" Tanya exclaimed. Grabbing towels, the girls hurried down to the water's muddy edge to claim a section of "beach."

After the stop to restock Evel's cooler, the guys in the Thunderbird drove around the lake. It was a nice day, and lots of folks were out and about. They saw a few people they knew, but Evel hadn't decided on a stopping point yet.

They drove through the picnic area. "There's that RV we passed out on the highway," Fuzzy said.

"You said it wasn't a Grandpa, right? I wonder who it is?" Evel maneuvered around the large vehicle that wasn't quite out of the way of through traffic in the parking area. Peering around and failing to see anyone near the motor home, he shrugged.

Charles pointed toward the large group of cars and pickups. "Hey, there's Daniel and Jackson and some of the other guys over on the other side of the park. Let's go over there!"

"Why not?" Evel shrugged and drove in that direction.

The three guys joined the others at a picnic table behind a large tree. Evel set his cooler on the concrete beside the table, took a seat on the bench and opened a beer.

"Hey, Evel. I was tellin' these guys you know a little bit about explosives. They don't believe me. Tell 'em the story—the one from high school," Daniel suggested. Evel frowned slightly in response. "Oh, come on. Jackson and Little Ricky haven't heard that story, and it's a good one!"

"OK. OK. Well, me and my old high school runnin' buddy, Tom Lewis, were always gettin' in trouble for things we did and some things we didn't do. There was this one guy that usually ratted on us. He kept his precious stuff hidden securely in his precious locker and wouldn't let anybody see what he had in there. Anyway, he ratted on us one too many times—that time for somethin' we *didn't* do. So we decided to get back at him.

"We was takin' tennis in P.E. about then, and Tom had one of those tall, round cans that tennis balls come in. He got into his dad's shotgun shell reloadin' supplies and got a bunch of black powder. We stole an egg timer from the home economics classroom and took that can and poured in some black powder.

We threw in a few ball bearings and some cotton balls and wood chips in so it would smoke a lot. Then Tom put some more black powder in and hooked a couple a' flashlight batt'ries to the timer. We waited till the break between classes was just about over and put the bomb in a locker underneath the rat's locker. Tom set the timer, and we ran to class. The hall was empty, and we was sittin' innocent-like in Home and Family Living class waitin' for a little bang."

"Did it blow up his locker?" Jackson asked.

"Oh, yeah. It sure did. Our classroom was way down the hall from where we put the bomb, and we heard this huge BOOM. The sound of glass breakin' and loud crashin' noises was over pretty quick, and everybody ran out into the hall to see what had happened. The whole bank of lockers on that side of the hall had blown clear off the wall. Metal and concrete and junk was everywhere. The glass doors at the end of the hall were completely blown out and just the metal framework was still on the hinges."

Little Ricky was enthralled. "Oh, man. But nobody got hurt? Did they figure out who did it?"

"No injuries, thank God. It was a little...well, a lot...more explosion than we planned for. But we figured with all that destruction no evidence would survive."

"You couldn't be that lucky!" Daniel was enjoying this—it was one of Evel's best stories.

"Yeah, well...anyway, when the smoke cleared, and the fire department sifted through the rubble, the only suspicious items they found was one ball bearing and the metal bottom of a tennis ball can with the initials TL in Magic Marker. Tom Lewis. His locker wasn't in that bank." Evel finished his beer. "He used the can that had his initials on it."

"So, they caught Tom, but did they get you?" asked Little Ricky.

Evel rose to his feet. "Hell, the Principal knew whatever Tom was into, I was, too. We had to work a whole month that next summer to pay for the damage. Moral of the story— if ya want some writin' to survive a bomb, use a Magic Marker. And if you wanna blow somethin' up—remember, it don't take much black powder to make a big boom!"

He reached for another beer and watched the effect of the story on new listeners.

The group laughed and clapped Evel on the back. The sound of a motorcycle distracted them—but the racket wasn't coming from the road. Curiously, it was down near the water.

"Hey! HELP! My bike is sinkin'!" called the rider.

Evel and the guys—some of them staggering—went down to the water's edge. "Hey, it's Big Rick!" cried Little Ricky, running toward the motorcyclist.

Big Rick's family had raised Little Ricky since he was ten years old. Because they already had a son named Ricky, they called him Little Ricky. They were both grown now but still called each other by their childhood names.

"Little Ricky! Help...I'm stuck!" Big Rick had obviously had way too much to drink. "Guys, help!" He kept trying to kick-start the motor, but it was flooded.

"Sure Big Rick. Just get off the bike. We'll pull it out," Evel instructed patiently.

"Yeah. And we'd better hurry. The tide'll be comin' in soon," said Daniel jokingly. Evel looked at him with a raised eyebrow. He chuckled, turning his attention to yet another vehicle in need of rescue.

"Oh, no. My bike—it'll be drowned. Come on! Let's get it out before the tide comes in!" Big Rick sounded scared and was still trying to start the motorcycle.

Little Ricky began running around in a circle. "Hurry—the tide's comin' in!" Evel and Daniel watched the spectacle some-what tickled for a minute.

As usual, Evel took charge of the crisis. "You two pipe down and get outta the way. This is a lake and a small one at that, not the ocean. Come on everybody."

They pulled the motorcycle out of the mud. With the help of the now calmer Rickys, they pushed it foot-by-foot up the hill to the picnic table. The exhausted and inebriated Big Rick collapsed to the ground.

"Ouch. He landed in some stickers," Fuzzy said, looking down at the prostrate figure in a patch of grass burs.

"He didn't notice. Let's load this bike up into Jackson's pickup, and when y'all leave we'll load up Big Rick. You can haul him home, too," Evel said with a laugh.

It took every one of them, but they hoisted the motorcycle into the bed of the pickup, where Rocky now stood guard over it. The bike was filthy, with muddy sand everywhere, but it was loaded. The guys dusted themselves off and settled down to talk and drink the afternoon away. Big Rick kept snoozing in the stickers, oblivious to the lack of the rising tide.

The girls spent a fun afternoon lying in the sun, playing in the water and consuming almost all of Janie's parents' beverages. Glenda noticed Janie seemed a little drunk. She was about to do her Superman imitation again—this time on the picnic table. Tanya grabbed her before she jumped, forcing her to sit down on the concrete bench.

"Janie. Oh, great, look at you. Now you can't drive us back. What're we gonna do?" she asked with agitation.

Janie smiled sweetly. She wasn't worried. "Glenda can drive us home. She can drive anything." Janie hiccupped. "Can't you, Glendee?"

She tipped over and laid her head in Glenda's lap, giggled, and hiccupped again.

Glenda glanced over her shoulder at the Winnebago, worried. "Maybe—I guess I'll have to. But it's gotta be about like drivin' an eighteen wheeler!"

"Breaker. Breaker. One-niner! Smokies better look out. Here come the WWAB's!" Janie laugh-hiccupped.

Glenda pulled her little friend up to a sitting position, to get close to her face. "Janie. Look at me. Don't giggle. Look at my eyes and breathe with me. Breathe in real deep and out real slow." Glenda put her hand on Janie's bare belly just below the sternum. "Sit up straight, now. Feel that inside—where the hiccup is—feel it? Now relax it. Consciously relax it. Breathe in and out slowly. Close your eyes and relax, relax, breathe innn....breathe outtt...relax. Shhhh." Glenda kept pressure on Janie's sternum with her fingers; everyone else held their breath. "Now swallow...easy-like. Take one more deep breath. There, feel better?"

Janie blinked, as if coming out of a trance. "Wow, yeah. The hiccups—they're gone, Glendee-girl. You can cure the hiccups! That's great! Now drive us home, please. I need a shower and a coke. Remember, we gotta be back by seven."

Janie stood up a little unsteadily. She held her arms out to regain her balance, shooing Tanya away. "I got it—I got it—thanks anyways," she said firmly.

Tanya backed away with her hands held up good naturedly.

The girls gathered their things and loaded them into the motor home. Glenda took her position in the driver seat, looking around at the dash and controls. She saw the clock: 6:10 p.m. She started the engine.

"OK. Everybody ready?"

A collective "YES" was yelled at the driver. Tanya rode shotgun. "Good thing they had Coca-Cola and that you don't like beer, Glendee. I'll feel better with you drivin' anyways."

"Thanks—I think."

Glenda braced herself before moving the gear shift into Drive. She tried the brake pedal and nodded again. Realizing the back tires were a long way from the front tires, she would need to take extra care on the turns, or the motor home might run off the road. She checked the view in the large side mirrors before stepping on the gas pedal.

Janie sang the beginning of "On the Road Again" loudly, but lapsed into humming the tune before slowly fading out.

Tanya looked back at her roommate, who appeared to be asleep on the couch. She laughed. "Glendee-girl. Try not to turn too hard to the left, or you'll dump Janie out on the floor!"

Barb-oh giggled from her easy chair behind Glenda. "Yepper. Or she'll come flyin' over here on me. Then we'll break this chair, and how will I explain that to her folks?" Barb-oh had downed a few beers herself, but she could handle it better than the younger and smaller Janie.

Glenda gripped the steering wheel with both hands. "Everybody please hang on. I'm not guaranteein' anything. I've never driven a vehicle this big!" She lurched onto the highway, and headed toward Dairyville. "Gosh, I'm glad we left before dark. Everything looks OK. Wait...crap...somebody's gonna pass us."

She gripped the wheel even tighter.

"There's that motor home again. Take it, Evel, but slow down a little when we go by and lemme git a look at the driver, OK?" Fuzzy suggested.

They left the lake just after the girls. With their good deed for the day now done, they were ready to go back to town. The Rickys and the rest of the group were left to fend for themselves.

"Right. It's clear—away we go."

Evel stepped on the accelerator. The Thunderbird whizzed up beside the motor home and hovered there for a few seconds. Glenda looked down with panic in her eyes and saw Fuzzy smiling at her. She looked surprised, but immediately frowned and waved her hand to impatiently send the message to go on around. She slowed down. The big silver car safely passed, moving over in front of the RV after proceeding a safe distance.

"Hey, that was that Glenda. The girl with the yellow Camaro!" Fuzzy had been sure it wasn't old people.

Evel looked at him like he was crazy. "You're kiddin'!" he quickly looked in the rearview mirror but could only see the large front grill of the taller vehicle.

Charles turned around to peer through the Thunderbird's back window. He waved at Tanya. "Yeah, that's her. And there's Tanya in the passenger seat. What in the world are they doin' in a Winnebago?"

"No tellin'. Somebody's got a rich daddy, no doubt," said Fuzzy with a laugh.

"They were at the lake, and we didn't see 'em," Evel said quietly, almost to himself. Then he raised his voice a bit. "That's our luck. A motor home load of college girls at the lake, and we spend our time with a bunch of ugly guys." Evel shook his head with mock disgust.

"Yeah. Oh, man. You're right. That was a hell of a good opportunity, and we missed it!" Fuzzy said dejectedly. Charles shook his head sadly.

Evel stepped on the gas to put some space between the Thunderbird and the Winnebago. He was inwardly kicking himself. He looked at his friends. They looked dejected, too. In front of the motorhome another vehicle moved slowly. The Thunderbird passed the green AC Cobra with Evel barely noticing, as he raced to escape feelings of regret.

Glenda watched the back of the Thunderbird shrink into the distance. It passed another vehicle and moved out of sight. "They didn't even notice us at the lake—or maybe he avoided us," she said quietly.

Tanya glanced over and saw her friend's thoughtful expression. Glenda's use of the word "he" was interesting. She almost didn't reply. "I bet they had no idea who it was in this monstrosity. They probably thought it was some old folks sunnin' at the lake in their skivvies. They sure wouldn't wanna see that!"

Glenda laughed and relaxed her grip on the wheel. "You're right. Boy howdy, did they miss out. The way Janie was goin', they mighta' seen quite a show!" She glanced up at the mirror on the sun visor, making eye contact with the girl sitting in the easy chair behind her seat. "Hey, Barb-oh, if we take this megamobile to your sister's house, how do we get back to the dorm?"

"Oh, that's no problem. Barb'll drive us—she won't mind. I'll give ya directions to her house when we're back in town."

Much like the Rickys, Barb-oh was raised in a family in El Paso with two Barbara's—she was the younger one, so she got the nickname. They weren't really blood sisters, but that didn't matter. They felt like sisters. She leaned up a bit and looked at Glenda in the mirror. "Or, I could call Mark," she offered with a smile.

"Hey, where is he today? Usually you two are together on Sundays," Tanya asked over her shoulder.

"He was playin' in a golf tournament over in Schmittville." Barb-oh looked at her watch and then her engagement ring. "But he should be back at the dorm by now. I'll call him when we get to Barb's house."

Barb-oh leaned back in the chair and relaxed. Tanya put her bare feet up on the dash and hung her arm out the open window. She liked the way the wind felt, as it caressed her fingertips—beneath the fingernails. Her fingers seemed fixed in a position that resembled a magician's hand casting a spell.

After a fairly uneventful trip back to Dairyville, Glenda carefully maneuvered the Winnebago down the streets to Barb's house. She pulled slowly in the driveway, thankful no cars were in it, and that it was long enough for the back bumper of the motor home to be off the street. Barb-oh ran into the house to find a ride back to the dorm. The other girls changed into their T-shirts and cover-ups and got their things together. Glenda left a ten-dollar bill in the refrigerator. She shrugged. It was an effort. Janie could explain later.

"Nobody's home here, but I called Mark. He can come pick us up. He'll be here in a few minutes," Barb-oh said with delight. She and Mark had been sweethearts since high school, and planned to get married after college. She gathered her things from the motor home and checked behind for any mess. All the trash had been dumped off before leaving the park. They made an effort to leave the motor home as clean as they had found it.

Mark quickly arrived at Barb's house and transported the tired group back to Horne Hall. The girls dragged themselves upstairs to shower and recover. Glenda reached the community bathroom before the others. As she put her things on the counter, someone approached from behind.

"Glenda. Oh, Glendee-girl. You're older than the rest of us, right?" the girl asked. She had her arms crossed over her bare breasts.

Glenda frowned—this was odd. "Well, yeah. I guess so. Why, what's the matter, Hope?"

Hope lived on the lobby end of the hall but was gone most of the time on basketball trips. "I just wondered—well, how can you tell if you're pregnant?"

Glenda felt her mouth almost drop open in shock. "Oh, Hope. I really don't know. I've never been pregnant. Are you late?"

"Yeah, two weeks." Hope closed her eyes as if in pain.

"You're not on the pill?" Glenda was nonplussed, as the girl shook her head in a negative response. Hope's boyfriend was a regular visitor to the dorm when Hope was in town.

"No. I was afraid to ask my mom. She wouldn't understand about Alex and me." Hope fought back tears. "What should I do?"

Glenda paused, took a breath, and gazed at the beautiful girl standing at the threshold of her whole life, now possibly facing a desperate situation. "I think you'd better go call your mom—and make a doctor appointment," she said firmly. "And call Alex."

Hope nodded slowly. "OK, yeah. Thanks, I guess you're right."

She sighed, turned, and ran to her room while still covering her breasts. Glenda looked around and saw Hope's clothes in a pile on the floor. She must have been about to take a shower but decided she needed to talk. Glenda shook her head sadly and got ready for her own shower.

Chapter Nine

THE GLIDER MADE A high-pitched squeaking noise as the two old people rocked on the forward stroke. The man smiled tenderly at his wife, and she flashed her somewhat crooked grin in return, emphasizing a dimple in her left cheek. He gently touched his index finger to that beloved feature, leaning over to kiss the love of his life. A yell from the street distracted him.

"Mr. Allen! Mrs. Allen! Hey!"

The couple turned in surprise at the interruption and heard a car horn honk. A tender moment shattered. When they saw the Camaro, though, both waved enthusiastically. After it passed, Winston Walker Allen happily turned back to his wife and received his kiss. Bettie laid her head on his shoulder with a contented sigh.

"Gosh. Are they sweet or what? Rockin' on the porch and holdin' hands. It even looked like he was about to kiss her. What a fine way to spend a Friday afternoon," Tanya said dreamily.

"Sure. They're lucky people, and I think they know it," Glenda answered thoughtfully.

"Lucky? How do you know?"

"Think about it. They've got that great house. They've got each other. What else could a person want?"

"How 'bout a million dollars or a new car?"

"Happiness is the most important thing, Tan-ay—not money. Those folks back there are happy, and that's all they need. Money and things and social pressures would just mess that up. See?"

"Yeah, I guess so. But it would still be nice to not have to work—*ever.*"

Anxiousness gripped Glenda. "Work! Oh, my gosh, I've gotta get back to the college and go to work from two to five. What time is it?" She never wore a watch, or any bracelet, for that matter.

Tanya checked her watch. "You've got thirty minutes—don't sweat it. Drive down past the Monarch, and let's see what's playin' this week."

"Why? You can usually see the same movie on cable at Jimmy Mac's apartment about the same time it finally comes to this backwater theater!"

Tanya giggled. "I know. But it's a lot more fun when we go to Tuesday dollar night at the Monarch. Remember when we went to *The Muppet Movie?*"

Glenda laughed. "Yeah, we nearly got thrown out for blowin' bubbles off the balcony. I couldn't believe they took our bubbles away!"

"You know, I'm still mad about that."

"Yeah. So what if little bubbles got in people drinks. What's a few more bubbles?" Glenda asked. Tanya nodded in agreement.

Glenda turned onto the same street where a few weeks earlier, the driver of the blue pickup truck had made a very big mistake. She slowed the car when she noticed a construction crew working near the front of the movie theater. Tanya read the marquis aloud. "*The Black Hole*. Crapola. No dollar movie this week," she said disgustedly.

Her attention was diverted by an unexpected loud pop from the direction of the construction equipment.

"Hey, look out!" Evel cried loudly. He and his coworker, Randall, were sandblasting paint off the low wall in front of the movie theater. Some boss at City Hall decided the yellow paint wasn't working and needed to be changed. Despite the bright warning color, people kept running into the concrete wall. He and Randall were assigned to remove the yellow paint. The running air compressor and sandblasting made a lot of noise—neither worker noticed the air hose fitting was about to break free. The loud pop, however, was audible above the din.

"Dammit, Randall. Turn off the valve!" Evel fought with the loose air hose. "The fitting blew off!" The hose kept flying around, this way and that, making awful hissing and slapping sounds. "OW! RANDALL!" Evel yelled even louder, as the hose wrapped around his leg like a boa constrictor. He wrestled wildly with the hose, struggling to get untangled.

Suddenly, all the animation disappeared. The black air hose flopped to the ground with a strange hollow sound. Randall stifled a laugh and turned off all the equipment. "Glenn man! You were dancin' around like John Travolta in *Saturday Night Fever*!"

Evel, relieved that the attack of the wildly flailing hose was over, joined Randall's laughing. "Well, now I can honestly say I've been beaten with a rubber hose!"

He leaned back against the city pickup to relax and noticed a car slowly driving by. Relieved and amused, his smile lines grew extra crinkly when he made eye contact with the surprised, bright blue eyes in the yellow Camaro.

Glenda smiled back. She was amused at the scene, yes, but there was something else. Evel winked at her surreptitiously, causing her to experience a curious response. Glenda nodded her head, ever so slightly, feeling the flutter grow larger. She hastily stepped on the gas pedal and was gone.

"Hey, hey, hey. Who was that?" Randall asked as the car sped around the corner and out of sight.

"Oh, just a girl. A girl I might just hafta get to know," he said quietly.

Evel stood very still, staring off in the direction of the car for quite some time.

The bell rang, signaling the end of the break between high school class periods. Chip emerged from the shrubbery by the east door to Hall B, as Larry pushed a tall motorcycle up the sidewalk toward him.

"OK, Chip. I think I'm ready," said Larry, mounting the dirt bike.

"OK. Shawn and Thomas should have the other doors open in time. I'll try to meet ya at the other end."

Chip opened the glass door—the way was clear for Larry to ride the Yamaha dirt bike into Hall B. Larry kick-started the motorcycle, revved it a bit and nodded once at his friend. Then he was off.

He roared down the hall, leaving a cloud of smoke from the motor and the spinning back tire. The bike slowed to a stop in front of Room B-10, Coach Fagan's room. Larry held the front brake and revved the engine. The back tire spun, squealed and smoked in a loud statement of defiance. Larry slowly released the brake, allowing the motorcycle to move forward again. Kids and teachers were coming out of the classrooms. The time had come to make his getaway.

Larry sped through the building toward the doors on the west side, down-shifting to slow the bike a bit when he saw—with growing panic—that the doors weren't open. He pressed on the foot brake harder to slow down more, getting closer and closer to the glass doors—still they did not open. He grabbed the handbrake and slammed his boot down on the footbrake but was going too fast. The Yamaha slid sideways, hitting the doors broadside. The metal framework was mangled; the glass shattered. Larry rolled away from the destruction into the grass, as the bike miraculously missed hitting any parked cars during its slide into the parking lot. A crowd gathered at the destroyed west entrance to Hall B at the Dairyville High School.

Chip emerged from the shrubbery beside the end of the building, breathless. "Larry! Are you all right? Are you hurt?"

Larry rose up on a scraped elbow. "Where the hell was Thomas and Shawn? The doors weren't open!"

"Obviously," commented Chip. He glanced up at some kids who were cheering and saw camo fatigues. "That figures. The Samsonites *would* find this entertaining."

Hearing someone else approach, the two boys looked up with dread.

"Mr. Allen, do you need an ambulance?" a voice asked from above.

Larry sat up and poked at his ribs. "No, Mr. Stickler. I don't think so."

"Then get up and come to my office. You, too, Chip. And Allen, if you *are* bleeding, don't drip on anything." The high school principal turned and walked through the crowd into the building. "Get back to class, everyone."

Chip helped Larry to his feet. The crowd parted as the two crunched their way across the broken glass to follow the principal to his office.

"Thank goodness it was safety glass," commented a voice from the crowd. Larry recognized that voice. He turned to glare at the traitor. Thomas. His eyes squinted in disdain, the promise of payback glowing from them.

Chip gripped Larry's arm. "Come on—let's get this over with."

The two walked through the stunned crowd into the hallway.

"Pancho! PANCHO!"

Evel turned sharply. A pickup approached driven by Ned—the oldest, feistiest man on the crew. For some completely unknown reason, Ned nicknamed Glenn "Pancho."

Evel quickly walked over to the vehicle. He sensed something was wrong. "What is it, Ned?"

"Your brother called the shop from school. He's in some kinda trouble, and he needs ya to go up there. Come on. I'll take ya back to the shop," Ned said, his voice cracking off word-rounds like an automatic weapon.

Evel turned to Randall with concern about leaving his coworker alone. "Go on. This job's at a standstill till that hose gets fixed. I'll be OK—go." Randall waved his buddy off.

Evel hopped in the pickup. Within ten minutes, he was speeding down Main Street toward the high school. He passed the yellow Camaro as it pulled into the college entrance and tapped his horn.

"Hey, that was Evel Knievel in the Thunderbird!" Tanya said, craning her neck to look back.

Glenda glanced over her shoulder. "Yeah, that's weird. We just saw him workin' down by the picture show. It looked like he was in a hurry. I wonder if somethin's up. Oh, well, I've gotta go to work. Want me to drop you at the Student Center?"

Tanya nodded. "Yepper. I gotta go see my spider, anywho. Although, I doubt any mail has come in to disturb the web he's built in my mailbox. But I do feel a responsibility to check on him."

She got out of the car and jauntily moved toward the Student Center.

"Right. See ya later." Glenda wondered if Evel Knievel, or whatever his name was, had an emergency. But it was Friday—he'd probably be out later, unless something was really wrong. She parked the car and ran to the Administration Building, arriving at her work-study job at 2 p.m. straight up.

Evel walked up the steps to the front door of the high school. He graduated from a different school before the family moved to Dairyville, so he had never been in this building. He stepped inside and looked around. To his right, chairs lined up outside a closed office door. Chip sat in one of those chairs, holding his head in his hands. "Principal's Office," the sign on the door beside Chip proclaimed. Evel walked toward his brother's best friend.

"Evel—I mean, Glenn. Oh, man. Am I glad to see *you*!"

Evel sunk into the chair by Chip. "What the hell is goin' on? They told me Larry was in some kinda trouble."

"Yeah. We really did it this time," Chip said dejectedly.

"What? Whatever it is, it'd better be bad enough to pull me away from work."

"Oh—it is. Larry decided to make a statement in front of Coach Fagan's classroom. You know what the coach did, don't ya?"

"Yeah. Same thing that happened to me at his age. Damn coaches. They think they can bad mouth kids...and get away with it."

"Right. Well, Larry borrowed a dirt bike and did a burnout in the hallway. Shawn and Thomas was supposed to have the doors open so he could ride out, but they didn't—he crashed." Chip shook his head.

"Crashed! Is he hurt?"

"No. Just scraped up some. Nothin' bad. But it could a' been worse—he went right through the glass doors!"

"Oh, man. So, why am *I* here?" Evel asked.

"They called our parents. But they couldn't get your folks, so Larry had 'em call you. You goin' in?" Larry was Chip's best friend. He realized Glenn was one of his best friends as well.

"I guess I have to. Here goes nothin'."

Evel stood up. He patted Chip on the shoulder. "Hang tight, Chip. This is gonna be interestin'—we might need ya for back-up," Chip cringed, nodding his head.

Evel entered the office. "Hello. I'm Larry Allen's brother. Somebody called that there was some kind of trouble," Evel said to the school secretary as pleasantly as he could under the circumstances.

She scowled at the man in a blue-collar type uniform standing before her. "There certainly is. Your troublemaking brother is in Mr. Stickler's office. He'll probably get expelled for this stunt." She spoke in such a nasty tone Evel knew he was facing a mean woman.

He lowered his voice a notch, assuming a more serious tone, as he felt the tension in the room. "Would you please call Mr. Stickler on the intercom and let him know I'm here, or should I just walk in?" He puffed up his chest a little in preparation for a confrontation.

The secretary scowled at him anew and picked up her phone. "Mr. Stickler. His *brother* is here." She spat the word "brother," snarling as though it left a bad taste in her mouth. "Go on in." Her icy voice could have punched a hole in the closed door.

Evel strode confidently into the office. Larry was sitting in a side chair. He looked up at his brother's crinkly smile. Stifling the excitement of seeing him, Larry glanced nervously at the figure sitting behind the desk. His gaze focused back down at the floor.

"Ah yes. Mr. Allen. Do have a seat and join us. Perhaps you can enlighten me on why your brother put on such a destructive performance as he did today."

Evel did not sit down. Instead, he leaned on the desk to face the Principal. "Mr. Stickler. I don't know exactly what damage Larry caused, but I do know what Coach Fagan did to Larry a couple a' weeks ago. I imagine my brother just wanted to show everybody that he didn't give a rat's ass about what the coach thought about him quittin' football. I had almost the exact same thing happen to me my junior year in high school. After workin' hard all summer for local farmers and ranchers and growin' a few inches, I wasn't the big fat left guard I'd been the year before. In fact, I looked more like a long distance runner and, boy, did the coach let me have it. He told me how worthless I was. He said how dare I slim down and ruin his plans—and then threw me off the football team. Now, four years later, this Coach Fagan gave Larry such a hard time for losin' weight over the summer and ruining *his* plans, Larry just quit. So, if my brother overreacted to bein' insulted and put down by a coach by ridin' a dirt bike down the hall and disturbin' this Coach Fagan's class, I can't really blame him. You should know sometimes your coaches and teachers treat the kids like crap. It's actually pretty sad that kids'll do stuff like this instead of talkin' to somebody or tryin' to straighten things out."

He sighed and sat down heavily in the chair beside Larry.

Mr. Stickler folded his hands and rested his chin on them. He looked intently at the brothers over his reading glasses. Closing his eyes briefly, the Principal seemed to come to a decision. He put his hands down flat on the desk and directed his gaze toward Larry.

"Larry. In the future, please come talk to me if you have a beef with a teacher. Believe you me; to avoid problems such as this, I'll gladly make time to listen to you. Now, go on back to class and keep quiet about our little conversation. If it gets out I let you off without getting out my paddle and giving you licks, my reputation will be ruined. We'll talk later about how to pay for the damages." He grinned slightly at the astonished, pleasantly shocked student.

Evel stood and extended a cordial hand to the Principal. "Thanks, Mr. Stickler. It's awful tough bein' a teenager. Maybe these teachers need to remember that. Now, I'd better get back to work."

"Thank you for coming in. You make a very good point, Mr. Allen. Larry, you have a pretty fine big brother here." He stood and shook hands with Evel.

"Yes sir. I know it. Thanks—to both of ya!"

"Now, get outta here. I have work to do. Oh, and tell Chip to go back to class and keep his mouth shut, too," said the Principal, as he opened a file on his desk. He hid his amusement as the brothers hurried past the flabbergasted secretary and left the office.

Out in the hall, the three guys silently saluted each other—then went their separate ways.

Glenda walked to the dorm after getting off work at five o'clock, looking forward to a fun night of riding around. But she frowned, noticing a pickup with boxes in the back and a very sad looking woman in the cab. She ran up the stairs.

"Is that everything, Hope?" A man's gruff, agitated voice echoed in the hall.

Hope was holding a box, and met Glenda face-to-face at the top of the stairway.

"Yes, Daddy," she called over her shoulder. "Bye, Glenda. Tell the girls bye for me." She turned away and started down the stairs with her box.

Confused, Glenda looked at the beautiful girl. Her father carried a large suitcase toward the stairway. He nodded politely at Glenda as he passed—then they both were gone. She was aware of someone standing quietly beside her but focused on the stairwell.

"Well. There goes a full basketball scholarship down the drain," Candace said with a gentle shake of her curls.

Glenda nodded. "And either the beginning or end of a whole life. I hope she keeps it."

"I know I would," Candace said firmly.

"Really? Corn flakes?"

"Cereally. No doubt about it."

Glenda stared for a moment then changed the subject. "You goin' home this weekend?"

"Nope, I'm stayin' in—got a party to go to Saturday night. You?"

"Noper. I had to work till five today, so it's too late now. Might as well hang around and burn up some gas locally."

Candace laughed, breaking the tension they'd witnessed. "Yeah. If y'all find somethin' excitin' to do tonight, lemme know!"

"Right. It's Friday night. Surely, we can find somethin' to do."

"Yes, we can." Candace turned toward her room. "And stop callin' me Shirley."

Glenda giggled at the *Airplane!* line and walked to her room. She found it full of people. "Glenda. We goin' ridin' around tonight?"

"Can we make a run to Riverview?"

"When will you be ready?"

"Wait a second—hold on a minute. Geez, gimme a break! I need a shower—then we'll think about it. You guys must be bored to tears. What have you been doin' or not doin' as the case may be?"

Tanya and Janie said in unison, "Waitin' for you!"

Glenda rolled her eyes good-naturedly and Linda Lou smiled at her roommate. "Go take your shower. I'll keep these two busy somehow, but we have been waitin' for you. We hear Taco Hut callin'!" Linda said. She directed her gaze to the other two girls. "Y'all go sit in the window and see who's out while we get ready, KO?"

"KO. Sure. We'll be right out here. Hurry Glenda—it's Friday!" Tanya said as they left the room.

The two shorter girls assumed their usual toe-to-toe position in the window sill, keeping watch. A few cars drove through, but it wasn't quite six o'clock; not much was going on. They saw Boots and Gene walking toward the Student Center. But even if they yelled, the guys were too far away to hear. At that moment, they saw the loaded pickup.

"Do you think Hope is leavin' for good?" Janie asked quietly.

"So it appears. You know, she's been gone a few days, and I heard she quit basketball. Now she's movin' out, so I guess it's true." Tanya was also speaking quietly.

"What?"

"You haven't heard? She's pregnant. At least, that's the word in the hall."

"Oh, man. That's too bad. Uh oh. There's Jackal Ann comin' this way," Janie said with a cringe.

Tanya turned to look for the dreaded vehicle, and both girls braced themselves for the usual honk and obscene gesture. Surprisingly, it didn't happen. "What the heck? She always honks and flips us off. That's weird," Tanya said.

"AAArrrooff!" Janie cried, as she fell off the window seat. She'd lost her balance looking back-and-forth down the hall and out the window. Tanya hopped down to help.

"Way to go, *Grace*. Are you OK?"

"Yeah. I guess so. But I ripped my pants. Crap, now I've gotta go change."

Embarrassed, Janie ran into the room, followed by with Tanya. She disappeared into the closet. "I hate all my clothes!" Janie's voice was muffled by the closet door. Tanya lay down on her bed to while away a few minutes.

It turned into much more.

"Hey! Are y'all ready?" Glenda walked into Tanya's and Janie's room—they were sound asleep. "Well, well. Lookee here. Are the two impatient partiers ready and waitin' for action, sittin' on the edge of their seats? Why no. They're in *bed* takin' a *nap* on Friday night. Amazin'. Are we goin' ridin' around or what?"

The roommates sat bolt upright, surprised to find they had been asleep for almost an hour. Janie got up to tidy her curls. Tanya went to the sink to brush her teeth. Glenda leaned on the door facing with her arms crossed.

"GLENDA!! Glenda, are you up there?"

Glenda went to the hall window and looked down to find the source of the voice. "I reckon I am up here!"

"Well, get down here. Somebody egged your car!" Gene yelled up at the window.

"What?" Gene's words didn't sink in.

"There are eggs broken all over your car, Glenda. You'd better come see."

Gene noticed the WWAB sign was still glued over the door. He was briefly amused, but looked intently at the window when he remembered why he was there.

Linda Lou overheard the exchange and tossed Glenda's keys to the distraught girl. "Go. I'll be down in a minute."

Glenda grabbed her checkbook. She ran at full speed down the hall, with Janie and Tanya close behind.

"Did you see who did it?" Glenda asked Gene as the entire group jogged to the other side of the Shoe Bench.

"No. I was just passing by on my way to the cannon from the Student Center and noticed it."

They arrived at the Camaro. Egg shells were littered all around; several were broken on the roof and the back glass. Egg yolk had run down onto the window's rubber seal and trunk lid.

Janie and Tanya stared at each other with wide eyes. "Jackal Ann—it had to be her! Glendee, she drove by a while ago and didn't honk or flip us off or anything. We didn't see what she did 'cause Janie fell out of the window. It had to be her," Tanya said. Janie nodded in agreement.

Glenda narrowed her eyes. "Janie. Tanya. Will y'all please go up to the room and fetch some wet wash rags and a towel? Hurry!" Both girls ran back to the dorm to fulfill their new mission.

Glenda turned back to her car and surveyed the mess. She swept her arm across the top of her car, flinging egg shells into the air. She was almost in tears. Gene put his hand on her shoulder.

"Hey, watch it!" a voice called from behind the car. Gene and Glenda turned in surprise to see the silver Thunderbird stopped behind the Camaro.

Glenda gasped and hurried out to the big car. "Oh, my gosh! I'm sorry. Did it hit your car?" she said with dread, looking distraught.

"No. But it was close." Evel pointed at the broken egg shell beside his front tire. He turned to Glenda. "What happened?"

"Somebody egged my car. The girls have gone to get somethin' to clean it off. Oh, my, I'm glad I didn't fling it on *you!*" Glenda's frown reappeared as she looked at her car.

"Who'd do that to ya?" Evel asked gently.

Glenda turned to face him. "We think it was Jackal Ann. You know the car hop that has the old Dodge station wagon?

We have a longstanding feud," Glenda explained. "It has apparently escalated."

Tanya and Janie had returned and worked vigorously on the mess, scrubbing yolk and egg white off the car. "It had to be her. She drove by about an hour ago and was bein' sneaky, so it had to be her." Tanya said as she scraped an egg yolk off the window.

"Revenge! We must have revenge!" Janie cried.

Evel nodded his head at the blue-eyed girl. He noted the girls had given the same nickname to the high school troublemaker as his buddies. "I might could help ya out with that," he said softly.

Glenda turned to him, feeling herself drawn to the crinkly blue eyes. Her heart fluttered a bit—she blinked in surprise. "How?" she asked, recovering herself.

"There's a high school football game at the college stadium tonight. Your enemy plays in the band, so her car should be parked over there durin' the game. Maybe y'all could get her then."

Evel's 8-track player had been in a pause between tracks; the loud music interrupted the conversation. He reached over to turn down the volume.

"You know her that well?"

"No. No. Only from the drag—and she goes to the same school my brother goes to. I try to stay away from her as much as possible." He realized Glenda had a real problem with the unpleasant girl.

Glenda nodded, accepting the explanation. "OK, that sounds like good information we can use in a plan. Whatever it may be." She leaned closer to the car. "Hey, is that "Stranglehold" I hear?"

Evel looked at her with surprise. "You like Ted Nugent?"

"You bet! Is that a tape?" Glenda's dimple appeared at Evel's affirmative nod. "That's one 8-track I wish I had. Oh, well, I guess I'd better go help clean up my own car."

Evel reached toward the dash to pop the tape out of the player. He held it out the window toward Glenda. "Here, you can borrow it—just get it back to me sometime, OK?"

Glenda gently took the 8-track tape from his hand. "Sure, thanks, will do. Uh...is it Evel or..."

"Evel Knievel!" Tanya supplied from behind.

"Tell you what. You can call me Glenn. And you are?" he asked, out of politeness rather than a need to know. He already knew.

"Glenda. Glenda Meadows. It's very nice to actually meet you, Glenn. Is that Glenn with two 'n's?"

"Yep. Most everybody around here calls me Evel, but Glenn's my real name."

"Righto. OK. Glenn it is. Ya know, my dad's name is Glenn with two 'n's, too." Glenda cast a charming look at him. "Thanks for the tip about Jackal Ann. We'll act on it, I'm sure."

"Then maybe I'll see ya out later?"

He gazed directly at her with his very blue eyes and crinkly smile lines. The look fluttered Glenda's heart again. She leaned on the door of his car for support and peered into his eyes, certain they both felt the spark.

She took a breath and leaned back. "Oh, yeah. We'll be out and about. After the payback on Jackal Ann, I'll get this tape back to ya."

Evel took a breath. "No hurry. Lemme know how the revenge goes. I'm outta here. See ya later!"

He put the car in Drive and took off with a rumble of mufflers. Glenda watched the back of the big silver car for a moment before turning back toward her own.

Tanya looked at Glenda with a curious expression. "Don't look at me in that tone of voice, Tan-ay," Glenda joked to avoid any questions.

Both were distracted by a new voice. "Hall-oh. Are you done? Here's another towel. I still hear Taco Hut callin'!" Linda Lou announced, as she approached.

"Right. Taco Hut. Hey, hey! That's a great idea! Bean Burrito Bombs!" Glenda exclaimed.

"With lots of onions and sour cream!" Tanya added.

"Candace wants to go with us. She said she'd be down in a minute," Linda said. "What's this about bombs? Wait—I get it. Payback?"

"Definitely. Glendee-girl, we'd better go to the car wash. This is dried on worse than we thought," Janie said firmly. "I brought my purse—I've got quarters."

Glenda turned to Gene and put her hand on his arm. "Thanks for lettin' me know, Gene. You wanna go with us?"

"Naa. Y'all go on and have your fun. I'll hang out here with Boots. He'll be along in a few. I do expect a full report later, however. Ah, here comes Candace."

"Linda told me what happened. Glenda, let's go get her," Candace said, her voice tinged with malice.

"All right. Load up everybody. Car wash, Taco Hut, Ted Nugent and REVENGE!" Glenda held up the 8-track tape. "We'll come back and report to Boots and Gene, later...much later!"

The girls piled into the Camaro.

After the car was satisfactorily washed, the girls stormed into the Taco Hut. Justin was on duty. Good—he made the best burritos. He prepared their food, then walked into the so-called dining area to sit with them and hear the story.

"So...you want some mega bean bombs. Well, that is somethin' I can do. I'll be back in a bit," Justin said after hearing about the egging. He rose from the table. A short time later, he handed a rather heavy sack to Glenda. "This oughta do it. It's the messiest, smelliest stuff I could come up with. It's just wrapped in the paper the burritos are usually in—no tortilla. All you want's the mess anyway, right?"

"Right. No need for frills—just spills." Tanya giggled.

"So, all we do is unwrap it a bit, aim and chunk?" Candace asked.

"Yep. There's five of 'em in there, so each one of ya can have a shot." Justin beamed at the group of girls. Each had a rather wicked smile on her face.

"A-OK. It's almost dark. They should be gettin' ready for halftime about now. Pretty soon little Miss Jacqueline Ann will be struttin' around with the band on the football field blowin' her horn," Janie said.

Glenda and the others rose from the booth. "Right. Let's do a run through and locate the car, so we can come back after while and bomb it. Thanks muchly, Justin. We'll cruise back through and let ya know how the bombs worked out."

"Happy bombing—or good huntin'—or whatever the sayin' is," Justin yelled from behind the counter. "If the story's good enough, I'll give y'all all a coke when ya come back!"

Dusk fell on the stadium parking lot, and the streetlights kicked on. They began to glow. The girls could hear a band playing on the field.

Glenda felt a bit nervous and changed the plan. "Let's find her car and bomb it now. Then we can make tracks and hide out for a while. Keep a watch out for Campus Cops—or anybody for that matter. Linda, pass out the bombs, carefully. I don't want that stuff spilled in my car!" she said, while looking around for the old station wagon.

Linda took the paper packages one-by-one out of the bag and passed them into ready hands. All were now armed and dangerous.

"There it is!" Tanya exclaimed. "One row over, Glendee-girl."

"OK everybody. Get ready. After we stop, if it's clear, everybody hit a different part of the car."

Glenda stopped the Camaro directly behind the target. She checked around to make sure the coast was clear. "GO!"

Both doors flew open. Girls tumbled out of the car wildly. Glenda plastered her bomb all over the windshield. Tanya hit the hood with a great splat. Linda Lou slammed hers on the back glass, and Janie and Candace each chunked their bombs in the open windows onto the front seat. They threw themselves back to the Camaro and Glenda took off, as Linda closed her door.

"I don't think anybody saw us!" Candace stated happily.

"I certainly hope not!" Linda Lou said nervously. "Seems like every time y'all go out—or is it we? Anyway, we get into somethin', or do you always do stuff like this?"

Tanya chuckled. "Sure, Linda Lou. Girl, you need to get out more! That was great. Oh, boy, will her car stink to high heaven. Justin really loaded on the onions and hot sauce!"

Glenda felt satisfied. "Oh, yeah. That was payback for *almost* all the times she's messed with us. Almost."

"Didn't somebody say somethin' about a run?" Candace asked. "Glendee-girl, that'd be a good place to go for a while, wouldn't it?"

"The beer store? OK. Sure. I guess so. Y'all earned it. That'll kill an hour or so, till the game is over, maybe. Man, I'd like to see her face when she sees that mess!"

"Oh, we'll see her—there's no doubt about that," Tanya said from the back seat. "We'll hafta ask Evel Knievel to protect us."

Glenda looked in the rearview mirror to see her friend's face. Tanya's glance was positively mischievous.

"He could do it, too!" Janie exclaimed. "Glendee-girl. Let's get him somethin' for helpin' us. That was great information."

"Indeed it was, but he doesn't need us to buy him beer!" Glenda laughed. "But that's not a bad idea, Janie. We'll look for somethin' while we're there. Somethin' unusual."

"Get real, Glenda. They don't have anything exotic at the Riverview beer stores. Leave it to me. I know what to get. I saw his brand in their cooler when I rode around with them that night a while back," Tanya said.

"That'll work. But first I want that coke Justin promised." She pulled around to approach the Taco Hut from the rear but couldn't see very well. "Hey, it's awful dark over here. What's goin' on?"

The Taco Hut, Dairy Queen, and The Pizza Place were all blacked out. No electric lights anywhere—only headlights. Cars were leaving the parking lots in all directions. Glenda pulled into the Taco Hut, surprised to see the silver Thunderbird right behind her. Evel parked beside the Camaro. Fuzzy smiled from the passenger seat.

"What's goin' on?" Candace asked.

Fuzzy looked over at Evel. They both laughed. Justin came out of the Taco Hut. He walked in a somewhat confused state toward the two cars.

"We was just throwin' a football around. But Charles got a little wild!" Fuzzy exclaimed with a laugh.

"Man. It just went dark. All of a sudden the power went out," Justin said.

"Yeah. 'Cause Charles knocked the wire down, or it shorted out or somethin'. 'Boom Boom! Out go the Lights'—git it? That Pat Travers song?" Fuzzy nudged the laughing Evel.

"Yeah, yeah. But we'd better get outta here. We'll catch y'all later," Evel said, as he looked around Fuzzy's hair. "When stuff like this happens, the cops always look for us!" He started the car and backed out of the parking space.

Glenda watched them, bemused. They were always in the middle of whatever was happening. No wonder the cops were always looking for them. She was about to turn and speak to Justin when they all heard—KABOOM!—and shortly thereafter, the backlash echo—BOOM! The girls exchanged knowing glances. The phantom cannon shooter had struck again.

Glenda looked up at Justin. "Well. Boom Boom—out DO go the lights. OK. Now that all *that's* over, maybe I can speak. Hey, Justin. I guess that coke you promised is out of the question? Oh, and the bean bombs worked great!"

"Glad to hear it. Well, with no power I got no fizz, but come on in anyways. We'll have flat Coca Colas by candlelight!"

"Glendee-girl, let's go!" Janie called from the back seat. "You can get a coke at the beer store!"

"Thanks anyways, Justin. I must say I prefer lots of fizz. We'll see ya later!" Glenda started her car with a roar. "We'd better get outta here, too!"

Chapter Ten

A SHADOW PASSED OVER an intense negotiation in the donut shop parking lot, as the sun sank behind the Marlboro Man. The bargaining was obviously one-sided; the parties were not easily coming to terms. An acquaintance of Charles' wanted a favor on this Saturday night—a big favor, considering what he was offering in return.

"Come on, Evel. Let's trade. Just for a little while. Please, man. I've got a hot date!"

"Red, I do not want to ride your piece of shit Harley all night," Evel said to the red-haired guy facing him. He stood protectively in front of the Thunderbird.

"Not all night—just a couple a' hours. Just enough to impress her—then we'll get on the bike. Please, man, it's full o' gas." Red was practically begging.

Evel glanced up at the darkening sky. "I don't know...I don't like it."

"Hey, Evel. We could ride the bike for a while. It'll be fun. We haven't got to ride since your brother wrecked his," Fuzzy said.

Evel glared at his buddy for the betrayal. "Oh, all right. But leave the cooler in Charles' car."

They transferred cooler and keys. A few minutes later, after some severely delivered instructions, the big silver car pulled carefully out of the parking lot with a stranger behind the wheel.

"Well, now what?" Evel asked with dread.

Fuzzy brightened and raised his eyebrows. "How about a drag back-to-back?"

Evel shrugged, then threw his leg over the motorcycle and started it. Charles waved, as they left—he was in charge of the cooler. Fuzzy hopped on—backward of course—and off they went.

Soon, they bounced over the railroad tracks. "Hey...thi-is thing...i-is...kind-da...rro-ugh...ai-n't i-it?" Fuzzy asked.

"Tha-at's be-e-cause i-it's a pi-iece o-of shi-it!" The bike still bounced long after passing over the tracks.

Fuzzy waved at the cheering crowd parked in the lot across from the Astro Drive-In and at the driver behind them. Then he realized who the driver was: Shakey. In response, Shakey waved a palsied hand. His happy face could be seen through the windshield. Fuzzy turned on the seat to warn Evel of the danger lurking behind them. But the bike weaved dangerously; Evel spat a curse at him to keep still. Fuzzy grimaced nervously back at Shakey, hoping Evel would turn into the college to avoid the possibility of becoming a traffic statistic.

He felt the bike move into the right turn lane at the college entrance and breathed a sigh of relief. But Shakey's fender was getting closer and closer to them. He elbowed Evel.

Evel opened the throttle. "I see him. Hang on!" The old motorcycle coughed once—then surged forward. Evel maneuvered the bike into the college entrance and away from Shakey's car, which had veered dangerously close.

"Dammit! How *does* he keep a driver's license?" Evel exclaimed, coasting up the drive toward the girls' dorms.

"Man. I thought he had us that time."

Fuzzy looked up at the dorm windows and saw the red WWAB sign, but no people. Evel swung the bike around the U and found a crowd at the cannon. He honked the horn. It was louder than either expected; Fuzzy lost his balance. "HEEELLLLPPPPP!"

Fuzzy fell off the back of the bike. The difference in weight distribution caused the motorcycle to surge ahead. The engine coughed and sputtered, forcing Evel to keep moving. Fuzzy stood in the driveway with his hands on his hips, watching his friend ride away. He shook his head and turned toward the cannon. "Well, how do you like that? My ride ran off and left me!" Fuzzy eyed the group of girls who were staring at him. He shrugged. "May I join you?"

"Sure. Come on up!" Tanya called, as Fuzzy vaulted his small frame onto the wall and strode over to the cannon.

"So. What's goin' on?"

"We were just relishing a little revenge we took out on Jackal Ann yesterday," Glenda said.

"Bean bombs!" Janie said. Fuzzy's face turned into a questioning look.

"You see, she and I have had this ongoing feud for over a year, but she went too far when she egged my Camaro yesterday. Your buddy told us where to find her car, and we bombed it with smelly bean burritos," Glenda explained.

"Wow. Remind me not to git y'all mad at me!" Fuzzy said. "I'm impressed. When did this happen?"

"Yesterday evenin' during the football game—right before y'all knocked out the lights all over town. We didn't see anything of her last night so she oughta drive by any time now. We've got water balloons ready if she tries anything," Tanya said. Candace and the Months of the Year stood ready as well.

"Water balloons?" Fuzzy asked. "That don't sound all that bad."

"Well, balloons filled with water with lots of green and red and blue food coloring ought to make it a lot more interestin'." Glenda's voice was conspiratorial, quiet, as if sharing a secret.

"It'll be great. We're waitin' for the flashlight signal. Linda Lou's on lookout near the front entrance. Barb-oh's coverin' the back way for us and she'll honk if Jackal Ann comes in that way. We found out when she was gettin' off work at the Astro. I hope the little bitch-Ann drives by. Just let her try and flip us off. I'll aim my balloon right at her spiteful face!" Janie said.

Fuzzy raised his eyebrows at the attitude of the irate little bomber. Another girl walking toward the dormitory caught his attention. He saw a way to avoid whatever was about to happen.

"'Vette or no 'Vette—that girl likes me!" Fuzzy said brightly. "See y'all later. Hey, Melinda!" He started running toward the girl, caught up with her, and they disappeared into the dorm lobby.

"Well, I guess he's not worried about gettin' a ride back to wherever," Tanya said with amusement.

She suddenly noticed a flashing white light. Gene saw it, too. "Hey, is that the signal from Linda?" he asked nervously.

"Yepper. Everybody take your positions!" Glenda instructed. The girls hid with their balloons behind trees, cars and anything else close to the driveway in front of the cannon. Boots and Gene climbed up on the cannon and tried to act nonchalant.

The old Dodge station wagon stained with brown smudges was driven by a livid Jacqueline Ann. She paused in front of WWAB Hall and honked. Peering up to see if anybody was looking through any of the brightly lit windows, she honked again, but no one appeared. She vehemently flipped off the building anyway. The windows were down, allowing the bean and onion smell to escape into the atmosphere. With a hateful, angry look on her face, she drove forward around the U toward the cannon. With one glance two guys were spotted, but no enemy was apparent. Then they struck.

"NOW!!"

From all directions multicolored balloons hit the car—colored water ran down the sides and the windshield. Jacqueline Ann seemed stunned and jerked the car to a stop.

Glenda walked slowly, holding a red balloon and stopped a few feet from the driver. She glared at the high-schooler who had tormented her for over a year. They had never before been this close to each other. The fight was over a good for nothing loser no longer in either of their lives. Jacqueline Ann saw the look on Glenda's face and flinched, as if she knew she was about to get hit.

Instead, Glenda tossed the balloon onto the pavement by the driver's door. Red water splashed onto the car. "That's it. I've had enough of you and this feud. Leave us all alone. Understood?"

Jacqueline Ann had a rather amusing dumbstruck look on her face. She brusquely snarled her lips and glared back at Glenda. "Fat chance. You just better look out," she said, so that only Glenda could hear.

"It's over. Kevin used both of us. He's gone. Let it go," Glenda demanded.

Jacqueline Ann shot a hateful look at Glenda and put the car in gear. Glenda reached behind her back so another water balloon could be slipped into her hand. She threw it with all her might at the open driver window. It hit the edge, sending green water down the side of the door and through the window onto a furious Jacqueline Ann, who sped off to escape the onslaught.

"Stay away from us—or there'll be more where that came from!" Tanya yelled at the fleeing vehicle, throwing one last balloon.

The girls gathered around Glenda quietly. She smiled, and everyone cheered at the success of the mission. They happily moved about to pick up the now empty balloons that were lying all around before any other cars came around the U. They chatted and laughed together, then headed toward the cannon.

Out on Main Street, Evel brought the motorcycle to a halt at the donut shop, slamming the kickstand down with an angry swipe of his very large foot. The bike's engine backfired and shuddered to a stop. He was aiming for the gas tank with his boot heel when Daniel strode up beside him. "Wanna make a drag?" he asked calmly. "I've got a bottle."

Evel put his foot on the ground. He nodded once, then stiffly followed Daniel to the Oldsmobile. "Get me away from that piece of shit," he said with clenched teeth.

"Where's Fuzzy?"

"Lost him in the college. I couldn't stop. The damn thing was tryin' to die. It finally did. Man, when I get my hands on that Red..."

Daniel mixed a drink and handed over the plastic Coke bottle. Evel took a long swig and a deep breath to calm his anger. Daniel pulled onto the drag, spinning his tires—an action which always made Evel feel better. By the time they came back by Tim's, Evel was in a much better mood, and they were having a good time. At the old Dairy Queen, they saw some friends—*very* young friends.

"Hey, Daniel. Evel. Take us ridin' around!" one called.

Two girls, both in high school, were cute and a lot of fun. They got in the car. Evel crawled in back with the bottle and the Cokes. He assumed the duty of keeping the girls out of the alcohol. "You're silly enough without booze," Evel said, as they tried to take the bottle from him.

Daniel plugged in a tape and turned up the music to distract them. Before long, the girls were dancing to the music and hanging out the window, yelling at any and everybody. Their activity drew the attention of a patrolling policeman; flashing lights appeared behind the car. Daniel gauged he could make it to the grocery store where he worked. As soon as was possible, he slowly pulled over. This gave Evel time to try to hide the bottle. But there simply was no hiding place in the small car. He hastily put the bottle in the seat and tried unsuccessfully to sit on it.

The cop hitched his pants up and sauntered toward the car. "What 're you boys and girls up to tonight?" He knew the guys well and happily gave them a hard time at every opportunity.

Suddenly, a flashlight shined in Daniel's eyes.

"Oh, just doin' the drag, Officer House," Daniel replied innocently. The flashlight panned over the passengers, settling on Evel. His head was pressed up against the top of the car. He looked very uncomfortable.

"Whatcha sittin' on there, Mr. Allen?"

"Huh? Me? Nothin', Officer House," he shifted his weight a bit. "Ow—nothin'."

"Hand it here," the officer said, holding out his hand. Evel adjusted his weight again and produced the bottle of whiskey. The officer knew these girls were underage.

"We didn't let 'em drink any, Officer House," Evel said simply.

The officer peered in the car at the young man sitting in the back and believed him. He straightened up and made a decision. "Daniel. Outta the car, and git ridda' this," he commanded.

Daniel unfolded his tall frame from the low car. He tentatively took the bottle from the officer's hand. Rearing back, he aimed to throw it as far as possible across the parking lot.

"Whoa. Whoa up, there. Not like that. Whattaya wanna do, make a big mess for somebody to hafta clean up? No, no—that's not the way. You see that dumpster there?"

Daniel looked stricken. He walked over to the dumpster. It appeared he was trying to carefully drop the bottle—perhaps with a thought that he could retrieve it later.

"Whoa again—pour it out first," the officer said sternly.

Daniel hung his head in defeat. He uncorked the bottle and poured the whiskey onto the asphalt pavement. Watching the amber liquid run across the white painted stripe of the parking space was downright distressful. When it was gone, he tossed the empty container into the dumpster, where it crashed and shattered.

"Y'all better take these girls back to their car. It's gittin' late," Officer House said. Satisfied with the work he had done, he chuckled, strutted back to his police car and drove away.

Daniel started the Oldsmobile. Everyone was silent, until one of the girls turned the music back on. The mood lightened, but for Daniel the night was over. After taking the girls back to their car, he drove to the donut shop to drop off Evel, then left without another word.

Evel watched the back of Daniel's car for a moment, shrugged and walked over to Charles. "What happened? We saw House go by with lights and sirens. Was he after y'all?" Charles asked.

"Yep. Oh, it's OK. Nobody got hauled to jail or anything. Any sign of the Thunderbird? Or Fuzzy?"

"Nope. Well, not in a while. The Thunderchicken went by about thirty minutes ago down toward town, but it hasn't come back by."

"Great." Evel was depressed. "Where's the cooler? I need a beer."

He leaned on Charles' car. Samson walked over and stood with him. He knew despair when he saw it and handed Evel a beer. Unexpectedly, he grabbed Charles, picking him up. Evel was amused at the sight. Suddenly, he felt much better.

The yellow Camaro pulled out of the Astro after the three girls had refueled themselves on corny dogs and tater tots. On the way out, Glenda waved at the high school kids sitting in the vacant lot across the street. They looked like a crowd at a concert. Most were wearing black T-shirts with multi-colored printing on the front. Larry saw the wave and returned it. He gave her a big smile, twirling his finger sideways. Glenda understood the signal, so she floored it. The back tires screamed as the rubber spun on the pavement. Tire smoke boiled from under the fenders—the engine roared. The car surged forward radically. She heard the cheers of the crowd at the vacant lot.

Driving past the donut shop parking lot, Glenda looked for the Thunderbird. The big car wasn't there, but she did notice a rather muscular man carrying another guy across the parking lot. So did Tanya. "Humph, that's strange." Tanya saw a familiar car up ahead in another parking lot. "Oh, lookee—there's Mike. Pull over, Glenda!"

Glenda parked so she could quickly escape from the small area should the need arise. Tanya quickly walked over to the guy sitting in a tiny Datsun pickup truck. He was known to smoke a lot of weed. Most weekends he was pretty messed up.

"Mike. Are you OK?" Tanya asked.

"Yeah—I'm *fine*—man," Mike answered slowly. He gave his signature limp peace sign—the one the girls had picked up from him.

"I'm *fine*. Just call me Squint." Janie narrowed her eyes to slits and sarcastically mimicked the peace sign. Glenda nodded in agreement.

Tanya came back to the car. "Let's go. He's wasted. Why does he smoke so much dope? He's so cute until he does that!"

"Don't worry about it, Tanya. If he does that kind of stuff, he's not worth the trouble."

Glenda pulled back out into traffic. The polka-dotted VW honked as it cruised past. As usual, the two drivers tooted their horns until they couldn't hear each other anymore. Glenda prepared to turn left into the old Dairy Queen.

"Evel Knievel! There he is!" Tanya pointed at the convenience store.

Glenda quickly changed direction, turning right into the store parking lot, and pulled in beside the parked Thunderbird. A quick thought that the big car was usually seen backed into a parking place crossed Glenda's mind. Janie handed the sack between the seats to Tanya, which held the six-pack they'd bought for him the night before. She grabbed the sack and hurriedly got out of the car.

"Hey Evel! We..." Tanya stopped short when a stranger with wild, red hair stared up at her with an equal look of shock. "Who are you?"

"Me? Who are you? Go away! My date'll be back in a minute!" the red-haired guy said anxiously. He nervously looked toward the store. Tanya looked back at Glenda, then glared at the stranger in a familiar car.

"What 're you doin' with this car?" Tanya was certain something was rotten in Dairyville.

"I just borrowed it for a while. Come on—go away. She's— look she's payin' out now!"

"Well...here—give this to him when you give the car back," Tanya said coldly. She shoved the sack in the open window and got back in the Camaro. She turned her face toward the strange guy in the familiar Thunderbird and spoke into the air. "Some date—he has to borrow a car and then makes her go in the store!"

"I knew somethin' didn't look right." Glenda hurriedly backed away from the Thunderbird and left the store parking lot. Before long they were almost back up the drag to the college.

"Pull in and let me off, Glenda. I'm tired," Janie whined from the back seat.

"What 're you tired of? Or, are you sickly?"

"I don't know. I don't think so. I'm just tired for some reason. Maybe I practiced my dance too much."

"Tell us about it. We was there, ya know!" Glenda chided.

"Oh, come on. Please drop me at the front. It's after ten o'clock, right?"

"Our sign is still there. Can you believe it?" Tanya said, oblivious to the conversation around her. Janie banged her hand on the back of the passenger seat.

"Hold your horses, Janie. Don't get grumpy with us. Tan-ay, get ready to let her out, so she can go beddie-bye. We'll make a quick stop—I wanna go back out there," Glenda said impatiently.

"Me too. I wanna see what's goin' on with the Thunderbird!" Tanya opened the passenger side door.

"Hey!" The voice came from the front porch of the dorm. The girls saw Fuzzy running toward them. Tanya stood up so Janie could crawl out. After a loud moan, Janie bade them goodnight, shuffling away from the car as Fuzzy arrived.

"How 'bout a ride? You goin' back out on the drag?" he asked cheerfully.

"Sure. Hop in!" Glenda readily agreed.

"Shotgun!" Fuzzy tilted the seat up so Tanya could slide into back. She punched him in the arm as she slithered into the back seat. "Just down to the donut shop. Hopefully, Evel got the Thunderchicken back by now."

"Thunderchicken? Hey, did you have a good time with Melinda, Fuzzy? Did you get your license back?" Tanya asked with interest.

"Yeah. They gave it back. Hey, how'd you know? Oh, never mind!" He was embarrassed that she'd figured out he'd been to Melinda's room.

Glenda and Tanya laughed out loud at Fuzzy's discomfort. He scowled and pushed the 8-track tape into the player. Ted Nugent's guitar screamed through the speakers. He immediately brightened. "Ted!"

Glenda's dimple slowly became visible. They enjoyed the music on the way to the donut shop. Glenda pulled in with a flourish but slammed on the brakes when a large figure jumped out of the darkness in front of her car. The figure quickly moved to the passenger side and opened the door. It grabbed Fuzzy by the arm, jerking him out of the car. The girls froze in place.

Suddenly, the figure sat in the passenger seat, slammed the door and smiled at Glenda. "Hi there—let's go. NOW!"

"Evel Knievel! You scared the crap out of us!" Tanya slapped at Evel's shoulder but was thrown backward when Glenda peeled out of the parking lot.

Evel nodded his approval at the exit. "OK. Now, let's go find my car. If you don't have anything better to do, that is," Evel said pleasantly to Glenda. She glanced over at him, but quickly turned her eyes back to the road.

Tanya couldn't contain herself. "We saw it. There was some weird guy with crazy, red hair in it. Go, Glenda!"

"No way they're still there, Tan-ay." Glenda glanced at her unexpected passenger. Still, she drove toward the old Dairy Queen end of town.

"Where?" Evel asked.

"At the little store across from the old DQ. He was there with a date—or so he said. Apparently, she was inside the store when we were there. We gave him your present."

Evel raised his eyebrows in surprise. "Present? For what?"

"For helpin' with the revenge. Oh, man. You should a' seen it." Tanya was again leaning on the console between the front seats. "We bombed Jackal Ann's car with bean burritos at the stadium last night—then again tonight with colored water balloons in front of the cannon. She left with her tail between her legs!"

"Yeah...well...I'm not sure. I just hope it's over," Glenda said.

"She was so mad—it was great!"

Evel nodded. "I'm glad to hear it was a successful operation," he said with amusement. "Nothin' succeeds quite like success."

"Very successful." Glenda's dimple showed as she responded. She thought she saw a twinkle in his eye and felt the little flutter in her chest. She quickly glanced at the road. "Where do we look for the Thunderchicken?"

Evel looked at her, surprised she knew his car's nickname. "You got a flashlight in here?" He opened the glove box and pulled out a flashlight, tested it and nodded his head once. "Pull into the DQ and park around in back. There's a cut-through where cars go over into the museum grounds and park. I have a feelin' that's where they are. Just try to keep it quiet. I'll walk over and check it out."

"Gotcha. KO," Glenda was ready—she didn't know what they'd find, but whatever it was, her passenger wasn't going to be happy about it. No doubt Mr. Red was going to be sorry he ever borrowed that car. Very sorry. She squinted her eyes to concentrate as the car turned into the DQ parking lot. Glenda cut off the ignition, coasting to a stop just past the dumpster, near a stand of trees.

Evel glanced at her with an approving look. "OK. I'll go ahead. Y'all just keep watch out here. If and when you hear my car start up, get outta here fast, 'cause I'll be haulin' ass this direction. If it's not there, I'll be right back," he said in a hushed voice.

Glenda nodded, her face filling with the look of mischief. His smile lines really showed in the look he gave Glenda before quietly exiting the Camaro.

"Stay back there, Tan-ay, until we see how this shakes out," Glenda whispered. "You watch behind. I'll listen and watch for him."

Tanya shifted positions for a better view out the rear window. Glenda's window was down. She leaned her head out of it slightly, so she could hear. A few cars were turning in the front of Dairy Queen to head back up the drag. Nobody ever came around the back. The pavement was so rough and full of potholes that most everyone not actually passing through the drive-thru avoided it. Glenda was briefly distracted by the memory of Candace standing by the dumpster covered with cow crap when her attention was diverted by voices and sounds beyond the shrubbery.

"Outta the car, Red. Now!"

Red's date started to scream—but stopped. She grabbed her purse and quickly got out of the passenger side door. "I knew this wasn't your car, you son of a bitch! I never want to see or hear from you again!" She slammed the door, turned, and started walking toward Main Street through the museum grounds.

"Wait! Jenny. Don't leave!" Red was also out of the car, yelling at his date. Evel shoved him away from the open door and hurriedly got in the driver's seat. He started the engine before he had the door closed.

"Evel! Don't leave me here. Oh, man!"

"You'll find your piece of shit bike at the donut shop. But if I was you, I'd leave it there for the sanitation crew to take to the landfill when they pick up the trash on Monday. Don't ever talk to me either, Red," Evel said with disdain. He put the car in gear, hoping Glenda was already moving.

Glenda had started the Camaro as soon as she heard the Thunderbird fire up. She saw the glow of headlights and glanced back at Tanya.

"All clear back here." Tanya was nervous.

Glenda floored it. As she whipped the wheel back-and-forth, she managed to dodge most of the potholes. Thankfully, no cars were in the way, so she popped onto Main Street after a quick check of the rearview mirror to make sure the Thunderbird was on the move. She saw the headlights and headed downtown.

Evel maneuvered the car through the opening in the trees. Pleased to hear the screech of the Camaro's tires on Main Street, he wasted no time getting out of the parking lot. But he slowed upon seeing a girl walking down the drag. Red's date.

"Hey. Can I give you a ride somewhere? I left him back there."

"Yes! Please!" Jenny ran to the car and got in. "I'm so sorry..."

Evel held up a hand to stop her. "No problem. We both made a mistake. I can't believe I let that nimrod take my car."

"We didn't spill anything—I mean, I don't think anything's messed up. Can you drop me at the vacant lot? Some of my friends are there."

"Sure, my brother should be there, too." Relieved, Evel's mood heightened greatly once behind the steering wheel of his own car.

"Oh, that's right, *you're* Larry's brother. I've heard about you. Hey, some girls in a yellow car gave Red somethin' for you. I saw 'em at the store. He didn't think I did. It's in a sack in the back seat. I think it's a six-pack."

"Girls? In a yellow Camaro?"

"Yep. Red didn't think I saw, but I did," Jenny said proudly.

Evel nodded slightly. The crew in Tim's parking lot cheered as he drove by; he waved out the window. He pulled off the street into the not-so-vacant lot and let Jenny off. He saluted to Larry and Chip, then made a U-turn onto the drag to return to the donut shop. Quite a crowd had assembled. Fuzzy and Charles held cold beers, then tossed another to Evel as he walked up.

"That's it. We're officially out," Charles said sadly.

Evel reached into the back seat of his car, retrieving the sack. "Not completely, but they ain't cold. I'll throw 'em in the cooler..." Distracted, he dropped the six-pack on the cooler lid, as Fuzzy was speaking.

"Ya know, Evel. You 'bout scared the shit outta me—pullin' me outta Glenda's car that way. My arm kinda hurts. What the hell? FIRE!" Fuzzy jumped up-and-down once and pointed at smoke pouring from the engine compartment of a pickup.

"Oh, no! My dad's truck!" one of the guys yelled. He ran to the pickup he'd apparently borrowed from his father and unlatched the hood.

"NO! Don't raise the hood!" Evel yelled. But it was too late. The three buddies ran over to the now raging fire. The added air from the opened hood caused the small fire to become a full-fledged flame-up. Evel looked around for something to use as a fire extinguisher. Fuzzy prepared to pop the top of his cold beer.

"Hey! Shake up the beers and spray the fire!" Evel ordered.

They violently shook the three beer cans. In unison, the tops were popped and beer spewed onto the fire. As Fuzzy emptied his can to completely extinguish the flames, he laughed sarcastically.

Evel crushed his empty can on the asphalt with his boot. "What's so funny?"

"Those were our last cold ones. Why didn't we use the hot beers to put out the fire?" he asked while sadly shaking his head.

Evel and Charles looked at each other with anguish. Evel shot a meaningful look to Samson, who was behind the crowd. He moved forward, scooped Fuzzy off the ground, and walked across the parking lot with him.

"Look. There goes Fuzzy. Hey, that guy's carryin' him!" Tanya said incredulously. While Glenda pulled into the donut shop, Fuzzy was returned to the ground.

Glenda brought the car to a stop. "Somethin's goin' on. Look at the smoke!" She leaned out the window. "Is everything all right?"

A collective "YEAH!" came from the crowd. The girls got out of the car. But they didn't get far before Charles and Fuzzy ran up. Evel stayed back a bit but also moved toward the yellow Camaro.

"Tanya! Did you see—we put out a fire with beer!" Charles, as usual, was glad to see Tanya. She looked at him like he was crazy.

Glenda looked at Fuzzy, then saw Evel standing in the background. "Did you find the six-pack we left you?" she asked.

"Yep. It's on the cooler. We used the last of our cold ones to put out the fire," Fuzzy stated as if it made the most sense in the world.

Glenda shook her head slowly side-to-side before raising her eyebrows with a thought. She moved a little closer to Evel. "Hey, I've got an idea. There's some in my cooler. We should 'a put your six-pack in, too. Say, if you'll let me keep Ted for a while longer, you can take our cooler. We can trade back sometime."

Evel smiled and nodded. For a moment, they regarded each other in silence. His eyes steadily became more crinkled. Glenda reluctantly broke away from the gaze. She leaned into the back seat to retrieve the cooler. Evel enjoyed the rear view of her tight jeans. "There's six or seven left. Maybe that'll get you through." She handed the cooler to Charles to give him something to hold on to besides Tanya, then opened the driver's side door. "See ya! Y'all be good!"

"Or—good at it!" Tanya added. The girls took off in a flash. The three buddies stood still for a second.

Larry pulled in and walked up to the staring guys. "What's up—what's the matter with y'all? Hey, that girl in the Camaro's pretty cool. She can do a hell of a burnout!" he said to anyone that would listen, as the three people in front of him seemed to be in some sort of trance. But they weren't.

"They gave us beer," Fuzzy said impishly, taking the cooler from Charles.

"Oh, great. Y'all still have beer?" Larry shook his head. On one of the shakes he noticed Samson moving toward him. "Oh, no, you don't. I'm outta here!"

He ran to his car, then peeled out of the parking lot. Those standing about burst out laughing—everyone except the guy with the burnt-up pickup.

"Can we make a drag in the Thunderchicken, Evel?" Fuzzy asked. "We haven't seen the other end of town all night!"

Evel calmly walked to the car. The others followed him with Glenda's cooler. After just a second, the car entered the drag. Just before the new Dairy Queen, Fuzzy saw Evel's tongue stick slightly out his pursed lips in a face of concentration—he knew to hang on tight. Sure enough, Evel grabbed the emergency brake, turning a quick one-eighty.

"Yee Haw! The Dairy Queen Turn Around!" Fuzzy was feeling pretty good now.

The Thunderbird rumbled down the drag. People honked and waved at the familiar vehicle. Boots and Gene had taken their usual places on the wall in front of the boys' dorm. They raised their hands in greeting when the passing Thunderbird honked. Fuzzy waved his hand over the roof of the car at the two guys.

"There they are. OK, the night is now complete. We've seen the King of the Drag," Gene said with a slap to his knee.

"Yep. Well, it's after eleven, and I've been up since six-thirty. I'm headed in," Boots drawled in his strong El Paso accent. It was especially pronounced when he was tired.

"You go ahead. I'm going to watch for Glenda," Gene said. He didn't have to wait long. Within two minutes, the yellow Camaro braked to a dead stop in front of him. The passenger side door opened a bit.

"Hey buddy—lookin' for a good time?" Tanya called, laughing as she flapped the door once. Glenda started to move forward but stopped when she saw Gene running toward the car. Tanya scooted over; he jumped in. They squeezed into the passenger side seat.

"You're squishin' me, Gene. GLENDA!" Tanya cried.

"Hang on. We'll rearrange at the Dairy Queen." Glenda laughed and drove faster.

"Where's Janie?" Gene asked—but got no answer. Tanya couldn't breathe. Glenda was too busy driving in traffic. He sighed, accepted his fate and tried to stop Tanya's incessant slapping.

As the Thunderbird cruised past the courthouse, the guys noticed a crowd beneath the Moo Lah statue. Evel pulled in and parked to find out what was going on. The people standing around were pretty drunk and rowdy. The guys joined them.

"Hey—Moo Lah!" a particularly inebriated fellow slurred. He turned to the crowd and said, "You know, somebody oughta ride that cow!"

Fuzzy perked up, looking at Evel expectantly. Evel shrugged his shoulders and smiled mischievously.

"And we're the guys to do it!" Fuzzy started climbing the fifteen-foot pole which supported the black and white fiberglass cow. Evel was close behind but moved more slowly. They both shimmied their way up to the platform. Fuzzy climbed up on back of the cow. "She's sturdy. Come on up, Evel. Giddy-up. Yee Haw!" Fuzzy held the chain attached to the fake cow by a halter of sorts. He was hopping up-and-down like he was trotting down the trail. Evel climbed up on the cow behind Fuzzy. He began moving his feet as though he were spurring and riding in a rodeo.

Glenda noticed a crowd looking up at something. The lights from the courthouse back lit two gyrating figures. She slowed, gaping at the sight. From the back seat, Gene gasped.

"That's Evel and Fuzzy—Oh, my gosh!" Tanya cried in shock.

Evel saw the Camaro and waved his arm. Tanya pointed at him. Glenda promptly pulled over to join the spectators. The two girls and Gene got out of the car. Suddenly, Glenda felt Evel looking at her. He flashed a smile that made her heart stop. She laughed at the ridiculous sight. The crowd cheered the two fiberglass cowboys, making crude jokes, until someone saw flashing lights.

"Cops!"

Most of the people cleared out of the area as quickly as possible. Glenda, Tanya and Gene made a quick exit, too, but she parked just out of sight around the first corner. The trio exited the Camaro and peeked around the building. Charles and a few others who didn't bother leaving leaned on the rails of a pickup bed, waiting for the inevitable.

Two police cars slid to a stop in the parallel parking spaces on the town square. The cops piled out and gawked at the sight fifteen feet above them. Fuzzy still yelled "Yee Haw," and Evel was now turned backward, facing away from his friend. He was looking for the Camaro, but saw the policemen and saluted them. He elbowed Fuzzy to get his attention. Fuzzy acknowledged the cops with a tip of an imaginary hat. All of a sudden, Evel slipped a bit—but he quickly grabbed hold of Moo Lah's tail.

"What on earth are you doin'? Are you crazy? You git down from there right now! I'm gonna arrest you. This time you two have gone too far! GIT DOWN HERE!" Officer Pettijohn was practically having a coronary.

Not surprisingly, the other cop, Officer House, was laughing uncontrollably. "Oh, my goodness gracious. Y'all pulled a good one this time!" He laughed so hard his eyes watered.

Charles and the other witnesses moved away from the raving cop toward the giggling officer, laughing with him.

"Stop laughin'. Dammit House. Make 'em git down here!" The red-faced Pettijohn shook his fist at Fuzzy and Evel. The riders stayed on the cow—way up high and out of reach—with silly grins on their faces.

"Come on down, boys," House said, trying to catch his breath. He waved his hand at the airborne pair, beckoning them to descend.

"Sure thing, Officer House. All ya had to do was ask nice like," Evel said amiably. "You first, Fuz."

Fuzzy slid off the cow, losing his balance and barely hanging on to the chain that had served as reins. The chain was longer than it first appeared—a fortunate thing, because he lost his footing and slipped off the platform. He dangled in the air for a second or two, his feet kicking, before one end of the chain came loose from its fastening to the cow. Fuzzy dropped several feet quite suddenly and twirled at the end of that chain for another second.

Not unexpectedly, the chain broke completely loose with a loud thunk. He fell to the ground. Charles ran over to help. But Fuzzy jumped right up on his feet, obviously not hurt.

"Git him! Handcuff him, House. Allen, you git down here now!" Pettijohn was still worked up.

"Calm down, Mad Dog. Take it easy!" House said to his colleague. "They're not hurtin' anything. I knew someday somebody would do this. Figures it was these two!"

"Don't you Mad Dog me. They've gone too far, I tell ya. Oh, hell, you wanna handle it? Then handle it!" Pettijohn yelled at House. He turned on his heel growling, as he marched to his car. He left the scene in a huff.

Meanwhile, the second rider slid carefully down the pole and landed on the pavement in front of the still chuckling House. When Evel's feet hit the ground, he fell backward to lean on the wide metal pole. His great sigh of relief was both visible and audible. Abruptly, his knees collapsed; his body slipped into a squatting position.

A shaken Evel looked up abjectly at the delighted policeman. "Oh, man. Why didn't somebody remind me I'm afraid of heights?"

Chapter Eleven

AFTER A SIMPLE LUNCH of ham sandwiches and corn chips, three of the local Allens lounged on the front porch of the historic house on Main Street. It was a cool afternoon; a light blue Norther had blown through the area overnight. A true blue Norther brings icy cold winds, sweeping down from Canada and the Arctic Circle, but the gentle breeze on this Saturday afternoon must have originated somewhere around Wyoming, as the temperature was pleasantly cool.

Betty and Dub were rocking in the glider, reminiscing. "Yep. That was good bread in those sandwiches, but there was nothin' like those hot, fresh biscuits mama used to bake in her old wood cook stove. Hot biscuits with fresh butter I'd churned just a few days before would melt and drip all down my fingers. I'd slurp up every drop from my fingertips down to my knuckles," Dub said enthusiastically.

"Now I keep my flowerpots and pottin' soil in that old cook stove in the backyard," Bettie teased. "Can you imagine? They toted that big heavy thing all the way from Missouri! And nobody uses real butter anymore. Dub, you know everything's better with Bluebonnet on it."

Dub ignored her remarks and cleared his throat. Evel glanced fondly up at his aunt from his perch on the top wooden step. They had heard Dub's stories many times and shared a moment of mutual understanding. They let him talk—it was good for him. It was good for all of them.

"Uhmmhmm. Where was I? Oh—and that strawberry shortcake! We picked all kinds of crops up there in Southern Missouri where Papa moved the family durin' The Depression, ya know. But our favorite was the strawberries. We got to keep all the over-ripe ones—those that was too soft to survive the shippin' to the big cities where people had some money, and *oowee* were they sweet! Mama would whip that fresh cream from Daisy, the milk cow—and bake mounds of sweetened pie dough, and she'd make strawberry shortcake in a dishpan. 'Course with twelve kids, we needed a lot of shortcake. Those were the days," Dub said with a sigh.

Sadly, many of his siblings had passed away and never saw 1980. Evel's father and Uncle Dub were the youngest of that generation, the folks that endured The Depression, fought and won a World War, survived the 1960's and were now watching the next generation build a nuclear power plant over in the next county. But the old memories are the best, perhaps because one has the option to forget the bad and recall only the good.

"You know, Glenn, I could never make pie dough like your grandma. Isn't that right, Dub? Well, at least never in that quantity!" Bettie exclaimed.

"Sugar Babe—now, that may be true, but you make the best homemade bread in the world." Dub patted Bettie's blue-jeaned knee.

"Yes. Well, that's another story."

"Tell us, Aunt Bettie!"

"It's pretty embarrassin', actually. My friend down the street gave me a loaf of this bread recently, and it was so good—I asked for the recipe. She gave a copy to me, but I couldn't quite make out all the details. So, I called her up, and she said she'd drop off the original so I could see it. The next day I found it in the mail box. It was my own recipe from fifteen years ago. I felt so silly!"

"Yeah, but no wonder it was good bread, Sugar Babe. It was yours!" Dub slapped his knee.

"Oh, Aunt Bettie. I'm sorry, but that's funny," Evel said. He laughed with his uncle.

"Yes. Well, at my expense, I suppose. While I'm at it, did I ever tell you about the time I rode a bus all the way from Lubbock here to Dairyville to see Dub? No? Well, that was one long ride, I tell ya. He was home on leave from the Navy durin' the war. He'd sent a letter to tell me he was here at home. So, I popped a note off to him, care of his mama, that I'd come see him here, since he'd already met my family a few months before. We actually met at college in Lubbock before the war, ya know. Anyways, Dad drove me to the bus station and dropped me off for a seven o'clock in the evening departure. The bus driver didn't show up and that delayed us an hour. When we finally got a driver, he didn't know the route and had never been very far from Lubbock. He got us good and lost. Somehow, he turned off on a dirt road out in the middle of nowhere and just about ran the bus into a lake. When he was turnin' the bus around, he got it stuck in the mud, and we had to wait till morning when a local farmer used his tractor to pull the bus out."

"Man! I guess they'd let just about anybody drive a bus back then!" Evel said with a laugh.

Dub smiled knowingly as Bettie continued. "Yes. Well, that isn't all. Even when he did find a town where we were supposed to stop, he couldn't find the bus station. He actually got off the bus and asked local residents where it was. They thought he was jokin', but unfortunately…he wasn't. Anyways, after a time or two of that hooey if nobody needed off at the next town, he didn't even bother tryin' to find the actual bus station. We just skipped that town. Luckily, the next major station was on the main highway, easy to find, and we were blessed with some more passengers and a new driver who seemed to halfway know where he was goin'. One of the new ladies had motion sickness real bad, and we had to stop and let her off to throw up pretty often. We finally got into Central Texas. My ticket was for Waco, because nobody in West Texas had a clue where Dairyville was. When I saw a sign for Dairyville, I got my bag out from under the seat, walked up to the front of the bus and asked to be dropped off. The driver said, 'You've paid to go to Waco', but I insisted this was my actual destination. He let me off right in the middle of downtown. I walked past the courthouse and over to the drugstore on the corner and called the Allen's phone number. Yes, they had phones back then. They said they'd send Dub's little sister Kay to pick me up. About a half an hour later, this teenaged girl walked up to me where I'd been sittin' on a bench in front of the store. She'd never seen me before, so I stood up since she was the one evidently there to 'git' me. I quickly discerned we did not have a ride to the house. We walked the half-mile or so up here in virtual silence to this very house. Only then did I find out what Kay had been avoidin' tellin' me all durin' that long walk. Dub had been called back to duty. He wasn't even here!"

This was a story Evel hadn't heard before. "Oh, no! But they got your letter?"

"Oh, yes. It passed in the mail with his to me sayin' he had to leave for Corpus Christi the day before I was to arrive. Mail service was pretty slow. There was a war on, ya know. Well, I had a nice visit with your grandma and Kay and got to know this house, so it wasn't a total loss," Bettie said.

"Yep. I made sure that didn't happen again. We got married during my next leave!" Dub said happily. "Thirty-five years later we're still goin' strong!" He leaned over and kissed his wife on the cheek.

"Wow. I know times were rough then, but some of it sounds pretty good to me. We're lucky these days if we have store-bought canned biscuits, and whipped topping comes in a squirt can, not from a cow!" Evel added jokingly.

"Maybe so, my boy. But at least you have your own wheels and money for gas. I do believe these are your good old days, ya know."

"Ya know. I believe you're right, Uncle Dub, and sometimes they're very good. In fact, I'd better get movin' and see what's in store for tonight."

Evel rose from the top step. He stretched a bit, but cut it short when a vehicle pulled into the circle drive behind the Thunderbird.

"Evel! Come quick. Larry had a wreck!" Chip yelled urgently. Dub and Bettie moved toward the steps, concerned.

"Where? Is he OK?" Evel ran toward Chip's open driver door. Chip was half-in and half-out of his Camaro.

"Yeah. I saw him. He's OK. But the car...Oh, man. I'm glad I found ya. You'd better get up there."

"Chip. Where is he?" Evel asked sternly. He noticed his hand was shaking, as he leaned on Chip's hood. Blood pounded in his ears as he tried to control his impatience. "Where?"

"Oh, sorry. He's in front of the college. You know—on the wall." Chip slid down in the driver's seat. Evel rushed to the Thunderbird and turned the key to start the engine.

"I'm comin' with you, Glenn," Dub called. He hurried as best as he could down the porch steps. He opened the passenger side door and got in. Evel glanced at his uncle and noted the resolve on the weathered face.

"We'll be back in a while, Sugar Babe. Maybe I can help," Dub called to his worried wife. Bettie waved and bravely watched the Thunderbird peel out of the driveway with Chip in close pursuit.

There wasn't much traffic on Main Street, so they made it to the site of the accident quickly. The police had already arrived, and Evel stopped behind the cop car. Larry hopped up from his perch on the wall when he saw his brother and uncle approach.

"Uncle Dub! Brother Glenn! Oh, man, am I glad to see y'all. The throttle stuck wide open. They don't believe me!" He leaned on his brother's arm.

"You all right?" Evel asked. Larry nodded. Evel returned the nod and handed him to their uncle. He turned his attention to the amazing sight of the Nova on the wall.

"Larry. How in the wide, wide world of sports did you manage that?" he asked loudly. The Allens and Chip walked over to the Nova. The engine was still running at a very high RPM.

"No doubt he was gittin' all over it around this corner and lost it," said the smug Officer Pettijohn from behind. "Throttle hung—hehe—yeah right."

The Allen men and Chip stood looking at the Nova in awe. It was perfectly astraddle and balanced on the stone wall in front of the boys' dormitory. The back tires were still turning fast, as if the transmission was still in Drive. The engine roared loudly. Evel walked over to the front of the car, threw one foot over the wall and stood with a leg on either side of the low wall. He noticed they were very close to where the college kids liked to sit at night to watch the cars go past. He faced the rumbling vehicle and opened the hood. Dub joined him. With a reach into the engine compartment, the older man touched the accelerator linkage with one finger. The engine immediately quieted and the back wheels slowed.

"See, Pettijohn? It WAS stuck!" Larry said triumphantly to the officer.

"Humph. Yeah...well maybe. But how you gonna git this car off this wall?" the officer asked sardonically.

Evel stifled a chuckle. "I can't figure out how he got it up there in the first place!" He reached into the car to turn the key to "off." The engine was immediately silenced. But the back tires kept turning for a few seconds—the car rocked ominously from side-to-side after he shut the driver side door.

Suddenly, Samson appeared from nowhere and walked up to the scene. He looked around intently—his eyes locked on Evel.

"No, Samson. You'd better not. I think we need more than your muscles to lift this car off the wall without tearin' anything else up," Evel said.

He clapped the strong man on the shoulder. Samson nodded with understanding, shook hands with Evel—then walked silently away. Evel shook his head side-to-side. That was truly an unusual fellow. Good as gold—but a bit strange.

Boots and Gene heard the commotion through their dorm room window. They walked across the grass in front of the building, startled to see a car sitting on the wall. They stopped and stared. It was the Nova they'd seen pass by many times. By all appearances, some giant somebody picked the car straight up from its normal, proper position on the asphalt street, moved it over some fifteen feet to the right and set it long-ways on top of the rock wall. There were people all around, but the police car was leaving.

"Hey, there. Oh, man, this is bad. Aren't they gonna get you a wrecker or something?" Gene asked in the general direction of the teetering vehicle.

Evel laughed sarcastically. "In this town? No way. Here, you're on your own. Heck, last month when that old man pulled out in front of Daniel's Monte Carlo—and we wrecked—we had to leave the car in the ditch and walk to his grandma's house!"

Dub looked shocked. The older man was appalled at what he heard. "We shall see about this. I'm makin' a phone call first thing Monday mornin' to the police chief," he said indignantly.

"You want me to go in the dorm and call somebody?" Gene asked.

"Yeah, that's a good idea. Call Hambone's Garage and see if they'll send Jackson with the wrecker. Tell 'em where we are and what's happened. They might need to bring a winch truck, too," Evel said.

Gene walked over to him and reached out to shake this surprisingly nice guy's hand. Evel returned the handshake with one of his crinkly smiles. "I'm Gene. Glad to actually meet you. This is Boots—I mean Jim."

Gene pointed to his friend in the cowboy hat. Evel nodded cordially at Boots—and received a tip of a cowboy hat in return greeting.

"Glenn Allen—otherwise known as Evel Knievel. Hell, I'll answer to just about anything. Thanks, man. Tell 'em to hurry. Larry's not blockin' traffic, but we are!" Evel chuckled. He was glad about Gene's offer to phone for the wrecker—it saved a walk to the pay phone at the Dairy Queen. And time.

Gene waved, grabbed Boots and said, "Come on." The two hurried back to the red brick building. Gene found a phone book, called the Hambone Garage and gave them Evel's instructions. Then he called Janie.

It didn't take long for traffic to back up. Not surprisingly, Jackson took some time maneuvering through traffic to reach the scene in the wrecker, what with another garage mechanic following in a flat bed truck with a long pole and chain attachment. He finally stopped behind the Thunderbird.

Gene returned to the unfolding spectacle, watched and listened to the group discuss the best way to remove the car from the wall with the least damage to both. He also kept an eye out for Janie and Tanya. After the girls arrived, they all became enthralled with the sight of removing a car from the stone wall.

Evel moved his vehicle to a position well in front of the scene. The winch truck backed up toward the Nova. Jackson took control of a mechanism that released a chain and a hook. With some strong straps, strategic positioning of the lifting devices and several steps of repositioning, they moved the car toward Main Street, inch-by-inch. After about ten minutes of careful manipulation, the Nova was placed successfully on its own four wheels on the asphalt. It had one flat tire—but otherwise, it looked all right.

Like a stock car pit crew, several guys worked together, quickly changing the flat tire. Evel watched to be sure the Nova was functioning properly with Larry behind the wheel. Satisfied, the drivers and their cars took off and disappeared around the curve. A few minutes later all the vehicles were gone—with traffic again resuming its lazy Saturday afternoon pace. The only evidence of this newest major dilemma was a rock and some mortar missing from the wall.

"OK—now what?" Janie asked excitedly. "That was quite a sight. I'm glad you called, Gene. Bring on the next entertainment!"

"Yeah. I wish Glenda had come with us. She'd have been real interested in how they moved that car around like that," Tanya added. "Hey, it's a little cool out, but why don't we go down to the city park?"

"Yeah! We could swing and climb trees and ride the merry-go-round." Janie liked the idea. Gene rolled his eyes, because he knew who'd be pushing the swings and the merry-go-round, but Janie chose to ignore him. "Tan-ay, you drivin'?" Janie asked. Neither she nor Gene had a car at school.

"Not I. I'm outta oil, and it's a week until I get my monthly allowance from Uncle Sam. What about Boots?"

"No chance," said Gene. "He must have something going on this afternoon. He disappeared when I went to call the garage. Let's go inside and call Glenda. She might want to go." The three headed to the dorm to make the phone call.

She answered on the fifth ring. "OK. OK. I'll be over in a minute to pick y'all up. I'm just about ready, anyways." Glenda said goodbye and hung the receiver back on the cradle. Linda Lou had ignored the ringing phone. She was standing very still, staring out their north window.

Glenda walked over to stand beside her. "Tan-ay and them wanna go to the park. You wanna go?" She followed Linda's gaze. A young man was leaning on a car that was parked in a space on the one-way street in front of the dorm. "Well, well. How long has he been down there?"

"Just a few minutes. He called while you were in the shower and said he wanted to see me. I don't know, Glenda. He's younger than most guys I've dated," Linda said in a whisper. She stood staring down at the male figure leaning on an extremely ugly car. "We're supposed to go to a reception tonight in his mother's honor. Why did he have to get here early?"

"Early? Too young? He's no baby. That's for sure. He drives all the way up from College Station to see you before the big party, and you ask questions? You've gotta go talk to him, Linda. Face it, he's taken quite a fancy to you, and I do believe the feeling is mutual." Glenda patted Linda's shoulder, then fluffed Linda's long brown hair, which had obviously been in hot rollers quite recently. "Besides, it appears you've gotten spiffied up for some reason this afternoon."

Linda Lou quickly turned to her roommate with panic in her eyes. "You goin' down? Walk with me," she sighed, reaching for her purse.

The girls approached the young man who was dressed in jeans and a brown plaid flannel shirt with the cuffs turned up. He casually leaned on the multicolored car with one knee bent and his hiking boot resting on the dented front bumper. Glenda was struck with the confident ease in his manner and the twinkle in his blue eyes when he saw Linda. There's a fellow in love, she thought to herself, glancing at her roommate and best friend. Glenda stopped herself from physically nodding her head, as she saw the small smile begin on Linda Lou's lips that was matched by the shine from her eyes. The two girls halted several feet from the young man.

"Hi there," he said brightly. "Hi, Linda." He stood up to face the girls. "Hi, Glenda."

"Hey, Lee. If you don't look like the lumberjack! All you need's a hatchet and a hat with ear flaps. You mean you drove that wreck halfway across Texas today?" Glenda teased.

"Naa. Just three hours...from A&M. Hey, better a lumberjack than an axe murderer! Please don't knock the spotted ape." Lee patted the hood of his 1970 Plymouth Barracuda. "It doesn't look like much, but it'll get ya where you wanna go. Linda, are you ready?"

Linda Lou didn't answer—she just stood there, rooted to the sidewalk beneath her feet. Her eyes glazed over a bit. Lee's eyebrows drew together with concern. Glenda leaned toward her friend to touch her on the arm. Linda turned her whole body away from Lee, looking into Glenda's eyes with what could only be called "fear." Glenda gently took her friend by the shoulders, turned her to again face the patiently waiting young man, and nudged the girl in his direction. He took the cue, moved forward to calmly take Linda's arm and led her to the passenger side of his car. After she was inside, Lee walked quickly around the front of the car, winked at Glenda and mouthed, "thanks." Glenda smiled as they drove away.

Glenda turned to walk to her Camaro—but stopped dead in her tracks. Kevin drove his Matador past Horne Hall on the west side. She involuntarily ducked down behind a car to hide until he was gone. Strangely, suddenly, Glenda felt alone—embarrassed—wondering why she was hiding. The terrible awareness settled so quickly—like a thick patch of fog—causing her to feel somewhat overcome.

After a moment, the foggy sensation lifted for the most part, but sadness remained. Glenda walked slowly to her car. She started the car's engine and slammed her new Little River Band tape into the player almost out of self-defense. Suddenly, the song "Cool Change" grabbed her senses. The words were so meaningful and strong that Glenda turned up the volume to flush the negativity out of the open car windows. The awful sensation was completely gone. She felt much more happy and contented upon arrival at the boys' dorm to pick up her friends.

The world was turning round and round and round. Clouds and trees were spinning wildly above Tanya and Janie. They lay flat on their backs on the floor of the merry-go-round, while Glenda and Gene pushed it faster and faster. The two girls were squealing—hanging on to the middle handle to keep from being flung into the dirt. As Tanya slid, her sneaker kicked Gene in the leg. She was losing the battle with centrifugal force.

"Ow! OK, that's it. OW!" Gene cried. Another foot hit his leg even harder. He limped away from the merry-go-round. Janie and Tanya were giggling uncontrollably as their rotations slowed to a stop. When they stepped onto the substantially slower rotating earth, they stumbled about.

"Wowie zowie. Now that *will* alter your state of awareness!" Tanya said happily, leaning against Glenda. Janie lost her balance and fell into Gene's arms—to his pleasant surprise. He closed his eyes and placed his chin gently on top of her curly head. Glenda looked surprised at the sight. Tanya whispered in her ear: "Didn't ya see this comin'?" Glenda shook her head "no," then helped Tanya to the picnic table.

Janie pulled back from Gene awkwardly. She hurriedly walked past her friends to stand next to the Sittin' Tree. In Central Texas, live oaks usually grow in groves of between just two and several hundred trees. Occasionally, the trees on the outer edges of the grove grow horizontally, rising only a few feet from the ground, stretching out from under the taller, older trees to reach the sunlight. The Sittin' Tree was such an oak, the lone survivor of a grove that stood in the path of a new road through the park. The trunk emerged from the earth near the edge of the riverbank and was about four feet in diameter. It rose no more than six feet in vertical height—but it stretched some twelve feet horizontally. The tree's eventual height was uncertain, as the trunk was quite long and the canopy reached across the narrow river. This configuration made it perfect for climbing and sitting.

Janie, apparently recovered from her dizziness and possibly trying to escape Gene, scrambled up the trunk, politely setting her butt down on the rough bark of the tree. However, Gene wasn't far behind. Glenda and Tanya looked at each other, shrugged, and in a most unladylike fashion started climbing. All four perched on the horizontal tree like "birds on a wire." Except these birds wore sneakers and swung their feet.

Tanya looked over her shoulder. "Remember when we practiced softball at that field on the other side of the river?"

"Yeah. We were the Mixed Nuts. I was Peanuts, and Glenda was Almonds!" Janie said.

"Right, and Glenda got the poison ivy. Ooowee. It was awful!"

"Sure was. She looked like she'd been in a motorcycle wreck!"

"When was this? I don't remember anything about that," Gene asked of Glenda.

"It was before we knew you, you silly boy. It was really horrible, the worst case of poison ivy I've ever had. Believe me—I've had it plenty," Glenda said with a shudder. "I'm extremely allergic to it."

"I guess I'm not—I've never had it. But what's this about a motorcycle wreck?" Gene still couldn't understand.

"If you've never had it, yep, you're probably not allergic, lucky you. OK, here's the whole story. I messed up and threw the ball over the fence down there," Glenda pointed across the river toward the ball field. "It had rolled down the river bank almost to the water. It was a nice day in February. We were in shorts and T-shirts, and I didn't even think about poison ivy. I mean, there's no leaves, right? I must a' scraped my left arm directly on a vine, as I slipped and slid my way down to get the ball. And some of my other parts apparently encountered the insidious stuff on the way back up. That was on a Thursday evening. By Sunday afternoon when I got back from Dallas, my arm was horribly swollen, and I was miserable. These sweet girls had just gotten back from the Udder Delight. They were laughin', as they walked down the hall—until they saw me sittin' there in tears all red and bumpy. They dropped their ice cream cones in the sink right then and there and took me to the hospital."

"Sure did. She couldn't even bend her arm, so Tanya drove us," Janie added.

"Anyway, the ever-so-clever doctor there at the emergency room gave me shots and medicine and wrapped up my whole left arm, part of my right arm, and three places on my legs in gauze and tape. Hence, the appearin' to have been in a motorcycle accident."

"I took a picture of you like that, Glenda," Janie said sweetly. "I have it somewhere."

"Gee thanks. I'll want a copy of *that one* for my scrapbook," Glenda said sarcastically.

"Hey, look!" Tanya pointed toward the park road where a car approached. She cupped her hands around her mouth: "HEY!!"

Evel was making a razoo through the park before heading home to shower and get ready for Saturday night. Slowing, he crossed the low bridge over the river, then turned a corner. Surprised to see the yellow Camaro parked by a picnic table, he let off the accelerator, slowing even more to take a closer look around. No one was at the table or in the car or anywhere in sight. Evel shrugged and stepped on the gas pedal again. He slammed on the brakes upon hearing Tanya's shout.

"Hello! We're up here!" Tanya's hands were still cupped around her mouth. Janie and Glenda waved.

What the hell? Evel backed up quickly and expertly slid the Thunderbird into a parked position directly beside the Camaro. He walked over to the tree with an amused look. "Ahem. There's no need to go out on a *limb* for me."

"Oh, don't worry about him. His *bark* is much worse than his bite," Glenda said.

"I'm *stumped* for something to say," Gene added. They were on a roll.

"I don't know about you *tree*, but I'm crackin' up!" Janie exclaimed.

"Look out. We might be at the *root* of all evil!" Tanya added.

Evel slapped his thigh. "If this is the way things are goin', I'm gonna *leaf*!"

"No, don't go...Ohhh!" Glenda cried.

She slipped and fell from the limb. Gene tried to catch her, but she dropped beyond his reach. It really wasn't very far to the ground, so she landed on her feet in front of Evel. But inertia took over; she fell toward him. Evel easily caught her by the elbows, steadying her small frame. Glenda felt his strong arms on hers and looked up into his eyes. Suddenly, she found herself peering deeply into the man whose very blue eyes were also gazing into hers. The attraction was palpable, almost tangible. Each felt the sensation of the connection like a lightning bolt.

They stood mesmerized for a few seconds. Then, as if on cue, the physical connection was broken, as each took a step backward and looked away.

"Will you be out later? Would you wanna go ridin' around?" Evel asked quietly, as his eyes returned to her face.

Glenda stood very still for a second—still feeling the electricity. She glanced up at him with a smile. "Oh, yes, I surely would."

"Good. Well, I'll see ya later." Evel felt awkward but relieved—an odd sensation for the King of the Drag. "Maybe we could drink a beer."

"No thanks. I don't drink beer—it looks like pee." Glenda startled Evel with the off-hand comment. "Besides, I'm silly enough without alcohol. Get me a Dr Pepper, and I'm a happy camper!"

Evel nodded, considering his curiosity of finding a good-looking college girl who didn't drink beer and drove a hot rod car. Amazing. He looked up at the three on the tree. "If y'all ever wanna *branch* out, let me know!"

"Now, that's what I call corny!" Tanya replied.

"Tan-ay! He's funny! But whack him for me anyway, Glenda!" Janie called jokingly.

Glenda moved toward Evel, attempting to smack his arm with her hand. But he dodged the blow and hurried to his car, laughing. He was gone in a flash of silver, so to speak.

Tanya watched the Thunderbird rumble away. "He really is pretty corny. Hey, I think I hear pizza callin'. Are y'all hungry?" Janie reached around Gene to slap her roommate's arm. He automatically put his hand on her back to steady her. Tanya leaned back to avoid the blow, but Janie was still able to deliver the whack.

"Yes. I'm hungry. Yeah, he's corny. But man, is he funny. Uhh ohhh, look out below!" Janie lost her balance and grabbed the others. They all fell laughing from their tree.

After a long, hot shower and a little extra cologne, Evel donned his best western shirt and boots. He drove back into town to find his running buddies. Fuzzy and Charles were ready for Saturday night. They were parked at Tim's, having already made the run to Riverview in Charles' car. The two guys joined Evel in the Thunderbird. Surprisingly, Fuzzy offered to buy gas for the evening.

"What's this, Fuz? You must a' got a raise," Evel said. He only had half a tank of fuel—it wouldn't hurt to top it off.

"Matter of fact, I did. Go to Curry's Quick Stop. You can gas up, and I can git some gum," Fuzzy said happily.

A few minutes later, Evel was putting the gas cap back on and Fuzzy was walking back to the car, looking down, struggling with the gum wrapper. Suddenly, a pickup truck raced into the station. The driver slammed on the brakes, but he didn't see Fuzzy until it was too late. The pickup truck slid—with the large bumper knocking Fuzzy off his feet. His body was propelled toward a metal sign weighted at the bottom and equipped with a spring. A strong wind gust could cause such a sign to pivot back-and-forth—with it eventually returning to the upright position.

Fuzzy's entire body landed on the sign. It bent completely to the ground under the impact of his weight. But the spring hinge did its work, catapulting the sign back to an upright position and Fuzzy to his feet. The sign was swinging back-and-forth.

Fuzzy had also come up swinging. "You son of a bitch! You HIT me! Where is he—where is he?" Fuzzy yelled and peered at the offending pickup in a rage.

Evel quickly grabbed his friend from behind, lifting him off the ground. "Lemme at him! I'll beat the shit outta him! Let...me...go!"

Evel held on to Fuzzy tightly—quite a challenge, since he was enraged, kicking and throwing punches into the air. Charles calmly joined the scene. He looked at the pickup driver who had unwisely gotten out of his vehicle.

"I'm sorry. I didn't see him there," the driver said loudly.

"Man, you better just hop in your truck and get outta here," Charles said firmly.

"It was an accident. He ain't hurt is he?"

"No. But *you* will be if you don't—get outta—here!" Evel managed to say, as Fuzzy continued to struggle.

"That's right. My friend can't hang on to this wild-man much longer. You'd better leave—now!" Charles insisted.

The driver took the advice, retreated and drove away as quickly as he could. Evel released Fuzzy, then stood back so the crazy little guy could settle down.

"He *hit* me with his pickup! Do you believe that? I could a' taken him, ya know. I was that mad!" Fuzzy was still angry, but a bit calmer. "Hey, Evel, you smell extra good this evenin'—what's up?"

Evel reached out to grab his friend, but Fuzzy was too quick, still fairly pumped up with adrenaline. The pack of gum was lying on the pavement by the still swinging sign. Evel picked it up. He smiled mischievously at Fuzzy, who was safely positioned on the opposite side of the Thunderbird, and tossed the gum across the hood. Fuzzy easily caught it.

"Just for that—you get to buy supper. How 'bout Pizza Place? Charles, doesn't that sound good?" Evel adjusted his sleeve cuffs—they had come unrolled while wrestling with Fuzzy.

"Yeah, you bet!" Charles slapped Fuzzy on the back. "Thanks Fuz—let's go!"

Fuzzy frowned—pulled out his wallet to check his stash of bills. He nodded, accepting his fate. Besides, The Pizza Place made the best pizza in town. It was a great hang-out. The second story windows looked out over the drag, and they gave out playing cards as claim tickets for your order. They also had video games—"Pac Man" and "Space Invaders."

As Evel drove toward The Pizza Place, he silently watched the green AC Cobra drive past. He really loved that car. Well, not that particular car. He'd probably have a different color—silver most likely. The driver gave him a salute; he nodded amiably in reply. He noticed Glenda's yellow Camaro parked in front just before turning into the restaurant parking lot, quickly altering his course to park on the far side.

Two of the three guys were puzzled. "Why'd you park over here?" Charles asked, shutting the passenger side door.

"I don't wanna be seen with you clowns…it's shady over here…what of it?" Evel said defensively. Apparently, the accused clowns hadn't noticed the Camaro.

"Forget it. Come on, let's go in," Fuzzy said.

They went in the side door and ordered. Evel checked out the first floor. Not seeing Glenda, he decided she was likely upstairs. Her friends were playing "Space Invaders", but concentrating on the game and hadn't noticed the new arrivals in the restaurant.

"Let's go upstairs," Charles suggested.

Before Fuzzy could answer, Evel did. "No, let's sit over here where we can see the car," he said nonchalantly.

The other two accepted the decision. It was not uncommon for Evel to want to watch over his car. They squeezed into a booth with tall sides and talked quietly. Before long, their food was ready. They devoured two complete pizzas. Evel slid his large frame out of the booth and stretched. They were headed toward the door when they heard people walking down the stairs behind them. Evel turned around—

—and found himself face-to-face with Glenda.

"Hi. Are you on the way in or on the way out?" She side-stepped him to walk to the counter and get her "to go" cup refilled with ice and Dr Pepper.

"We were about to leave. Y'all wanna go with us?" Charles asked.

"Noper. Not me. I've gotta go back to the dorm for a while. But Glenda can go," Tanya said sweetly.

Glenda took her drink from the young man behind the counter, throwing a question at Tanya with her eyes. Tanya just widened her own eyes a bit, so that Glenda got the message she'd been set up. It couldn't have been prearranged, but she wondered. She also wondered why didn't he come upstairs and say "hello." She didn't like it when things got out of her control.

"But we're in my car. Are y'all gonna walk back to the college?" Glenda asked.

Janie and Gene had overheard the conversation. They joined the group at the foot of the stairs. "I know. We could take your car out and meet you somewhere later, Glenda," Janie suggested.

Glenda laughed out loud. "Y'all take MY car OUT? Yeah, *right*. Neither of you has driven anything lately. That just leaves Tanya, or you walk," she said.

"Great. Gimme the keys!" Tanya said to a surprised Glenda, who grudgingly handed over her keys. She hadn't considered Tanya would take her up on it.

"One drag—just ONE. Then park it. Got it?" Glenda commanded.

"Sure, sure. But where?" Tanya asked impatiently. She was anxious to sit behind the wheel of the famous Camaro.

"You can stop at the donut shop. Just don't park too close to the building or you'll get blocked in. We'll meet up with y'all there after we make a few drags," Evel said evenly. "Be careful," he added, with a glance at Glenda

"Right. And be alert!" Janie giggled.

"Yeah. We need more 'lerts!" Tanya exclaimed, as she and the others ran out the front door to the Camaro.

Glenda turned back to the guys. "Oh, mah *good*ness. Ah have been de*suht*ed by my com*pan*ions, and they have *stol*en my *cahh*. May Ah make a drag or two with y'all?" she asked, rolling out her Southern-damsel-in-distress accent. Evel smiled his crinkly smile at her.

"Sure. But I got shotgun. You're in the back with Charles!" Fuzzy said happily. Evel's facial expression turned quickly to a glare. But Fuzzy didn't notice. He was already out the side door of The Pizza Place.

Being out on the drag in the Thunderchicken, as Fuzzy called Evel's car, was a strange and unique experience for Glenda. Almost everywhere people waved, yelled, or otherwise greeted Evel in his very large and distinctive vehicle. She thought it must be a little like being an extra in a movie—in the shadows behind the stars. Fuzzy sat up front like a grand marshal in a parade. Glenda was amused at the thought and took a sip from her drink. The liquid was nearly gone, so she shook the cup quickly side-to-side to loosen the remaining ice. The rattling noise was rather loud.

Fuzzy jumped. "Snake! Rattlesnake!" he screamed, jumping up-and-down in the seat.

"Calm down, Fuz. It was just Glenda's drink!" Charles and Evel laughed, as Fuzzy turned to look in the back. Glenda held up the cup, shaking it again to make the same noise.

"Man. That scared me!"

"Fuz. Why would a rattlesnake be in the car with us?" Evel asked wistfully.

"You don't think logically when you hear things like that, Evel. It just sounded like a rattlesnake!"

"Truth is—you don't think too much, do ya Fuz?" Charles asked, as he slapped the back of his friend's fuzzy head. The *slapee* turned around in the seat to get at Charles.

"Stop it now. We're pullin' over. Get out you two!" Evel commanded. He whipped the car into the donut shop parking lot. He was relieved to see the Camaro already there. As soon as the Thunderbird came to a stop its passengers quickly exited to escape the driver's wrath. Except Glenda.

Evel turned slightly to look over his shoulder at Glenda, finding her leaning up toward him. He quickly turned back toward the windshield. "Sorry about that. That didn't work out like I'd hoped. Would you...wanna ride around again later?"

He felt a light touch on his shoulder. "Yes, I would. But next time, I wanna sit up there," Glenda said softly, removing her hand from his shoulder and pointing beside him. She noticed he smelled really good and was turning to look at her. She quickly withdrew her hand, sliding over to the right—to exit the car. But she paused to make eye contact with Glenn Allen.

"So...I'll see ya later?" he asked hopefully.

"Definitely. Tell ya what. I'll park my car at the college and be at the Shoe Bench across from the dorm about ten. If ya can—come by then. See ya later, Glenn."

Glenda found herself again looking deeply into his blue eyes and saw the edges crinkle into rather charming smile lines. She committed that smile to memory, returning it with her own unique smile. She jauntily handed her empty cup to Fuzzy—then turned to run toward the Camaro.

"How did it go?" Tanya asked.

"Don't be so nosy," Janie said sternly from the back seat. Gene remained silent.

"I'm not nosy. I'm on a quest for knowledge," Tanya said— her pride injured.

"You most certainly are nosy, Tan-ay!" exclaimed Glenda. "For your information, I may go ridin' around with him later. Besides, I need to return his Ted Nugent tape and retrieve my cooler."

"Really? Wow, Glenda. He's the King of the Drag. Before, I thought he was kind of a scary character, but he actually seems all right," Gene said.

"Yeah. I'm not sure what I think, but somethin' tells me he's OK," Glenda said philosophically. "Anyway, I reckon I'll find out. My mama always says 'you never know till you try'!"

"And she's right, you know, ya just might be on to a good thing," Janie agreed.

Tanya and Glenda looked at each other meaningfully. Sometimes, they knew what each other was thinking.

"And too much of a good thing is…" Tanya began.

"Wonderful!"

Glenda finished the statement from a poster with the Mae West quote on her dorm room wall. All the occupants laughed. Gene took Janie's hand and held it to his chest—then kissed it. Janie looked at him with surprise. Tanya pulled out the Ted tape, purposefully tossed it into Glenda's lap and plugged in REO Speed Wagon. They sang, honked and jammed their way up the drag to "Lucky."

Chapter Twelve

A LATE-MODEL "ARREST ME" red Mustang pulled into the donut shop parking lot, rolling slowly to a stop. The passenger side door opened, but no one appeared. The guys standing around the parking lot speculated on who would emerge from the unfamiliar car. Fuzzy gasped, recognizing the Mustang, and was surprised to see it out on the drag on a Saturday night. Evel and Larry were leaning on the Nova.

"Thanks. I'll see ya 'round, OK?" the passenger said, extracting his large frame from the sports car. He shut the door, took a step backward and put his hands on his hips.

"Chip?" Larry took a step toward his friend. "What the hell are you doin'?"

Chip waved to the car, watching it pull out onto the street. He swaggered over to the guys who stood waiting for an explanation. "Hey y'all. We were just ridin' around. She invited me, so I took her up on it. Man, that's a nice car, and I think she's pretty nice, too." He turned to watch the Mustang drive away, sighing. "I hope I get to see her again."

"Who is she?" Larry asked. "I don't remember seein' that car around."

"She said her name is Sherry." Chip's answer sounded rather dreamy.

Fuzzy appeared from behind the Nova, walking quickly up to Chip. "That's it! Miss Bland!" He laughed and slapped his hand to his thigh.

"Bland? That's real nice, Fuz. She wasn't bland at all. Matter-of-fact, she's pretty good lookin'!"

"No. No. I don't mean that kind of bland. I mean she's Miss Sherry Bland. I knew I'd seen that car before—at the elementary school."

"Whatcha mean the elementary school? I thought she was a college student. Maybe she's a student teacher or somethin'?"

Now Chip was confused. He had just celebrated his seventeenth birthday. Dating a freshman or sophomore in college wasn't out of his realm of hope. Fuzzy chuckled while shaking his head sadly. The explanation was funny, but it was sure to hurt Chip's pride.

"More like a teacher with students." Fuzzy clamped his hand on Chip's shoulder. "Chip, she was my little sister's fourth grade teacher, and that was two years ago. Man, she's gotta be twenty-five or so!"

"Ohhh," Chip groaned, holding his hand to his chest, as if he'd been shot in the heart.

"Yeah, git this, Chip—you're jail bait to her!" Larry guffawed.

"Oh, man. She said she liked me..." Chip slumped against the Nova. "And that we could go out sometime."

"Maybe she thought you were older than you really are," Evel teased. "Or—she could a' been just messin' with ya, Chip."

"Yeah, that's it!" Larry exclaimed. "She was playin' with ya, man. We can't let her git away with it. Everybody—off the car. Chip—load up. We're gonna go git somethin'. I've got an idea!"

Evel laughed nervously, quickly moving away from the Nova. He grabbed Fuzzy by the sleeve. "I don't wanna know!" he called to his brother, as the two got into the car. Larry smiled and waved, but Chip still looked depressed. They drove out of the parking lot.

"Wha..."

Evel stopped Fuzzy's question with a raised hand. "Forget it. The less people involved in his shenanigans, the better. I'm pretty sure we'll find out what they're up to soon enough, and it's better not to know till it happens."

Fuzzy nodded in agreement. He and Evel leaned casually on the Thunderbird. As vehicles drove by and honked, the two politely acknowledged the various greetings.

Without warning, a car practically flew over the railroad tracks, skidding as it hit the pavement. The girls inside were screaming. Fuzzy and Evel jumped to their feet, their eyes following the action. The yellow Camaro, under Glenda's control, roared past. The guys thought they heard a short honk, but definitely heard somebody yell something they couldn't make out, before the car whizzed past. The shout didn't seem to be a distress call, so Evel relaxed a little.

Right behind them, another car sped by—a green four-door Chevrolet of some sort. Apparently, it was chasing the Camaro. A police car pursued with flashing lights, intent on overtaking the Chevy. The officer caught up with the green car in front of the donut shop. By all appearances, the driver of the big Chevy gave up the chase. He pulled over, stopping at a closed gas station at the end of the block.

"Well, looks like Glenda got away scot-free," Fuzzy said with a giggle. "That girl sure can drive, and that car runs pretty good, too."

"MmmHmm," Evel mumbled, while peering past the red and blue flashing lights to make sure the Camaro did indeed get away. He saw taillights and a gleam of yellow in a distant streetlight just before it disappeared from sight. Evel breathed a sigh of relief, clapping his hand on Fuzzy's shoulder in a friendly gesture of triumph. "Yep. That's quite a car—and quite a girl."

Fuzzy's eyes widened, his jaw dropping open with surprise and sudden insight. "No wonder you were mad back at The Pizza Place. Man, why didn't ya say somethin' if you wanted her to ride with ya? Never mind. I know...I know. Me and my big mouth got in the way. Sorry about that, man."

Evel checked his watch. Just nine o'clock. He nodded his forgiveness, maintaining his silence. They walked away from the Thunderbird to join some of the other guys hanging out in the parking lot. Evel heard someone mention "the girls in the yellow Camaro."

Those words grabbed his attention.

"Yeah, it was last spring. They were ridin' around in that Camaro, and I was ridin' with Brian—you know—he drives that dark green Road Runner. We play on the company softball team every summer. Anyway, he yelled somethin' at the passenger in the Camaro, and she yelled somethin' back, and before I knew it the chase was on. I can tell ya that car *will* run, and that girl *can* drive it. She lost us two or three times. But each time she pulled back out in front to see if Brian would take up the chase. Which, of course, like a fool, he did. Finally, she really lost us. We were drivin' all over town lookin' for that Camaro when suddenly, there she was. The car was comin' toward us on Sandy Road. Brian knew he'd been beat, so he saluted to the driver.

She waved back—then they disappeared. It was pretty fun. She still waves at Brian—like there's no hard feelin's."

"Why'd you keep chasin' 'em?" Evel asked.

"Why? Hell, I don't know. I guess when you see a bunch of pretty college girls in a hot car, why not?" He shrugged and laughed.

"I see what ya mean," Fuzzy said. Movement out of the corner of his eye distracted him. "Hey, ain't that Larry's car down there?" He pointed to the old gas station next to Tim's building.

"Oh, boy. Here we go. We'd better get back to the Thunderbird. We might hafta make a getaway or cover 'em or somethin'," Evel said with dread. He noticed the police car and the four-door Chevy had both left the area. "Good, the cop's gone. I'm sure we won't want whichever cop around whenever whatever is gonna happen to whoever."

"Easy for you to say. As long as *whichever* cop ain't Pettijohn. He has absolutely no sense of humor," Fuzzy said with disgust. "House—that's different. I think he gits us."

"Gets us? Oh, you mean he understands us? Ha! That's a laugh. Fuz, *we* don't even understand us!"

Evel leaned casually on the hood of his car, reflecting on Officer House—nicknamed "Court House" who, additionally, had the audacity to name his daughter "Jayle." Evel cheerfully pictured the confusion at the County Courthouse if Officer "Court" House had to testify if Jayle House was ever in danger of going to her namesake.

"Here comes Chip. Maybe we'll find out what they're doin' now," Fuzzy said anxiously.

"I hope the hell not." Evel brought his attention back, crossing his arms in front of his chest, as Chip approached.

"Hey, have y'all seen that red Mustang I was in a while ago come back by?" Chip asked nervously.

"Not yet. Why?" Fuzzy asked.

"No, Chip. Don't say nothin'," Evel commanded. He held his hand up to halt any more words. He still believed ignorance was the best way to avoid becoming an accomplice.

Chip obeyed—but had a request. "Just watch for it to come over the tracks and wave or somethin', so we can see the signal down there at the corner. OK?"

"This isn't gonna be dangerous or hurt anybody, is it?" Evel asked sternly, noting Chip's nervousness.

"No. It shouldn't. It's just a little pay-back for Miss Bland playin' with my affections that way. Just wave real big when you see it. Will ya, Fuz?"

"Sure. Sure. Go on. We'll keep watch. Relax!" Fuzzy suggested.

Chip hurried back to the corner where Larry waited. Evel could see his brother was crouched down. It also appeared someone else was with him. The Nova wasn't in sight.

"Well, I might as well have a beer while *you* watch for the red car to aid and abet the crime I'm sure *my* little brother is fixin' to commit," Evel said sarcastically.

"Hey. He learned from the best, right?" Fuzzy slapped his buddy on the arm.

Evel ignored the comment, reaching into the cooler in the back seat of his car. He resumed his position at the front of the Thunderbird with the can concealed in a foam coozie. Lots of cars passed the donut shop—but not the red Mustang. It only took a few minutes for Fuzzy to lose interest. He stuck his head in the window to plug in the Boston 8-track tape. "Smokin'" kicked off in the middle of the instrumental when Evel calmly made an announcement...

"There she is."

Startled, Fuzzy banged his head on the roof while trying to pull his upper body through the car window. Running toward the street, he waved his arms about wildly. The driver of the red Mustang noticed the seemingly crazy person flailing about in the donut shop parking lot—she stepped on the gas to avoid the entire scene.

Suddenly, Miss Sherry Bland smashed her foot down hard on the brake pedal and screamed. Somebody was lying in the road. She couldn't stop the car in time. Feeling the thump-thump as she ran over the person, she veered first one way—then the other. The car skidded to a stop with the driver's hands pressed tightly over her face.

Glenda was approaching the donut shop area from the opposite direction when she saw the Mustang in the oncoming lane having trouble. It dipped and swerved and came across the center line a bit. Glenda sped up to move through the area as fast as possible. When the two cars passed, a large projectile flew in Glenda's open window, landing with a thud on the steering wheel. Petrified by the thing in front of her, she slammed the brakes without a thought to what was behind her. Tanya screamed: the thing was a severed arm. It fell off the steering wheel into Glenda's lap. The car screeched to a halt.

Glenda was about to scream—jump out of her skin—and out of the car right there in the middle of Main Street. But, she noticed the otherwise real-looking disembodied limb was dented and creased, as if it were a carelessly handled doll's arm. The panic and adrenaline settled a bit, as she touched the appendage. It was plastic—like part of a mannequin. Curiously, a watch was in place on the arm. Tanya was still screaming.

"Tanya. TANYA! It's...OK. It's a fake! Oh, my gosh. Oh, thank goodness..." Glenda said, panting with relief. Tanya quieted down, but Glenda's brows creased with anger, as she peered intently out the window. The Mustang had pulled over into the old gas station. An animated conversation seemed to be taking place. Glenda stared. "What in the world is goin' on? Oh, CRAP. That lady thinks she ran over somebody REAL!"

She jammed the accelerator pedal down, hurriedly turning and sliding to a stop in the area between Tim's parking lot and the old gas station. As she got out of the Camaro, she observed the driver of the Mustang was out of her car and apparently all right. She was in the center of a small crowd on the other side of the parking lot. The lady seemed calm. Larry, Chip and the others were standing around casually. Everything appeared to be all right. Glenda could barely make out the crushed mannequin in the dim lights. One person waved a leg at passing cars. She nodded, taking a deep breath to settle her heart rate, while walking with Tanya toward the Thunderbird. Evel and Fuzzy were also realizing what had just happened.

"Anybody around here need a *hand*?" she asked, holding up the mannequin arm.

Evel and Fuzzy chuckled. Gathering his charisma, Evel strolled over to Glenda and held out his hand. Looking up, she gladly gave him the arm.

"I didn't know you were *armed*!" Evel joked. Fuzzy laughed but Glenda didn't. Evel noticed she was shaking. He looked at her with concern. "How'd you get hold of this?"

"Get hold of it?" Glenda said with shocked surprise. "Gee, well it's like this. I broke a store window and pulled the arm off some unsuspecting dummy. How do you think I got hold of it? I was mindin' my own business drivin' up the drag, and it flew in my window! It practically grabbed hold of the steering wheel!"

He felt the shaking of her voice. "OK! OK! Oh, my. Are you all right?" he asked softly. "That was a dirty trick of Larry's. I'm sorry you got dragged into it." He now understood her edginess.

Glenda consciously attempted to calm herself, breathing almost as deeply as when she cured hiccups. She took a moment—then risked a glance at the man standing in front of her, seeing a worried look.

"Oh, *way*, that's the *well* it goes. No harm done—though it did scare the crap out of me and Tanya," Glenda said, not knowing why she was still standing there. She considered a better plan would have been to throw the arm at them and leave. Although...she appreciated that he was being pretty nice about it and decided to roll with the flow.

Glenda took another deep breath. "So. See ya at the college at ten?" Exhaling, she took a longer look at his face.

"You bet. And I'll take care of this," he said jokingly, holding the arm up slightly. He noticed the watch on the arm's wrist and turned it slightly to read the time. He laughed. "Check it out. It takes a lickin' and keeps on tickin'! I'll see you in...twenty minutes, Glenda."

Glenda rolled her eyes skyward, shook her head side-to-side. She looked at Tanya.

"I've heard corny before, but, Evel, you take the *cornbread*!" Tanya exclaimed.

Glenda moaned good-naturedly. She glanced again at Evel. His smile lines deepened.

"Tan-ay, I reckon we've *fingered* that out by now. See ya' in a few, Glenn!"

Glenda released a backward snort of amusement—then turned and hurried back to her car. When she looked back, he was waving to her with the arm. She again shook her head side-to-side, spinning her tires leaving the parking lot.

Tanya was unusually quiet. Glenda glanced over as they approached the college entrance.

"What's the matter Tan-ay? Still upset about the flyin' arm?"

"I don't know. Maybe...it's just a funny feelin', I guess."

"Funny strange or funny ha-ha?" Glenda asked lightly, testing her friend's mood.

"Funny strange." Tanya said stone-faced. "Pull in—let's find Janie. I need to see Janie for some reason."

"You think they're at the Shoe Bench?"

Glenda was concerned about Tanya's mood. It was quite out of character for her to be this serious. But that arm thing had been quite a shock.

"Probably—let's go see," Tanya said urgently.

Glenda tried to break through the heaviness hovering around her. "I need to shut this ride down for tonight anyway. Glenn's supposed to pick me up at ten. Hey, maybe there'll be an Amen Corner parkin' place this early on Saturday night." She drove toward Horne Hall, actually finding a fairly good spot to park— not the Amen Corner, but close. "So what does one call the place across from the Amen Corner parkin' place, I wonder?" Glenda asked as she climbed out of the Camaro.

"That would be the Satanic Spot!" a voice called from the Shoe Bench area.

"Janie! Are you there?" The urgency in Tanya's voice caused Janie to peer over the high back of the Shoe Bench.

"Here, there and everywhere—even in your underwear!" Janie exclaimed happily. Gene stood up, too. He had a strange expression on his face.

"What's goin' on? Have you been drinkin'?" Glenda asked. She and Tanya walked toward the bench area. They sat across from the still startled Gene and Janie.

"No. Just feeling good—a natural high." Gene's voice was calm, which belied the funny look on his face.

"Janie—really. Is everything all right with you? I had this funny feelin' a while ago." Janie nodded amiably...nothing wrong with her. "Where's everybody else?" Tanya still wasn't satisfied all was well.

"Let's see...Candace is off at some party with April, May and June. Linda's still out with Lee. They all left hours ago—we haven't seen anything of them. Mark picked up Barb-oh a long time ago, so they're probably together. You know they broke up a couple a' weeks ago but got engaged again this week," Janie explained. "You are there, and I am here. All accounted for but not necessarily present, madam!" She saluted Tanya.

"OK. Maybe it was just that arm that landed in the car," Tanya said casually.

"Arm?"

Glenda relayed the story of the mannequin in the road in detail. But when she got to the point where Glenn looked at the arm's watch, she gasped. "Crap, I've gotta go brush my hair and my teeth. What time is it?"

Glenda rose from the bench, nervous. Tanya stood up too.

"Five till ten. Why? You got a date?" Gene asked.

"Sort of—we'll see. He might not even show up," Glenda looked toward the college entrance. One couldn't see the street through the trees, but it helped somehow to look that way anyway, so her friends wouldn't see the apprehension in her eyes.

"Ha. He'll show, all right. I'd bet on it," Tanya said with confidence. She was looking toward the drag and noticed a car heading in their direction.

Glenda saw it, too. "I gotta go—but I'll be right back!" Glenda waved at the driver, as she ran across the road in front of him. She tentatively pulled on the dorm door. It wasn't locked yet, so she disappeared inside.

"Hey! That's Jimmie Mac!"

Tanya ran over to the stopped Corvette. Jimmie Mac started to climb out, but Tanya hurriedly hopped in with him. They quickly drove away.

"Well, bye Tanya—see ya later!" Janie said sarcastically.

"She was acting kind of strange. Like she wanted to get away, but she was sure worried about something," Gene said, concerned. They sat back down and held hands.

"I'm sure I'll find out later," Janie said, resting her head on his shoulder. He leaned his cheek gently on her golden brown curls, sighing contentedly.

"Well. Ain't that sweet?" A cynical voice split the darkness. The two heads snapped upright in surprise. The Figment appeared, sitting down on the bench Glenda and Tanya had just vacated.

"Hey, Brent. And yes, it is sweet, as a matter-of-fact," Gene said.

"Well, I'm glad for you two. I just saw Mark back at the dorm, and he said you were out here." The Figment was acting strangely, even for him.

Janie was perplexed. "Mark was at the dorm, already? Was Barb-oh with him?" Barb-oh and Mark often spent weekends together at Big Barb's house.

"Nope. He said she wanted to be dropped off at her sister's, so he came on back to the dorm. That's not why I'm here," the Figment said firmly.

Janie took Gene's hand, holding his fingers next to her cheek. She suddenly felt very nervous.

"What is it already, Brent?" Gene asked, his patience running thin.

"What it *is*—is Kevin. He's here. I saw him. He's prowlin' around and sayin' he's lookin' for Glenda, but she's not that hard to find. He seemed pretty drunk and wanted to play Risk with some of the guys, but they chased him out of the TV room. I expect he'll find his way over here sooner or later, and I thought Glenda and y'all should know."

The long speech complete, the Figment rose from the bench. "Gosh. I sure hope Evel Knievel shows up on time," Janie said softly. Gene nodded.

The Figment raised one eyebrow and walked away. "Thanks, Figment," Janie called to the retreating figure.

"No problem," he replied from the darkness—and then was gone. Janie and Gene looked worriedly at each other and sat back down.

Glenda peered out her window for the Thunderbird, but it was nowhere in sight. She looked at Linda Lou's new digital clock and noted the time—9:59 p.m. Linda needed a special alarm clock that didn't beep. This one made a constant noise when activated. Linda had a peculiar contrary trait to her normal low-key personality—she reacted excessively to unexpected sounds while sleeping. Usually, this manifested with her screaming at the top of her lungs. The thought amused Glenda as she slid her checkbook into her back pocket and hurried out of the room. She burst through the side door just before the dorm monitor turned the lock.

As she emerged into the semi-darkness, Glenda surveyed the parking area. She noticed large red taillights mirrored in some chrome flicker—then cut off—in a parking space one down from her Camaro. Two figures got out of the car. She paused on the top step, determined the car was the Thunderbird, and the figures were Glenn and Fuzzy. "Imagine that—he's here—and right on time," she said softly. She watched them walk to the Shoe Bench.

"Who's here?" a voice asked softly from beside the steps. Glenda was startled at the sudden disembodied question. She quickly realized the voice belonged to the Figment. She glanced over and saw him standing in the shadows. She couldn't make out his features, but it didn't matter.

"Brent. You show up in the strangest places. To answer the question—Glenn," she said quietly. "Glenn is here."

"And?" The Figment continued his query.

"And...he's on time. I'm—ha-ha—not used to that. We're goin' ridin' around in the Thunderbird at ten." She turned her attention toward the Shoe Bench.

"Ah. Well, yes indeed—he's on time. I'd get out there and be on time, too, if I was you."

"You know, Brent—sometimes you're pretty weird," Glenda said with uncharacteristic impatience.

"I do try my best," the Figment commented calmly. Of course, Glenda didn't know he was there to watch for Kevin. Brent left it like that—assuming the Figment-like silence.

To avoid further conversation with the irritating voice in the darkness, Glenda hurried down the steps. She started to cross the drive to join her friends at the Shoe Bench and face the next adventure—but had to wait for several vehicles to pass by. Jimmy Mac's Corvette was the last car in the line of traffic. She was surprised to see Tanya sitting calmly in the passenger seat. He stopped in the middle of the roadway. It wasn't uncommon to do so, and there weren't any more vehicles coming up the drive.

"Tan-ay! Are you all right? Hey, Jimmy Mac." Glenda leaned on the open car window frame.

Tanya flashed the limp-fingered peace sign their druggy acquaintance, Mike, liked to use.

"Fine, man. Just fine," she said lazily. "Just call me *Squint!*" She laughed out loud.

"Apparently. That's good. You really do feel better?"

"Yepper. But it's weird. When we drove up toward the stadium on the back streets, I felt somethin' bad. As we headed back down toward town, the feelin' went away. When we went toward the boys' dorm, I felt somethin' bad again. So, I told Jimmy Mac to stay from here to downtown, and I'd be fine," Tanya explained with mock seriousness.

Glenda raised her eyebrows skeptically. "OK, whatever you say. So, you're usin' Jimmy Mac to avoid somethin'?"

"Yeah. I'll use him, then throw him away like a dirty dish-rag!" Tanya said with a laugh.

"All right, little miss, you can get out right now if you're gonna act like that," Jimmy Mac teased.

"Not really, Jimmy. Please, I was kiddin'!" Tanya said earnestly.

All of a sudden, she realized he, too, was kidding. She whacked him on the arm with the back of her hand and looked fondly at Glenda. "Have a good time. He's really nice, ya know," she said with a nod in the direction of the Thunderbird.

"Yepper. I think so, too. My mom would say, 'Dive in—nothing ventured—nothing gained,' and 'Run it up the flag pole and see if it flies' and clichés like that."

"Holy Cow. They're comin' over here!" Gene whispered to Janie when he saw Evel and Fuzzy headed in their direction.

"Oh *paleeze*. You'd think the President of the United States was walkin' by." She stood, pulling Gene up with her. "Hi! Glenda should be here pretty quick. She just ran up to the room for a minute. Won't you sit down and join us?" she swept her hand generously toward the bench.

"Why, thankee, ma'am—don't *mahnd* if *ah* do," Fuzzy said with an extra heavy Texas drawl. He plopped down on the bench across from Janie. Evel remained standing but propped one boot up on the center structure designed for such propping. They chatted for a minute, but Janie was getting nervous.

"Uhh…Evel. I think you should know somethin'. We just heard Glenda's ex-boyfriend is around here somewhere and is pretty drunk. He is such a butt-face. I hope he doesn't cause any trouble." Janie's concern sharpened her tone.

"Well, if he wants trouble, we can give him trouble—right Fuz? What's this guy's problem?" Evel's own tone had hardened to ice.

"You remember, Evel," Fuzzy said, leaning forward. "Tanya told us about that guy that Glenda had been engaged to. He got some girl pregnant and had to marry her."

Evel nodded slightly.

"Right," Gene confirmed. "We heard a little while ago he was at the boys' dorm and that he was looking for Glenda. But he hasn't shown up over here yet, so I don't know for sure what's going on. Even if he found her, I'm sure she'd tell him to go to hell. Well, I'd tell him that. She'd tell him to jump in the lake."

"Yepper, it was rough," Janie explained, looking intently at Evel. "She was really hurt for a long time, and is just now gettin' back to herself. Anyway, keep her out as long as you want to, but if you'd drive through here every now and then, I'll tell you if we've seen him and give you the thumbs up sign if I think it's safe to drop Glenda off. Would that be OK?"

"Sure," Evel said quietly. "This guy sounds like a raging asshole. What's the signal for Mr. Butt-Face is in the area?"

"How about Janie waves you on, and I point to where he has been sighted?" Gene offered.

"So we're supposed to keep Glenda far away from this nimrod, right? Sounds like he really needs his ass kicked," Fuzzy said.

Evel nodded. "You seem very protective of her, but you say I can keep her as long as I want?" He seemed amused at the irony.

Janie was laughing, too. "Well, within reason. I'm not stayin' out here all night and gettin' dewed on!"

Fuzzy was perplexed. "Dood on?"

"You know, when the moisture in the air condenses on surfaces—usually early of a mornin'—you get *dewed* on."

"And y'all called *me* corny!" Evel exclaimed.

"That was Tan-ay. Matter-of-fact, I defended you. I'll have you know I think you're dad-gum funny!" Janie said, laughing.

"OK! OK! Thanks. Y'all are all somethin' else. It's a deal. I'll watch for the thumbs up—and don't you worry, I'll make sure everything is OK. Remember, you're in good hands with Glennstate!"

Evel cupped his hands like the logo for the insurance company. Expecting a volatile reaction, he walked quickly away.

"Boo! Hiss! Bad cinema!" Janie yelled. She ran toward the big man who had turned tail to escape. She stopped short, though, when she saw Glenda looking over the top of Jimmy Mac's car at them.

"Well. Here goes." Glenda patted the top of the car with the flat of her hand. Jimmy Mac understood the cue and pulled away, leaving her standing alone in the street. She cocked her head to the side to watch the antics at the Shoe Bench, while gathering her courage. She walked toward the Shoe Bench with expectation.

"What 're you goof-balls doin'?" she asked—but raised her hands to stop the explanations. "No, no. Never mind—don't tell me. I don't have that kinda time."

She looked with anticipation at Glenn. He motioned for her to accompany him.

Fuzzy ran to the big silver car and opened the passenger door. With a flourish, he motioned for her to enter. "Madam. Ladies first—*you* git to sit on the crack," magnanimously offering her the spot in front where the sixty-forty seat was split.

Glenda looked around nervously. She saw Jimmie Mac's car stopped on the far side of the Shoe Bench and all her friends looking at her. "Good grief, can't anybody just go ridin' around anymore?" she said, ducking quickly into the Thunderbird.

Glenn waved to Janie and Gene before he slid into the driver's side. He knew Glenda was nervous—he quickly realized that he was, too. He stiffly moved his hand to start and back the car out. The three people in the front seat of the Thunderbird remained silent during its exit from the college. Fuzzy broke the silence with a joke. Before long they were all laughing and joking around, having a pretty good time.

Glenda was again amazed at how many people seemed to know Glenn. Just about every car on the drag honked—every person not in a vehicle waved or yelled. He pulled into the Astro Drive-In, parked on the un-nerd side and hit the order button. The voice in the box asked for their order.

Glenn leaned toward the speaker. "Right, Ralph. Re need a rurty-reven rent Croke rand phree strawrs prease. Rorry, re're broke."

The voice in the box laughed—then cut off. Right away three large drinks were delivered by a giggling car hop.

"Boss says that's always a good one. These are on the house!" The car hop handed in the large Styrofoam cups one by one. Glenn passed two of the drinks down to Glenda and Fuzzy and stuck one between his legs.

"Rell Ralph rhanks!" he called. The girl laughed on her way back to the building.

Glenda took a sip from her straw, pondering the situation for a moment. She decided to ask about it. "That was Astro talk, right? Are you really broke? I mean, I could have paid with a check."

"Rright, Rastro! It's a tradition now," Glenn explained. "A while back we were here, and all we had between us was thirty-seven cents. We really were broke that time. So, I ordered a thirty-seven cent Coke with three straws in the Astro voice as a joke. It worked, so we do it now and then to keep it goin'. Right, Fuz?"

"Huh? Yeah, right. Hey, there's Charles!" Getting out of the car in a flash, Fuzzy poked his head back through the open window. "I'll go ride with Charles for a while. See ya later."

Glenda realized she was sitting very close to Glenn—and that without Fuzzy in the car, there was a lot of open space in the front seat to her right. Unsure of what to do, she began to slide away from Glenn. He gently laid his hand on her knee.

"Stay right there—it's OK," he said quietly. He slowly returned his hand to the steering wheel.

Glenda froze and gripped her drink cup with both hands to have somewhere to put them. Glenn left the Astro, driving toward downtown. She was aware of his warmth next to her arm and leg across the small space between their bodies. The strange sensation she felt in the park earlier that day now churned deep in her chest.

"You wanna go to the park?" He continued to fix his eyes straight ahead.

Glenda jumped. She was startled to hear the word "park" at the very moment the memory of falling out of the Sittin' Tree and into his arms crossed her mind.

Glenn quickly noticed her discomfort, sensed her physical withdrawal. He mentally kicked himself. "What I meant was—we could sit at one of the picnic tables and talk—if ya want to." He approached the turn to the park when he felt her relax a little. She might have said "OK"; he headed into the park.

When the Thunderbird stopped in front of the picnic table near the Sittin' Tree, Glenda again was faced with a decision— get out on his side or move over toward the passenger door. She looked apprehensively in that direction and realized she was in a really big vehicle. The exiting decision was made when Glenn held out his hand to help her out of the car. She placed her left hand in his. Before she knew it, she was standing very close to him. Her hand was still in his. "You have cold hands," he said softly into the top of her head.

"Cold hands—warm heart," Glenda answered automatically. Her hands were notoriously cool, even cold. She often replied to the observation with this comeback. She gently pulled her hand and climbed up on the table top, placing her feet on the seat. Glenn sat beside her. He measured his cowboy boot against her sneaker. "And small feet."

"Not so small. Yours are just big. What size are they?"

"Boat size—twelve sometimes thirteen. With feet like this I should a' been six foot five instead of just six foot."

"Well, we can't help how our mamas made us," Glenda said philosophically. Glenn nodded at the truth of her statement. Glenda was much more comfortable than she had figured. In fact, he was easy to be with—a big relief. Before long they were so at ease, they were telling their life stories. His tales were substantially more exciting than hers, but they laughed a lot. Very soon, their shoulders were touching.

"It appears you turned out all right. You couldn't have been all that bad!" she said, nudging him slightly with her elbow.

"Maybe not, but back in school the teachers thought I was, so I tried not to disappoint 'em. It started when I ambushed an older kid—he'd been harassing me for months. I was just eight years old. He was twelve, and I licked him good. The school was real small and so old they had an outdoor bathroom. It was a tiny metal building with an access door screwed on the back. When this kid went in to do his business, I took that panel off and grabbed him by the neck. I pulled him out of the back of that outhouse with his pants down and all that. Then I beat him to a pulp. And well, he didn't bother me anymore after that."

"But you were only eight? What about high school?"

"Oh, there was all kinds of pranks and shenanigans, but I guess my crownin' achievement, besides blowin' up the lockers, was weldin' the Ag teacher in his office," Glenn said with pride.

Glenda turned her head slowly to look at his profile, waiting for the story. His classic nose seemed too straight to belong to such a notorious fighter. She saw Glenn looking off into the distance, so she brought him back in by resting her fingers lightly on his forearm.

That slight movement got his attention. He cleared his throat. "OK. Well, ya know in Future Farmers of America, kids raise project animals—mine was a heifer calf. She was a beauty. I walked and halter-trained her to get ready to show. The Ag teacher was supposed to come out to our ranch and see my project, but he never did. And he gave me a D. He never saw it, and he gave me a D." The unfairness of the situation still irked him. "So, anyway, this teacher didn't have a class third period, and he usually went in his office in the Ag shop to take a nap. We'd learned to use the welder—plus, I had done some weldin' and cuttin' out on our ranch. First, I skipped class and checked to make sure he was asleep in his chair. Next, I moved the welder from the shop so it would reach. It was easy to weld the steel office door to the metal door facing in several places. All the metal got pretty hot. When that was done, I put everything back in its place as quiet and quick as possible. Then I ran down the hall and pulled the handle on the fire alarm."

"Oh, no. Was there a panic?"

"Naa. It wasn't all that strange to have a fire drill or even a bomb scare. Mostly it was an excuse to get out of class. Anyway, the Ag teacher woke up and tried to leave his office. The door was hot and wouldn't open. Now, *he* did panic. I guess he thought there was a fire and that it was right outside his door. He banged on the glass window that looked out on the hallway and acted pretty anxious to get outta there—but everyone just passed by and waved at him. I flipped him off—it was really funny."

Glenn concluded with a chuckle.

Glenda spoke into the sheer darkness. "Sure is. But did you get caught?"

"Nope. That's one I got away with to this very day. At least I hope the statute of limitations is up. How 'bout you, or are you a miss goody two shoes?" he asked mischievously.

"Not hardly. Though it took coming to college to bring out the rebel in me. I used to be painfully shy. But I guess I came out of my shell a few weeks after I got here. In fact, one time Dean Stickler called me in and said I was ugly and sour and had a chip on my shoulder."

Glenn glanced over sharply at the mention of the familiar name. "She really said that? What brought that on?" Glenn was very glad to know she wasn't as straight as she seemed to be, since she didn't drink, smoke, or curse.

"Oh, yes, indeed. You know that window that looks out over the road through the college—the one in the middle?" Glenda again nudged him with her elbow and continued. "We'd sit in the window sill, and the screen tended to get ripped—or pushed out or otherwise damaged—and it had to be replaced a couple a' times. They tried everything to keep us from sittin' there: barricaded it with benches, roped it off, and even threatened us with expulsion if we were caught. It was really ridiculous. Anyways, the Dean summoned me to her office. We exchanged heated words, and she said that about me havin' a chip on my shoulder. I yelled back that she was sure tryin' pretty hard to knock it off. As I left her office, I hit the wall with my coat so hard somethin' fell off, and we haven't spoken since. It wasn't very nice." It still hurt, the way the Dean so misjudged her and quickly turned the conversation away from her. "Maybe someday you'll tell me about the lockers."

"It's gettin' late. How 'bout we get together tomorrow?"

"Late? What time is it?" Glenda asked but didn't wait. She reached for his left arm to look at his watch. "Ah, a real live arm—and whoa—it's almost one a.m.? Man, no wonder my feet are goin' to sleep from sittin' here. If we stay much longer, we'll get dewed on!" She chuckled. "Ya know...it might even be the purple sock hour."

Amused, Glenn recognized one comment and chose to ignore the other. He helped Glenda to solid ground, pausing as she stomped her feet to regain the feeling. When she stopped stomping and looked up at him, he felt the need to hold her, but was unsure of himself. The same impulse seemed to take hold of Glenda; she leaned a little toward him. He gave in to the desire, wrapping his arms around her gently. He could almost feel her heart beating. Glenda felt his chest rise and fall with measured breath against her cheek and found her breathing matching his.

After a few seconds, she took a deep breath to break the trance. She pulled away and bowed her head. "Tomorrow, I could get some tacos and stuff and if you'll meet me here at one *p.m.*, we could have a sort of a picnic. And you can tell me the locker story."

She ventured a look at his face, a risk that paid off big-time: looking back was as sweet a smile as she had ever seen.

"You bet—that sounds great," Glenn said softly. "I'll bring a cooler with beer for me and Dr Pepper for you, deal?"

"Deal. Drive me back to the dorm, please, before the purple sock hour really sets in."

She began to laugh. Glenn realized that the purple sock hour was not a time or event, but a description of when people act silly late at night. He was again amused, mostly at himself, as he opened the car door for her to enter from his side.

Drive by the dorm. Oh, shit, I forgot. He plopped down into the driver seat—slightly surprised to find Glenda right beside him. The look she gave him melted some deep piece of his heart and startled him so much that he quickly drove them out of the park.

Chapter Thirteen

*A*LOUD VEHICLE RUMBLED by the Shoe Bench. Startled from a deep sleep, Janie blinked hard to force her contacts back in the right places and sat upright.

"Hi," Gene said sleepily. His eyes were almost closed—his arm was wrapped protectively around her shoulders.

"Hi." Her brain cells woke up. "Oh, my, what time is it? Where are they? Is she all right?" Janie threw the questions into the air around her, turning her head rapidly, looking this way and that.

"Whoa. Slow down. I don't think that fast this late at night. Let's see…it's almost one a.m. I have no idea. But, whichever she you're talking about, I'm sure she is. How's that?" Gene asked in a not-so-humble fashion.

Janie took a deep breath to calm her jumping heart. "OK. OK. Man, I wish I knew what was goin' on here. I'm worried. I just had some kinda bad dream, but I can't remember what it was."

"You were twitching and stuff," Gene joked. "I just figured that was normal for a feisty little fireball like you!"

Janie jabbed her elbow into his side. Grabbing her before she hit him again, his arms gripped her tightly. He sighed when she relaxed into the embrace—but she suddenly shivered.

"Are you cold, sweetheart?" he asked softly, shifting his weight to look at her face. They had stayed in virtually the same position on the wooden bench for several hours—discomfort was definitely an issue. They both fidgeted.

Janie stomped her feet and wiped a tear that had fallen from her eye. "No. Yes. I don't know. I don't like it. Somethin' ain't right. Dang it—where is Glenda?"

"Maybe it's that your butt is as tired of this hard bench as mine is. Oh, man. I start my new job tomorrow. I'd better turn in soon." He stood up to look around the area. "Hey, look! There they are now."

Gene reached down to help an unconvinced Janie to her feet, so she could see the Thunderbird really was approaching. She grabbed Gene, pulling him back down on the bench—so *they* couldn't be seen.

They crouched together, well below the top of the Shoe Bench's high back. "Gene! I thought you were kiddin'! Crap, how long have I been out of it? Is the coast clear? Do you think Kevin is around? Do I give the thumbs up?"

"All is well—no sign of the butt-face as far as I know. I can confidently report that it is safe to allow Glenda to exit the Thunderbird."

Janie couldn't help but giggle at his formal manner while poised in such an awkward position. "Whew, that's a relief.

Thanks for keepin' watch. I didn't mean to conk out completely, but you *are* somewhat softer than this bench," she said slyly.

Gene looked at her fondly. She nudged him good-naturedly before nimbly turning around to kneel on the seat, so she could peek over the high back of the bench. She ducked her head, thrusting her hand up in the air in an effort to give the thumbs up sign. But the signal more resembled a thumbing a ride sign. Unfortunately, her thumb had a bit more horizontal orientation than customary for giving the thumbs up.

"Do you want me to turn right and drop you off in front?" Glenn asked. They were approaching Horne Hall. He was looking to his left toward the Shoe Bench. He thought he saw something but wasn't sure if it was the right signal.

"Matters not. You can drop me here, and I can walk around so you don't hafta go down that narrow one-way street. Oops! No…that a' way." Glenda said, as he turned left to go around the U instead of right to go toward the lobby entrance.

"We gotta go around again—just hang tight." As the car approached the Shoe Bench on the other side, Glenn saw Janie waving and giving the thumbs up. He nodded and relaxed. "Hey, there's your friends," he said, just before Glenda was about to ask what he was doing.

She was surprised to see Janie jumping up-and-down waving—making quite a scene for one o'clock in the morning.

"Yeah. Please go ahead and stop. I'll hop out here and see what they're doin' out here at this hour…as if I didn't know."

"Oh, yeah?" he asked with raised eyebrows.

"Oh, yeah, indeed. Those two have recently decided they were meant for each other after just bein' friends for over a year."

"Oh. I thought you were gonna say they were waitin' up for you," Glenn stopped the Thunderbird in the roadway and assisted her out of the car. She gave him a little half-hug goodbye.

"Tomorrow at one. At the park bench. Bring me a real Dr Pepper, OK?" she asked softly.

"You got it. Get me a couple a' Gringo Burgers—if ya don't mind." He felt her head nod. "It's a date." Glenn gave her a little extra squeeze.

Glenda backed up, as Janie came running over. "Glenda! Gosh—I'm glad to see you."

"You goober heads. Y'all were waitin' up for lil' ol' me? I'm touched." Glenda rolled her eyes.

"Now wait a second, little miss. You were out on the town with a notorious troublemaker—*me*. Janie had a right to worry!" Glenn liked this little group of college kids.

"That's not it at all—silly boy—I was afraid you'd taken her off and made her Queen of the Drag!" Janie teased.

"Geez. I'll say it again. Can't anybody just go ridin' around anymore?" Glenda again rolled her eyes. She realized she was very tired, and both Gene and Janie looked sleepy.

She turned to Glenn. "See ya tomorrow—please don't forget," she whispered.

"I'll be there. You can count on it. See ya," Glenn whispered back. He flashed that crinkly smile that crackled through her body like electricity. Glenn slid behind the wheel of the Thunderbird and gazed at her. Two hands raised in a subtle wave goodbye.

Then he was gone.

Glenda was quivering. She got hold of herself and turned to her friends. "Let's go in, Janie. Hey, did you see Linda come in?"

"Yepper. Lee dropped her off *and* kissed her good night on the front lawn about midnight. I s'pect she's havin' *very* sweet Lee dreams about now." Janie spoke in her gossipy voice.

"Listen to Little Miss Nosey. Glenda, she actually ran over there by the building and hid behind the bushes to spy on them!" Gene said.

"Well, certainly. She was on a quest for knowledge, and it was successful. See ya, Gene. I've gotta take my contacts out. I think they're stuck to my eyeballs." Glenda grabbed Janie's arm.

"Me, too. I know mine are. I went to sleep a little while ago," Janie said sheepishly.

"Hey wait!" Gene ran over to Janie and pecked her cheek. "Good night, sweetheart. See ya tomorrow," he said a bit too sweetly before stepping back to avoid the blow he knew would be coming. Glenda held on to the hot-tempered Janie to keep her from hitting the retreating young man.

"Run, Gene, Run!" Glenda joked. Gene ran a few steps— then turned and waved. Glenda waved. Janie blew him a kiss. All was forgiven. The girls made their way to the front door and walked into the dorm lobby. No men were around, because they had to be out of the building by midnight on weekends. In fact, the only person in sight was the dorm monitor...snoring on a couch.

"You think Linda will be asleep, really?" Glenda asked as they climbed the lobby stairs to the second floor.

"Sure. She's been back for a while, so you'd better be careful."

"Amen. Last time I sneaked in while she was asleep, I banged around, took out my contacts, put on my pjs, brushed my teeth, and when I put the toothbrush down—it made a 'click' noise on the sink. Linda screamed and came clear out of the bed like she'd seen a ghost!"

"I remember that. We thought somebody had crawled in the window and grabbed her or somethin'. Yeah, please do be quiet, or she'll wake up everybody. Everybody that's home that is," Janie added quietly.

They walked through the door into their hall. As she passed by Candace and Barb-oh's room, Janie stopped and looked in. Neither was there. Her awareness filled with an odd impression lingering from the mysterious dream she had while sleeping on the Shoe Bench. She shrugged off the sensation as weirdness due to the late hour. She caught up with Glenda to say good night.

Janie stepped softly into her room. One fan was humming—turned up toward the ceiling. Instead of cooling the room on this night, it served to drown out the noise of the outside world. Tanya was asleep, so Janie tiptoed around their room and got ready for bed. She truly expected to hear Linda scream at any time.

Across the hall, Glenda tried to move about the room quietly. Neither fan was running, so she felt like every sound she made echoed loudly against the high plaster ceiling. She greatly feared Linda Lou would cry out. She *did not* expect to hear actual crying.

Glenda walked over to her friend's bed. "Are you awake? What's the matter?"

Linda Lou babbled something. She sobbed uncontrollably—her words incomprehensible. Glenda quickly knelt on the floor beside the bed, put her arm on Linda Lou's back and felt the heaving sobs. The girl was almost hyperventilating.

Glenda grew alarmed. "What the heck is goin' on? Talk to me!" She shook her friend to gain her attention. "Tell me. What's the matter, Linda?"

"Leeeeeeeeee..." Saying his name seemed to cause Linda Lou pain.

"What about Lee? Is somethin' wrong? Did he do somethin' to hurt you?" Linda Lou was a basket case; Glenda had never seen her so upset.

"Nooooooo! He...told me...he said..." Linda Lou clamped her mouth shut. Her eyes widened with fear.

"What?" Glenda's question was patient. She could wait. The answer would come out, slowly. But it needed to surface, whatever it was. She gently patted her friend's back. "He told you what?"

Linda tried to calm herself with a deep but gasping breath. "He said—he told me—'I love you'—Oh, Glendee-girl. I don't know. He can't—I can't—I DON'T KNOW—I JUST DON'T KNOW!" She began crying again.

"Linda Lou, Oh, my gosh. That's wonderful! You gotta know you love him, too. I can see it when you look at him!"

Glenda was quite relieved to hear this good news. She was beginning to think something bad had happened.

"No. No. I can't—I don't!"

"Yes, you do!" Glenda said gently. She rose to her knees beside the bed, placing her head next to Linda's on the pillow. "Yes...yes, you do. Face it, Linda Lou, you do love him," she said softly into her friend's hair. Slowly, Linda's sobbing breath settled down. The girls shared the moment of understanding in silence.

After about a minute, Glenda raised her head. Linda sighed. "You're right—I think I do. I just don't know what to do."

"You'll know what to do when the time comes. Meantime, just try to let it soak in. You gonna be OK?"

Linda nodded.

Glenda stood up slowly. "You wanna drink of water?"

"Yes, thanks. That would be nice." Linda rose up, leaning on one elbow.

"Comin' up. And I think a wet wash rag is in order. You're a mess!"

Relieved, Glenda filled Linda's plastic cup with water and moistened a wash cloth in the corner sink. After delivering those items to her friend and squeezing her outstretched hand, Glenda walked over to the front window to look out at the still of the night. The parked cars were glistening with dew—they'd been dewed on. Her dimple appeared at the thought. She remembered that, curiously, Glenn had used that same phrase earlier. She looked out at the stars visible between the trees and the roof of the dining hall and wondered where he was—where he lived. Her emotions were causing a commotion in her chest again. She took a deep breath to settle down.

"Did you have a nice time?" Linda asked softly from her bed.

Glenda turned around with a smile. "Oh, yes, very. And we're meetin' for lunch tomorrow in the park. He's really nice and funny. Really different from all these stuck-up college guys. He acts wild, but on the other hand, he also appears to be very solid and dependable. Or so it seems. I guess we shall see."

She answered with words she hadn't really thought through—but decided they were true. Instinctively, she felt he was a good guy. Feeling a bit strange—nice, but strange—she wondered about it for a second.

Her name being called from outdoors interrupted her reverie. "What the heck?" Glenda murmured, turning back to the window. She raised the sash about a foot and leaned over: "Who's there?"

"Glenda, baby—it's me. Come down and see me," the voice called softly.

Glenda's blood ran cold after hearing the voice more clearly through the open window. *Kevin.* She stood upright and froze in place. Linda approached from behind.

"Don't you dare do anything. Stand back outta sight, and I'll tell him to get the hell outta here," Linda told her friend firmly. She put her arm around Glenda to support her, as she was swaying a bit.

"No. I'll do it. Don't worry. I ain't goin' down there. But get ready to call the Campus Cops if..."

Glenda's voice trailed off. She shook her head slightly, squinting her eyes a bit to focus. She moved to the window, raised it higher and leaned on the sill.

"What on God's Green Earth do you want?" Glenda asked through the screen in an even, yet frosty, tone.

"Glenda! I wanna see ya, baby. I wanna pay you back the money I owe ya and your folks. I wanna make it up to ya. Please...down...here..." Kevin slurred the words. Glenda was disgusted.

"You're drunk—and you're married. Mail me the money. Go away and never ever come anywhere near me again—you understand?" she said firmly. "Go away."

"NO! I need you! Pleeeeease baby! Gimme the address!" Kevin was begging on his knee.

Linda snickered sarcastically at the sight. "He has a habit of gettin' down on one knee, doesn't he?"

Glenda caught the joke and couldn't help but giggle a bit in relief. She reached out to touch Linda on the shoulder in thanks. She turned back to the open window with a new attitude. "You need the address? Gimme a break. We shared a post office box for over a year. You know good and well what the address is. Feel free to send a money order—no checks will be accepted. Now, go away or we're gonna call the Campus Cops!" she yelled out the window for all to hear.

She pulled the window down as hard as she could. It closed with a loud slam. The window panes rattled ominously.

"We already did!" a voice called from below—loud enough to be heard clear across campus. Kevin's shoulders slumped dejectedly. He stumbled away. Glenda turned her back to the window, closing her eyes. She didn't see Kevin leave. The Figment emerged from the shadows to follow, having kept guard for several hours to ensure Kevin left his friends alone.

"Thank goodness. Thank you, Lord. Thank whatever powers that are out there that he is out of my life," Glenda said softly into the air.

When she opened her eyes, Tanya was standing in front of her. The two embraced, and Glenda cried one last time over Kevin. Linda threw her arms around the two girls. Suddenly, it was a group hug.

"Men—can't live with 'em—can't live without 'em," Janie said philosophically from the doorway. "You know, that must a' been the bad vibe we've been feelin' all night. The butt-face!"

The girls laughed loudly to relieve the tension. Janie ran in and joined in the big hug. The lights came on, and the girls sat on the cool tile floor to talk far into the night. The discussion included a little about their strange feelings and dreams—but far more about much more pleasant things. Eventually, they were ready to go to their single beds. When they did, each girl fell asleep as soon as her head hit the pillow—except Janie. She still felt uneasy and couldn't understand it. She shuffled quietly down to Candace and Barb-oh's room, finding it was still unoccupied. A troubled Janie returned to her bed and listened to the upturned fan rattling the Queen *Jazz* poster on the wall for a very long time. She finally drifted off, joining her friends in slumber.

Glenda leaned on the Taco Hut counter, impatiently awaiting her order. She was running late for her lunch date—and the food maker, Justin, was moving excruciatingly slowly.

"Justin! Hurry up! I've gotta go!"

"You should a' gotten here earlier. You say ya want extra special Gringo Burgers—so extra special you shall have!"

With a flourish, Justin delivered a perfect dollop of sour cream onto a bed of taco meat. He squeezed some hot sauce over everything and crowned the sandwich with the top of the bun. He expertly wrapped it in paper and placed it carefully in a sack with his other creations. He handed the sack to Glenda without a word.

Glenda pulled her checkbook out of her back pocket. "Sorry, Justin. How much do I owe ya?"

"On the house. And here's some chips and guacamole, too. Good luck, Glenda." Justin congenially handed her another sack. "Who's the lucky guy attendin' this picnic?"

"Well, you know the guy that drives the silver Thunderbird that was here the other night?"

"Heck yeah. That's Evel Knievel. I don't know his real name. He's your picnic partner?" Justin's tone was incredulous. "I don't believe it."

"Why would I make that up? His name is Glenn, and he's very nice and very funny. He asked for a Gringo Burger—so here I am."

"Hey, calm down. It's just hard to picture the King of the Drag on a picnic in the park. But hey, a man's gotta eat," Justin said.

"Yes. And I've gotta go. What time is it?" Glenda asked—but didn't wait for the answer when she saw the clock above the door. "Crap, five minutes till one. I'm outta here. Thanks muchly, Justin. I owe you another one."

Glenda walked quickly to the door. Justin leaned over the counter, waving goodbye. His plan was to make himself an extra special Gringo Burger with lots of hot sauce. The lunch rush, such as it was on Sunday, was over—he could take it easy the rest of the afternoon.

Glenda, on the other hand, carefully placed the sacks of food in the passenger seat and proceeded to drive like a maniac all the way down the drag to the park. She even passed some grandparents headed home from the café after church. It was a pretty wild move to make on Main Street in broad daylight. "Thank you, Lord, for keepin' the cops away," she said into the wind, while turning into the city park.

Glenn had parked the Thunderbird by the designated picnic table at 12:45 p.m., and was sitting backward on the bench, his back against the edge of the table. He glanced at his watch briefly before surveying the entrance to the park. A streak of yellow between the trees moved at more than the posted speed limit; he released the breath he had unconsciously been holding the previous few seconds. He reached down into Glenda's cooler and brought out two dripping wet, cold Dr Pepper cans.

The yellow streak slowed and parked next to his silver car. He saw Glenda struggling with some sacks, so he hurried to her.

"Hey, there! Lemme help. I used to be a COB. Wow, did you get everything on the menu?" He grasped one of the sacks she shoved through the open window.

"I'm sorry. Am I late? That dang Justin took his good, sweet time makin' the Gringo Burgers." A bit nervous, Glenda exited the Camaro with the other sack.

"Right on time. I like to be early. These are Gringo Burgers? What'd he put in 'em—lead? This is heavy for fast food!"

"Oh, yeah. He made them extra special and loaded down with all kinds of stuff. I grabbed a bunch of napkins. Hey, you got the Dr Pepper!" Glenda put down her sack and picked up the canned drink. "Ooh, and it's cold!"

"That's what ice'll do. There's more in your cooler, here. See?" He opened the lid briefly. "Let's eat—I'm starved. I don't think I ate as much as I drank last night."

"Good thing Justin gave us this extra stuff then," Glenda spread everything out on the table. "What's this about bein' a COB?"

"Carry-out boy at the grocery store. It was the best job in the world for a kid. The work was fun, and it was a great way to meet girls," he explained with a wink.

Glenn and Glenda enjoyed their food and talked, finding they had quite a bit in common—a pleasant surprise. Both loved spinach and beets and didn't care at all for country music. They laughed a lot; he even told her the story of blowing up the lockers in high school.

"Gosh, that is crazy. I bet you were glad nobody got hurt," Glenda said, nudging him with her elbow.

"Crazy—that was us—all right. I remember when me and some of the guys pulled a trick on a teacher that had a little red convertible sports car. It was a Triumph or maybe an MG, I think. We picked up that little tiny car and set it down sideways on the front steps of the high school. The driver side tires were on the top landing, and the passenger side tires were on the bottom step."

"Wow. She must a' been a pretty bad teacher to get that kind of treatment."

"No, not really. We had the chance, so we did it."

"How'd they get it down?"

"They, nothin'—we did. We put it up there—then we thought—hey, she's a pretty nice teacher and didn't really deserve that kind of treatment even if it was easy to do. Anyway, we felt kinda bad, so before anybody else noticed, we picked it up again and set it back down on the pavement. The tires ended up almost exactly where they started out. Then all the guys ran like hell. She never found out what we did."

He flashed the smile that made his blue eyes sparkle and lines crinkle.

Glenda threw her head back, laughing out loud. She glanced up into the blue sky briefly, then looked back down directly into those eyes. She again felt the curious stirring deep inside her soul. Her smile slowly faded—so did his, as their eyes locked—and for a moment time stood still. A different sort of look of understanding dawned in both sets of blue eyes. They were transfixed for a few seconds. With great effort, Glenda pulled her gaze from his to watch some leaves blow by in a gust of wind. That burst of air caused a strand of her hair to fly into her face. Before she could reach up to brush it off, she felt Glenn's fingers gently push the hair back into place. She almost turned her head to look at him but instead got off the picnic table and onto her feet.

Glenn quickly withdrew his hand, leaned back a bit and took a breath. "You wanna go ridin' around? I've got a need for speed," he said, sliding off the table to stand beside the trembling girl.

"Yeah, that's a good idea. Your car or mine?" Glenda's heart still pounded, but the excitement she felt was good. It wasn't fear. It wasn't nervousness. She felt a bit of thrill, while turning toward Glenn. His face first took on a look of surprise, then one of gladness.

"Mine. Let's go." He walked over to the Thunderbird—and opened the driver's side door. "Ladies first."

"Why. Thank ya, kind suh," Glenda replied with her Southern Belle accent. She gently tapped his chest with the back of her hand before quickly ducking into the car. Glenn froze for a moment before folding his frame into the driver's seat.

A few minutes later, they sped down a two-lane highway out in the country a few miles south of Dairyville. Glenda noticed the occasional mailbox and the barbed wire fences with their tight horizontal lines passing by at a faster-and-faster rate. She glanced over Glenn's forearm at the speedometer through a gap in the steering wheel, shocked to see the needle touch 90 mph. She had taken her Camaro to speeds around 100 with confidence, but she felt rather vulnerable as a passenger with no steering wheel to hold. She braced herself against the seat and planted her sneakers in the carpet on the floorboard. A movement from Glenn caught her attention. He sat up even more upright to grasp the wheel firmly. She saw the tip of his tongue press against the corner of his slightly opened mouth—his eyes squinted in concentration. Glenda's eyes widened, as she looked straight ahead. Her hands gripped the seat a little tighter.

The world outside the car was a complete blur. Glenda thought she heard Glenn yell something about 120, but wasn't sure exactly what was said due to the extreme roar of the wind coming in the open windows. Glenn lifted his foot from the gas pedal to allow the car to slow—but not before they came upon some railroad tracks that crossed the highway at a slanted angle.

"Hang on!" he yelled. The car launched off the uneven tracks. Glenda involuntarily let out a squeal as the big vehicle settled back on the road, slowing to a more comfortable sixty-five mph.

Glenn jabbed her gently with his extremely sharp elbow. "Oh, so there is a Glenda alarm, is there?" Without warning he gasped, pulling his foot completely off the accelerator and lightly tapping the brakes. A deer jumped out in front of them—barely getting off the road, as the big car passed by.

"Shit! That was too close!" he cried.

"Oh, ho, so there is also a Glenn alarm?" Glenda returned the elbow jab. "By the by, you have sharp elbows. And yes, that was close. Geez, I'm glad we didn't hit it goin' 120 mph—you did say 120?"

"Yes, yes, and yes ma'am. These sharp elbows have come in very handy in the many fights I've found myself in over the years."

Glenda studied his profile, again noticing the perfectly shaped nose. Kevin's nose was a bit crooked from an untended break from his high school football days. She was strangely moved by the striking difference a straight nose made in a man's face. She reflected on the thought—well, this man's face. "Wait a second. If you've had so many fights, why's your nose so straight?"

Glenn held out his right arm, demonstrating its extreme length. "With these long arms, I could reach out and touch them before they could get to me. Plus, I always protected my face!"

"Wow. What is that—a thirty-six sleeve length? My dad wears thirty-three!"

"Yep. Thirty-five, thirty-six—that sounds right. I'm used to sleeves bein' too short, so most of the time I roll the cuffs up a time or two anyway."

"My main problem is just bein' plain ol' average and havin' to wear contacts, I guess," Glenda said.

Glenn let off the accelerator, glancing briefly at the girl sitting beside him. Feeling a jolt inside his usually tough exterior, he took a moment let it settle. His long arm stretched over Glenda's head and rested on her shoulders. She looked up at him expectantly.

"Not so average, Glenda. No, you're not average at all," he said softly. He squeezed her arm for a moment, then retrieved his own, returning his hand to the steering wheel.

Glenda remained still for a moment, clearing her throat. She decided to change the subject. "Thanks. Umm, tell me about the worst wreck you've ever had."

"What makes you think I've ever had a wreck?" he asked. Glenda chuckled at his show of innocence. "OK. OK. Car, truck or motorcycle?"

"Car," Glenda looked at him out of the corner of her eyes.

"Awright, let's see. Well, back when I was a kid, there was a guy who ran a gas station out where I grew up—way out in the country. He had a '67 Mustang that was pretty fast. Anyway, I was workin' at his gas station one summer, and he let me take that Mustang to town for a car part or somethin'. I was only fourteen and didn't have a license or nuthin', and well, I got a little carried away. Before long, I was goin' too fast for a curve that was comin' up, and I lost it. The car launched off the highway, cleared a fence and landed in a great big oak tree branch about ten feet off the ground. The car literally broke in half. The motor compartment hung up in the tree, and I fell with the back half of the car. We slid down the branch of the tree and landed back bumper down with me still sittin' in the driver seat. It was weird that the steerin' wheel and windshield weren't in front of me anymore—just the parts of that poor old oak tree that nearly reached the ground. It's amazin' I wasn't hurt one bit—well, until the owner saw what I did to his car! OK, now how 'bout you?"

"Wow. Nothin' that excitin'. I guess the most interesting incident was when I hit a steering column in the middle of the highway," Glenda said.

"A steerin' column? Not attached to vehicle?"

"Righto. Some scrap metal fell off a truck, and I hit a steering column with both right side tires. It flattened the tires and bent one of the wheels. Then it slid over to the other side of the highway and took out a guy's transmission. Tanya and I were stranded. I had one spare, but who would a' thought you'd need two? We walked to a house and called the boys' dorm. Thank goodness it wasn't long distance. We called phone number after phone number—the room phones are all sequential—until we got hold of somebody that could come fetch us. It was pretty bad. Also bad was when I had an axle break goin' over the railroad tracks on the drag. Now that was an interesting ride into the donut shop parking lot!"

"I'll bet it was. Hey, now that you mention it, seems like I remember your car was parked at Hambone's Garage for quite a while. Was that it?"

"Yepper. Long enough for Jackal Ann to egg it. That was the first time, and it ate the paint off the trunk lid in a couple a' places. That's why everybody was so paranoid when she egged it again."

"Mmmhmm, yep. I savvy," Glenn said, sliding his hand onto Glenda's leg. He glanced at her, seeing it was OK. Both were feeling a bit euphoric as they headed back to Dairyville.

Janie lounged on her bed with an open book on her lap, but with her gaze locked firmly toward the window.

"Hey, Janie!" The voice in her doorway startled her.

"Barb-oh! Where on earth have you been? Are you OK?"

"Sure, better than ever," Barb-oh reached out to hug Janie with surprising fervor.

"I was so worried when you didn't come back in last night. You and Mark OK?"

The two plopped down on Janie's bed. "Of course," Barb-oh said, waggling her ring finger so the diamond engagement ring flashed in the late afternoon sunlight that streamed through the window. She lay back on the bed, sighing heavily. Janie also sighed—one of relief. Barb-oh, and Mark had problems from time-to-time, and Barb-oh was often rather moody. But apparently she was feeling pretty good, as she appeared to be quite happy.

"Whew! That's good—I was kinda worried. Hey, don't forget the dorm meetin' tomorrow after supper. Don't you have almost all day classes on Monday?" Janie asked, visibly relieved Barb-oh was back.

"Yepper. Until early afternoon." She sat up and took a deep breath. "But, I'll probably go over to Big Barb's to study tomorrow afternoon after class, so don't worry if you don't see me. I'll be fine."

Janie cocked her head in curiosity—but shrugged. Barb-oh spent a lot of time at her sister's house. "It should be quiet. Big Barb's back home in El Paso with the kids for a few days. I've got a big test comin' up and need to concentrate." Barb-oh stood up, holding a hand out to pull Janie to her feet. "But right now I've gotta go meet Mark for Sunday night pizza. Wanna come along?"

"No thanks. Gene's supposed to get off work soon and bring us some burgers. He started workin' at Mac's today, ya know," Janie said.

"Oh, yeah, that's right. I'm really glad you two are a couple, Janie. Well, be good." Janie gazed after Barb-oh but was distracted by the phone ringing. She slid over to the black phone hanging on the wall to grab the receiver.

"Janie's Bar and Grill," she said jokingly.

No answer from the other end—only heavy breathing.

Janie leaned out in the hall. "Obscene Phone Call Guy's at it again!" Returning the receiver to her mouth, she said, "Thanks for callin'. I was beginnin' to feel unloved!"

She hung the phone up with a bang. She counted to five and walked across to Glenda's open door just as the phone rang. She lifted it, listening for the heavy breathing.

"Hi there! So, it's you again, isn't it? Gosh, we've gotta stop meetin' like this!" She hung the phone on the hook softly. She counted to five again. The phone rang in the next room. But she was tired of the game and let it ring. She stopped in the middle of the hall to wave at Candace. "Obscene Phone Call Guy's comin' your way. Give him hell!" she called. Candace flashed the OK sign. Janie was about to run up the hall to listen, when her phone rang again.

"Tanya's House of Horrors—no, not Whores—Horrors. How may I help you? Oh, Mom! Sorry about that...yes, everything's fine. I love you, too, Mom. Gosh, I'm glad it's you and not the Obscene Phone Call Guy again. Oh, never mind—tell me what's happenin' back home!"

Janie stepped into the closet with the receiver.

Glenn and Glenda were driving down the drag on their way back to the park when Glenda noticed the infamous blue Nova parked in front of Mr. and Mrs. Rocker's house. *Allen*—she corrected her thought. She saw Glenn's brother and Mr. Allen waving at them from the circle driveway in front of the beautiful Victorian house. Glenn honked, waving out the window.

"Isn't that your brother? You know Mr. Rocker—I mean—Mr. Allen?"

"Rocker?" Glenn was perplexed. "Know him? Sure, that's my brother, Larry, and my Uncle Dub." He turned a bit to glance at Glenda. "You know Uncle Dub?"

"Kind of. He and his wife Bettie gave Linda and me a little tour of the house one afternoon a couple a' weeks ago. They're very nice, and the house is fantastic. Until we met them—we always called 'em the 'Rockers,' since they were usually on the porch in that rockin' chair. I can't believe it. They're your aunt and uncle? Wait a second. Allen—that's their name, too. Of course, now I see."

Glenda peered back, waving at the man who was still staring at the Thunderbird. Turning back, she noticed Glenn had gripped the wheel with both hands.

"Damn. Time's gotten away from me. We were supposed to help Uncle Dub with hopefully the last yard mowin' of the year. Man, I hate bein' late. I'd better drop you off and get to it." Glenn turned the wheel sharply to return to the park. Glenda relaxed and reflected on this new information. Deep in thought, she was startled when Glenn spoke again. "The Rockers. That's pretty good. Technically, it's a glider. So, you like it—Uncle Dub's house?"

"Oh, yes. Everything about it's wonderful."

"Yeah, everything except the plumbin', the electrical wiring, and the roof's cavin' in—but yep, other than that it's great!"

After parking next to her Camaro, Glenn turned toward Glenda. She looked up into his very blue eyes, remaining silent. Before she knew what was happening, he placed his arm around her shoulder—his hand gently held the back of her head. He tenderly pulled her close and kissed her. And she kissed him back with everything that had been stirring inside her since their first meeting. As the kiss deepened, Glenda felt the connection with this man reach very far down into her soul. The butterflies she had experienced before became a tornado of emotion. Breathless—they drew slightly apart—but with him holding her head to his chest and wrapping his other arm around her waist. Glenda felt his warmth—heard him whisper, "Wow..." into her hair. She drew a deep, shuddering breath. Her eyes closed to allow the new emotion to seep into her consciousness. She took in his smell—his presence—his heart beat—then heard him sigh deeply. She felt calmer within, also. Well, not really all that calm, but at least more under control. She thought so anyway.

Glenn cleared his throat, releasing the girl from his embrace. The kiss had surprised him. He certainly didn't intend to kiss her—well, not like that. Leaning back in the seat, he felt her move slowly away. He noticed her eyes were still closed. He, too, closed his for a moment. He gulped and peeked at her through hooded eyelids.

"Well, wow. So, what 're you doin' tomorrow night?" he said in an effort to sound light-hearted.

Glenda turned to face him. "Hmm…I don't know. What am I doin'?" She pressed her chin with her index finger, as if in thought. They both chuckled—and climbed out of the Thunderbird.

"How 'bout we meet right here about seven and play it by ear?"

"That's doable—Monday evenings are usually pretty boring. Maybe we could liven it up a little!" Glenda said happily. Her brow creased with a little frown. "Or will your usual runnin' buddies be upset?"

"My buddies? They're big boys. They can take care of themselves. What about your gang? They depend on you to take them ridin' around, don't they?"

"Heck, they can stay home and study for a change. Speakin' of, I'd better go back and check on 'em. Plus, I have to study for two big tests this week. Really, I think the professors get together and plan it that way. Maybe they do that to prepare you for life. Ya know? When things always seem to happen in bunches?"

Glenda realized she was rambling but felt happy—something she hadn't felt in a very long time. She closed her mouth, gathering her thoughts. "Thanks for a wonderful afternoon," she said, moving closer to Glenn.

She placed her right hand tentatively on his chest. He took a deep breath, momentarily trying to resist, but just couldn't stop his arms from wrapping around her. He instinctively knew he didn't dare kiss her again—realizing with surprise that he might not let her go. He held her closely for a few seconds—then released her. All in good time—take it slow—those were his thoughts, as she backed away carefully, her eyes on the ground.

Glenda walked toward her Camaro, somewhat in a daze. As she shut the car door, she looked back at the man who had just reached inside and touched a part of her being she didn't even know existed. His smile lines crinkled, causing the butterflies to stir again. She returned the smile and gave him a little wave. Driving away, she could feel him watching. She savored the thought of his blue eyes looking deeply into her soul.

Chapter Fourteen

"*H*EY, DON'T KILL THE messenger," called a voice from the lobby doorway at the dark end of the hall. The large group of grumbling coeds turned as one away from both dorm monitor and message at the end of the Monday mandatory floor meeting.

"Damn it all straight to hell," Candace said, her voice venomous, tossing her curls angrily. "It's all my fault because of that stupid sign."

"Don't worry about it, Candace. Like I told you before—we're all in this together," Glenda said. They broke away from the main group to walk back toward their end of the hall. Janie and Tanya merely nodded. Linda Lou looked stunned. The dorm monitor had stated rather loudly that the Dean of Women had sent word that five of the girls known to be associated with WWAB had five mandatory appointments on Tuesday beginning at 1:00 p.m., except for Glenda. Hers was at 9:45 a.m.

"But why 9:45?" Linda Lou asked, concerned. She had lived in Horne Hall for three years, and though she was heavily involved in various shenanigans, she had never before been called to the Dean's office.

"Ah, yes. It's all becoming very clear to me now. She must a' looked at my schedule—I have eight o'clock and eleven o'clock classes on Tuesdays—and my work-study job in the afternoons. So, she gets me in at 9:45—right in between those two classes. That way she gets at me first. This is just great. I've got that chemistry test at eleven, and it's a big one," Glenda said, disgusted.

"I've got it," Tanya said.

The five girls entered Glenda's room, landing on whatever surfaces they could find. "Glenda can say I did it—I'll say Janie did it—Janie says Linda did it—Linda says Candace did it—and Candace says Glenda did it. By the time Dean Stickler is through with us, she'll be so confused maybe she'll forget all about it!"

"Not a chance, Tan-ay. Not this time. This sounds pretty cereal with her calling us all in separately," Linda Lou said, a sense of dread in her words.

"I'm afraid Linda's right," Glenda agreed. "This is corn flakes cereal for sure. I think it would be best to just say we don't know who did it and leave it at that. Just take *the fifth*. Dang it. And things were goin' so well lately. Is that plan OK with you, Janie?"

Janie had been uncharacteristically quiet—but looked up at the mention of her name. "Uhh, yeah. Sure, fine. Did anybody see Barb-oh at the meetin'?"

"No. I haven't seen her since before lunch," Candace answered quickly. Janie looked sharply at her tall friend. "She wasn't at dinner either."

"Yeah, I know," Janie said quietly.

"She's probably just studyin' or somethin'," Tanya said, as she moved closer to her roommate. "After all, it's only six-thirty."

Janie nodded absently, looking out the window at the setting sun. Glenda watched closely for a moment, then jumped from her chair. "Oh, my. I've gotta get ready to meet Glenn at seven. Shoo everybody—go home and make room." She waved her arms as if chasing away unwanted pests. Subconsciously, she was trying to use all her bluster to purge the undefined pall that had somehow fallen on her friends. "No, no! No questions—not now!" She could see the inquiries forming in her friends' eyes and minds.

Linda Lou knew what was going on. "GO!" she yelled.

The room cleared out pretty quickly. Glenda and Linda chuckled at the fact the other girls actually did leave upon request. The soft laughter also broke the nearly palpable tension that had built up in the room.

Glenda heard Janie across the hall on the phone. "Mark? Hey, have you seen Barb-oh? I mean, she was supposed to be at dinner and a floor meetin', but she didn't show up. You think we should go look for her? OK, I'll call Big Barb's—then I'll call you right back."

A shadow of tension returned. Glenda glanced at Linda Lou but saw her roommate had picked up a book, apparently unaware of the conversation or the worried tone in Janie's voice. Janie hung up the phone loudly. Glenda heard no more, so she shook off the feeling as much as she could before walking into her closet to change clothes. She was dressed and brushing her teeth when the sensation returned.

Someone was watching her.

She noisily spit toothpaste into the sink and whirled around to confront the intruder. Tanya was standing in the middle of the room. "Where are you meetin' him?" she asked.

Glenda sighed rather heavily with relief, grabbing the towel from the rack on the wall by the sink to wipe her face. "Down in the park—same as before—at the Sittin' Tree," she answered through the towel. "Why, what's the matter?"

She looked hard at Tanya. A troubled look crossed the girl's face. A disturbing situation, as usually this girl didn't worry about much of anything.

"I don't know. I just wanna know where you'll be, I guess. In case we need ya." She turned abruptly, leaving the room without further comment.

Glenda and Linda exchanged perplexed looks. "Hmm. Very strange. You're startin' to like him, aren't ya Glenda?"

Glenda's nonverbal answer was only a hint of her dimple. Linda Lou nodded knowingly, lowering her eyes to her book. "Have a good time!" she said in a low voice.

"I certainly hope so." Glenda checked her reflection in the mirror mounted on the plaster wall. "Well, here goes nothin'." She grabbed her keys, checkbook, and hurried out of the room.

Janie stood at the phone, dialing Barb-oh's sister's phone number again—letting it ring ten times. She hung up and dialed it again. This time it rang twenty times before she gave up. She called Mark; they decided to go look for Barb-oh.

She turned to Tanya. "Mark's comin' to get me. We're gonna go see if Barb-oh is at Big Barb's or what. I know she walked over there—so she'd hafta walk back. Maybe she sprained her ankle or somethin'."

"OK. I'll stay here and wait for you." Tanya rose from her chair, picking up on her roommate's apprehension. Janie nodded absently and left the room. She hurried out of the dorm, ran down the outside steps and hopped in with Mark. He drove out of the college the back way—into the neighborhood behind the campus—then pulled into Big Barb's empty driveway a minute later.

He glanced over at Janie. She looked back at him. Neither spoke as their eyes met. Janie squeezed her eyes closed—then opened them, gazing at the house. She felt the skin on the back of her neck prickle. Mark turned the key off. The only sound was the pickup door softly clicking when Janie pushed it part of the way shut. Mark stayed behind the wheel. It was uncharacteristic for him to make no move to exit the truck. Janie walked up to the front door. It was slightly open.

"Barb-oh?" she called softly. She pushed the door open a few more inches and called out in a louder voice, "Barb-oh? Are you here?"

She stepped inside the doorway, hearing only silence.

Janie walked through the living room toward the kitchen. Kids' toys were scattered around the room in a strange, still arrangement. Everything was quiet—not even Janie's footsteps made any sound. As she passed the hall bathroom, she glanced through the half-open doorway and froze in her tracks. Her eyes widened when she saw Barb-oh in the bathroom. Janie's long time friend—her best friend in the world—was on the floor—slumped against the bathtub—with a gun in her hand.

She took a step closer—then froze again. She could see a pool of blood in the bathtub and instantly knew what had happened. Hearing Mark walk through the living room, she remained involuntarily fixed in place, unable to stop him from seeing Barb-oh, his fiancée. Janie was breaking inside and feared he would break down, too. Mark stopped beside Janie, then looked into the bathroom. He yelled something unintelligible before running out of the house; he collapsed and retched in the front yard.

Janie remained stationary—in shock. Somehow, she knew Barb-oh was dead; nothing could be done to save her. Death brings a profound stillness to the body when the lungs no longer draw in and expel breath. The body, the skin, the muscles, the very bones are completely still—nothing moves in any way—

save perhaps a strand of hair stirred by some nearby air current. That's what she saw in Barb-oh.

Janie withdrew from her place in front of the bathroom door. She couldn't bring herself to move any closer—she couldn't even touch her friend. She took a deep, deep breath and walked stiffly to the master bedroom, where she knew there was a phone. When she entered the room, she saw evidence of Barb-oh's search for the gun. Drawers were open and clothing was strewn all over the floor. Janie felt frozen again, like she was caught in a dream where she needed to run away, but she could only move her legs in slow motion. Finally making it to the bedroom, she opened the small phone book on the nightstand and fumbled through the first few pages to find the emergency numbers. Police—she needed the police number but couldn't find it.

Frustrated, Janie shook her head furiously to regain her senses. Brain cells finally started working, and her index finger dialed zero. The line connected. She had to report a suicide—but her mind could not convince her mouth to form the words.

"Operator? Operator? I..uhh...we...uhh...the police. My friend—she's...police—we need the police, please," she said desperately into the phone.

The operator connected her to the police dispatcher. She had to start over. "We need the police. My friend, she's...she's...suicide. Address? I don't know. It's on Pecan Street, Big Barb—no wait. It's Jimmy's house. I mean James—James Griffin's house. Thank you. I'll wait outside for 'em."

She replaced the handset gently onto the cradle and remembered Mark. She walked through the house, eyes locked straight ahead, and found him in the front yard, sitting on the grass next to a tree. He held his head in his hands, sobbing. Janie wanted to cry, too—to let it out—but she knew she had to maintain control for Mark's sake, and also for herself and what was yet to come. Janie left him alone under the tree. He didn't appear to have recognized she was there anyway, so she walked back into the house. Bracing herself, Janie quickly passed again by the shocking scene in the bathroom, keeping her eyes focused on the table in the kitchen. Her mind must have reasoned subconsciously that most people would sit at a table to write something down on paper. Therefore, she had formed a thought that Barb-oh had left a note. She walked into the kitchen with anticipation.

The bottom edge of the piece of paper lay on the straight edge of the table perfectly—carefully placed there. It was a page from a yellow legal pad, neatly torn at the top perforation. Janie glanced around. An ordinary notepad for jotting down messages or grocery lists lay on the kitchen counter beneath the wall phone by the back door. Except this time, the paper recorded the last thoughts of a twenty year old girl. Janie looked again at the note in front of her, seeing words in Barb-oh's handwriting. Controlling the urge to touch the note, she slumped heavily in the kitchen chair to read it where it lay. It spoke of apologies and regrets, but the actual words were lost in the flood of memories and ideas that bombarded Janie's mind.

Understanding came to her in that single moment, as she remembered all of Barb-oh's bad breaks in high school—all those times life in general seemed to go sour for her—and the times she was blamed for and accused of behaviors that now seemed understandable. Janie remembered that Barb-oh's oldest birth brother had committed suicide in 1973. Her birth mother had always suffered from mental illness; she had been in a mental institution from the time Barb-oh was seven. All of it added up in Janie's mind as to Barb-oh's birth family's predisposition to mental illness. She looked up at the ceiling, silently appealing to God to explain why she didn't realize all this before it was too late. Maybe she could have gotten her friend some help. Janie closed her eyes against the hot tears threatening to burst from her breaking heart. Why hadn't she been alarmed at the calm, happy-go-lucky Barb-oh of late? That should have been a sign, a beacon declaring that a decision had been made—the ultimate decision. Janie breathed deeply to banish such thoughts. *Strength*—she told herself—*be strong*. She fought off tears and left through the back door to avoid the inside of the house.

As she walked around the side of the house, she saw two police cars parked at the curb in the street. Two officers were attempting to ask Mark some questions. Still completely in shock, he stood helplessly.

Janie approached. "Officers. I'm Janie Gentry. My friend, Barbara Lane, shot herself in there—in the house," she said with surprising strength. "I'm pretty sure she's..." Janie hesitated and looked imploringly at the policeman closest to her, as her resolve waned. The large man took her arm and steadied her.

"Just show us where, sweetheart. Then come right back out here, OK?" Officer House said with compassion.

Janie got a grip on herself and nodded. She silently guided the two officers through the living room and to the bathroom. After taking a few steps to keep herself out of the range of sight of Barb-oh's body, she motioned for the officers to follow her to the master bedroom. She mutely pointed at the evidence of the search for the gun before leading them to the kitchen and motioning to the note on the table. She answered their questions mechanically from the same kitchen chair she had occupied earlier.

"It came from this pad," Officer House said softly. "I mean the note. Ya know, it's odd. The kitchen phone cord's on top of the notepad. It's like the pad was set down here—the phone was picked up—and then the phone was put back—leavin' the cord to rest here on the pad—after that note over there was torn off." Janie's sharp intake of breath caused him to look up.

"Oh, no. Maybe she tried to call me, or Mark, and we weren't there? Oh, my God," Janie cried in a voice close to panic. She rose from the chair, stumbling to the back door. The officers followed her wilting figure around the house to the front drive. Another vehicle had pulled in. Officer House went over to identify the driver.

Alarmed at coming home from work to find policemen on his front lawn, Jimmy Griffin nearly jumped out of his car. "What's goin' on?"

Officer House put his hand on the man's shoulder. "There's been a suicide. Barbara is dead," he answered.

Janie's head jerked up at the sound of Jimmy's sharp intake of breath. "But, Barb. She and the kids..." he said with a fading voice. He began to sway on his feet. "My wife's in El Paso."

"Your wife?" Officer House turned toward Janie.

Janie quickly ran over to this man she had known all of her life. "Jimmy! Oh, Jimmy! It's Barb-oh. Barb-oh killed herself in there—in the bathroom."

She sank into his arms. She felt the wave of relief initially come over Jimmy, realizing his wife Barbara was all right. But as he comprehended the current situation, a different tension grew. Janie looked up at him with compassion—then pulled away, so they could return their attention to the officers.

After a period of questions and police interviews, an ambulance crew quietly went into the house. Eventually, Barb-oh's body was wheeled out the front door on a gurney, completely draped in a white sheet. Everyone stood statue still until the doors of the ambulance were closed, and the vehicle was out of sight. Jimmy walked very slowly into his home which now held a tragic memory, knowing his next task was to call Big Barb in El Paso with the terrible news. A doctor had been contacted to prescribe a sedative for Mark, who still seemed to be in shock. The Dean of Men was called to take him to his dorm room. The police officers gathered their notes and checked the scene one last time. They clumsily voiced condolences before driving away in opposite directions on Pecan Street.

After everyone disappeared, Janie stood very small and alone in the driveway. She swayed a little, sighed and looked blankly at Mark's pickup. She got in the driver's side, found the keys in the floor right where she expected them to be, and drove herself back to the girls' dorm parking area. It wasn't easy being the strong one, she realized. She shut the pickup door, pocketing the keys. Janie walked up the stairs to the second floor of Horne Hall, instantly conscious that the primary thought in her mind was that she wanted her mama.

Janie walked down the hall with dread. She feared having to tell everybody what had happened. Barely believing it herself, she had no idea how she could say the words over and over. As Janie paused at the threshold of her room she heard voices, and breathed evenly to work up some courage. It was Tanya and Candace—good—two for one. Her feet wouldn't move at first, but she looked down and willed them to take steps forward.

"Hey, Janie. You're back. Whew, I was worried, though I'm not so good at that. I was—I mean..." Tanya began rambling. But she stopped in mid-sentence when she saw Janie's face. "Oh, my God, what's the matter?"

Candace walked over to Janie and guided her to Tanya's bed. She and Tanya hovered and waited. After a few seconds, Janie spoke in a weak and very quiet voice: "She killed herself. Barb-oh's dead."

Tanya and Candace both cried out in shock. Each began babbling questions Janie could not comprehend. She held up her right hand to stop the gush of words.

"I need to call home. I need Gene, and I need Glenda. But most of all, I need to talk to my mama," she said, as tears began to fill her eyes. She almost couldn't think—she looked desperately to her friends for help. "Gene's at work."

Candace rose from the bed. "I'll go call Boots and ask him to find him."

"And ask him to go down to the park, too. Glenda should be there with Glenn, I hope." A strange realization hit—she must have known they'd need to find Glenda. "Janie, I'll dial your mom's number. Here, scoot over here." She helped Janie move down the bed to within reach of the phone.

Tanya picked up the receiver and dialed the number posted on the bulletin board. She quietly asked the operator to connect the collect call. After a moment, she gently handed the phone to Janie. She backed away silently.

"Daddy? Oh, Daddy, Barb-oh is dead. She killed herself!" Janie cried into the phone and attempted to tell the news. She had never seen or heard her father cry, but he was crying with her now. Hearing his youngest daughter falling apart 600 miles away, he was overcome with helplessness. His voice faded away, as he handed the phone to Janie's mother. It took a long while, but eventually the talk and love her mother sent to her across the phone line allowed Janie to finally let the emotions and tears flow. Mama did help her feel comforted and safe.

"Thanks, Mama. I love you, too. Tell Daddy I love him. I guess I'll probably see y'all in a couple a' days." Still sobbing, Janie nodded her head slowly and whispered, "Bye." She laid the receiver on the floor, collapsed on Tanya's bed, and covered her head with a pillow.

Candace walked in, saw Janie, and turned off the light. She motioned to Tanya to join her in the hall. Tanya quietly replaced the phone receiver, pulling the door almost closed, as she left the room.

"OK. I got hold of Boots. He's gonna go get Gene and Glenda. Word is spreadin' fast. April and June and some of the other girls think we should get everybody together downstairs. For Janie," Candace whispered.

"Yeah. That's a good idea. Let's let her rest for a little while. Will you grab something to do and some quarters for the coke machine, then let everybody know to meet us down in the lobby? I'll bring Janie down—say, in half an hour. Gene and Glenda should be here by then. I'd better go back in and see if she needs anything. Thanks, Candace," Tanya said, resting her fingertips on the taller girl's elbow.

Candace nodded and headed down the hall to her own room. She stopped stock-still at the threshold. Barb-oh's things were lying about. Her shoes were on the floor by the bed, a pair of jeans lay neatly folded on the desk chair. Candace took a deep breath, remembering the time they had a contest to see who could balance a beer bottle on her head the longest. The cloud of sadness grew, as her mind's eye pictured Barb-oh sitting in that very chair in rapt concentration, completely straight-faced with a beer bottle on her head. Barb-oh won that contest. Candace focused on the good memory and tried to shake off the sadness. Grabbing a deck of cards and her change purse from a shelf, she turned her back on the sadly abandoned items and the room.

As the door slammed shut, a hollow sound echoed throughout the hall.

Glenn straddled the seat of the picnic bench, while Glenda faced the table. She felt his leg behind her and found herself leaning toward him. They talked about their backgrounds and family. They had much in common, as they had realized the day before, though they were very different people. He had an aura of danger, yet safety—she had a manner of peace and patience. They both had corny senses of humor. Glenda felt his gentle hand on the small of her back. She gave in and moved closer to rest her cheek on his chest. Her arms were crossed, but she relaxed as his other arm encircled her, holding one elbow in the cup of his hand. It felt natural and right. She placed the flat of one hand on his chest by her face.

The talking stopped. Without the other knowing, they both closed their eyes. They breathed together—hearts beating—he smelling her hair—she feeling his warmth. Glenda sighed after feeling him kiss her hair. The knowledge that if she looked up they would kiss caused her to pause, suspecting he was shy and self-conscious about that sort of thing. So, she just snuggled a little closer.

Glenn couldn't believe his luck, having this adorable college girl in his arms. He had never experienced this type of contentment—satisfied with just sitting somewhere—being with somebody. As he unconsciously kissed her sweet smelling hair, he held her with his arms and thoughts. At that moment, everything was very, very good.

"Boots? What the heck are you doing back here?"

Gene was quite surprised to see Boots at the kitchen door. He jauntily waved the large metal spatula he was using to flip the Mac Burgers, until he saw the look on Boots' face. His expression changed to concern. "What's the matter?"

"I need to take you to see Janie." Boots quickly held up his hand, seeing the alarm in Gene's face. "Janie's OK. It's Barb-oh. She killed herself this afternoon. Janie found her."

Gene's mouth fell open. He dropped the spatula to the floor, the loud clanging sound causing nearly the entire crew to turn around to see what had happened. Gene swayed a little, reaching back toward the grill to steady himself.

Someone grabbed his arm to hold him up. "Whoa there, son. That's a mighty hot spot to lean on. Lean on me instead. I heard what your friend said. Whatcha need to do?"

An older man dressed in a shirt and tie spoke with compassion. He held on firmly to the younger man's arm.

"Janie. My God, Janie! I've got...got to go, Mr. Mac..." Gene recovered himself. He began removing the apron he had been wearing. "But, but...the food?"

"Don't you worry about that, son. I've flipped a few burgers in my time in this joint, don't ya know? Go. Go to your friends." He attempted to tie Gene's apron around his ample belly, while the two young men practically ran through the kitchen and out the back door.

"One down—one to go," Boots said to himself, after Gene ran down the sidewalk toward the front door of the girls' dorm lobby. He didn't wait to see his friend to go in. He wasn't ready to see the girls. Plus, he still had someone else to find. "The park. Candace said Glenda would be in the city park with that Evel guy." Boots continued his conversation with himself. "Well, he's not all that evil—he actually seems to be OK."

He mashed his foot down on the accelerator—the car sputtered a bit, as it wasn't driven often. But it responded, taking off with a roar.

It only took a few minutes to drive to the city park. Boots drove down the winding road, craning his neck, looking this way and that for Glenda's yellow Camaro. Daylight faded—tall oak trees cast dark shadows on the park grounds.

Boots saw a reflection to the right, as his headlights swept over the area. "Ah ha. Two sets of taillights. Well, here goes. Man, I hate this." The car stopped behind the Camaro and Thunderbird.

"Company." Glenn removed his arms from around Glenda's waist. She rose upright slowly, like a stretching cat, peering at the vehicle that had interrupted their peaceful moment. She saw the cowboy hat rise above the roof of a familiar car in the fading light.

"Boots?" She stood up, shaking her head a bit to fully awaken. "Boots? Man, what 're you doin' here? You hardly ever drive that old heap!"

Glenn stood beside her, touching her elbow to let her know he was there. "Come on, and meet Boots," she said over her shoulder.

They walked forward, as Boots moved around to the rear of his car. He held his hand up in the air. "We know each other... sort of." Boots leaned on the trunk of his car. "Glenda, you need to go to the dorm lobby. Something has happened."

"Lobby? What 're you talkin' about? You sound strange, Boots. What's wrong?"

"Glenda. Barb-oh killed herself this afternoon. Janie found her—she needs you," he said as gently as he could. He heard her gasp and moved toward her, but Glenn firmly gripped her arms, moving her forward so she could lean on the Camaro.

"Oh, my God," Glenda said, her voice suddenly hoarse. "Oh, no—not Barb-oh. And oh, my...my little Janie! Glenn, I—I've gotta go!"

She turned to the man standing very close to her. He took her in his arms for a count of three—then released—but held fast to her shoulders.

"Go. Or do you want me to take you? We can get your car later."

Glenda shook her head slowly, taking a deep breath. "No, I'll be OK. I may need my car later. But thanks," she said, looking up into his blue eyes. She knew he could see the tears beginning to form; she blinked heavily to control them. "I'll be all right. I've gotta go to Janie. Thanks, Boots."

Boots seemed embarrassed. "I'm just glad I found you. Sorry to interrupt, but..."

"No problem man. Glenda—go, but be careful. I'll be around if you need me for anything." Glenn knew this was a terrible situation; he felt compelled to be strong. "Tell Janie...well, I'll be glad to help, if I can."

Boots and Glenda both looked at Glenn with admiration. She gave him a thankful half smile before sliding into her car. Boots stood still—both men watched the Camaro's taillights disappear around a corner. *Well, that's done,* Boots said to himself.

Glenn looked at the cowboy and his vehicle. The car was a big brown two-door of a quite rare vintage and style. Glenn was curious about it. "Nice car. Man, you don't see many of these around," Glenn said to change the subject to something more comfortable. But anything to do with automobiles caught his attention. Boots decided he was right about this being an OK guy. They discussed the car in great detail—all about the engine and transmission and cars like it, with engines of slightly different sizes and different transmissions.

The streetlights flickered on. They'd been standing in complete darkness for quite some time.

"Well, I'd better get back to the college. Maybe most of the cryin' is over by now," Boots said. "Nice talkin' with you, Glenn."

"Yeah, you, too. Hey, if anybody needs me, I'll probably be at Tim's until late."

"Right. That T-Bird's easy to spot. I thought I had a big coupe till I saw that car!" Boots walked over to the driver's side of his car and opened the door.

"Land yacht. That's what it is. The Battleship Allen. Glenn returned to a more somber attitude. "Good luck, man. I don't know what else to say."

"Yeah. I know whatcha mean. See ya later," Boots said, as he sank into the car. The engine roared to life and the vehicle slowly moved away. Glenn watched it disappear around the curve just as the Camaro had earlier, listening, until there was no longer any sound. He slid into the Thunderbird—shut the door to extinguish the light and disappeared in his own way. He had some thinking to do—some hard thinking.

When Boots entered the dorm lobby, he immediately saw quite a few people assembled. They were extremely quiet for such a large group. The incongruity struck him firmly. Some were playing cards—some were talking quietly—whispering actually—but most were just sitting. Janie and Gene were huddled together, her face puffy from crying. His eyes were red as well. Friends circled Janie like a bull's eye: Glenda, Tanya, Linda and Candace were the closest; April, May, June and some of the other Horne Hall girls huddled in the next concentric ring. On the outskirts of the group were other people he recognized but didn't actually know. Candace was directing things—she appeared to be taking orders for drinks, though the only sound he actually heard was the quarters jingling in her hands. She vanished through a door into an unknown area where no male could go—other than the guy who stocks the coke machine.

"Hey. Thanks for comin'," Linda said quietly. Boots jumped as if he'd been goosed from behind. Linda elbowed him gently. Glenda and Tanya joined them. The concentric circles of people dissolved into smaller, individual groups. The four friends walked silently up to the large front windows that offered a wide view of the poorly lit front lawn of the dorm.

"This is terrible. It's gonna to be a long, rough night," Tanya said sadly. The others remained quiet. They stood shoulder-to-shoulder, blankly looking out the windows.

A streak of blue whizzed by the dorm lobby. Brake lights flashed briefly, as the car slowed to make the turn to zoom away from the campus and out of sight.

"Hey. That was Jimmie Mac," Glenda said softly.

"That's weird. He didn't have his lights on," Linda Lou said.

"And he was in a *real* big hurry," Tanya added.

BOOM! It sounded from the area of the cannon. The windows of the dorm lobby rattled. A few people cried out with surprise. Tanya looked out the window, toward the direction in which the Corvette had sped.

"What the heck?" Boots asked.

Tanya and the other two girls gazed at each other with sudden comprehension. Each smiled for the first time in several hours. The longstanding mystery of who had been firing the cannon was finally solved.

Chapter Fifteen

*J*ANIE LAY AWAKE in her dorm room. Almost two weeks had passed since she had slept in that bed. For a Saturday night, the campus was strangely quiet. She sighed; of course no one was ridin' around—it was very late. Everyone else in the dorm was asleep. An almost full moon appeared in her window. It was perfectly framed in one of the old panes of glass above her bed. She gazed at the Man in the Moon, letting her mind wander over the past two weeks since Barb-oh's death.

The day was the longest of her nineteen years. Her friends stayed up with her until the wee hours of the morning, playing cards and keeping each other company. Gene stayed as long as he could, but at midnight the dorm monitor made him leave, despite very valid and logical arguments from Tanya and Glenda for him to stay. Janie was grateful her close friends stayed with her as long as possible, but eventually even they had to go to bed. Candace was the only person who saw the night through with Janie, joining her to watch dawn's light promise a new day. During that seemingly eternal night, Janie could not close her eyes without seeing Barb-oh lying on the floor of that bathroom. Candace couldn't face being in the dorm room with her roommate's things, knowing Barb-oh would never return to claim them. So, they kept each other company—and awake.

The next morning, Dean Stickler cancelled all the WWAB's appointments, except Janie's. She could now see the Dean acted more out of curiosity about the manner of Barb-oh's death than the offering of any true sympathy. Janie nodded her head on the pillow, realizing she could finally think of the terrible experience without a shudder or tear. Believing she might always hold that offensive interview against the Dean of Women, she hoped to never have to face the Dean again. Tanya informed Janie the WWAB sign had mysteriously disappeared shortly after she left for El Paso. It didn't really matter anymore.

The moon moved into the next pane of glass to the right. Janie stretched her legs under the sheet. She thought of the recital the following afternoon in the Fine Arts Building. Having missed several modern dance rehearsals on the big auditorium stage, Janie sighed heavily and wondered if she was ready. But her mind continued its tour of memories.

Barb-oh's funeral arrangements had been made by noon the day after her death. The task of packing her friend's things fell on Janie. Also, she had to pick out the clothing in which Barb-oh would be buried. She remembered sitting on Barb-oh's bed, wondering how a person makes a decision like that. Do you pick something she'd wear every day, like jeans and boots? Or maybe a dress—like to wear to church on Sunday? She finally decided on the only dress in the closet, recalling Barb-oh wore it once. Boxes appeared outside the door without explanation, so Janie filled them with her friend's things, holding back only a few items that held fond memories of their friendship. She would cherish them always.

That second night, the exhaustion finally kicked in. She finally got some sleep. Good thing, as the next morning, she and Barb-oh's belongings sadly made the long 550 mile trip to El Paso in Jimmy's van. Barb-oh was buried in a desert cemetery outside the city. Her institutionalized mother was brought to the funeral, but she didn't really understand what was happening. She just looked around happily, showing everyone the red rose she had been given. Very sad. It was all so very, very sad. But somehow Janie had to find a way to go on without her life-long friend.

The moon travelled past two more panes of glass and approached the right side of the window frame. Janie closed her eyes and thought about the recital the following day. Her dance to "September" had been perfected in the previous weeks, but she hadn't actually performed the full routine until the Saturday afternoon rehearsal. On Thursday, she'd returned to Dairyville with Jimmy and Big Barb—only to skip classes on Friday. In fact, she had almost pulled out of the recital. Tanya and Glenda insisted that they didn't endure the endless repeated playing of "September" for weeks—just for her to quit. Janie nodded. She'd do it. It would be a good step forward. She sent a silent kiss across the campus to Gene and turned away from the Man in the Moon—who was about to disappear from view. She settled in, finally at ease, and fell right to sleep.

The silver Thunderbird was rolling through downtown Dairyville. It was quite late—Glenn was making his last drag before dropping Charles at his car and Fuzzy at his house. Glenda had ridden around with him earlier. She'd ridden around with him a lot lately. He looked forward to seeing her the following afternoon.

"You're beginnin' to like Glenda quite a bit, aren't ya, Evel?" Fuzzy asked, noticing the look on his friend's face.

Glenn looked sharply at him but quickly relaxed. "I was just thinkin' about where we might ride to tomorrow. I'm gonna pick her up after some dancin' thing her friend Janie's doin'."

"Oh, yeah. Melinda's in that dance recital, too, but she didn't invite me. She did make it a point to mention there's a big cast party or some such thing afterward, and that everybody was goin'. Except me, apparently. Come to think of it, I'm not so sure I like her so much after all," Fuzzy paused. "Maybe I never really did."

"Party?" The thought that Glenda would rather go to the party with her friends than ride with him caused his brow to furrow. He hated to break a date, but she may have forgotten she had something else to do. Glenn had almost decided to show up at the appointed time, when his thoughts were interrupted. Having been so preoccupied, he almost didn't notice a girl walking on the sidewalk beneath Moo Lah. Glenn instantly shifted into high alert, scanning the area for trouble.

Fuzzy looked around, too, full of questions: "Hey, look. That's Debbie, Ben's girl friend. Why's she out here alone? Where's Ben?"

Charles leaned up between the seats to see what was going on. Glenn quickly turned the Thunderbird to pull into a parallel parking place directly under Moo Lah's head. Debbie walked quickly over to the car and leaned in the passenger side window.

"They've got Ben. I was walkin' to find some help," Debbie said forlornly.

"Who's got Ben?" Glenn asked, leaning across Fuzzy.

"The cops. They stopped us and found the cooler full of beer and arrested him for possession of alcohol with a minor—me. They had to let me go, but they've got the Trans Am down at the police station, and Ben's locked up inside. Do you know how we can get bail money?"

"Fuz, scoot over. Debbie, get in. Where's the car exactly—and where's the beer?" Glenn asked firmly.

Debbie rattled a key chain. "The car's right in front of the cop shop, and the cooler's still in the trunk, I think. But I got away with the keys."

Glenn pulled out from the curb. Abruptly, he turned right, driving very slowly. A plan formulated in his mind, which he explained to the others. All agreed it might work, so he killed the headlights and headed to the police station.

He stopped the Thunderbird about half a block from where Ben's Trans Am was parked in front of the police station. No one was around. Fuzzy looked to Glenn for the sign the operation was a *go*. They got the nod. Debbie silently opened the Thunderbird door. Fuzzy caught the door and closed it carefully. The girl walked quickly to the rear of Ben's car, knelt and opened the trunk without a sound. Debbie then carefully reached through the open window, placing the keys in the driver seat. She strolled calmly toward the trees near the building, becoming virtually invisible in the shadows.

The Thunderbird sat uphill from the Trans Am, so Glenn shifted into Neutral, letting the big car roll silently down the hill. He braked to a stop right beside the Trans Am. Fuzzy and Charles moved quietly to the rear of the other car and lifted the cooler out of the trunk. Charles silently closed the Trans Am's trunk lid, while Fuzzy carried the cooler to the Thunderbird. Fuzzy quickly placed the cooler inside Glenn's open trunk, but not before grabbing a beer. He popped the top as Glenn carefully closed the trunk lid.

"Fuz! What the hell are you doin'?" Charles whispered nervously.

Fuzzy slammed down most of the beer and stifled a belch. He grinned crookedly, sauntering toward the front wall of the police station. He stood on his tiptoes and reached for the lighted letters mounted on the brick wall that spelled "POLICE." He couldn't stretch far enough. Glenn snuck over to help out. He lifted Fuzzy a foot or so, allowing him to place the beer can directly on the horizontal part of the L in POLICE. They hurried back to the Thunderbird. Glenn coasted down the hill before starting the engine to make a fast getaway.

"We did it!" Charles said with relief.

"Too bad we didn't have a camera. I wish I could a' got a picture of that 'L' with the beer can on it!" Fuzzy was delighted at the joke.

They decided they couldn't end the night until they knew what happened with Ben, so Glenn parked the Thunderbird at the donut shop. A few beers later, they saw the Trans Am rolling up the drag. Fuzzy flagged it down. Ben was driving—Debbie was with him. They both got out of the car.

"Ben! What happened? They let you go?" Fuzzy asked.

"Sure, they did. When Debbie came in the police station to tell the cops the cooler was gone, they didn't have any evidence. So, they couldn't charge me with anything. They had to let me go. No evidence. That was a mighty fine trick, fellers." Ben was clearly relieved. "But say, can I have my evidence back—if there's any left, that is?"

"He'll never learn," Charles said with a good-natured shake of his head. Fuzzy closed his eyes and stifled a cackle.

"No, probably not," Glenn snickered. He opened his trunk lid.

The next afternoon the sunlight felt extra bright, which was understandable after spending more than an hour in the artificially lit Fine Arts Building. The recital had been a success for the performers, but somewhat excruciating for the audience.

Tanya shaded her eyes. "I can't believe four different people did dances to Janie's song. I never wanna hear 'September' again!"

"And it's no surprise Melinda did hers to Boz Skaggs, either," Candace said, her sarcasm also in fine form.

Glenda smiled. "Oh, give 'em credit. At least they had the guts to jump up there and perform, especially Janie, considering. You wouldn't have gotten up there in front of everybody and danced by yourself, would ya?"

"No way—not me. Not in a million years. Now, go to the party afterward—that I can and will do!" Candace replied.

"You drivin', Glenda?" Tanya asked. "Janie's ridin' with some of the other *so-called* performers. Come on—let's hurry."

"Not I. Candace, you'll hafta drive. You forget...I don't have any hurry bones. Besides, I have a date with Glenn—he'll be here at five. You guys know I don't go in for partyin' all that much anyways."

"Right, right. I knew Glenn had somethin' to do with it!"

The three chatted happily as they walked back to their dorm. After just a brief pit stop upstairs, Tanya hopped in the truck with Candace, and they hurried off to the cast party. Glenda watched the truck through her window until it was out of sight, then turned to check the clock: 4:45 p.m. Just enough time to freshen up a bit and have a Dr Pepper before Glenn arrived. She sighed contentedly.

At 4:59 p.m. Glenda made one last check in the old mirror. In her reflection, she saw more happiness than she thought she'd ever feel again. Checkbook in back pocket, cash in front—all was ready. She practically skipped down the hall and stairs. She came to a sudden stop on the concrete porch, peering around for the Thunderbird. It wasn't in sight. "Whew, made it," she whispered. She walked briskly over to the Shoe Bench—briskly for her—and sat down.

A few cars drove through every now and then, but she didn't see the Thunderbird or Glenn at all. Thirty minutes passed before she became somewhat disheartened. More cars drove by, but none stopped. Her butt told her she'd been waiting on the hard bench for over an hour, and she listened to it. Glenda rose to her feet, fighting back tears. She walked dejectedly back to her room.

The dorm hall was eerily quiet. Glenda was relieved no one was around. She felt like such a fool. As she plopped down on her bed, the anger began to rise. How dare he stand her up like that? She counted on him, but he didn't show. The anger turned to fear when it occurred to her that something might have happened to him or members of his family. There *had* to be an acceptable reason that he didn't show up for their date. While fighting back tears, a motherly endearment came to mind, "You shouldn't wear your feelings on your sleeve." A sardonic chuckle erupted from her throat. She tried to shake off the negative sensation. Searching for something to do, she found it...there, an overflowing laundry basket, ignored for the entire weekend so she could ride around with Glenn. Sighing, she gathered her spirits and her laundry. Escaping the temptation to look out the window was paramount. Glenda grabbed a book, threw it in the basket and marched off to spend some not-so-quality time in the laundry room, far from any window to the outside world.

The next morning, Glenda could barely sit through her ten o'clock class. The professor finally dismissed the students at 10:58 a.m. She tucked her spiral notebook under one arm and pulled the car keys from her pocket. She almost made it to the Camaro without being noticed.

Janie ran up. "Hey, Glendee-girl, where you goin'? Aren't you comin' to the dinin' hall for lunch?"

Glenda opened her car door. "Hi. No. I've gotta go do somethin'. Y'all go on. I'll get somethin' to eat later."

"Later you have to work. Glenda, what's wrong?" Linda Lou had joined the pair by the Camaro.

"I'll be fine. I gotta go now. Don't worry—everything's fine."

Glenda shook her head when she realized she was babbling. She shut the door. Janie and Linda Lou stood back, their mouths hanging open. She waved and smiled so they wouldn't worry, even though she was very nervous.

As she stopped at the traffic light, Glenda looked down at the note written and rewritten several times. The final version was the best. She tore it out of the notebook, folding it in half. She tucked it under her right thigh, so it wouldn't blow out of the open windows. At the first flash of green, she turned left out onto Main Street. At the far end, she kept going past the old Dairy Queen and the historical chapel. On one of their many turns around town Glenn had pointed out the service center where he worked. Glenda knew she could find it again. In just a few minutes she was looking at the unobtrusive entrance to the service center. The place appeared quiet—no people were around. She sighed with relief, spotting the shiny silver Thunderbird.

The yellow Camaro coasted into the service yard beside the silver car. Glenda hurriedly got out, put the note under the driver side windshield wiper—and left. She pulled into a restaurant parking lot a block away and caught her breath. Glenda closed her eyes to send a mental message to Glenn. *Please read the note. Please.* She decided to pick up a to-go sandwich from the restaurant and try to get to work on time.

Lunch time at the service center meant sandwiches, thermos bottles of coffee or sweet tea, and dominoes at straight up noon. The guys played religiously every day. The old guys were good, real good, but Ned liked having Pancho as a partner. He was young but sharp. Glenn enjoyed the dominoes, though the old guys were hard to beat.

At quitting time, Glenn felt disgustingly dirty, gritty. It had been a rough day of handling the worst job duty—again. He had washed at his hands and face before giving up on that as wasted effort. Real soap and hot water—under pressure—was sorely needed. Nearly exhausted, Glenn dusted off his pants, so he would deposit as little dirt on the red seat covers as possible. He practically fell into the driver's seat.

It was then Glenn saw the note under the windshield wiper. He looked around suspiciously, waiting for the rest of the crew to leave the service center. When the yard was empty, he took the note off the windshield. It was folded once and had apparently been torn from a spiral notebook. He read silently:

Glenn,

I was worried that something bad happened when I didn't see you yesterday. Please come by, if you want to. If you don't, that's OK too. But, I'd really like to talk...

Glenda

The note shook in his trembling hands for a moment. He placed it gently on the seat, drew in a deep breath, exhaled, then breathed deeply again. Glenn closed his eyes for a moment—only a second really—before opening them and peering through the windshield intently. He started the Thunderbird, spinning the back tires all the way down the gravel driveway. The big car slid sideways as it burst out onto the street, leaving a cloud of dust in its wake.

Glenda and her friends were at the Shoe Bench. Supper was over for them, although a long line still stretched out the dining hall doors.

"I'm glad we go early and beat the rush," Janie was saying.

She leaned on Gene. Their relationship had become even stronger after Barb-oh's death. They were practically inseparable except during classes, Gene's work schedule and after midnight.

"Yeah, but now what 're we gonna do?" Tanya asked.

"You're never satisfied, are ya? Can't we just sit here for a while and digest?" Glenda faced the dorm so she could watch the inbound traffic. "What time is it, anyway?"

"Quarter after five. We've got a whole evenin' ahead of us," Boots answered.

"Do you think he'll...?" Janie began—but stopped when she saw Glenda's eyes were closed. The others kept talking about nothing in particular. Tanya was chatting along until she stopped in midsentence. She threw an elbow into Glenda's side. Glenda sat upright, immediately recognizing what had halted the conversation.

"Oh, my gosh." She rose to her feet to look at Glenn. He was standing beside his car, motioning for her to come over to him. The car was stopped in the main traffic lane, but no other vehicles were around. Glenda paused only a second before hurrying over toward the car. She stopped short, until she saw his smile—and felt her own.

"Pardon my appearance, ma'am. I just got off a major shit detail, and I'm sure it'll take an hour or so of scrubbin' to get cleaned up. But after I do, would you wanna go ridin' around? I mean…I'd like you to—if you want to."

"Oh, yes. I would. You got my note?" Glenda risked a glance into his eyes. The glance lengthened into a gaze; she liked what she saw. She had that fluttering feeling in her chest again. It made her catch her breath.

"I got it. I'm here. I'm dirty. I'm sorry about that, and I'm sorry about yesterday. How about I meet you back here at seven o'clock, and I'll try to explain?"

"Deal. I'm so glad to see you, even if you are under a layer or two of dirt," she answered, relieved.

"I'll be here—seven or before." He said it as though it was a promise. They both knew it was. He got back in the car and winked at her as he took off.

Glenda stood there for a second, breathing with relief. She turned around to find Tanya staring at her. "Well?"

"Seven o'clock—he'll be back. He'll be here this time."

"He'd by golly better be here," Tanya said. She looked over at the Thunderbird. Glenn waved out the window as he passed the Shoe Bench. "I do believe he will. But what do we do till then?"

Glenda first rolled her eyes skyward, then firmly whacked Tanya's arm. "Oh, Tan-ay. Go fetch the Ted tape. I still haven't given it back to Glenn. Let's go ride around a little while. I hear a cherry limeade calling!" She chuckled, holding her hand to her ear as if listening to a faraway voice.

Tanya smacked and licked her lips noisily. "I feel like a Twist. Forget Ted—let's go now!" She turned back toward the Shoe Bench. "How 'bout you, Janie?"

"Naa. No Twist for me. I've gotta watch my girlish figure!" Janie squealed when Gene pinched her rear end. "Besides, somebody's gotta go fetch Ted for Glenda!"

Tanya and Glenda beamed at each other. Boots applauded and Janie laughed, as the two girls performed a quick "twist" dance in the street. They hopped in the Camaro for a trip to the Astro Drive-In. The Twist was a simple, yet delightful dessert of soft-serve vanilla and chocolate ice cream dispensed side-by-side and twirled together in a small cup. At only fifty-nine cents, it was a bit of happiness at a bargain price.

"Oh, no. Jackal Ann is on duty," Tanya said.

"No matter—it's time to put that behind us. Let's pull in and order our Twist," Glenda said.

Jacqueline Ann passed by the yellow Camaro with an order for another vehicle, not even looking their way. Glenda looked at Tanya with a hint of her dimple showing. "I knew it was over, Tan-ay."

"Imagine that." When their Twists were delivered, they took great joy in the treat.

A little later the girls were making a drag, when Tanya noticed the Allens on their porch, enjoying the fall weather. She waved heartily at them, receiving a greeting in return. She remembered that Glenda had visited them once and that Mrs. Allen made a mean cookie.

"Hey, Glenda. Next time by let's stop and say hello to the Rockers, KO?"

"Heck. Let's stop now. I'll turn around right up here. We have a few minutes before I have to be back at the college."

Glenda turned her Camaro quickly into a deserted parking lot, then popped back onto Main Street. She turned into the right side of the circle drive in front of the grand old house, to better position the car to merge easily with traffic later. She stopped in front of the wide wooden steps.

"Hi!" Tanya called. She got out of the car. The Allens rose from their glider with wide smiles. Glenda ran around the car to stand beside her friend.

"Hello. How are y'all? This is my friend Tanya. Tanya, may I present Mr. and Mrs. Allen?" Glenda swept her arm to the side gracefully. Bettie Allen chuckled.

"Good grief, girls. Come on up here and save this bum knee-cap from those dangerous steps!" Dub said happily. "Glenda, it's good to see you again, and it is very nice to meet you, Tanya."

Glenda and Tanya jogged up the steps to the porch. The older couple resumed their gliding. The girls leaned on the porch railing, grinning at the couple.

"So, are y'all out cattin' around or what?" Dub asked mischievously. "Hey, you're the gal with the little smoke-mobile, aren't ya, Tanya?"

"Yes, we are. And yes, I am. In fact, I'll probably hafta go buy a quart of oil after while, since Glenda won't be drivin' us around tonight," Tanya said with a jab to her friend's side.

Dub and Bettie focused their attention on Glenda, who was glaring at Tanya good- naturedly. But Tanya wasn't finished. "She's got a date with a guy in a T-Bird!"

"You mean with our Glenn?" Bettie asked.

Tanya looked surprised. Glenda laughed out loud at her friend. "Tan-ay, this is Glenn's aunt and uncle! Didn't I tell you that?"

"No, you didn't. Boy, do I feel stupid."

"He is indeed. My favorite nephew—I always say!" Dub said with delight.

"You say that to both of your nephews, Dub!" Bettie held out her hand for Dub. The man took his wife's hand tenderly.

"That's right. But don't tell them. Hey, is that true, Glenda? You're goin' out with our Glenn?"

Glenda looked uncomfortable. She wasn't sure how to answer. So, she didn't. Tanya, however, felt perfectly comfortable. "Well, he's been takin' her ridin' around a lot lately, and he's comin' to the college to pick her up at seven. In my opinion, that's pretty close to goin' out!"

Glenda glanced up from the spot on the porch she'd been studying and found herself looking into Bettie's eyes. Their happiness and approval caused her to happily sigh with relief.

Dub pulled out his pocket watch and flipped it open. He looked up sharply at the girls.

"Then, you'd better get a move on, gals. It's ten till seven now! Course I could be a little fast."

"Yikes. Glenda, let's go. Nice to meet y'all. See ya later!"

Dub stood up a little too quickly and swayed a bit but caught his balance on the glider armrest. He held up one finger, a signal to wait. After shuffling around the corner of the porch, he returned with a quart of oil, handing it to Tanya without a word. He shooed the girls away with waving hands. Glenda, however, did not immediately shoo. Instead she walked over to Bettie to kiss her cheek. The two women gazed at each other, sharing what seemed to be a secret message. Glenda soaked in the feeling, then turned to run down the steps with Tanya.

Tanya yelled her thanks for the oil to Dub as the car pulled out onto Main Street. Glenda sped back to the college, luckily finding a decent parking spot. The two girls ran to their rooms. Glenda quickly got herself in acceptable shape to see Glenn. She checked in the old mirror—patted her pockets to be sure she had everything—took a deep breath.

"Glenda. He's here. He's down there!" As usual, Janie ran into the room. "He parked right next to you. Are you ready?" She pulled Glenda into the hall.

"Ready as I'll ever be. Y'all stay up here. I mean it. I'll see you later. Tan-ay, if you go out—be careful. I know how distracted you can get," Glenda said in her most serious voice.

Tanya chuckled from her seat in the hall window but remained silent. A lighthearted Janie joined her there in their usual book-end positions. Glenda looked at them warmly before turning away to walk as calmly as possible down the hall.

By the time she moved beyond her friends' line of sight, Glenda was really hurrying, so she quickly exited through the big wooden doors somewhat out of breath. Casting her gaze toward the area where her Camaro was parked, she caught her breath when she spotted exactly what she was looking for. He was standing tall and casually beside the Thunderbird, his full attention focused on her. Gladness spread across his face. Glenda felt the flutter as she descended the steps. It was like some force pulled her toward him; she couldn't stop if she tried. She certainly didn't want to try. Suddenly, she was there—facing him—close to him.

"Hi, there."

Glenn turned to open his car door. Glenda accidently brushed against his chest, as she moved to slide into the car. He nearly gasped. She took her place on the split of the red seat. As he put the car in Drive, she propped her elbow on the back of the seat, letting her hand fall gently onto his shoulder. He cast a quick glance in her direction.

"Where to?" He felt her shrug. "How 'bout the park—the usual place?"

"That's fine. Let's just please get outta here. I can feel Tan-ay and Janie lookin' at us." *Calm down.* "I mean, sure, let's go down to the park."

Glenda wanted to lay her head on his shoulder, but resisted the urge. He kept his hands on the steering wheel while driving to the picnic area they had often visited the past few weeks.

Glenn turned off the ignition and turned toward Glenda in one movement. She removed her arm from his shoulder. They looked deeply into each other's eyes. Glenda wanted to melt into his arms.

"First of all—I'm sorry about yesterday. Second, I want you to know that I'll never let you down again," he said earnestly. His eyes had almost closed, but they opened to observe her reaction.

Glenda took a deep breath to still her pounding heart. "Thank you," she whispered.

She looked at him with such a yearning gaze that he could stand it no longer and took her in his arms. Glenda pressed her ear against his chest to hear his heart, allowing her senses to take in every sensation. They kissed, long and deeply, until each was breathless. Glenn shifted his weight in the seat a bit—Glenda suggested they get some air. A few moments later, they sat side-by-side on the picnic table, their feet on the bench. He was holding her hand with both of his.

"I know this might sound kinda silly, but I believe I'm in 'heavy like' with you, Glenda."

Glenda felt her heart almost stop. "Oh, Glenn, it's not at all silly. It's just right. But calling it 'it'—we do have somethin', don't we?"

"Oh, yeah, we sure do. Come here."

They embraced tightly. Glenda could feel their spirits touching and intertwining. Letting it soak in, she breathed his essence in deeply. As she exhaled slowly, the quivering flutter calmed at last. It was too soon to call it love, she knew. But it definitely was "heavy like."

"Damn it. Somebody's comin' this way."

They pulled away from their embrace, but Glenn again took her hand in his. When it appeared the approaching vehicle was headed right for their picnic area, he got down from the table and helped Glenda to descend safely. However, the vehicle did not stop. It proceeded farther into the park and disappeared.

"Now then—where were we?" Glenn reached for Glenda's shoulders. She playfully ducked out of his grasp.

"You were takin' me ridin' around, remember? Besides, if we're gonna be out carousin' around, I'd better fetch a jacket or sweater from the dorm," she remarked cheerfully.

"You won't need a jacket. I'll keep you warm."

"Oh, paleeze. You'll be off talkin' to the first motor head that comes along!" she teased. He looked stricken, so Glenda relented. "I'm kidding. Come on—let's go make a drag, then cruise through the college. It really is gettin' chilly out here. Please?"

Glenn tickled her side as she got in the Thunderbird. He insisted on one more kiss before he started the car. Glenda gladly complied.

As the big car gained speed, her left arm rested on the back of the seat with her hand on the back of his neck. His right hand was on her leg with his fingers playing with the inside seam of her jeans just above the knee. It was a comfortable feeling. Glenda finally gave in to the urge to lay her head on his shoulder. Glenn briefly let off the accelerator as he felt her hair against his face.

Glenda rejoined Glenn in the Thunderbird after retrieving her favorite sweater. The car windows were still down—the evening was not yet overly cool. Glenda snuggled up close to Glenn as he waited for some people to cross the roadway.

Something grabbed their attention. Both were quite shocked to see Fuzzy running at full speed from the front door of the dorm lobby.

"EVEL!! GLENN!! WAIT UP!!!"

"What in the holy hell?" Glenn asked no one in particular.

"Oh, my goodness!" Glenda pointed to her right. "Look! Somebody's chasin' him!"

They watched the spectacle unfold on the lawn in front of the dorm. Fuzzy eluded an apparently very angry female who swung her purse as if she would beat him to a pulp should she catch him. Fuzzy wasted no more time yelling. He ran straight for the Thunderbird and dove through the open window. His head was in Glenda's lap, but his feet still hung outside the window. He wiggled into the car and to an upright position, as Glenn spun his tires to escape from the fast approaching pursuer. "Go! Git me outta here!"

Glenda waved across Fuzzy's face as they sped by the cannon.

"Who you wavin' at, Glenda?"

"Boots and Gene," she answered casually.

"Boots and jeans? What? Jeans and boots?" Fuzzy asked quizzically.

"No, goofball. They're guys, friends. You remember? Boots and Gene from the wall and the flying underwear?"

"Oh, yeah," he said quietly. "How'd you know about that? Oh, never mind." No one said anything for a bit.

Glenn pulled into an elementary school parking lot and stopped. "OK, Fuz. What's the story? Why was that gal chasin' you, and why were you runnin' for your life?"

"Well, you remember I went out with that college girl a couple a' times?"

"Melinda." Glenda provided the name. Glenn nodded.

"Right...well...when she didn't invite me to that party after the dance thing Sunday, I decided I didn't really like her all that much. So, I wondered what was I doin' tryin' to be with her. Evel, you remember I took that psychology course when I was goin' to college? Well, it occurred to me what I was doin' with Melinda was just a social experiment."

"A *social experiment*? What do you mean?" Glenda was aghast. Glenn shook his head side-to-side sadly, waiting for Fuzzy to keep talking.

"Well, it's like this. Charles dropped me off a little while ago. I went in and called Melinda to meet me in the lobby. I told her I didn't appreciate her purposely excluding me from that party. I explained that she had just been a social experiment for me. You know—a local workin' guy with no car dates a pretty college girl to see how she reacts. She seemed kind of hurt about that. When I told her the experiment had run its course, she got pretty upset."

"I guess so. That was cold-blooded, Fuzzy!" Glenda exclaimed.

"Oh, Fuz. What were you thinkin'?"

"Apparently, I wasn't thinkin' at all, Evel, because she started hittin' me with her purse. Man, there must be somethin' really heavy in there. It hurt! I ran outta the lobby, and she was close behind. Ya know, she's pretty fast on her feet. Then luckily I saw you. Boy, am I glad y'all were there!"

"Lucky for you I didn't know what you'd done, or I might a' left ya there to take your beatin'," Glenn said grimly. Fuzzy looked surprised. Glenda gave the unwelcome passenger a dirty look before turning pointedly away.

"Gosh, I'm sorry. I mean, I know that wasn't the nicest or smartest thing I've ever done, but geez—give a guy a break!"

Glenn ignored Fuzzy's remark. He quietly drove out of the parking lot, retracing his way to the back entrance to the college. The Thunderbird passed the cannon, traveling very slowly down the outbound lane. It made a U turn in the median near the Shoe Bench, circling back up toward the girls' dorm where Fuzzy had appeared a few minutes before.

"Evel...Glenn, buddy—what 're you doin'?" The car turned right onto the one way, stopping directly in front of the girls' dorm lobby. "Oh, no, man. Please don't."

"Get out, Fuz. Here. Now," Glenn commanded. Fuzzy looked dismayed but obeyed his friend's somber order. He firmly shut the passenger side door. Glenn quickly drove out of the college, leaving a pitiful looking Fuzzy standing on the sidewalk.

When he stopped at an intersection, Glenn put his arm around Glenda. They chuckled together for a few seconds. "Hey, where's the Ted tape? HIC. Oh, damn," Glenn said, as he hiccupped and laughed at the same time. "I have—HIC—the damn—HIC—hiccups. I hate—HIC—it when—HIC—this happens."

Glenda turned to face him, and advised him to put the car in Park. No other cars were around. Glenda placed her index and middle fingers firmly against his sternum and looked straight into his eyes. "Forget Ted for now. OK, try to concentrate. Look at me and breathe with me."

Glenn started to laugh. "No, don't laugh! Come on—cooperate. OK, now breathe in real slowly. Right—just like that. Now hold it and try to feel where the hiccup is." She moved her fingers around a little as the spasm happened again. "Ah, right there. Now, slowly let the breath out, easy, and try to relax the muscles I'm pressin' on. Breathe in again, slow, real slow—hold it and stretch out your sternum with the breath. Now let it out real slow and relax. Relaxxxx. Breathe in normally a few times... Better?"

"Well, I'll be damned. You can cure hiccups!" Glenn exclaimed. "Wow, I've never seen anything like it. That's amazing. No drinkin' water upside down or anything. You are really somethin', ya know it?"

He kissed her forehead. Sometime during the hiccup cure, he had put his hands on her arms. Leaning toward her, without thinking, he placed his own forehead firmly against hers. Each felt a sudden and strong connection, savoring the unusual contact. He moved his head side-to-side, so that his forehead rolled back-and-forth on hers. When he leaned back, he released a satisfied moan.

"Mmmm, that was strange, but it felt good. Do it again," Glenda requested, as she lowered her chin. He took the bait, rubbing her forehead with his again for a few seconds. He pulled back—but this time raised her chin with his hand gently to kiss her lips.

Headlights appeared behind them, interrupting the magical moment. Glenn hurriedly got the Thunderbird moving. Shortly after he pulled out onto Main Street, he saw Larry and several other people in the parking lot of a store that had closed for the evening. Larry waved at the Thunderbird.

Glenn shot his big car across the road. "Looks like the Samsonites are out in force tonight." He clicked off the ignition. Glenda looked at him with a question in her eyes.

"Come on. You need to meet Samson," he said with a chuckle. "But he's probably tellin' a war story about now, so we'll wait till he's done."

He helped Glenda out of the car. They moved quietly toward the people gathered in a semi-circle around Samson. Glenda recognized the figure. She glanced at Glenn as if she would speak, but he shushed her. Sampson was in action.

"So, see in 'Nam, we got this new wet-behind-the-ears lieutenant fresh and tender right out of officer's school. He was always studyin' a map but didn't know north from south and was always gittin' us lost. We called him Lost Lieutenant Luke. Well, we was out on patrol, and we was wanderin' around the jungle—him with a map in his hand—us followin' him around like sheep. But we knew where we were. Lost. Most of the guys was on their second tour and had been around the palm tree a time or two. But Lost Lieutenant Luke wouldn't listen to none of us, oh, no. He had his map."

"How'd you find your way back, Samson?" asked one of the Samsonites.

"I'll git to that part. It's like this, see, on some unknown signal one of the guys said, 'Hey, Lieutenant', and Lost Lieutenant Luke looked right at 'em. That guy snapped to attention and saluted the Lieutenant right smart like. We all took the cue and saluted'm, too. He looked real satisfied-like, as he saluted us back. That's when the shot hit'm."

"Shot? Who shot him?"

"The Viet Cong! Charlie, that's who. Everybody except Lost Lieutenant Luke knows you don't salute anybody in the jungle. That's a sign a sniper looks for to take out an officer, ya see." Samson got quiet.

"Did he die?" someone asked hesitantly.

"Hell no—that sniper must a' needed glasses. He got'm in the leg. But he went down and acted dead, I tell ya. Then he realized he wasn't dead, and he was lookin' around for us, but we was all hidin' in the bush. We had a big long discussion on whether or not we should take'm back to camp or leave'm there for Charlie. Finally, I said, 'Oh, hell. I'll git'm.' So, I did."

"Wow. Did they shoot at you, too, Samson?"

"Nope. Charlie usually took a quick shot and then ran away expectin' that we'd shoot back. So, I just went over to Lost Lieutenant Luke—picked'm up off the muddy ground and threw'm over my shoulder. Like this!"

Samson grabbed a person who was at the front of the crowd. He held tightly to the struggling body, ignoring the kicking feet. "Except he bled on me and got me muddy." Samson calmly walked away with his victim. When he turned, the observers in the back recognized the person.

Larry shot a grin at Glenda, then to his brother. "He's got Fuz again."

Glenn nodded. He took Glenda by the hand, and they made their way through the little crowd. The Samsonites cheered on their hero.

Samson turned around, noticing Glenn's arrival. "Hey there, Evel Glenn! And who do we have here?" he asked casually, as though there was no grown man slung over one shoulder.

"Samson. This is Glenda—the girl in the yellow Camaro."

"Hi, Samson—nice to meet you." Glenda smiled, feeling quite awkward. She pointed over to their left. "Uh oh, lookee over there. Here comes Melinda, and it appears she has assembled a group of vigilantes!"

Samson's eyes brightened. "Female vigilantes? Them's my kinda gals! What 're they after?"

"I would imagine they want Fuzzy. And I bet they'd be pretty obliged if you'd hand him over to 'em. He pulled a dirty trick on one of the girls."

Fuzzy struggled and squealed like a piglet. Samson whacked him on the leg, firmly instructing him to keep quiet. The strong man stood very still for a moment—then nodded. The group of girls stopped at the edge of the parking lot. Samson casually carried Fuzzy toward them. After a discussion and subsequent agreement, Samson stood the captive feet-first and released him to Melinda. Fuzzy took off running; the chase was on again.

Samson laughed heartily while walking back to Glenn and Glenda. "Why can't I git college girls to chase me like that?" All the Samsonites laughed with him, surrounding their hero. The whole group moved away from the pickup bed that had served as Samson's stage.

Glenn noticed Charles in the small assemblage. He and Glenda walked over to talk to him. A few moments later, the three bade good night to Samson and Larry and were happily ridin' around in the Thunderbird, listening to music and laughing at each other's jokes. Suddenly, Glenn sat straight upright, rigidly placing both hands on the steering wheel. Glenda leaned away from him, surprised by his mood change. He was obviously very tense, with his tongue pushed into the corner of his mouth, the tip protruding slightly from his lips. She looked at the oncoming traffic. Headlights appeared to be coming right at them.

Charles touched her on the shoulder, sensing her uneasiness. "Don't worry. This happens all the time—just hang on."

Glenda didn't have time to answer. Glenn abruptly turned the steering wheel, sending the Thunderbird to the opposite side of Main Street. The driver of the other vehicle honked his horn as he sped past on the wrong side of the road. Glenn whipped his vehicle back to the right side of Main Street, releasing a sigh of relief. They sped by the college entrance before Glenda could regain her voice.

"Umm, well, that was pretty scary. Hey, that's what y'all did out on the highway the day we went to the lake in Janie's motor home, isn't it?" she asked.

"Yeah. That was us. We didn't even know it was y'all in that motor home that day," Charles said.

"I thought so. No matter. I can see Glenn has everything under control," Glenda said somewhat unconvincingly.

Glenn pulled his emergency brake, spinning the Thunderbird around 180 degrees in a perfect Dairy Queen Turnaround. Glenda was thrown onto Charles and then back against Glenn.

"Hi there," he said with amusement. "Remember, you're in good hands with Glennstate!"

He returned his hand to her thigh. She wrapped her arm through his and pinched the underside of his arm ever so lightly. A good-natured squeeze of her leg caused Glenda a surprise amount of pleasure.

As they approached the college entrance, she realized she'd better call it a night. "I hate to be a party pooper, but I've got an early class tomorrow. I'd better get back to the dorm."

"Oh, my, it's almost eleven, and it's a school night, Evel!" Charles teased.

Glenn chuckled but turned the big car into the entrance as requested. Glenda figured he'd drop her at the Shoe Bench or at the side entrance to the dorm, but he kept driving. He made the U in front of the cannon where most of her friends were gathered. They were waving excitedly, while Charles waved back with his usual animation. Glenn pulled the car into a visitor parking space. Charles bailed out, quickly walking toward the cannon. Glenn and Glenda also got out to lean on the car—out of the direct glow of the streetlight. On an unheard signal, each turned toward the other. He took her in his arms and kissed her.

"Hey, Charles!" Tanya walked toward him from the cannon area. Janie, Linda, Candace and the Months of the Year strolled toward the wall behind Tanya, distracted by a group of people running toward them

"Keep on truckin', Fuz!" Charles called. Fuzzy was still being relentlessly pursued by the scorned woman and her comrades.

"Get him, y'all!" Janie yelled and shrugged, not certain what was happening.

"Hush, I hear a noise!" Boots called from behind the group.

Tanya moved toward him. "I hear it, too. It's a hissin' sound. Maybe it's a snake!"

"No. No. It's not a snake. I don't know what—hey look!"

A blue car darted from behind some trees, streaking toward Main Street. Glenn and Glenda were so involved they didn't notice it go past. But Tanya did.

"That was Jimmie Mac. What the...wait a second. Oh, no! Everybody run away—the cannon—it's gonna go off!" She yelled to the general area. The others stood still for just a second—but were soon in motion. Each jumped off the wall and ran as fast as possible straight down the road, in the same direction that Jimmie Mac had just escaped.

"Come on, Glenda! Run! Everybody run!" Boots yelled as he passed the Thunderbird.

Glenn looked up briefly—then back down at Glenda.

"Glenda! Run! Oh, and here's Ted," Janie called, veering toward the couple, gently tossing the tape on the trunk lid. "Come on, y'all. Run!"

"Hey, that's my line," Glenn said jovially.

"I'm not runnin'. Are you?" Glenda asked with an expectant look in her eyes. Glenn's smile lines appeared. He answered with a firmer embrace and a tender kiss.

A bright flash of light shattered the darkness. The resulting sound reverberated over the entire area. People were running about, screaming and yelling before and after the...

KAAAA BOOOOOOOOMMMMMMMMMM!!!!

But Glenn and Glenda didn't notice it or any of the pandemonium erupting around them. They retreated farther into the shadows and kept on kissing.

Epilogue

THE AIR WAS SOMEWHAT warm on the wide front porch—
and the glider made a familiar squeak—as they gently rocked
in the early September afternoon breeze. They loosely held
hands, content and happy, as the woman stretched her blue-
jeaned legs out in front of her body. The man propelled the
glider back-and-forth.

"They'll be here in about thirty minutes or so," she said
quietly. "I think everything's ready—at least I hope so."

"Hmm. Then there's enough time to make a drag in the
new car?"

"Oh, yeah. You bet!" She hopped up to her feet on the forward stroke of the glider. "I have an anniversary present for
you, baby. Meet me at the car in a few minutes."

She disappeared into the house behind the slam-slam of the
front screen door.

The man sighed and waited a minute. He knew he could take
his time. She always took longer getting ready than she intended.
He rose, stomping a bit on one tingling foot to stimulate the
circulation. This action also caused his jeans to unbunch from
the top of his boot. A car honked as it passed by. His hand
automatically raised in a casual greeting. He walked down the
wide steps where he had rested his bones so many times over
the years and turned the corner of the house.

The new car was sitting in the driveway beside the grand
old home—backed in as always—and he was slightly surprised
to find his wife already standing beside it. The happiness in his
face shined, as he walked toward her and the car.

"OK. You know you're a lucky guy, right? You have this house—you retired early—you have your dream car and your dream girl!" She handed him a small bag, giving him a quick kiss on the lips. He took the tiny item out of the bag and looked at her with a question on his face.

Glenda couldn't contain her excitement. "I figured since this car—much like the cars we used to have—doesn't have the capability of mobile music—I got you—OK, I got us—an MP3 player with a docking station. It's battery operated and will play hours of music for us or at least until the batteries run down. Happy Twenty-Seventh Anniversary, my baby!"

Glenn glanced at the gift briefly before placing it gently in the seat. He reached for Glenda's shoulders and rested his forehead against hers. They rocked their heads side-to-side gently for a few seconds before pulling apart.

"Thanks, baby. Happy Anniversary to you, too. Wow, twenty-seven years. We had 8-track tapes back then—now this little electronic device can probably hold the same amount of music as we had in a whole tape box. All right—we gotta go try it out. Come on. Let's go ridin' around before the party starts. Wait—you sure you got enough food ready?"

"Certainly! With Tanya's four kids, and the nine between Linda, Candace and Janie, plus grandkids and all the rest comin', I've got enough hot dogs and hamburgers to feed an army!"

"Okeedokee, hop in!" Glenn stated happily. "Let's make a drag past the old chapel."

"Yeah, imagine—twenty-seven years ago we walked down the aisle of that old church, and it was old then!"

Glenda opened the passenger side door of the AC Cobra, glancing at Glenn seated behind the wheel. It was a beautiful car—a dream come true for Glenn. He'd always wanted a Cobra. It was silver, with a big Ford engine. It looked and sounded like a race car. She sank into the black upholstered passenger seat, resting her elbow on the red pillow she had purchased especially for this purpose. The new car needed some red in the interior to remind them of the Thunderbird.

Glenn started the car and warmed it up. He looked over at her in the passenger seat. Love sparkled from her eyes; he couldn't resist the urge to kiss her again. Glenda got the player ready, as Glenn put the roadster in gear. After the initial roar of engine and rush of wind to get up to speed, she activated the little, modern music device. She grinned, anticipating the first song to begin. She lovingly watched the smile lines by his right eye become more pronounced, as he drove past the concrete slab on which once sat the old Dairy Queen. A flash of chrome reflected on a nearby building; he turned around in the museum driveway. They took a moment to admire the still beautiful historical chapel. The car headed back toward town with Glenn smiling even more broadly when the first song blossomed into full volume.

Glenda looked at him. The bond between them was almost visible.

The music was loud, as it should be. It was Ted. "Hey Baby" filled the air. Each burst out laughing, as the small red taillights passed underneath Moo Lah. They were, as always, very happy just ridin' around.

So, did our stories of ridin' around bring back memories? If you have funny or touching stories you'd like to share, please send them to Elaine@blazingstarbooks.com and we might use them in the next book, "Ridin' Too—Capers on Cassette."

Watch for other Blazing Star Books releases at *www.blazingstarbooks.com.*